Dedalus Europe 2006
General Editor: Mike Mitchell

The Lost Musicians

Illustration by Zacharias Heinesen

William Heinesen

The Lost Musicians

translated from the Danish by W. Glyn Jones

Dedalus

Dedalus would like to thank The Danish Arts Council's Committee for Literature and Grants for the Arts in Cambridge for their assistance in producing this book.

Published in the UK by Dedalus Ltd, Langford Lodge,
St Judith's Lane, Sawtry, Cambs, PE28 5XE
email: info@dedalusbooks.com
www.dedalusbooks.com

ISBN 1 903517 50 8
ISBN 978 1 903517 50 5

Dedalus is distributed in the United States by SCB Distributors,
15608 South New Century Drive, Gardena, California 90248
email: info@scbdistributors.com   web site: www.scbdistributors.com

Dedalus is distributed in Australia & New Zealand by Peribo Pty Ltd,
58 Beaumont Road, Mount Kuring-gai N.S.W. 2080
email: peribo@bigpond.com

Dedalus is distributed in Canada by Disticor Direct-Book Division,
695 Westney Road South, Suite 14 Ajax, Ontario, LI6 6M9
web site: www.disticordirect.com

Publishing History
First published in Denmark as *De fortabte spillemaend* in 1950
First English edition published in the USA in 1971
New translation by W. Glyn Jones published by Dedalus in 2006

The Lost Musicians copyright © William Heinesen 1950
Translation and Introduction copyright © W. Glyn Jones 2006

The right of William Heinesen's estate to be indentified as the proprietor and W. Glyn Jones to be identified as the translator of this work has been asserted by them in accordance with the Copyright, Designs and Patents Act, 1988.

Printed in Finland by WS Bookwell
Typeset by RefineCatch Limited, Bungay, Suffolk

A C.I.P. listing for this book is available on request.

THE AUTHOR

William Heinesen (1900–1991) was born in Tórshavn in the Faroe Islands, the son of a Danish mother and Faroese father, and was equally at home in both languages. Although he spent most of his life in the Faroe Islands he chose to write in Danish as he felt it offered him greater inventive freedom. Although internationally known as a poet and a novelist he was also highly regarded as an artist. His paintings range from large-scale murals in public buildings, through oil to pen sketches, caricatures and collages. He published *The Black Cauldron* in 1949, Dedalus translation 1992 and his masterpiece, *The Lost Musicians* in 1950.

It is Dedalus's intention to make all of William Heinesen's fiction available in English in new translations by W. Glyn Jones.

THE TRANSLATOR

W. Glyn Jones read Scandinavian Studies at Cambridge and was subsequently appointed Lecturer in Danish at University College London. His career took him to Newcastle upon Tyne, where he was the first Professor of Scandinavian Studies, and finally to the University of East Anglia as Professor of European Literature. He also spent two years as Professor of Scandinavian Literature in the Faroese Academy. He has written widely on Danish, Faroese and Finland-Swedish literature and together with his wife is the co-author of the *Blue Guide to Denmark* and *Colloquial Danish*.

The Faroese poet and author William Heinesen (1900–1991) must be counted one of the major writers in Scandinavia in the 20th century. The writer of novels, short stories, poems and a small number of works of non-fiction, he was considered for the Nobel Prize but asked to be left out of consideration since he wrote in Danish and believed that any Faroese receiving the prize should write in Faroese. He was in addition a painter of note and a gifted pianist who also composed a modest amount of music.

Born in 1900, Heinesen grew up in a Faroe Island community in transition. Until 1856, the islands had been a Danish colony and trade monopoly closed off from the outside world. However, once the Danish monopoly was abandoned, what had basically been a medieval society underwent a period of both economic and cultural change. One result of this process of opening up to the world was the advent of various sectarian movements who made – and still make – a huge impact on Faroese life. The most important of them, the Plymouth Brethren, locally known as "Baptists", still has an influence rivalling that of the established Lutheran Church. One of the achievements of the sectarians was the introduction of total prohibition at the beginning of the 20th century. *The Lost Musicians* is centred on the fates of a small group of life-asserting amateur musicians facing the threat and apparently final triumph of these life-denying sectarians.

Poor as they are, the musicians represent a joy in life, yet one by one they are overcome by the anti-life forces of the sectarians led by the formidable savings bank manager Ankersen and his scurrilous putative son Matte Gok. Yet, typical of Heinesen, hope survives nevertheless when Orpheus, the child of one of these doomed musicians, is finally taken off to Copenhagen to embark on a musical career there.

However, this is no dry piece of social realism, but a fast-moving, rollicking account that verges on the fantastic. Ankersen himself is a fanatic, blind to the reality around him but nevertheless not portrayed in an entirely negative light. Matte Gok, one of the most thoroughgoing scoundrels in 20th-century Scandinavian literature, has on the other hand no redeeming features. On the other side of the divide there is the enormous, hen-pecked blacksmith Janniksen, a huge man who would enjoy life if it were not for his determined sectarian wife. It is he who organises a grand traditional wedding festivity for his daughter, which turns into a battle between the two forces each struggling to take possession of the bridal couple. To offset this we have the tenderness and kindness of the ordinary people of the little town in which the action takes place.

Only by stretching the term to its utmost could this be called a historical novel, though there is a vague link between it and actual events in the Faroe Islands at the beginning of the twentieth century. There was indeed at that time an amateur quartet such as that portrayed in the novel, and there was indeed a savings bank manager by the name of Danielsen who led the sectarians and obviously had at least something in common with the Ankersen of the novel. One of Heinesen's many caricature paintings is of this Danielsen, and to it the painter has added the telling words "that hellhound Danielsen". The struggle for total prohibition took place at the time at which the novel is set of course, though it was scarcely as amusing and grotesque as it is portrayed here. And the visit by the Hamburg Philharmonic Orchestra did in fact have its parallel, though the visiting orchestra's programme was not such as would emphasise the struggle between life and death reflected in Heinesen's interpretation of Schubert's Eighth Symphony.

Constructed as a classical symphony, the novel has music at its heart and is at the same time a wonderful mixture of caricature, satire and poetry. On a higher plane it represents the cosmic struggle between life-asserting and life-denying forces. It is set in an unnamed town in an unnamed tiny country in the North Atlantic – for those who know it quite clearly and recognisably the capital of the Faroe Islands, Tórshavn. For those who do not know it, it is of no matter, as the novel's theme is one of universality. Seldom can such great themes have been treated in such an approachable fashion.

One of the great Danish novels of the 20th century.

FIRST MOVEMENT

*in which the musicians and their family and friends
are presented*

1

On the Aeolian harp builder Kornelius and his sons

Far out in a radiant ocean glinting like quicksilver there lies a solitary little lead-coloured land. The tiny rocky shore is to the vast ocean just about the same as a grain of sand to the floor of a dance hall. But seen beneath a magnifying glass, this grain of sand is nevertheless a whole world with mountains and valleys, sounds and fjords and houses with small people. Indeed in one place there is even a complete little old town with quays and storehouses, streets and lanes and steep alleyways, gardens and squares and churchyards. There is also a little church situated high up, from whose tower there is a view over the roofs of the town and further out across the almighty ocean.

One windy afternoon many years ago, a man and three boys sat up in this tower listening to the capriciously varying sounds of an Aeolian harp. It was the sexton Kornelius Isaksen and his three sons, Moritz, Sirius and Young Kornelius, and the Aeolian harp they were listening to was the first of a considerable number deriving from the sexton's hand, for this remarkable man gradually developed into a builder of Aeolian harps such as is seldom encountered. So for a time there were no fewer that seventeen Aeolian harps hanging up there in the tower, and the concert of sound they produced went right through you.

But let us return to the day when the magical music from an Aeolian harp came to the ears of the three boys for the first time and stirred a curiously insatiable longing in their young souls. Before this, they had not heard any music apart from what came from the asthmatic old organ that Lamm the organist sat and murdered on Sundays.

"Daddy, who is it playing the Aeolian harp?" asked Young Kornelius, who was about six years old at the time.

"It's the wind, of course," replied his elder brother.

"No, it's the *cherubs*, isn't it, Dad?" asked Sirius seeking to catch his father's gaze with his wildly open eyes.

The sexton nodded in absent-minded confirmation, and the three boys' listening became still more breathless and rapt. They sat staring from the belfry lights out into a wind-swept space where huge solitary clouds scudded past with an observant mien, as though they, too, were listening to the distant music. The three brothers never forgot this wonderful afternoon in later days, and as a grown man Sirius gave it a lasting memorial in his poem "And cherubim passed by".

As already said, the sexton's Aeolian harp-making later got out of hand. Kornelius Isakson was in general a man given to excess; he was for ever subject to some crazy idea, and he often set himself impossible tasks. When he failed to achieve them, he was deeply upset and abandoned himself to melancholy, and while in such a state he not infrequently turned to the bottle.

He was nevertheless a kind and considerate father to his sons. And so it was at his instance that their musical gifts were placed in the meticulous care of Kaspar Boman.

Kornelius became a widower at an early age and he himself only lived to be thirty-four. So the three sons were left to themselves at an early age and had to manage as best they could. But the Aeolian harp builder's restless spirit lived on in their souls, among other things resulting in an inordinate love of music.

2

About a wedding, a wake and an angry man, and about the name Orpheus

At the age of only twenty-two, Moritz, the sexton's eldest son, married the eighteen-year-old highly musical bottle-washer Eliana, whom he had met in Boman's choral society, and who had already long been much courted. It was about this Eliana that Sirius later wrote his justly so much loved poem "Sunshine in a Cellar", in which he pictures a fair-haired girl standing washing out bottles in a greenish twilit room, wet and a little dishevelled, but young and happy like an Aphrodite who had just come ashore. Eliana really was like that, as though made of lighter stuff than other mortals; indeed, she had that goddess-like gaze that is a remarkable quality in certain female creatures who are specially favoured: a gaze that as it were looks right through everything in a blithesome and practical way without for a moment seeming pensive, and in addition there was something light and airy about her entire person, an innate sense of agile movement, which had certainly not been lost on Lindenskov the dancing teacher, for in his classes he usually pointed Eliana out as a model of natural grace and plasticity.

It goes without saying that Eliana was a beautiful bride. Moritz, too, looked smart: a tanned and handsome young sailor, upright and full of confidence and with the medal for life-saving shining on his jacket lapel. In general, the young couple were surrounded by the atmosphere of freedom from care and of innocent happiness that can make certain solid citizens so strangely bitter and distrustful. And soon there was plenty to gossip about; even the wedding provided the occasion for worries and much shaking of the head, and neither can it be denied that the end to the wedding was as ugly as its start had been beautiful.

17

It began with a male voice choir, in which the bridegroom himself took part as first tenor, singing "In the Wondrous Hour of Dawn", written for the occasion by Sirius and set to music by Young Kornelius, who here made his first appearance as a composer. Then a string quartet in which the bridegroom himself played first violin performed Haydn's well-known Andante cantabile for solo violin and pizzicato. That, too, was a great success and resulted in much praise for the soloist. After this, the assembled company ate and drank and then danced, and in many respects in a very animated fashion, though not more animatedly than is customary in this society. But unfortunately the celebration cost one man his life, as an old shoemaker by the name of Esau – a fine old man of seventy-seven years, whose only fault was that he was incorrigibly devoted to the bottle – was found drowned towards morning in the little cove known as the Kelp Trench, only a few steps away from the house where the festivities were taking place.

The wedding was to have lasted at least two days, but now it naturally came to a standstill. The guests wended their way home. It was a sad affair and extremely unfortunate.

The old shoemaker was buried a few days later, and the male voice choir sang beautifully and movingly at the grave-side. That evening, Moritz gathered his friends together for a wake. Here, the remains of the interrupted wedding feast were eaten and drunk, but all naturally took place in a suitably subdued and decorous atmosphere.

Nevertheless, the manager of the savings bank, Mr Ankersen, found reason to interfere. He turned up in the midst of the wake, red and frothing at the mouth as was his custom, and spoke of blasphemy, retribution and damnation. The little gathering listened obediently to this impassioned castigator. Ankersen looked dreadful; he had no control whatsoever of his bearded rubicund face and its wrathful spectacles; his voice broke several times in sectarian fury, and as it danced on the wall, his double shadow was the very image of the Devil himself. Two candles were burning on the table; and they fluttered in the blast from his mouth, and he blew one of them right out.

Finally, he grasped an almost full bottle of Dutch gin that was standing on the table, went outside and emptied it in the gutter. Not even this prompted a word from Moritz and his friends in the dimly lit room.

But when the bank manager finally left, Moritz took out a new earthenware bottle of gin and opened it. Averting his eyes, he sighed: "Of course it was a terrible thing that Esau, poor blighter, should go and drown, of course it was. But I surely can't be given all the blame? I hadn't even invited Esau; he came as an uninvited guest, but of course I didn't throw him out. But on the other hand I couldn't be his nursemaid. But what's done is done, and after all he was a lonely old man. Let's drink to him!"

Despite the fact that Moritz only plied the simple trade of a ferryman, he was, as already said, a man who had a rare and all-absorbing love of music. He had an excellent singing voice and never played difficult to get when he was asked to sing at weddings or funerals, and in addition he played at dances when the opportunity arose. He played the violin, the viola, the French horn, flute and clarinet. Not in the sense that he mastered any of these instruments in the manner of a real musician. But he was magnificent when taking part in music making, especially when playing the violin.

Aye, Moritz was more musical than most people, and when about a year after the wedding he had become the father of a little boy, he also wanted to give this child a truly musical name. On this question he asked the advice of various people who were more versed in the history of music than he was. Kaspar Boman, the gardener and music teacher, who at that time was tied to his bed, drew up a whole list of musical names. Moritz preserved this list; it still exists and in all its touching meticulousness, this is how it looks:

Franz (Schubert)
Christoff Willibald (Gluck)
Wolfgang Amadeus
Amadeus or Amadé
Wolfgang

Franz
Felix (Mendelssohn)
Ole Bull
Paganini (not good)
Papageno (not good either)
Johan Sebastian Bach
Corelli
Giovanni Battista Viotti? No
Franz (Schubert)
Orpheus (crossed out)
August Sødermann
Ludvig (dreary name)
J.P.E. Hartmann
Carl Maria v. Weber
Franz Schubert

Why from all these names Moritz selected Orpheus, which into the bargain had been crossed out, has remained a mystery, but in any case Orpheus became the boy's name.

Many years later, along with the list here reproduced, which Moritz kept at the bottom of his seaman's chest, Orpheus found a faded letter from old Boman. It ran thus:

Dear Moritz,
I am really sorry I cannot come to the christening party, but I am still not well enough, but I had otherwise put a little speech together for my godson. Now it had better wait for his confirmation if God allows me to live so long, which He probably will not, but please do not refuse this little present, and please do not make too much of the bottle, Moritz; promise me that, and remember Ibsen's beautiful words:

> With music ravishing and chaste in tone,
> Orpheus gave soul to beast and fire to stone.
> Make music so the stone strikes sparks.
> Make music so our carnal shape departs.

3

Of a trip one night to the Orken Isles

Poor Sirius. He finally became a recognised poet, but not until many years after he had suffered an untimely death, as so often happens. While alive he was seen as an idler and as impossibly stupid.

Of course, Sirius did also have many peculiar ideas and crazy habits, among which was that of wandering around at night, especially in the light summer nights. And then he could be completely unmerciful in disturbing his slumbering fellow creatures.

Thus, one mild night in August he had taken it into his head that it would be a splendid idea to go out to the Orken Isles and watch the sun rise, and for this purpose he first woke Young Kornelius and then the young couple from the house by the Kelp Trench. Of course they all wanted to go with him, for such were these people from the young and innocent dawn of time. Even little slumbering Orpheus, who then was only three years old, was taken along, carefully wrapped between blankets in a wash basket. The Orken Isles referred to here were naturally not the well-known Scottish group by roughly the same name, but merely a small cluster of rocks by the entrance to the cove. It was Sirius who had invented the bizarre name.

While Eliana made coffee and buttered bread and biscuits, Sirius and Young Kornelius sat in the living room working eagerly together to produce a hymn to the morning. Such was their nature, these sons of the Aeolian harp builder; there was always something to celebrate. Sirius sat there, tall and thin and with his hat pushed to the back of his head, writing in his crumpled poetry book with a well-chewed stump of a pencil, and Kornelius hummed as he peered over his shoulder through his pince-nez. There was something infinitely helpless about this pince-nez of Kornelius's. This was possibly because it was too small and too loose, or because he had no idea how to wear it with the correct, dignified nonchalance. Moreover, the pince-nez, which was in fashion at that time, hardly goes well with an honest and straightforward face with an under-hung jaw and protruding ears. There was no saying that Young Kornelius was handsome; he had a tendency to squint, in addition to which he had a stammer.

When the poet and the composer had finished their work, they discovered that the *Crab King* was present in the room. He was sitting in a rocking chair and staring morosely, as was his wont. It is this dwarf Sirius has immortalised in his moving poem "The Man from the Moon".

Moritz came back, bringing Ole Brandy the first mate with him. Ole Brandy was fairly inebriated; Moritz had found him sitting half asleep in a beached boat. Ole had half a bottle of brandy with him and was keen to hurry home and fetch some more.

Finally, the little group embarked in the boat. The night was inexpressibly quiet. Ole Brandy's bottle went round from mouth to mouth. The Crab King was the only one to drink nothing; as usual, it was impossible to get a word out of this strange shadow of a human being. Kornelius tapped his shoulder to cheer him up, and the dwarf gave him a devoted look. Kornelius was the only living soul for whom the Crab King is known to have felt any affection.

The ocean breathed in and out in long, resplendent billows populated by silent eiderducks. A full moon on its way down had the happy idea of revealing itself in the west between motionless clouds. It imparted to the darkened landscape a reddish glow that might seem to have been produced by some kind of spiritual trumpet blast.

When the little party had seated itself on the Orken Isles and while Eliana laid out food and coffee on the spotlessly clean rock, Moritz took out his violin and with verve and difficult double stopping played the extraordinary, blissful andante from Pergolesi's Concertino in f minor.

The bottle continued to circulate, but the men remained silent. Only the Crab King glumly cleared his throat, as was his habit, and stared out across the sea with a great careworn face which seemed once and for all to have drunk its fill of sombre superior knowledge. In the meantime, the moon had gone down, and the dawn sky in the east had started to derive colour from the sun, which was still below the horizon like some sunken Soria Moria castle. When the coffee was drunk and the bread and biscuits eaten, the first blush started to trickle forth from among the long linear cloud formations and to strike fire in a mantle of merry fleecy clouds.

Then Sirius stepped forward and in an emotional voice declaimed his morning hymn, a kind of song of praise to the sun and to life. The Crab King took off his bonnet and folded his hands. Moritz sat with the bottle on his left knee, and with his right arm he held his young wife close to him. Ole Brandy had stretched out on the rocks and lay emitting clouds of smoke in the air from his crusty chalk pipe. The morning sun shining on his broken red nose made it doubly red and played in his golden earrings. But all at once, Sirius stopped declaiming and pointed out across the water: Look!

They all rose to look. Out there on the furrowed water, which had now adopted a dazzling bronze glow, a pod of dolphins could be seen. They were flapping their tails and performing somersaults on the surface of the water as though in excessive joy as they hastened away in the current and disappeared in the distance.

Little Orpheus had awakened in his basket just in time to see this sight. He stretched his arms up and cried out, beyond himself with delight mixed with fear, and the image of the massively happy fish in the sunrise imprinted itself on his memory for all time.

Sirius read his poem to the end. Ole Brandy lit his pipe, which had gone out, and grabbed for the bottle, and now Kornelius had his melody ready. He handed the paper with the scribbled notes to Moritz, who took his violin and played the melody through a couple of times. He nodded approvingly and launched into singing the new song. Kornelius and

Sirius sang in harmony and Ole Brandy hooted in the empty bottle, and thus was born the beautiful hymn to the morning of which the literary historian Magnus Skæling says in his beautiful essay on Sirius Isaksen that with its powerful, naïve portrayal of nature it is reminiscent of Thomas Kingo himself.

When the song came to an end, merriment and the dawn broke forth in earnest. Ole Brandy smashed the bottle against the rock and embarked on a strangely merciless sea shanty. Ole's eyes had become clouded. Moritz, too, was somewhat tipsy. He went over and shook Ole's hand and listened patiently to a raucous and incoherent story of life at sea in his young years, of unforgettable voyages to distant parts on the bark the "Albatross" and of the Red Indian girl Ubokosiara, who bit the ear of the respectable Norwegian sailor known as Uncle and tore it to pieces.

Sirius had discovered a sea anemone by the water's edge and clambered cautiously down to take a closer look. The fleshy flower reached out with vaguely amorous movements up towards the darkish sunshine, as though in some melancholy yearning.

A breeze now started to blow from the south. Eliana packed the blankets more tightly round the child; feeling rather cold, she started gathering cups and jugs together. But suddenly there was a cry and a splash. Sirius had disappeared! Eliana uttered a scream that produced a loud and ominous double echo from land, and the Crab King's face twisted in a new and hopeless expression of grief. But Moritz had immediately thrown off his jersey and leapt into the water, and before long he appeared with Sirius, who was flapping about blindly with his arms and legs and uttering gurgling noises. Ole Brandy managed to haul him ashore; he remained on his stomach, groaning and with the water pouring off his worn clothes. Eliana bent down and with a sigh of relief kissed him on the cheek. She set about wringing the water from his long hair and soothed him as though he were a little child. Ole Brandy took off his dirty, alcohol-perfumed jersey and dressed Sirius in it. Moritz prepared the boat for departure, and the little party quickly embarked.

Sirius was trembling, and his teeth were chattering. Little Orpheus was howling and inconsolable, but it helped when his mother took him on her lap and reminded him of the lovely big fish that had been playing and leaping so amusingly for him out there in the sea. He met his mother's reassuring gaze and fell silent, lost in the memory.

4

Aspects of life in the basement of the Bastille and in Skindholm in general

During his childhood and early youth, Moritz had sailed the great seas, but now he lived by ferrying travellers and sailors out to ships. This was in the days before the harbour and the quay installations came, so that a ferryman was much in demand. Occasionally, Moritz also ran a kind of freight and passenger service out to Seal Island and other small landing places near the capital. These routes were mostly in sheltered waters, but Moritz's vocation was by no means without its dangers. Ferrying, especially during the winter months, often demanded a considerable amount of bravery and resourcefulness, and when misfortune was abroad it could turn into a game of life and death.

Moritz enjoyed a well-earned reputation as a sailor. He was both experienced and bold, and the rescue he had carried out at the age of twenty when single-handedly he had brought seven men and a woman safely ashore from the wrecked Finnish schooner the "Karelia", added undying lustre to his name.

But one pitch-black night close to Christmas 1904, Moritz was unfortunate enough to wreck his boat. He was on his way back from one of the large ocean-going steamers, which had dropped anchor far out on account of the strong on-shore wind. Together with a far too hospitable agent on board out there, he had drunk a couple of glasses of some unusually strong green liquid that the agent had jestingly called "Certain Death".

As though by a miracle, however, Moritz escaped death, but the boat, which had drifted ashore at Punt Point, was smashed to smithereens, and it was not insured.

Moritz wandered around for a time feeling ashamed but secretly happy, for of course his life had been saved, and that means quite a lot to a young man with the future before him. After some discussions with his young wife, he decided to sell the small, but well-kept house near the Kelp Trench and to buy a new and bigger boat for the money. The family, which incidentally had seen the arrival of two lovely, frizzy-haired twin girls, Franziska and Amadea, then had to rent accommodation in the *Bastille*, the big, dilapidated building on the east side of Skindholm.

In its day this house had been the home of the wealthy consul Sebastian Hansen, "Old Bastian", as he was called. The basement flat there was vacant just at this time due to the death of the former tenant, Sundholm the photographer. Sundholm had been a morose and lonely man of indeterminate origin. But although he was now dead and gone, it was as though impossible to be quite rid of him. In spite of having been thoroughly cleaned, the flat still smelled of Sundholm's tobacco and photographic fluids, and in the first nights after the new tenants had moved in, little Orpheus kept on dreaming of the late photographer. He dreamt that Sundholm was sitting on the edge of his bed, morose and brooding, in his shiny, worn jacket from the greasy lapels of which the pince-nez hung glittering in its chain. Occasionally, the boy would wake up in the middle of the night with the strangely mournful smell of the dead man's medicines in his nostrils. One night he dreamt that Sundholm's spirit opened a trapdoor in the floor and took him round a hidden apartment below, an endless series of rooms that were all bathed in a vague, sinister light from a hanging lamp, and in one of these terrible rooms sat the figurehead Tarira, staring at him with pale eyes. This figurehead otherwise belonged below the bowsprit of the old bark, the "Albatross". It represented a pale angel imperturbably staring ahead. But it frequently came to him in dreams, and it was the most ominous thing he knew. Not because it wasn't beautiful and kindly enough in itself, for that it certainly was – indeed it even reminded him a little of his own mother. But it was a baleful ghost nevertheless, and then you had to make the best of a bad job and call it by its name and pretend you were fond of it.

Otherwise, the Bastille was not a dismal place by any means. It was a big, overbuilt house with space for several families. In addition to the people from the Kelp Trench, the cellar was inhabited by a sprightly man called Fribert and his toothless old dog, Pan. Fribert delivered coal for Sebastian Hansen & Son; he always had black rings around his eyes, which produced a penetrating quality to his gaze, and he had the good-humoured habit each evening of singing himself to sleep with old ballads, especially "Ole Morske lay dead in the loft".

There were two flats on the middle floor in the Bastille. In one of them lived the Adventist family, the Samsonsens – husband, wife and daughter and little son. They ran a kind of laundry and mangle shop and kept Saturdays holy by playing the harmonium and singing defiant songs. In the other flat, which faced east and was very small, lived the carpenter known as Josef the Lament because he was a willing and much used singer at funerals. Josef was also an active member of the male voice choir, where he made a good contribution among the tenors. His hair and skin were curiously colourless, and his eyes were reddish, rather like two round portholes behind which a weak light can be seen glowing. His wife Sarina had been a maid out in The Dolphin, and it was generally known that she had married Josef the Lament because she had been seduced by a commercial traveller who had since disappeared abroad without trace. Meanwhile, Josef was ecstatic about his wife and daughter and slaved away to make them both content.

At the very top, in what were known as the "towers", two small flats had also been set up. Young Kornelius, a man who made much of his independence, lived in one of them. The other tower flat was the home of Mr Mortensen, a man who had known better days, and for whom all felt sympathy, but who nevertheless was known as a sourpuss and something of a bighead. He was a widower and had a daughter who was not quite all there.

Orpheus loved to stand at his Uncle Kornelius's tower window and look out. It was almost like flying, for not only was the Bastille a tall building, but it also stood on a promontory. From here there was a view out across the sea and of Skindholm with its winding alleyways, cramped gardens and confusion of roofs, some of which were covered with turf and populated by poultry.

Skindholm, which incidentally was no holm but a long rocky tongue of land, was the oldest district in the town. Here lived old Boman, Ole Brandy and the Crab King and many other odd characters, for instance Pontus the Rose, whose windows were painted with a profusion of roses and lilies and on whose door hung a showcase adorned with cheerful pictures of girls and ladies. Or Ura the Brink, the fortune teller, of whom all the town was secretly afraid and who couldn't be persuaded to leave her tiny ramshackle house on Cliff Rise, even though it seemed almost to be hovering freely in the air and indeed one day did disappear into the depths. Or the three maiden ladies by the name of Schibbye, who ran the smallest fashion shop in the world and looked like three skeletons. Here, too, was the old tavern, Olsen's Hotel, or "The Dainty Duck", where King Frederik the Seventh had stayed as a young prince, and further out on the point was the bigger hotel "The Dolphin", which didn't have a good reputation either.

Out on the very southernmost tip of Skindholm stood the High Warehouse and the other ancient houses and shops from the days of the monopoly. They were now owned by Sebastian Hansen & Son and served as stores for timber, salt and coal.

In Old Bastian's day the Bastille had been a distinguished edifice, but gradually as the town grew, Skindholm became a curiously out-dated and neglected place that respectable people moved out of. This tightly packed area was unhealthy and a fire hazard, and all the cellars were full of damp and rats. Skindholm had been left behind, and the new districts with their airy houses and gardens now constituted the real town.

The big room that had served Sundholm as a photographic

studio and had a pent roof with skylights overlooking the yard, was turned into a living room by Moritz and Eliana, but the sparse furniture from the Kelp Trench scarcely filled the large room. It was resoundingly empty here, cheerless and raw, and outside there was the wintry pale inlet where the black ships lay at anchor, dismantled and agape, surrendering themselves to their hopeless rocking backwards and forwards.

But there was one good thing about the former studio: it was splendidly suited to music. Moritz was not long in discovering that, and during the winter many pieces were practised, some for the string quartet, some for strings and wind instruments, occasionally also for Boman's choir.

The string quartet, which could also be expanded to a quintet and on a single occasion had counted no fewer than eight men (the Minuet from Schubert's Octet), was, like the choir, Kaspar Boman's work. At that time it consisted of Moritz, who played first violin, Sirius: second violin, Mr Mortensen: viola and Young Kornelius: cello. More often than not, the old music teacher was also there to conduct. Apart from the family, the audience usually consisted of the music-makers' friends and acquaintances, who came and went as it suited them: Ole Brandy, the one-legged sailmaker Olivarius, Pontus the Rose, Lindenskov the dancing-master, occasionally Janniksen the blacksmith and Mac Bett the decorator, and on special occasions Count Oldendorp and Judge Pommerencke, both of whom were great music lovers.

Orfeus liked these evenings. He would sit in a corner and enjoy himself. The stove was red hot; there was a reddish glow from the big tin lamps under the ceiling; the musicians were red-faced, and the music itself acquired a roseate tone, as it were. On occasions such as these, Sundholm the photographer was as though blown completely away. Old Boman bustled about, pointing and eagerly gesticulating or else sitting in rapt attention, stroking his grey goatee beard with his small veined hands. There was sometimes a curiously happy smile on his face, and on such occasions, despite beard and wrinkles, he looked like a boy, a rather shy boy at a birthday party. There was in general something childlike about these men as they played, especially when they were well on the way in a piece and it began to move forward of its own accord. They sat there with relaxed features and eyes dreaming as they humbly listened. The stern and suspicious Mr Mortensen looked like kindness itself. Kornelius was pale and sweating with emotion, sitting there with his projecting lower lip and his wispy hair hanging down over his glasses. Sirius sat with his head on one side, fondly stroking his violin. He was actually only a moderately good violinist and often the object of irritated remarks on the part of the other musicians.

But Moritz, the leader, sat bolt upright, and the notes emerged from his instrument like happy glimpses of sunshine.

Outside could be heard the seething of the dark waters, and when you looked out you could just see the outlines of the ships rocking in the darkness. But they, too, lay in a hint of red and with expressions of longing and listening, as though yearning to be freed from the prison imposed on them by their anchor chains and to set sail for the unmatched freedom of the windswept ocean.

5

On the kind-hearted and contented composer Young Kornelius and his secret plans

Now if these music-makers whose story is to be told below had seen to their work down here on earth instead of striving to reach the heavens in that curious way of theirs, then things might perhaps have gone far better for them in this, the pettiest of all known worlds. But that was simply not to be. Each in his own way, they were *possessed*, just as real musicians are by their very nature.

This applied not least to Young Kornelius. He was said to be a person not to be taken too seriously, for he was always happy and in good spirits and rarely produced what in the eyes of the world was an entirely sensible remark.

The latter quality was to some extent connected with the fact that he stammered. This unfortunate stammer came over him when he became excited, and it could take over to such an extent that he had to stand completely silent and make himself understood by means of hand movements and mimicry.

In everyday life, Kornelius was a compositor on the newspaper The Messenger. It provided a small regular monthly income that was just enough to keep the wolf from the door but which offered no future prospects whatever, in addition to which it was dreary and unhealthy work. That Kornelius was nevertheless a young man with few real worries, was due partly to the music to which he dedicated himself heart and soul. But it was also thanks to his innate ability to detach himself from that oh so important but immaterial web of petty everyday activities and to lose himself in curious visions, peering into things that were veiled from him and expecting the unexpected.

"You're a simple compositor and fiddler today, but who says you're not going to be the very person to find the *treasure*? It must be buried somewhere or other out here on Skindholm if we're to believe a persistent old legend, and he who seeks shall find. Why couldn't this treasure be lying hidden in the old churchyard just as well as anywhere else?"

In days long gone, a certain man by the name of Sansirana or Sansarasena lived out here on Skindholm; he was a free-booter and lived the depraved and dangerous life of a great nobleman, and one day retribution came to him, too: pirates arrived, took his robber's castle, forced their way into his houses, murdered him and his people and sailed away again with what they could lay their hands on. "But they didn't get hold of much, for Sansarasena was a man with foresight, and he had put his money and valuables out of sight before the pirates managed to come ashore. Since then, there has been no sign of this treasure, but it *is* still there, wherever it may be. And one thing is certain – no one apart from you gives a thought to this treasure and no one is doing anything to find it, and if you are lucky enough to come across it, at least you won't need to wear yourself out as a compositor on the smallest and, in many people's opinion, most ridiculous newspaper in the world. And just think how you would be able to spread goodness and blessings around if you suddenly went and became a rich man." Kornelius didn't only think of his own good, he thought of his brothers as well and of lovely, hospitable Eliana and her children, and then of old Boman and the unhappy, penniless Mr Mortensen, and finally of course, Ole Brandy and other friends, not forgetting the Crab King.

In brief: it can take a man all his life to find this treasure, but if fortune favours him he can just as easily find it tomorrow as any other day, and in any case he has a chance that other mortals don't have.

And Kornelius had made a start. From Sebastian Hansen & Son he had rented the long disused churchyard on the west side of Skindholm on the pretence that he wanted to establish a kitchen garden there. He had cleared the dense undergrowth of angelica and dock that had flourished there for centuries and collected all the mouldy old bones from the skeletons into a common grave, for which Josef the Lament had made a beautiful wooden cross with the words "Rest in Peace". And at the same time he had secretly searched for the treasure.

It was not there. But then that was *one* thing he knew.

The attempt had not been completely fruitless, however. On the one hand, during his gardening he had had the idea for a string quartet in three movements and had sketched two of them in his head, an *allegro ma non troppo* and an *andante con moto*. And on the other hand the kitchen garden provided the eager treasure seeker with an extra bit of income. He put the money aside. He was saving up for diving equipment, for his next plan was to search for the treasure on the bottom of the little Commander's Deep just off the old churchyard.

He had come to the conclusion that this was probably the very place where the treasure lay. But probability had now almost grown into certainty, thanks to Ura the Brink. For this woman was psychic. If people had lost something valuable they would secretly make their way up the Cliff Rise to see Ura, and if it suited her and the spirit was otherwise upon her, they were told where to look, and in an amazing number of cases her predictions turned out to be correct.

Meanwhile, Ura was not one of those who obliged anyone and everyone. Lots of people had gone to her in vain, and others had been given a vague hint, as though it were up to themselves to decide how to interpret it. Those bringing gifts for her were well received and she promised to do something for them. But she was otherwise an unpredictable creature, feared and hated by many, partly on account of her witchcraft and partly also because of the scandalous, sinful life she had lived in her youth.

On the day before Christmas Eve one year, Kornelius decided to visit this strange woman and present her with a well-fed, plucked duck and two red cabbages. Ura seemed to be quite overwhelmed at the sight of these things, but when she heard what it was Kornelius wanted her to do, she shook her head energetically, sniffed and looked up at the ceiling.

"No, no, a thing like that is far beyond my power," she said. "Remember, I'm an old woman. If I'd been in my prime, it would have been another matter. But since Dr. Manicus took my spleen, it's as if I'm finished. No, you'd better just take your wonderful gift back, Kornelius; I don't think I can do anything for you, much as I'd like to."

Ura started to laugh, as she often did. She produced these bursts of laughter at the most remarkable junctures, so they often had a confusing and somewhat disconcerting effect on whomever she was talking to.

"No, the duck's yours in any case," said Kornelius.

Ura laughed again and gave in: "Yes, well at least come inside and have a cup of coffee, Kornelius."

Ura was quite touched, as was quite plainly to be seen in that big reddish, shiny face of hers with its high cheekbones. There wasn't the slightest sign of grey in her black hair.

"Aye, I'd do anything for you, Kornelius," she said sorrowfully. "You're a wonderful person; goodness radiates from you, and I only wish I'd been able to help you to find this treasure, for you truly deserve it. But, you know, it's a terribly difficult thing you're asking of me."

"Erhh, I suppose we're alone here?" Kornelius asked cautiously. "I mean . . . I think . . . it would be best to keep that . . . that about . . . a strict secret."

"Of course," Ura confirmed him. "And as for Kornelia over there, you've no need to be afraid, 'cause she never meets anyone but me, and she's as reliable as gold."

Kornelius looked around in the faded little kitchen; his pince-nez had steamed up, and it was some time before he discovered Kornelia, Ura's young great-niece, who was sitting over by the fire nursing a big black cat. He remembered immediately that the poor girl was blind, of course. Perhaps he ought to go across and say hello to her.

He went over and took her hand. Kornelia got up shyly and put the cat down. A very young girl, not bad looking, not bad looking at all. What a pity that she was so hopelessly blind. But – there was nothing strange about her eyes; they were big and open, in fact it even seemed to him that she actually met his eye, something that gave him quite a strange feeling.

"Yes, it's one of the young men who play such lovely music," Ura explained. And she added as though confiding in him: "Yes, because Kornelia is so terribly fond of music. You know, she nearly always stands outside listening when you are playing out there in the Bastille. The poor lamb doesn't have much pleasure."

Kornelia blushed and sank back on her bench. Kornelius felt dreadfully sorry for her. It gave him quite a jolt to think she was so fond of music, this blind creature with a name almost the same as his own. Stammering and fumbling for the words, he said, "Well . . . why don't you come inside to us instead? Tell her she'll be heartily welcome . . . and then she'd hear so much better and she could sit down in the warm instead of standing shivering outside."

"No, you'll never ever get her to do that," smiled Ura, " 'cause Kornelia's terribly shy."

She set about filtering the coffee, and Kornelius sat down at the table. While they were drinking the coffee, Ura was silent and preoccupied, though her smile never completely left her face. But suddenly she stared excitedly at him and said with an eager little smile: "One thing I *can* tell you, Kornelius, is that your treasure *does exist*, and it . . . it's . . . it's lying somewhere damp where lots of something or other grow."

"Yes, seaweed," Kornelius confirmed in delight.

A shadow crossed Ura's face. She got up and said quickly, "It's here, Kornelius, aye, I could almost point to it, but errhh, I can't after all."

"No, that's almost enough in any case," said Kornelius animatedly, "For I can see now that it's in the water, isn't it; at the bottom of the Commandant Deep. I've had a feeling of that all the time, and I even dreamt it one night."

Kornelius felt a burning desire to press the old woman's hand, but suddenly Ura got up and her eyes assumed such a sharp and evil look that he felt a cold shiver run down his spine.

The old woman stood looking out of the window. "We're about to have an unwelcome visit," she said.

Kornelius had also got up to look out of the window. Three elderly figures were clambering up the steep Cliff Rise. They were Ankersen the savings bank manager and Mrs Nillegaard the midwife and her husband. They all three looked very serious.

"It's the welfare committee from the Christian Temperance Association Ydun," said Kornelius in surprise and without any sign of a stammer. "What do *they* want here? Oh well, it doesn't concern me, so I'll be off, Ura, and many thanks for your help."

The welfare committee had come to a standstill outside on the slope. The savings bank manager, out of breath and close sighted, was pointing with his walking stick to one of the four rusty iron ties that were holding Ura's little house fixed on the cliff, and Mrs Nillegaard was shaking her head in an energetic protest. Ankersen raised his stick and administered a fierce blow to the tie, and lo, it broke! It had been completely eaten away by rust.

"I call you to witness," exclaimed Ankersen and in righteous indignation he grasped Kornelius by the arm, but let go again when he discovered who it was: "Oh, you're not one of us at all, young man, go with God."

In his confusion, Kornelius bowed slightly and stammered as he backed away, "Thank you, Mr Ankersen, thank you very much."

6

More about the Ankersen phenomenon and his remarkable charitable and revivalist activities

The welfare committee of the Christian Temperance Association had a busy day that 23rd of December. The three representatives were coming straight from Pontus the Rose, to whom they had been talking on account of some obscene publications on display in his outdoor showcase, and they were on their way to none less than Captain Østrøm, the owner of the notorious tavern The Dolphin. But on their way they were going to have a serious word with that pig-headed woman on the Brink. As Ankersen said, this was a matter of vital importance.

"Up in the loft you go," Ura nudged her great-niece. "I want to be alone with them."

Kornelia disappeared without a sound up through the trapdoor to the loft, and Ura received her three visitors with a smile but no warmth. She invited them to sit down and herself adopted a reserved, non-committal posture.

Ankersen sat down heavily on the kitchen bench, puffing vigorously after the ascent. Mrs Nillegaard, too, who was dressed in an old, black-green plush cape, sat down. Her husband remained standing in the doorway. Nillegaard, the assistant teacher, was a prudent man who kept out of things.

Ankersen's capacious chest rose and fell, and he drew his breath with an audible rush of air through his hairy nostrils. "Ugh," he said staring at Ura through his thick glasses. "Getting up here's like climbing a mountain! And then your house is almost free-floating in the air, Ura. Aye, it's worse than it was the last time I was here, for the iron clamps are almost completely eaten away with rust. The next gale will see you down in the depths, Ura. Oh, yes. Even when I used to come here as a young man, Ura, this house was on the point of falling apart."

He now turned towards the Nillegaards and in a voice resonant with dark self-accusation, he said: "Yes, I deliberately mention the fact that I used to come here as a young man, for I have decided to use this opportunity once more to ask Ura Anthoniussen to answer a question that it is a matter of increasing urgency for me to have answered, and I wish that you, my dear friends, should be here as witnesses."

He polished his glasses with his handkerchief and put them back on his fleshy nose.

"Let it be in an atmosphere of tolerance," he said in a hoarse voice. "Indeed in an atmosphere of love. I have no desire to destroy, but to reconcile and build up. I come not to reproach you, Ura, for being so mired in the path of sin and prostitution during your youth. And I have the *right* to approach you on this, Ura, for at the same time I am giving myself away. Is that not true? I am not sparing myself."

Ankersen bent his bull-like neck and said in a voice that was filled with brooding self-reproach: "*I* was one of those who trod yon dreadful path of sin. Even though it only happened twice!"

He slowly took his glasses off. The expression on his face alternated between tears and laughter: "It happened while I was intoxicated. Intoxicated! And *how* that has tormented me day and night, year in and year out."

Ankersen turned a distorted face to Mrs Nillegaard, blindly pointing a finger in the direction of Ura: "That is why I have visited her so often, in secret, alone! But she has refused to answer my question and so give my conscience the comfort it so desperately needs and for which it sighs."

Ankersen now turned with a groan towards Ura herself: "For whether it *is* I or *not* I who is the father of your unfortunate, vanished son Matte-Gok, Ura, the full truth will lift a heavy burden from my breast."

Ankersen breathed out a little. He replaced his glasses on his nose and adopted a detached expression: "And that is why I today fully and unreservedly confide in my friends the

Nillegaards and bring them up here with me to have them as witnesses when once more and for the last time I ask you, Ura Anthoniussen: In the name of God: Is it I who am the father of that unfortunate child of yours that was begotten in blackest sin and has perhaps since been destroyed?"

There was a curiously knowing look in the corner of the savings bank manager's eye, and an almost imperceptible smile could be seen in his beard: "No, you don't need to answer at all, Ura. I will relieve you of that entirely. For if you continue to remain silent, Ura, I will take it as an affirmative answer this time. And I will not only call upon these two Christian souls as witnesses, but on God himself, who is and shall be to all eternity. Do you understand now, Ura?"

Mrs Nillegaard hurriedly took out a handkerchief and wiped her nose and her eyes. Her husband had half turned away in the doorway.

Ura was silent. She stood there with her face turned upwards and with raised eyebrows, but her eyes were closed, and a tiny, dogged smile played around her nose.

A few minutes elapsed. Ankersen looked at his watch. He was breathing heavily, almost snorting. Finally he spoke, saying in a low voice: "Let us pray."

He directed an impatient, embracing movement to the Nillegaards, and they all knelt at the settle. Ura remained in her place, standing. Ankersen's prayer took the form of a profound self-accusation, a plea for mercy, during which in a trembling voice he made a solemn promise to do what was humanly possible to find his lost son, poor Mathias Georg Anthoniussen, and to bring to him the blessings of faith and salvation.

Mrs Nillegaard was very touched, and it could be seen by her back that she was sobbing.

The prayer was finally at an end. Ankersen rose with difficulty; his full lips were open, and the thick, wolf-grey hair fell around his forehead. Confused, he sought to catch Ura's eye, and sitting down again on the settle he said, "And then, Ura. Then there was something else! You see, we are coming to you with a purely practical proposal as well, for the Christian

Temperance Association has the offer of the late Mangle Mary's little house down by the stream, and we will let you have it if you will move down there." In an increasingly stern and firm voice, he added: "Yes, for our welfare committee is very keen to help where it can. The town council doesn't mind people living in dangerous houses; they don't care about that any more than about anything else. And as for the Church! Well, you have presumably never ever had a single visit from the Reverend Lindemann? Have you, Ura? And your old father Anthonius, when he fell down off the ridge here and almost drowned at the age of seventy-nine . . . the vicar wasn't interested, was he? No, he couldn't even be bothered coming out here and administering the Sacrament to the old man when he died in his ninety-second year! But we, on the other hand, Ura, we will help. We will do our best. Not out of arrogance, Ura, but in repentance, in faith, in justice. Do you understand?"

Ura restrained herself and remained polite, but she said in a firm voice, "That is nice of you, Ankersen, but I am going to stay here where I've lived all my life and had my joys and my sorrows. And that's that."

Ankersen shook his head as he exchanged glances with Mrs Nillegaard. He rocked uneasily and continued in a lower voice: "And then there was something else. Erhh . . . well, you see, we would also like to help you in another way, Ura Anthoniussen, so that you don't . . . so that you don't need to live by these strange prophecies, you know what I mean. Our association would very much like to help you to get away from all that. For you remember that it is written: Thou shalt not practise witchcraft. And of course, you can easily say that that is not what you are doing, Ura. But would it not in any case be better for you to have a nice, decent living, for instance a little mangle business, and then come over to us and be converted and repent and surrender yourself entirely to our Lord and Redeemer Jesus Christ?"

"There's no reason for all that fuss," replied Ura. She turned to Mrs Nillegaard, as though to avoid Ankersen: "I see to my own affairs, so you look after yours, for God's sake.

I have never been a burden on anyone, and neither will I ever be."

"Ah, but listen, my dear. . . ." Mrs Nillegaard tried to speak, but Ankersen gently pushed her aside.

"Fuss, you say, Ura? *Fuss?*"

His voice rose into a falsetto, breaking as though in infinite tenderness and amenability: "Aye, but there is bound to be a certain fuss when God summons human souls! For we blind sinners, we kick against the pricks, for we know not what is best for us and we know not the time of our visitation! We know not Ura! We struggle. Until one fine day it is no longer any use. And then we yield. Then we become small and weak, sinners imploring mercy."

Ankersen's voice now slipped back to its customary level. He raised his head and wrinkled his brow imperiously: "The time of your visitation also approaches, Ura. Just think about what I have said and what has happened here today. I believe and sincerely hope in God's name that great events will soon come to pass that will also affect you, Ura. But whatever happens, we will not abandon you. We will be back, Ura. We will be back."

7

The poet Sirius makes a fresh attempt to establish himself on firmer ground

Sirius earned enough to live on by joining his brothers to play dance music in The Dolphin and by writing occasional poetry, but as neither of these two activities produced very much, he also worked as a painter and decorator and lived at the home of his master Mac Bett. He had once had an office job, which, despite his good middle school examination and uniquely beautiful handwriting, he had not been able to hold down, and for a time he had been an assistant teacher in Miss Lamm's school for infants.

Although the job of painter and decorator did not exactly fill Sirius with enthusiasm, he had nevertheless achieved a certain level of skill at wall papering. He rather liked wall-papers, he was almost fond of them, at least the flowery ones which with their constant repetitions could have an almost conjuring effect rather like the sight of spreading meadows, endless gardens in bud, mysterious underwater forests, snow-fall, indeed sometimes like the distant and lonely majesty of the firmament. But despite this and in spite of the fact that his master Mac Bett, who was otherwise extremely demanding, had to admit that Sirius had an obvious flair for wallpaper-ing, the poet daily felt a constantly growing aversion to this profession. For his part, Mac Bett could also often wish his assistant were far away, especially when he had overslept, as was often the case with Sirius because he often lay reading for half the night.

As emerges from Magnus Skæling's elegant essay, Sirius was well read, and he did not only turn to popular literature, but he also possessed Dante's Divine Comedy in a Swedish translation. Otherwise, Sirius's reading consisted mainly of biographies and books on cultural history, as can be seen from the record of books he borrowed from the library.[1]

One sunny morning in May, when all the gardens in town were celebrating the coming of their new leaves, Sirius went up to Mac Bett and said that his paper-hanging had to come to an end now. The master painter, who was of Scottish extraction and could be fearfully quick-tempered, set about belabouring his apprentice with a ruler, and when the poet climbed up on a table and tried to defend himself with a roll of wallpaper, the angry master hurled a pair of scissors at him. They caught his cheek, and he started to bleed a little.

"Oh merciful God, lad," shouted Mac Bett in horror. "I could have hit you in the eye, and then we'd both have been unhappy for the rest of our lives!"

He helped Sirius down from the table and examined his cheek, still trembling with rage.

"It's only a surface scratch," he decided with relief, sitting down exhausted on the floor, stroking his silvery whiskers and going on with a sigh: "Oh dear me. Yes, of course it's best you give up, Sirius, for otherwise I'd have done you an injury sooner or later, and you never hit back, I must admit that. But what are you going to do now, you poor wretch? You've nothing to fall back on, penniless and bone idle as you are!"

Sirius smiled and said plaintively, "I write, Mac Bett, I write poetry!"

The old master had no answer to this. He sent Sirius a perplexed look hiding both scorn and compassion.

Meanwhile, Sirius had a plan. He would set up an infants' school of the same kind as Miss Lamm's. For three days, he trudged around the town with the aim partly of finding some pupils and partly of discovering suitable accommodation. Both turned out to be more difficult than he had imagined.

---

[1] For instance the life of Johannes Ewald, Ahlberg: Victor Hugo and Modern France; F. Petersen: Søren Kierkegaard's Concept of Christianity; H.S. Vodskov: Selected Studies; Nissen: W.A. Mozart; and Notes of Ben Jonson's Conversations with W. Drummond.

While wandering around the spring-bedecked town, but without achieving his objectives, he again came across Mac Bett, who grasped the lapel of his collar with a sigh and offered to give him back his old job. Sirius thanked the master painter for his offer, but rejected it and initiated him in his plan.

"Come back home with me and have a bite to eat," said Mac Bett. "I think I've got a good suggestion for you."

This suggestion was that Sirius should run his school in the room behind Mac Bett's little picture frame shop. It was not to cost him anything, but in return, Sirius was to serve the shop's customers in the mornings.

"Then we'll save the wages I pay that dullard of a girl who serves down there otherwise," said Mac Bett. Encouragingly, he added: "And it won't be difficult, of course, because on the one hand I'm afraid there aren't many customers, and then you already know the trade so well."

Sirius gratefully accepted this offer. And within a week he also managed to recruit four pupils, his nephew Orfeus, the gravedigger's son Peter, the Adventist boy Emanuel Samsonsen and Julia Janniksen. Julia was fifteen years old and the daughter of Janniksen the blacksmith. She was enormous for her age, but rather lacking in intellectual capacity.

The window in Mac Bett's back room overlooked Janniksen's garden. There was a lovely view, especially now in spring, but it was soon to emerge that the proximity of the smithy had an unfortunate influence on the teaching. The first two school days went well enough; the three boys were keen and easy to teach; the girl was rather heavy going, but thanks to her advanced age she was able to keep up, and the customers in the picture frame shop were also easy enough to cope with. The sight of the smith's flowering red currant bushes provided spiritual refreshment.

The third day, too, which was a Saturday, started with sunshine, bird song and a feeling of contentment. There was not a sound from the smithy; the blacksmith was having a visit from Lindenskov, the dancing teacher; the two were friends and regularly played skittles behind the house. But at about twelve o'clock, the blacksmith suddenly appeared in the garden with a bottle in his hand, followed by Lindenskov. They were both already very drunk. With a heartbreaking lack of consideration, they both settled in the midst of a bed of purple crocuses and started pledging each other. It was not long before the blacksmith started to sing. Sirius ordered his pupils not to look out of the window and by speaking in a loud voice and banging his ruler, he sought to drown the smith's singing, which adopted an increasingly unrestrained character.

Neither the children nor the teacher, however, could be persuaded not to look out now and again. Janniksen the blacksmith was a big, strong-limbed man with a great, hairy chest. He had a Franz Joseph beard and a black hollow in the middle of his forehead. The dancing master was small and wizened, with staring fish-like eyes, protruding front teeth and a dangling moustache.

Julia sighed. She had an expression in her eyes as though she were about to weep. "Look," she said suddenly. "Dad's starting to dance."

Sirius went across to the window. Yes, the blacksmith had indeed started to dance. The huge man was leaping about, wildly and clumsily, turning round on himself, gesticulating with his enormous arms, stamping and roaring. This was what was known as the "one-man dance". Sirius knew it well from rumbustious evenings out in The Dolphin; it was a kind of show of strength on which the smith always embarked at a certain stage in his inebriation. The dancing-master sat knocking two empty bottles together in place of music. But what is this now? The blacksmith bends down over Lindenskov and lifts him up, rocks him in his arms like a baby and . . . suddenly hurls him into one of the big red currant bushes!

"Oh no," exclaimed Sirius. "Now he's ruining the whole garden."

"That's what the blacksmith's like," commented Grave-digger Peter soberly. "He wrecks everything when he's drunk."

"Look, mother's coming now," shouted Julia, biting her finger.

Sirius sighed. Yes, Mrs Janniksen was in the offing right enough. She was big and swarthy like her husband; her protruding eyes had an expression of composure and dark determination.

"Listen, Julia," said Sirius sternly. "You must stop looking now and come and see to your work."

Sirius himself went away from the window and sat at the wallpaper-covered packing case lid that served as his desk. Julia sat down and uttered a subdued but confused laugh. Some customers came to the shop, so Sirius had to go and attend to them. When he returned, the children were naturally over by the window. Julia was weeping profusely.

"Back to your seats," commanded Sirius. But the children showed no sign of moving.

"She's killed the blacksmith," announced Gravedigger Peter quietly.

"What's she done?" said Sirius excitedly.

Oh, fortunately that was not so. The smith was admittedly lying on his back in the flower bed, but he was certainly not dead; he lay there ululating gently, either from pain or delight or simply because he was so drunk. His wife was busy extracting the dancing-master from the red currant bushes' confusion of red blossoms and tiny, round, innocent leaves. Lindenskov had some scratches on his face and blood was coming from a gash near the corner of his mouth.

"Oh no, this is going too far," said Sirius and clacked his tongue piteously. He stood tightly clasping the fat girl Julia and stroking her hair with his thin hand. "Don't cry like that, girl; it won't do any good in any case."

Shortly after this, he was down in the garden. The blacksmith still lay there moaning. Lindenskov was groaning, too. There were red currant flowers in his clothes and hair; his moustache was dripping with blood, and he was humming in a broken, almost contrite, voice:

> Of all the flowers of spring,
> So fine they were and fair,

There's one apart,
Close to my heart . . .

Mrs Janniksen came out with a rag and wiped his face clean. Then Sirius grasped him by the arm, led him out of the garden and took him home.

As usual, Lindenskov's house was full of womenfolk. He had seven daughters, but the Misses Schibbye were there as well along with some other ladies, and there were gold-edged cups on the table – it looked like a major chocolate party. Lindenskov clung on to Sirius and wanted him to come in with him, but the ladies made a dreadful fuss and were out-raged and quite beside themselves with fury; they accused Sirius of being a drunkard and seducer, and his attempts to convince them of his innocence were mercilessly brushed aside. The little dancing-master reluctantly disappeared into a confusion of skirts and puff sleeves, and the door was closed with a demonstrative bang.

Sirius sent the children home. The boys immediately ran off, but Julia stayed behind. She had stopped crying but was spasmodically gasping for breath.

"Do you really not want to go home?" asked Sirius sympa-thetically. "Oh well, then just you sit here and wait until Mac Bett comes back."

Sirius himself sat down at the desk. He had taken out a pencil and was working at a poem. He got up now and then and walked across the floor and into the shop. It was a poem that had long been haunting him. Now it came as though of its own accord. The poem about spring and the new leaves, the multitude of flowers and the sunshine that as though by a miracle liberates the soul from its shabby apparel of worry and longing and prepares a refreshing bath for it. Curious that it should come now, in this midst of all this mess.

Julia sat in her place and stared at him, quite lost in thought. Mac Bett came back and pottered about in the shop, grum-bling quietly to himself. Sirius had his poem finished. He took Julia by the hand. They went out to the Bastille. Sirius found Eliana and said earnestly: "We must look after this girl a bit;

she's not particularly bright, but she has a good heart, and it's not much fun for her at home, as you know."

Eliana made some coffee for Sirius and Julia. The girl followed her everywhere with her eyes and looked so touching that Eliana had to give her a kiss on the forehead. But in the midst of it all, the blacksmith's wife arrived. The big woman's face was all puffed up and grimy. She didn't say a word, but took a firm hold of Julia's arm and went off with her.

That afternoon, Sirius made a fair copy of his poem. He read it through several times until he knew it all by heart. It was a good poem, perhaps the best he had ever written. In his state of elation he went to see the editor of The News. Here, at last, was a poem that deserved to be seen in print.[2]

Olsen, the editor, glanced through the poem and handed it back with a shake of his head.

"You don't like it?" said the poet.

Olsen took off one of his canvas shoes and started examining the inside. Then he fetched a hammer from the composing room. Downcast, Sirius watched how the big man struggled to get a nail pulled out of his shoe with the help of the cleft hammer head. Finally, the editor abandoned the experiment and knocked the nail down into the sole. Then he absent-mindedly went back to the composing room and was not seen again.

Sirius folded the paper up and put it in his pocket, but he had not yet abandoned all hope of seeing this poem in print. He went up to Jacobsen, the editor of The Messenger, the radical newspaper. Jacobsen gave the impression of being very busy, but he nevertheless took the time to run through the poem. He laughed, looked at Sirius over his glasses and sat down for a short while in an American rocking chair.

"It's no damned good," he said. "There's no point in all this romanticism. We live in an age of realism, not a golden

[2] See Sirius Isaksen: Posthumous Poems, "Spring", p. 57. In his history of literature Professor Christian Matras says of this poem that it is written with such a happy and light touch and is infused throughout with such fine and ecstatic music that one is reminded of no less a poem than H.A. Brorson's "Be still, my soul, rest yet, my soul".

age of writing, my dear sir. We have no need of idylls, Sirius Isaksen. Note that for your own sake. Write a satirical poem about conditions here, the parish pump, the reaction spreading everywhere, Nillegaard and Ankersen with their hysterical Christian temperance nonsense. Teach them a lesson, all of them, then you'll be doing something useful. Sunshine and birdsong are things you can amuse yourself with at home on your own if you can be bothered and if you've got time."

He handed back the paper to Sirius and lit a dead cigar stump. Jacobsen was much in need of a shave, and there were splashes of yellowish froth in the corners of his mouth. Drawing eagerly on his cigar, he added: "But you're gifted Sirius, by God you are. You're *daft* like your brothers and your father with his Aeolian harps. But you're all bloody gifted when you pull yourselves together. The song you wrote for Captain Østrøm's silver wedding wasn't at all bad; you managed to get everything in. But then it *was* copied straight from my leader in The Messenger, ha, ha. But it was well done. But, as I say, romantic poems about the spring – oh, not on your life. Write something with a bit of a bite in it."

He emphasised these last words by shaking his head violently, causing his great flabby jowls to quiver.

Sirius wandered the streets dejectedly for an hour or so. Then he went up to Kornelius who had just arrived home from work and was having a cup of tea and some ship's biscuits.

Kornelius read the poem, nodded as he quietly chewed away, and said he would set it to music that very evening as soon as he had shaved and changed. Sirius was given a cup of tea. Kornelius took his cello and set about strumming and humming.

That evening, the weather was particularly beautiful. Kornelius and Sirius fetched their brother and his wife to go a walk. Moritz took his horn. They walked out along the shore as far as Punt Point, where they sat down at the very end of the seaweed-scented point. Moritz played Kornelius's new melody through a few times and then produced some cheerful improvisations on the theme on his horn.

8

On old Boman and his godson

Orfeus had long ago started to learn the violin from his godfather Kaspar Boman, and he was making good progress.

It was obvious that he had inherited his father's gifts. The old music teacher was strict and scathing as long as he was teaching, but outside the lessons he sank into a characteristic boundless and melancholy kindness and talked to his pupil about music and its masters or lost himself in reminiscences from his own life.

Boman had been born on the little island of Hveen as the son of a gardener and accordion virtuoso, but he had left home at an early age, becoming something of a rolling stone and living partly as a gardener and partly as a musician. For a time he had taken lessons from a well-known musician in Copenhagen, and he might well have become something good in the world of music, but fate had decided differently, and here he was now, God help him, as a lonely, childless old widower. But oh, no, he was not lonely, for he had his pupils and friends and his flowers, and music had gone with him as well, and as long as you had that, you had all the heart could desire.

Boman's little parlour resembled a garden. On the window ledge and everywhere where there was room otherwise, luxuriant potted plants stood or hung, and vines covered almost the entire ceiling. Here and there on the walls there hung faded portraits and prints of composers and musicians. They all had the same kindly, attentive expression as Boman himself, but they also looked as though they could be fierce and determined when it came to the point. They were certainly all famous and fine men, but they had almost all started at the bottom as poor boys often in difficult circumstances. Boman talked about them as you talk about old friends you have known as children and seen grow up, achieve glorious things and then die from it all, for most of them died young, indeed some as mere boys, and those were perhaps even the very best of them.

One day when Orfeus came for his lesson, he found Boman stretched out on his threadbare chaise longue. The old man was lying there with his eyes tight closed and had an unfamiliar, suffering expression round his mouth.

"Is it Orfeus?" he asked in a whisper. "Sit down, my boy. I hope this'll soon pass; it's only a bit of a turn." Orfeus spent a quarter of an hour in great inner turmoil, for it was almost more than he could bear to see the kind old man lying there suffering. All the plants, the pictures on the wall and the big double bass standing in its linoleum cover looked like some human creature – all sharing in Boman's suffering in their own silent wait-and-see manner. The composers looked as though they were thinking: "This is bad, but these things happen after all."

In time, the old man started breathing more easily; he sighed and stretched out on the chaise longue, opened his eyes and smiled with a wrinkled nose: "There, that's better."

He was all right again before long. He pointed to the portrait of Weber on the wall: "Aye, what are we to say to it? I'm an old man, a real old man soon, but this chap here was a poor sick weakling throughout his life. Not to mention him across there, Beethoven, the greatest of them all; he became as deaf as a post, aye, what do you say to that? And even in his prime as well."

Boman quietly shook his head and for a moment looked quite confused, but then he suddenly assumed a determined look and started on the lesson.

Orfeus had gradually become quite accustomed to the many faces on Boman's wall; he could picture them in his mind, and they would occasionally reveal themselves to him in dreams, sometimes individually, sometimes in whole groups, sometimes together with Boman, but at other times in the company of Sundholm the photographer or with the figure-head Tarira. It wasn't always equally nice, especially when Tarira was there. Things went completely wrong one day when Orfeus had measles and lay with a very high temperature. The Bastille cellar was invaded by a host of men dressed in wigs or with half-long hair like that of a woman; they smiled at him and winked sarcastically and ambiguously, and one of them was especially nasty, a slight man with a thin nose, thread-like spectacles and a huge fur collar. He stood all the time over in the semi-darkness in the corner, blinking and making the most extraordinary faces.

Boman, who heard of his godson's remarkable visions from Moritz, came out to the Bastille towards evening and sat for a long time by the boy's bed.

"I really believe that the ghost he's talking so much about is none other than Carl Maria von Weber," Boman whispered with a worried smile. "Don't you think, Moritz, it would help if you played something on your violin? Something by Weber, perhaps? No, of course I don't know. Perhaps it's a daft idea."

"No, not at all," said Moritz animatedly.

He fetched his violin. In his dazed state Orfeus heard how the notes came drifting, some from deep down and some from high up, and then suddenly everything became light around him and the strange guests from his fever made for the doorway and quickly left.

Finally, there was no one left but Tarira. But a tender, attentive expression had come into her pale eyes, and now she came across to his bed and gently smoothed his pillow.

"Don't you know me, dear?" she asked reproachfully but at the same time with a smile, and yes, now Orfeus knew her all right . . . it wasn't Tarira at all, it was only his mother!

SECOND MOVEMENT

In which remarkable things start to happen

Moritz is swallowed up by the ocean, while a singing count and his sweetheart are left alone on a desert island

Boman's choir occasionally gave concerts for charitable purposes, and naturally Moritz and the other musicians from the Bastille also took part in them. Now there was to be a concert in aid of a new organ, a church concert with bazaar, tombola and wheel of fortune. It was the new vicar, the Reverend Fruelund who had had the idea, and he turned up in the Bastille one day to ask Moritz to take part.

"But of course, we can only use good music, indeed the very best music," he impressed on him. "You do understand, don't you?"

The Reverend Fruelund was a tall, commanding figure. His voice was beautiful and resonant, and he spoke loud and clear as though he suspected everyone of being a little hard of hearing.

"What would you think about Mozart's Quartet in D minor, the one, you know, the one with . . .?" And Moritz made to hum the andante, but the clergyman shook his head: "Well, yes, but I'd been thinking of a lovely little piece called 'Nazareth'. Do you know it? I can't for the moment remember who it's by, but my wife has the music for it, and as you are supposed to be so musical you'll soon learn it. I thought it would be nice to have it played on a trombone and organ."

"I know that piece all right, it's by Gounod," said Moritz. He wanted to add: "It's a deadly dull slow waltz. Mrs Fähse, the apothecary's wife once sang it, it was simply awful." But he desisted.

The clergyman nodded and added in a didactic voice, "Trombone, you see. A trombone is suited to a church, but not music for a quartet, no, certainly. And then we should have a couple of hymns for male voice chorus. I rather fancy conducting a choir of that sort if you for your part will assemble it and practise the hymns – you know, in a rough sort of way."

Then he added, "I was a member of the Students' Union Male Voice Choir in Copenhagen for three years."

He nodded with his handsome curly head: "Then the rest of the programme will consist mainly of organ music. And I will recite a religious poem by Paludan-Müller, and then Mr Lamm the organist's daughter will sing "Jairus's Daughter" and Count Oldendorp will sing "By brothers called the little one".

"Lamm?" said Moritz. He wanted to add, "Lamm can't play anything but Thorvaldsen's Funeral March, and when he does you'd think the organ had broken down."

"Yes, *Lamm*," said the pastor and gave the ferryman a glance that made it clear that any quips would be unwelcome.

The great day arrived with sunshine and a strong wind and flags fluttering in the breeze.

At midday, Moritz left for Østerøre in his ferryboat. He had Count Oldendorp with him as a passenger; the count was to fetch his fiancée, who was a daughter of the Reverend Schmerling of Østerøre. Count Oldendorp was in a splendid mood and sat learning by heart the text of the hymn he was to sing in the concert. "It looks better when you don't need to stand and sing from a book," he said. "Here, Moritz, what about testing me?"

He gave Moritz the book. Then he took half a bottle of cognac out of his back pocket. "We both need to get our strength up," he said seriously. And with a sigh, he took a huge gulp and handed the bottle to Moritz.

The two men sat in the back of the boat, which danced merrily over the lively waves. The count was a youngish man of unusual dimensions; his powerful, somewhat wobbly voice made itself heard above the sound of the motor and the roar of the waves.

The count stepped ashore happy and refreshed at Østerøre. His fiancée Anna-Iris, a thirty-year-old girl with a maternally concerned, earnest look, was waiting on the landing stage, wrapped in shawls and scarves. He lifted her down into the boat in his gigantic arms and then attended to a basket of well-packed bottles.

"Oh, do take care, Karl Erik," said Anna-Iris. "That's red currant wine from our garden. It's a little gift to the Chief Constable from father."

The vicar of Østerøre, who was in bed with sciatica, waved excitedly from his bedroom window, and the young couple waved back. The boat put out to sea. The count gave his fiancée the book so she could test him. His raised his happy, ruddy face and in voice transcending all around him, he sang:

> I wandered carving, lost in thought
> Firm of finger, keen of voice
> A lyre I found, a tune I caught
> Pure as harp with note so choice.

The boat rocked violently off Mermaid Holm; they had the current with them but the wind against. Anna-Iris clung nervously to her fiancé's arm; still singing, he stroked her cheek to keep her calm. But suddenly the engine stopped.

Moritz handed the rudder to the count and started examining the engine. The boat drifted sideways in the direction of the northernmost tip of Seal Island. Anna-Iris moved still closer to her fiancé and spread a corner of her shawl over his knee.

"There's nothing to be afraid of," said the count comfortingly and resumed his singing.

Moritz was working away to get the engine going again. He was sweating and there were black splashes and streaks all over his face. The boat drifted away apace. The wind was stronger than on the outward trip. In the middle of the channel, where wind and stream were battling for mastery, contorted ramparts had formed of intractable, sun-glittering water. Moritz got up from the engine and took the rudder for a moment. "We must be sure to keep well away from the whirlpool," he said.

The count went on singing. He had closed the book and put it in his pocket. "Get a move on and get that bloody thing working again," he shouted between two verses while at the same time glancing comfortingly at his fiancée in a rather exaggerated attempt to allay her fears. Moritz set about the engine again. It turned over a couple of times with something of a judder; the boat gave a start and turned its prow in the right direction.

"Bravo," shouted the count and took his book out again.

But a moment later, the engine stopped once more.

Moritz shook his head. Anna-Iris started whimpering nervously. The count laughed and yawned as though nothing was wrong. He went across and stuck his head down into the engine room to Moritz: "I think this requires a pick-me-up." Moritz felt the neck of a bottle against his chin. The count returned to his seat alongside his fiancée and resumed his singing.

The wind increased in strength; the foaming waters seethed happily and mercilessly around the drifting boat. Again Moritz managed to get a sign of life from the engine, and they made for the coast, into the shelter of Mermaid Holm, and Moritz leapt ashore on the islet and fixed the mooring rope to a jutting rock. Laughing merrily, the count helped his fiancée up on to dry land, where they seated themselves in the shelter of a rock, and he took out his book again. Moritz, who lay with his head down in the engine room could hear the count's exuberant singing:

I wandered carving, lost in thought. . . .

The wind was really getting up now. Along the coast of Seal Island a line of white foam had appeared, and a confusion of foam and froth adorned the ramparts of water out in the sound.

"Oh, you could at least stop that ridiculous singing now," scolded Anna-Iris. "I hardly think this is the place for it. And besides, you're singing the same verse over and over again."

"Yes, but it's a lovely verse," replied the count, "where he's going around carving. That's just the thing for me. You know, going around lost in thought and carving."

He got up to see how Moritz was doing with the engine, but there was no sign of the boat.

"What the hell . . .?" he exclaimed laughing loudly, and started to look out to sea. Anna-Iris, too, had got up. She was on the point of tears as she pointed out across the rushing waves: "Oh no, just look. He's right out there."

Now the count, too, saw the boat . . . a black dot far out in all the white turmoil.

"It's worked itself free," moaned Anna-Iris.

"Oh, I'm not sure about that," said the count. He slapped his thigh violently in a kind of ecstatic gesture. "Yes, it bloody well has; see, it's left a piece of the painter behind."

"Well, is that anything to be so amused about?" said Anna-Iris, looking at him in astonishment. "We've been left behind all alone on this desert island. We might never get back to shore alive, Karl Erik."

"Of course we shall," hooted the count. He scrambled up to the highest point on the islet. A sobbing Anna-Iris followed him. Wind and foam swirled around them. The count took out his handkerchief and waved, but there was not a living soul to be seen on the windswept shore.

"Oh, do come down again," shouted Anna-Iris. "Where are you taking us? Let's at least get down where there's some shelter."

"Yes, just a minute, just a minute," said the count in an effort to pacify her. He bent down behind a projecting rock and took a long, lingering gulp from the hip flask. Then he returned to his fiancée, radiant with joy and singing lustily.

Anna-Iris stared at him. There was fear in her eyes, but scorn and cold despair as well together with a certain determination.

"Never in all my born days have I seen anything so foolish and so terrible," she said.

He laid a hand on each of her shoulders and sang his calm and ponderous reply:

61

> I wandered carving, lost in thought
> Firm of finger, keen of voice

"Oh, do stop it," she complained. "You'll be the end of me with all your nonsense." And she added in a threatening voice, "I don't *trust* you, Karl Erik. I've no *faith* in you."

Completely calm, and intensely and emphatically, he replied:

> Then I came upon a lyre
> Chaste as a harp with organ sound

"Chaste as a harp," he repeated emphatically. "*Chaste as a harp.*"

Busy as he was with the engine, Moritz had nevertheless noticed that the boat had worked itself free, but he left it at that. There was no point in shouting out, for the count couldn't help in any case. The boat was drifting off to the east in the seething channel. He was forced to seize the rudder and try to steer a course round the whirlpool, and he managed more or less. The boat came out into crested waters that were as stony as a frozen road and was rapidly being carried east towards the open sea. It was like being swept away along a swiftly moving river full of boulders. But in time it glided out of the current; the mighty ocean received it with broad and benevolent indifference, raised it up on mighty waves where a fierce wind was blowing amidst a continuous shower of foam, and then it again drew it down into a trough where there was shelter for a moment.

Moritz started to consider the situation. Yes, there was a pretty strong wind, but there was no question of a real gale. The count and his fiancée had fortunately been left in safety. People at least don't die on Mermaid Holm, so close to inhabited land. At the most they might be rather cold, but then they had their blankets and could stay on the sheltered side of the islet.

But the boat was still drifting east out into the desolate

ocean, and there was no vessel to be seen, not even the tiniest fishing boat.

And the hours passed. The long late summer afternoon was ebbing away. The sunlit waves were taking on a darker shade, the sea was becoming greener. It wasn't an entirely attractive prospect to be placed at the mercy of this boundless expanse of water.

The concert! It was supposed to start now at six o'clock. Oh well. He would probably be missed, and so of course, not least, would the count and his fiancée. And they would start a search. Probably in Consul Hansen's big motorboat, the Triton, and perhaps with the little steamer, the Neptunus, which was in port just at that moment. The count and his fiancée would be found first, and they would be able to indicate the direction in which the boat had disappeared. It was only a question of patience.

Moritz got up and flapped his arms about in order to keep warm. There was the basket of wine over in the stern.

Contrary to his expectations, the wind started to increase at sunset. The sun burst forth for a moment and endowed the ocean landscape with a touch of coppery brown. The hump of Seal Island stood out dark violet against the sky. It would at least be a few hours before *that* was out of sight.

Moritz set about the engine again. But it was pretty hopeless. It slowly began to grow dark. The roar of the waves rose to a fierce howl. The stars appeared sporadically. The bare horizon began to fray; the darkness hospitably opened up its cavern. It did indeed. But still it was unthinkable that this was to be the end. It was only a matter of being patient.

He got up and swung his arms about, warmed his body a little and abandoned all melancholy thoughts. Various pieces of music glided through his memory. A broad and as it were sunlit largo by Haydn. He could hear the individual instruments, the cello's hesitant little chromatic solo, during which the piece grows darker for a moment as when a cloud drifts in front of the sun, only to emerge into the kindly warming light again. Yes, there was something rather nice about that largo, sunshine and happy times.

Other music for strings. Horn solos, marches. Schubert's three marches militaires. Meanwhile the wind blew around the boat in long gusts, and night began to fall.

Moritz went back and forth, humming a little, and started fiddling with the engine, more or less at random. It *might* just happen by some miracle that it would start up again in spite of everything. But the damp, greasy metal showed no sign of life.

He turned his back on the engine and now once more stood face to face with the dark wastes. Aye, what was one more than a speck of dust in the night? He suddenly remembered the words: In the beginning God created the heaven and the earth, and there was darkness upon the face of the deep and so on. This biblical text again made him think of his father and his remarkable doings up in the church tower where he had his Aeolian harps. When the wind was howling in the dried sheep's gut in these harps, it was as though entirely supernatural powers were at play. This was music for the departed and those mouldering in death. They could hear it in their graves. Ugh!

And thus he again came to think of "The Dance of the Blessed Spirits" by Gluck and in this connection of Eliana, who had a habit of singing this melody. Yes, she had hummed it by Orfeus's cradle, musical as she was. She used it as a kind of lullaby. That, and then the charming little minuet from Schubert's Octet.

No, by God! Moritz again turned away from the darkness upon the face of the deep. He considered tasting the Reverend Schmerling's wine and came to the conclusion that he could justify this under these unusual circumstances. The wine was sweet and heavy and tasted like liqueur. The quiet, rubicund priest certainly knew how to brew a good drink.

Moritz was hungry, the wine went to his head, and the music again started bubbling up in his memory. He quite consciously used it to banish all melancholy thought. Eliana . . . what would become of her and the children if he remained out there? Oh, get lost! Here came Søderman's "Wedding at Ulvshøg". It was one of Boman's favourite pieces and reminded him of summer and sunshine and an endlessly carefree life.

But then the Dance of the Blessed Spirits once more sneaked its way in, and the thought of Eliana forced itself on him and couldn't be forced out of his mind again. Struggle against it as he might, her image hovered in front of him all the time. He saw her as she looked in those insane days of first love when she was a waitress out in The Dolphin and radiated – radiated in competition with the sun-glittering waters outside the windows, a vision of a fair-haired creature, admired and courted by all, but not to be conquered. He still had the feeling that it was almost unreasonable that it was *he* who captured her, he, the poor sailor, and not for instance the elegant Mr Storm the head clerk, or Wenningstedt the wealthy lawyer, who had also paid court to her with a vengeance, indeed, the middle-aged old fool had even written several letters to her asking her to marry him.

But it was music that had helped Moritz. Eliana and he shared a common delight in music. And ultimately it was Boman they could thank for it all.

Aye, there was a great deal to thank Boman for.

Moritz took another swig from the bottle; he could just as well empty it at a go straight away. At least he was alive. He sat there holding the wet rudder. He was cold and wet and alive. And there was a whole basket full of bottles left. And tomorrow was Monday.

It was Monday. However you looked at it. Monday at sea. Monday in isolation. Monday in cold and hunger and lethargy. Monday in distress at sea all right, but at least Monday. And everything else was of no importance for the time being.

And thank God for that.

It was more than four hours before help reached Count Oldendorp and his fiancée on Mermaid Holm, despite the fact that one living creature on the shore had watched the couple's frantic waving right from the start.

But this creature was the Crab King. He was sitting by a

small pond of brackish water, which he sometimes visited to observe some hermit crabs that lived there.

It may be that this inscrutable dwarf failed to realise that these people shouting and waving were stranded beings who had a right to be rescued. It may be that their constant waving, sometimes with scarves, sometimes with fluttering shawls only made the little manikin fall into a reverie. At all events, nothing visible happened to him except that he settled down more comfortably and abandoned himself to watching them with interest.

Occasionally, the wind carried singing and laughter and curious words and sentences to his ears, and he listened attentively: "You hopeless fool!" "You wretch!" "Yes, that's what I said!" "I'll remember that, you bet I will. Just you wait!"

The Crab King heaved a deep sigh and stroked his black, silver-sprinkled beard. It will for ever remain a mystery whether his disquieting passiveness was due to ill will, indifference or ignorance. Even Dr. Manicus, who was an excellent doctor and a shrewd judge of character could never make out what was really hidden in the Crab King, this acondroplastic dwarf with the flipper-like short limbs and the marked and as it were frighteningly experienced and brooding face.

2

Of Moritz's subsequent fate and of the excesses of Mr Ankersen, the savings bank manager

The daily grind in a small town, the constant repetitions and minor irritations of everyday life make people foolish and irritable, jealous and petty. So there can be something elevating in seeing the change for the better that occurs when something *unusual* occasionally takes place and raises things out of their acerbic and finicky everyday. It is as though the town for a moment becomes conscious of standing on the edge of the enormous chasm that is the ocean.

A man, a fellow human being whom we are accustomed to seeing every day and who as such could be any one of us, has suddenly been swallowed up by the great unknown surrounding us.

He has vanished in an all powerful and unfeeling wasteland which, if not the irrevocable annihilation of death, is nevertheless the merciless wilderness of the sea. There is still hope for this man, and this hope spreads like wildfire and creates a spark in souls both great and small; the entire town congregates down by the wharf to see the decked boat the Triton and the little steamer the Neptunus sail off if possible to wrest a quarry from death.

"It'll be all right, you'll see," people nod encouragingly to each other, and they talk of Moritz as a magnificent chap, a gifted musician, a good father and husband, and even a *hero*. Yes, they lose themselves with pride and pain in the memory of Moritz Isaksen's deed in November 1899 when all on his own he had saved seven sailors and a lady from the schooner "Karelia". That was a heroic deed if ever there was one. That winter Moritz had been on people's lips more than anyone else, and he had indeed been awarded the life-saving medal as well.

Aye, Moritz was a fine chap through and through.

But there are naturally a few individuals who don't think like the others. There is for instance Mr Ankersen, the savings bank manager. Without mincing his words he declares that this thing now happening to Moritz Isaksen has been sent him as a punishment for his worldly life and his fondness for the bottle.

"Yes, but it would be a shame if . . .?" objects Ankersen's clerk, Fat Alfred.

"Shame?" snarls Andersen, rising and frothing at the mouth. "Yes, *shame* indeed. The shame of sin. And sin brings sorrow and unhappiness in its wake. The wages of sin is death."

Ankersen is in a state of great agitation. He walks back and forth, spluttering like burning pitch. Fat Alfred watches his boss in a mixture of deference and fear and thinks, "After all, Ankersen's fundamentally a good man. Ankersen wants the best for everyone. But he is terrible when this mood takes him."

Yes, Andersen was terrible. To the accompaniment of a great fuss, he put on his galoshes and went straight across to the Bastille, where he launched a veritable attack on Moritz's wife and the little group of friends and comforters who had gathered around the poor woman.

"This was inevitable," he thundered. "This is the hand of God, the chastising hand of God! Think not that you can avoid this hand touching you! Believe it not, all you who believe it makes no difference how we live our earthly lives, you who speak scornfully of the life to come, which is nevertheless the only thing of any real interest."

With bloodshot eyes, he surveyed the group, an assemblage of pale, confused faces, four women: Magister Mortensen's housekeeper Atlanta, Josef the Lament's wife Sarina, the Weeper and her daughter Mira, and a few men, including Josef and Fribert the old coalman and that ne'er-do-well Sirius. The Weeper wept consistently and unceasingly and was for ever drying her eyes. Moritz's son Orfeus was weeping, too, and hid his eyes in the sleeves of his jersey. But as for Eliana herself! She looked anything but repentant; on the contrary, she gave Andersen a kindly and cheerful glance and said something to the effect that it would probably be all right.

"I'm not afraid," she declared. "I'm convinced that Moritz will come back."

"Come back!" Ankersen mumbled threateningly. "He'll not come back by virtue of his own doing. Do not believe that, you poor, foolish, arrogant woman. You must think again, you must humble yourself, you must pray and confess your sins. Come, let us join in a quiet prayer . . .!"

Ankersen made a great, all-embracing gesture, but at that moment the door opened and Magister Mortensen entered, tall and gaunt. He adjusted his lorgnette on his nose and addressed Ankersen in a subdued but grating tone: "Hey, what the devil's all this, Mr Ankersen? What kind of behaviour is this? What right have you to be out here at all, if I may ask?"

Ankersen involuntarily made a gesture as though warding him off with his great hands, and a strangely peppered smile emerged in his beard. It was some time before he collected himself sufficiently to make a reply, but then it came in a ferocious, merciless torrent: "Oh, so you think you can take a liberty like that! An unbeliever like you. A . . . errh . . . a child of the Devil. Yes, that's what I said, a child of the Devil! Yes, for you're an apostate, that's what you are, you who once studied for the priesthood. Will you really come here to prevent me from joining in prayer with these poor frightened creatures . . . a prayer for the rescue of a missing husband?"

He stretched out his arms and with deep emotion in his voice said: "Is that not right, my friends? Are we not to pray to the Almighty to give us succour against sin and punishment and the evil machinations of Satan?"

And suddenly, Ankersen threw himself on his knees, closed his eyes and folded his thick, podgy hands beneath his chin.

"The man's mad," Mortensen shook his head. "You could come up to us if . . ."

"I was thinking exactly the same thing," says his house-keeper, looking questioningly at Eliana.

But now Ankersen suddenly rises from his knees. His face is puffed up, his nostrils are pulsating in and out, and he is groaning unrestrainedly. "Oh, generation of vipers! Oh, *generation of vipers!*"

"Now, that's enough, Ankersen," says Mortensen in a tired voice. "But you could simply have minded your own business. No one sent for you."

But all at once, a remarkable change takes place in Ankersen. He clears his throat, coughs, takes off his glasses, wipes the sweat from his brow and during this process becomes quite friendly and speaks in a low voice; indeed, he almost becomes polite.

"No," he says imploringly. "No, that mustn't happen. Just listen to me and understand me. You mustn't go. It mustn't come to the point when I drive you all out. Oh, just sit down again and be a little patient; allow me to explain myself."

He goes on, addressing Magister Mortensen: "Errh, I'm a little quick-tempered, I suppose. But the intention was truly good. But now I'll be so . . . calm. Yes, for you see, Mortensen, you, who are a learned man, you, you're even a theologian, you'll probably understand me. Errh . . . when you are a believer, you know, and feel this urge . . . this *duty* to . . . as it says: go out and make all men my disciples. No, perhaps you don't understand me, but let us remain good friends even so, I ask you."

He sighs profoundly and casts a gentle, paternal look around: "Oh yes. There we are. Now . . . it's gone, if I can put it that way."

The little group had fallen quiet; even Magister Mortensen sat down and became accommodating and peaceful. A distant little smile played behind his pince-nez: "Indeed, Mr Ankersen, I don't doubt that the intention was fundamentally good. But if I am to be honest, I don't really think you are suited to that trade."

"No, perhaps not," nodded Ankersen and bowed his head a little. "Perhaps not."

For a moment he flushed scarlet again, and his nose pulsated. But then he again fell quiet and nodded in silence. He got up with a sigh, went across and stroked Orfeus and little Franziska's hair, nodding in distress. There was a little foam left in his beard. Then he held out his hand to take leave, went round and shook everyone by the hand, still nodding, but without a word.

Out in the vestibule he snorted as he rummaged around to find his galoshes. Then he returned one last time, nodded silently and made the sign of the cross. A weak rattling sound could be heard from his nostrils.

The Weeper stopped weeping, but sat staring and sniffing. A clear drop was hanging from the tip of her nose.

"Ankersen's so good, so he is," she said plaintively. "He does so much good in secret."

At dusk, when the two little girls had fallen asleep, Eliana took Orfeus by the hand, and they walked out along the shore. It was blowing, and the sea was empty and gloomy. Orfeus was battling with tears, and he had to swallow deep all the time and gradually became prey to hopeless, ridiculous hiccups. It was as though he could not think for immense sorrow and unabated hiccoughing, and he wondered at his mother's calm and constant assurances that all would be well in the end.

"I just have a feeling," she said. "He'll come back."

Out at Stake Point, they sat down in the shelter of a projecting rock. There was a solitary scent here of seaweed and sea, and the wind whistled in a little bunch of dry sea starworts.

Eliana pulled her son close and put her cheek against his. "I'll tell you why," she whispered. "I'm so sure and relaxed because Ura the Brink has twice told my fortune, and each time she said that I would die before your father. And Ura never gets it wrong."

"No, you mustn't die," sobbed Orfeus, filled with a new indeterminate sorrow. He pulled at his mother's hand. She replied with a deep and calm little laugh: "No, of course not . . . we'll worry about that when the time comes."

The hours passed. The wind was settling. The sun appeared

for a moment through the clouds that were indifferently scudding past. There is nothing in the world as indifferent as a scudding cloud – it takes no interest in anything, not even in itself.

Moritz sat nodding; he was cold and fell half asleep; he woke again and took a gulp of the last bottle, listening to fleeting interior music. The wind was still blowing, and the boat was thrown here and there among waves the colour of grey filth. Drizzle and spray from the sea was running down his face and clothes; he was drenched, but had long ago settled down in a state of dull and defiant indifference. Only now and again did he start, as though wakened by some distant trumpet blast from the depths. But as soon as he came to himself and shook himself free from sleep and dream, all was as before. You can accustom yourself to anything, even to drifting around at sea in a boat without oars.

Aye, he was still there, and then the night had passed. A confused and accursed night, full of painful misunderstandings and mistakes. The engine had started working for a time, however that had happened, but while he sat steering the boat up against the wind, he had fallen into a merciless, death-like sleep for which the parson's wine was responsible, of course, and when he woke again the engine was once more as cold as ice and the boat was half full of water. But, as he said . . . here he was again; he *was alive*; he was breathing and shivering and cold.

But suddenly he sat up: there was smoke on the horizon. Before long a trawler came into view. Was it coming closer? With a beating heart, Moritz tried to attract attention. He took his jersey off and waved it about. Then he took off his shirt; perhaps that could be made out better from a distance. But the steamer appeared not to have seen anything. It drew away. Then he poured some petrol on to a tuft of machine twist and made a little fire. That was not noticed either, not even when he sacrificed his shirt to the flames. The steamer went its way, deaf and blind and disappeared in the wilderness.

And now it came on to rain heavily. There was still half a bottle of wine left. Moritz emptied it at a draught and immediately regretted his greed. Visibility had been reduced to nothing. It was like being locked up in a room.

As the hours passed, it cost him an ever bigger effort to stay even more or less awake, although he was now completely sober again. After a great deal of resistance, he fell into a painful torpor, full of ridiculous, frightening dreams. He dreamt that he was up in the church tower with his father, listening to the polyphonic humming of the Aeolian harps. But then he was suddenly an Aeolian harp himself, with the wind blowing through his ribs and forcing music from his half-dried-up intestines . . .

He woke, shivering with cold, but pulled himself together again, got up and started baling. Otherwise, nothing had changed: Monday and a desolate ocean, drifting clouds and empty bottles.

It was not long before he fell asleep again. The boat could look after itself; he noticed it was shipping water, but he left it to it. The music inside him was behaving in a curious way; there was no longer any continuity in it; it wanted to burst out like a great orchestra, an immensely boundless and foaming orchestra in which trumpets as big as the funnels on steamships played sombre and meaningless solos.

There was especially one of these celestial trumpets that sounded terrifyingly fateful; it was playing a monotonous bass note and gradually turned into the dogged organ note around which the other voices gathered as in a whirlpool just before dying down, for now the piece was finished. Aye, dozing and slumbering as he was, he heard it nearing the end. But suddenly it took an unexpected turn: the enormous trombone went on doggedly playing on is own account, long after the other instruments had said their last word, and smoke and a greasy smell was issuing from its mouth.

And suddenly, Moritz woke with a start: there was a steamer nearby, he could both hear and smell it, and yes, right enough, it was quite near, and it was the Neptunus! It looked so worn and kindly, so blessedly ordinary and reasonable, homeless and delightfully trite. And yet nevertheless such a wonderful vision.

A dinghy was launched. And Ole Brandy was one of those in that dinghy. Ole Brandy with his tousled moustache, broken nose and gold earrings. Ole Brandy, so old and yet so new. He was smiling blissfully like an apostle stepping from a descending cloud. Kornelius was there, too, and Olivarius and many other good men whom it produced a quite supernatural delight and peace to see again, healthy and well, old and new.

Moritz was helped up to the deck of the steamer. His boat was taken in tow. They were on their way home.

The impression of something *sacred* refused to leave Moritz. He sat in the mess and drank coffee and schnapps, and good, familiar men sat and stood milling around him. They looked so inordinately gentle and kind. The clear midday sun had come out and was shining on the worn linoleum cloth on the table.

"See, just you lie down on the bench and have a sleep," suggested the skipper. "You'll have to make sure you make a good impression when you go ashore, 'cause there'll be a lot of people looking on."

Moritz quickly fell asleep. Now and again he sat up with a start because he had been dreaming he was still in the boat, surrounded by death's rattling Aeolian harps, on his way to the abyss. But then it was true after all that he had been saved and lay here at the edge of the sacred oilcloth.

There was a party in the basement of the Bastille that evening. It came of its own accord. Members of the male voice chorus sang happy songs; Kornelius and Moritz played horn duets, and they all danced and drank laced coffee. There was a bountiful flow of wine; no one really knew where it came from, but it was later discovered that Count Oldendorp, who himself had been there for a time, had made a generous contribution.

But what about Ankersen at the Bank?

This amazing man naturally didn't miss the time of his visitation. Through his spy, Fat Alfred, he had been informed on what was taking place in the basement of the Bastille; there were not only drunken men, but also women present, not only topers like Ole Brandy and Janniksen the Blacksmith, but many others.

"Oh, who?" asked Ankersen fervently. "Magister Mortensen?"

No, Alfred hadn't noticed him. But . . . Lindenskov the dancing master, Josef the Lament, Olivarius, Lukas the grave-digger, Pontus the rosepainter, Fribert the Coal, Atlanta and Black Mira and lots more . . .

Ankersen shuddered and closed his eyes. Before long he put on his galoshes and crept out himself to Skindholm to make sure that Alfred was telling the truth. You could see it all through one of the windows in the outhouse. Ankersen shook his head so energetically that his cheeks and ponderous double chin quivered violently. He was so agitated that he took Fat Alfred by the hand as though he were a little boy, and breathlessly said, "Dreadful! Dreadful! Do you know where we are going now? We're going over to fetch the new vicar. He has his chance now. He can have his baptism of fire. And then we'll clear them out of this den. In the name of God. Come along!"

"Janniksen'll kill us," laughed a flustered Alfred.

"Laugh not," admonished Ankersen, "for it is possible you are speaking the truth. But it will be as I have said. Nothing ventured, nothing gained."

It was with a mixture of curiosity and amazement that the Reverend Fruelund saw the distraught Ankersen, who most of all looked as if he himself had had rather too much to drink. The savings bank manager had gone straight to the point and completely forgotten to introduce himself, but then, breathing heavily, he made up for it.

"Please sit down and rest a moment, Mr Ankersen," said the vicar and pulled out a chair. But Ankersen refused to sit down; he stood vibrating like an engine, his small, near-sighted bull's eyes constantly blinking behind his spectacles, and there was foam in his beard near the corners of his mouth.

"These are people on their way straight to damnation," he said.

The vicar had to suppress a smile, and in so doing he came

to look extra serious. Ankersen raised his hands enthusiastically and shouted: "I can see already that you understand me. You are on my side. Your predecessor, Lindemann, was a good-for-nothing, he couldn't be bothered getting up out of his easy chair; he became my enemy, my bitter enemy. Never, never did I become reconciled with him."

Ankersen lowered his arms.

"He drank port wine," he hissed confidentially. "Yes, he drank port wine together with Fähse the apothecary."

"Oh yes?" said the vicar absent-mindedly.

"Yes," shouted Ankersen almost in triumph. The savings bank manager had suddenly moved into falsetto and went on as in some hair-splitting ecstasy: "He tried to hide it from me, but I caught him, I caught him I can tell you."

The vicar stood uncertainly as he considered the situation. Ankersen looked almost in love as he regarded the slender young man with the elegant curly hair.

"Come," he said. "Come."

"Yes, but listen for a moment," the vicar said in a clear, loud voice. "I really don't know anything about these people you're talking about, do I. I am completely new here. They're drunk and will naturally resent our coming. We shan't achieve anything in that way, shall we? Wouldn't it be more reasonable to talk to them when they're sober? We could for instance . . ."

Ankersen broke him off with a low, threatening roar: "Resent us? Resent us you say, man? Are you afraid of being resented? You, a priest? A disciple?"

He turned away and started moaning in anguish.

"No, of course I'm not *afraid* Mr Ankersen," he said in an icy voice. "And I could well defend myself purely physically. No, but, as I say . . ."

"Yes, you're young and strong," said Ankersen collapsing for a moment on a chair. "You are young and strong. I'm only an old man who can't defend himself. But I am nevertheless never afraid. Oh, no, not the least little bit. The only frailty I know not at all is fear."

Ankersen's voice now again rose into a chirruping, plaintive descant: "Don't let me down. I had begun to think so well of you. Come. Follow me. Help me. I believe in you, young Mr Fruelund. I am placing my trust in you. You are strong and healthy. You have the warmth of faith."

"Just a moment," said the vicar. He went into the other room and rang to the parish clerk, Mr Bærentsen the senior master. Yes, Bærentsen knew Ankersen well. An honest man. An excellent man. A good administrator and financier. A great deal of selfless work for the Christian Temperance Association. A fiery soul.

The vicar returned. His forehead was flushed. "Let's go," he said.

Ankersen became humble with delight; he rubbed his shoulder against the vicar's arm, silent and overcome with gratitude.

It was some time before the merrymakers in the Bastille basement realised who was in their midst. Ole Brandy poured some schnapps into two glasses and pushed one across to Ankersen, who nodded unctuously, and Black Mira danced over to the vicar with a charming smile. An unusually well-proportioned girl, noted the Reverend Fruelund, taking shelter behind Ankersen. The situation was intolerable. The savings bank manager sat down and played with the glass of schnapps as though he was looking forward to emptying it. But suddenly he got up and wailed: "Ye fools. Woe unto you, you generation of vipers! This gathering ought to have been a thanksgiving because one of you, quite undeservedly, has been returned to this accursed vale of tears . . . because with no credit to himself a Lazarus has been awakened from the dead . . . And you have turned it into a celebration of the Devil! Think again before it is too late. Repent, you poor blind souls, on your way straight into the bottomless pit of damnation . . ."

Mr Fruelund turned away in shame. He was not accustomed to this slum tone, which he only knew from the Salvation Army's stupid meetings in the streets of big cities. And in any case Andersen's cries were quickly drowned in the general pandemonium of voices and song.

The vicar felt anger and shame welling up within him. He actually had to force himself not to give this foolish and presumptuous man a well-deserved rebuke. Shameless fellow! Several of those present laughed heartily at the scene. And suddenly, Ankersen burst out in a great, scornful laugh!

His face all distorted, the Reverend Fruelund made his way out towards the exit. He remained in the doorway. "*Ankersen!*" he called out harshly.

But Ankersen had disappeared in the crowd and was not to be seen anywhere . . . Yes, he was over there, kneeling in front of a music stand and . . . uttering a prayer! A crowd gathered around him, listening. His pulsating red nose glistened with sweat or tears.

The clergyman turned away in disgust. He went out into the entrance. But could he really just go home alone and leave that madman in the lurch? The sound of hymn singing was now coming from the room. Hymn singing! It was one of the hymns Mr Fruelund himself had chosen for the church concert that had so sadly come to nothing: "Rejoice ye now, all Christian men"!

He opened the door and with a strident, commanding voice shouted: "Mr Ankersen!"

But Ankersen simply did not hear him. He stood there, broad and thickset, and with unseeing eyes behind his glasses he was singing the last verse of the hymn at the top of his voice.

The vicar felt confused. The thought crossed his mind for a moment that Ankersen had been right in a way, and might had. . . . won. The entire party was obviously joining in the hymn. What kind of hocus-pocus was this?

When the last verse of the hymn had been sung, he made a quick decision and went back into the room. Ankersen discovered him and hurried over. The savings bank manager's face was distorted with pain and anger; he turned towards the vicar in doleful accusation: "You ran off! You ran off, so you did! You who ought to have taken up the arms of the spirit against them, struck them down with the thunderbolt of the Word, these despairing sheep! You who should have led them back to the fold! You ran off like a wretched coward . . . frightened for your . . . your *handsome skin!*"

Ankersen laughed loud for a moment, but then suddenly stopped, went and stood in front of the vicar, spat him in the face with all his force and roared: "I spit on you! You are no friend of mine, you are my enemy. Be off with you, you Levite, you Pharisee!"

The clergyman tightened his lips and left the building. He was very pale.

Ankersen stood in the doorway and threatened him with raised fists: "Never dare to cross my path again, you hypocritical dog!"

3

A remarkable contradictory amorous fate awaits the young poet Sirius

The so-called Leonora poems occupy an elegant and important place in Sirius Isaksen's lyrical oeuvre. As Dr. Matras puts it, they are "love poetry of a remarkable transcendental and serene kind that at times can remind one of Shelley himself".

It has long been assumed in literary circles that the *Leonora* who is at the centre of these poems was a pure abstraction, something by way of the "poet's muse", but later studies have shown that this assumption is incorrect, as the Leonora of the poems really did exist and is identical to Leonora Maria Pommerencke, the daughter of the local and subsequently regional judge Ib Thorlacius Pommerencke and his wife Elizabeth, née Paludan-Müller.

The following will provide a closer account of the poet's relationship with the young woman.

Sirius's elementary school was a success. During the eighteen months it had existed, it had attracted thirteen new pupils. Three of the old ones had left. These were Peter and Orfeus, who had gone on to the council school, and the smith's daughter Julia, who had grown up.

However, Julia had not quite left the elementary school, for she had been given a job in Mac Bett's picture frame shop and also had the task of keeping the schoolroom clean. It was Sirius who had arranged this; he felt sorry for this big, dim girl who didn't have a particularly congenial home, and who had moreover started to become the target for certain louts whose intentions to her were scarcely of the best. For her part, Julia was devoted to her former teacher, something that she never missed an opportunity of showing. Indeed, Sirius had just a suspicion that she was really in love with him in her own quiet, silly way.

But at this time, Sirius had thoughts only for Leonora.

Leonora was like a nun, a saint; she was very fair and very gentle, but there was something faraway about her fresh young features. Sirius knew that she read a great deal and was particularly fond of lyrical poetry.

Alas, Leonora! *She* was the daughter of a high-ranking public servant; *he* was a poor schoolteacher. There was a gulf between them. And yet things developed in such a remarkable way that fate – admittedly hesitantly and dubiously – built a bridge across this gulf.

It started with his writing a poem to her in which he simply declared his love to her. This poem never got any further than the drawer in his desk. But he sent her another, "Marsyas", which he thought contained things just as he wanted to say them.

Sirius had read about this curious legendary figure in the History of Music. His heart had beaten indignantly and tenderly for this mighty musician who with his flute had made Apollo himself so furiously jealous that he had had him flayed alive and his skin hung to dry in a windy cave. The young poet had for a time been virtually pursued by the idea of that poor human skin hanging there alone and deserted in its cave, writhing in the darkness each time there was the sound of music. And in his poem he had sought to achieve peace of mind by letting *Psyche* take pity on it and cut it into strips and then twist these strips to form the strings of an Aeolian harp from which divine music was played to all eternity.

Sirius accompanied this poem with a few humble words in which he expressed his hope that Leonora would not look down on this modest effort. He sent the letter off as though in a state of intoxication, and when the envelope had disappeared into the letterbox, he felt heartily ashamed of himself and bitterly regretted what he had embarked on.

But the following day, just as the children were going home, none other than Leonora herself turned up in the picture

81

frame shop, not in order to buy anything, but to meet Sirius and thank him for his poem.

"It's promising, very promising indeed," she said. "There's *passion* in it."

Sirius was speechless, but he nevertheless pulled himself sufficiently together to invite Leonora into the schoolroom. He took her umbrella and reverentially placed it in a corner, drew out the chair from the desk and invited her to sit down, and then he placed himself humbly on one of the pupils' benches.

"If you have any more poems," said Leonora, "I'd like to see them."

Sirius had a great many poems in the drawer of his desk. Like a sleepwalker, he rummaged through the pile of papers, but he felt strangely overwhelmed, and before he really knew what he was doing, he had shoved all the papers down into the drawer again and shut it.

"No, but . . . perhaps I might be allowed to send you some poems later . . . some of the best ones," he said emotionally.

Miss Leonora smiled. "I think you are a real poet," she said gently.

Leonora had a beauty spot on one cheek. She was fair-haired, but had brown eyes and long eyelashes that were darker than her hair. She went on with a smile: "*Sirius* – that's a lovely name even if it is rather unusual. It's the name of the brightest star in the sky."

"I'm called after my mother; her name was Sira," he replied almost apologetically.

Leonora regarded him warmly and said, "By the way, do you know who you remind me of? Yes, of Lord Byron. Really. There is something about your eyes and your profile and your hair. Do you know Byron?"

Sirius knew virtually nothing about this famous poet. There were none of his works in the library. Leonora promised to send him Byron's Don Juan in Drachmann's translation.

Sirius once more expressed his profoundest gratitude and fetched Leonora's umbrella, which he delivered to her with a little bow.

It was some time before he came to himself again after Leonora's unexpected visit. He sat for a long time deep in thought by the desk. What was this that had happened? Leonora! *Leonora* had come and visited him!

Overcome, he bowed his head and hid his face in his arms.

When he raised his head again, Julia was standing staring at him. The big, red-faced girl had a dejected look about her and was not far from tears.

"Hey, what's the matter with you, Julia?" he asked gently. But he really knew what was wrong: she was jealous! He smiled and stroked her arm: "There, Julia. I'm going now, lass, so you can start to tidy up."

She gave him a disconsolate look; he had to stroke her arm again; she leaned in to him; he felt her hair against his cheek; she was trembling all over.

"What's wrong, love?" asked Sirius and patted her back comfortingly.

"Nothing," said Julia but immediately threw her arms round his neck. He felt her firm, elastic breast, and without really knowing what he was doing, he took her head between his hands and tenderly kissed her on the cheek and mouth . . . once, several times. It finished with him taking her on his lap. She clung passionately to him.

Sirius sent a selection of his poems to Leonora. Some time later, she returned them with a little letter in which she thanked him and asked him to send her some more. He kissed the little scented letter with her elegant handwriting and throughout the entire evening and night surrendered himself to his immense and desperate longing.

But the following day after school, he again had a tender moment with Julia. This big, clumsy and dim-witted Julia . . . she had in fact grown up to be quite pretty. It was only now he saw that. She had become an entirely different person; she had blossomed and turned into a rose; indeed in a way she was almost enchanting, a new, plump, sparkling rose. Sirius had probably been taken by young girls before this, but things had never progressed so far that he had had anything much to do with women. Julia was the first one he had kissed and held in his arms.

And yet it was Leonora he loved, of course. Her and no one else.

He despised himself for playing this double game. But it had really been forced on him. For a long time he didn't know what to do. He worshipped the distant, sublime Leonora and wrote poems to her and about her. But at the same time he satisfied his love with Julia – she was warm and close. It all happened as it were against his will, and yet like something that was unavoidable.

But Leonora was simply unattainable, and that was that. She was not fated to be his; she probably already belonged to another. She was said to spend a lot of time with one of the officers from the inspection vessel Poseidon.

Spring came; the bushes in the smith's garden sprang into flower, and one day Sirius read in The News that Miss Leonora Maria Pommerencke had become engaged to First Lieutenant Rasmussen. Although this news in no way took him by surprise, he was nevertheless desperately upset and shed his secret tears. But that afternoon, he stilled his pain at Julia's breast.

During the following time he wrote a series of passionate, desperate poems to Leonora, one after the other, and in his extraordinary infatuation he sent some of them to her in a letter, without heeding the fact that he had used her name several times.

One day he received an unexpected visit from Miss Leonora and her fiancé.

"This is my fiancé," she said by way of introduction. "And here is my poet. Can you see he's like Lord Byron?"

The officer laughed politely; Leonora and Sirius also laughed, and it all passed in a perfectly delightful way. The unknown young man, who incidentally was a freckled little chap with thin red hair, complimented Sirius on his poetry and bought a couple of boxes of drawing pins.

That afternoon, Sirius decided that his engagement to Julia should be made public.

Julia was very unhappy and totally opposed to his going and talking to the blacksmith.

"He'll kill you," she said morosely.

"But why on earth . . .?" asked Sirius in amazement.

"Well, because they want me to marry Jartvard, Consul Hansen's warehouseman," said Julia, hiding her face in her shapely white arms as though she was afraid of being hit.

"But surely there can be no question of that?" said Sirius uneasily.

"I'm afraid there's nothing else for it," groaned Julia, kneeling in front of Sirius and stroking his hands in despair: "It's half way been decided . . .!"

"Decided?" asked Sirius, now becoming quite breathless with emotion. "They can't just decide for you in that way! You just say no, you *won't*. You're a grown girl! And that's that."

"Oh, I don't know," sobbed Julia, rubbing her eyes.

Sirius decided to laugh. He laughed, heartily and forbearingly: "You say you don't know. But surely you don't like this Jartvard, do you?"

Julia's sobbing grew more intense, and she replied in a thick voice: "Yes, I almost think . . . I almost think . . . and besides, *he* thinks so, too . . . and he's talked to mum and dad."

"Now listen here," said Sirius. "This is the craziest thing I've heard of in all my life. Don't you love me at all, then, Julia?"

"Yes," she replied and started shaking violently.

Sirius went on in a harsh voice: "But perhaps you love the other chap as well?"

Julia's reply was indistinct, but it was yes, she did.

Sirius got up and went across to the window. The big flowering bushes were half in the shade. In the light, they were red, in the shade blue. He turned round frantically and asked her imploringly: "Do you love *him* more than you love *me*? Answer me, Julia."

"I almost think so," whispered Julia.

"I'd no idea," murmured Sirius on the verge of tears. "I'd no idea. That's caught me out completely."

Julia had sat down on one of the school benches. Her luxuriant young body was shaking, and she swallowed her sobs. Then she said in a low, but clear voice: "We were to be married this autumn, him and me."

"So I can understand you've actually been engaged," said Sirius dully.

Julia nodded.

"Oh," said Sirius and his eyes closed. "Oh, Julia. Why haven't you told me before?"

"I thought you knew," sighed Julia. As a kind of explanation, she added, "And I thought that you . . . that you were in love with her, the other woman . . ."

Shaking his head, Sirius took his hat and threw a last look at Julia, who was sitting on the bench, big and round and ripe and with her plentiful brown fringe in disorder and wet with tears.

He drifted around aimlessly all that afternoon. It was an unusually fine day with light feathered clouds in the sky, bushes and trees in bud and the scent of new grass. Everything was sparkling, glasses and roofs and the water in the bay, and the big steamship Mjølnir at anchor out there was surrounded by dazzling white gulls. By the bridge across the river, Sirius met Leonora and her fiancé. He greeted them politely and they both returned his greeting with a smile.

As it grew dusk, he met Ole Brandy down on the shore, sitting in a boat that had been drawn up on the beach. Sirius could see that Ole was drunk and made to tiptoe past without being noticed. But Ole called him down to the boat in a loud, imperious voice. The upshot was that he sat down beside Ole and drank a little of his rum.

"Aye, I'm giving rum this evening," said Ole Brandy. "I'm giving rum this evening, and do you know why? Because today's a special day in my life."

"You see," he went on earnestly. "Fifty years ago today, this bloke you're talking to now set foot for the first time in his life on the soil of the great wide world, that's to say Constitution Dock in the English town of Hull. And when night falls it will be exactly half a century since I had the first foreign girl on my knee."

And Ole Brandy slapped his knee enthusiastically, took a drop of the rum and went on in a confidential tone: "She was called Mary. I can still clearly remember her. She was a dreadful bitch."

He sighed and started singing an old ditty, and Sirius listened in distress to its sad words:

> Sailor struggling on the ocean
> Drink to quell the pain now starting,
> Rapid is the light day's motion
> T'wards the bitter hour of parting.

> The ocean's wild and seething water
> Will surely pull you down apace
> And in the depths there'll be no quarter
> There you'll find your resting place

> She you worshipped as your woman
> Scarcely now recalls your name
> Dances with your evil foeman
> Basking faithless in his fame.

The twilight had grown deeper; the lapping of the waves against the shore was gentle and spoke of summer. There were strips and delicate rings of light, horizontal mists across the bay, as motionless as cigar smoke indoors.

Sirius felt himself sorely divided. The brandy ignited wild flowers of melancholy and boundless longing in his breast.

Ole Brandy had placed an arm on his shoulder, singing in a subdued but jubilant voice:

> But from the darkling depths of death
> The day will come when you shall rise
> And then your song with mighty breath
> With angel hosts will reach the skies.

4

Magister Mortensen has an unexpected and not particularly welcome guest

"I will naturally not directly oppose your paying a visit on this Magister Mortensen. I don't know him personally and can only go by other people's accounts. And of course, it *might* be that he is better than his reputation."

Prefect Effersøe smiled at his brother-in-law, the Minister of Culture, who repaid this slightly dry smile with a distant nod that seemed to indicate that he understood and forgave everything. The minister had spent a summer holiday at the prefect's home. He had mentioned on a couple of occasions that he would like to visit Mortensen, but he understood from his brother-in-law that the idea did not entirely appeal to him. But now, as the day for his departure was approaching, the minister had again, with the amiable stubbornness that was characteristic of him, insisted that he ought to pay a visit to Mortensen before leaving. Østermann and Magister Mortensen knew each other slightly from their student days, and the minister had derived a modicum of profit from reading the book Mortensen had written in his youth on Søren Kierkegaard. It was an interesting though somewhat immature little book. Østermann had even made use of a couple of quotations from it in the dissertation he had written on Kierkegaard for the degree of Doctor of Theology. It had pained him to hear that things had gone so badly for Kristen Mortensen, who had actually been a man of some promise.

The prefect stared ahead with raised eyebrows: "You see – if it were only that Mortensen was something of a bohemian, well all right. But he has also behaved like a *ruffian*. I'm thinking of his attack on Berg, the headmaster, a few years ago. It was this scandal, you know, that led to his having to leave the school. Physical assault – not exactly what one would expect of a so-called *learned* man, eh? When all is said and done, there are other ways of dealing with disagreements, and there is no need to act in such a plebeian manner just because you are quick-tempered."

"No, of course not," nodded Østermann, "Of course not."

The prefect cleared his voice, slightly impatiently, and continued, "And then there is another thing if we are to be perfectly frank: Mortensen is living in . . . what shall we call it . . . in promiscuity with certain loose-living womenfolk as far as I can understand. But, as I say, this is all only something I am telling you so that you don't go there *unprepared*."

Østermann continued nodding and regarding his brother-in-law with his clear, patient eyes, and the prefect added with a smile, "Of course, you could take the *count* out there with you. I mean just in case you were exposed to something directly unpleasant. Count Oldendorp is as strong as an ox. And then he knows the way. In fact, he has some rather unusual acquaintances in town. It's what he calls his 'ethnological interest'. Hm."

The prefect and the minister both smiled condescendingly, by no means maliciously, far rather suggestive of their approval, in brief in the very way in which one after all tends to smile at a somewhat reprobate aristocrat.

The count was willing to go out to the Bastille with the minister. On the way he talked in his carefree way about Mortensen, whom he knew personally and, as he said, had had many an amusing argument with. Mortensen was a gifted man, a brilliant man, and his unfortunate fate had anything but broken him.

"Is he *very* dependent on drink?" asked Østermann sorrowfully.

"Errhh." The count hesitated. "He has a binge now and again, as people do in these latitudes. But for God's sake don't think of him merely as a rowdy and a drinker, no – far from it. And his living together with *Atlanta* . . . good heavens, in many ways Atlanta is a wonderful woman. She's not at all bad looking either, and in one sense it's quite extraordinary that she sticks with Mortensen and keeps both him and his poor mentally deficient daughter going. You've damned well got to take your hat off to her. For if Mortensen hadn't got her . . .!"

Østermann stopped and cleared his throat, somewhat ill at ease: "Yes, but . . . Mortensen doesn't actually live off this woman? Or how . . ."

"Good lord, no," laughed the count. "Mortensen isn't a *pimp*! Is that what you were thinking? No, by God, he is as honest a man as both you and I. He earns an honest living by giving private tuition and as a librarian. And then he's something of an astronomer. At least he has a curious telescope set up in the loft. And then he's very musical. And he's working on a *book* as well."

"What kind of a book?" asked Østerman, lowering his voice confidentially.

"Well, Mortensen won't really say. But it's something about philosophy, a book on religious philosophy."

Østermann nodded, and a watchful expression crept into in his eyes. "I see. I see. Well, you know," he added, "I knew Mortensen a little in his student days. We both lived in Regensen for a time. He was a tall, handsome chap. Farmer's son, I think. From Jutland. He used to roll his r's. And he was a bit noisy. But something of a gentleman nevertheless, and extremely fond of the ladies according to what I have heard."

Østerman spoke with an indistinct voice as though seeking for words and repeatedly blinked and cleared his voice: "Mortensen was for a time engaged to an extremely charming girl. Someone from the best circles. A lady. Jewish family, I believe. But then it all went wrong. I believe it was she who . . . fell for someone else, as they say. Oh well, and then . . . well, one day Mortensen had simply disappeared. And then, to my amazement, it turned out that he had ended up *here*. Tell me, what was his wife like?"

His wife? Well, Oldendorp had really never talked to Mortensen about her. The idea had never struck him.

"And how old can this mentally deficient daughter be, do you think?"

"Oh, seven or eight. Something like that."

Østermann's eyes became round and staring. "It must be very, very sad for Mortensen," he said. "Very, very sad."

It was some time before Magister Mortensen thawed out. Østermann's visit had caught him quite unawares. Admittedly, he had for some time thought it possible that Østermann would pay him a visit while he was there on his summer holidays. Indeed, he had in reality imagined this meeting in somewhat polemical terms. But such a long time had passed now, and he had fundamentally not realised that the minister had not left again.

And then, suddenly one afternoon, there was Østermann sitting on the chaise longue and he had not gone away again at all. Christian Frederik Østermann, Doctor of Theology, Dean, Minister of Culture, talked of as a potential bishop. In the midst of all this mess. Yes, there was a dreadful mess in the little turret room ... Vibeke's matchsticks and cardboard boxes lay scattered all over the floor; Atlanta's sewing machine, surrounded by patches and pieces of material, sat in state on the writing desk together with the two empty coffee cups, one of which even lacked a handle. And there was a slight, lingering smell of fish cakes in the air.

In the midst of all this confusion he had been playing the viola by the old music stand, broken and held together by string as it was, when the visitors entered. It didn't usually look as bad as this, for Atlanta didn't leave things like this. On the contrary. But it was Saturday afternoon. And so on.

But now, there sat Dr Østermann, the government minister, the most important visitor to town that summer.

Rubbish: in reality the resplendent embodiment of theological discretion and fatuous careerism. So at the last minute the famous man had presumably deigned to come up to see this supposedly down-at-heel former fellow student. Deigned? No, he presumably had the curiosity of an old gossip and couldn't keep it under control.

"Yes, just you stare," thought Mortensen to himself, and at that moment, for the first time in ages, he became aware of the big blob of ink on the wallpaper above the broken-down chaise longue. It had happened once when he had thrown the inkwell at the wall in a fit of fury. Fortunately, you couldn't see that. And yet, perhaps after all you could?

And what did he himself look like in these clothes: the patched dressing gown and the worn-out slippers. And he'd hung his collar and tie on the bookcase so as not to be bothered with them while playing. And then what was it he'd been playing? He, who otherwise hated bad music and had that very afternoon spent two hours on end practising his devilishly difficult part in the Death and the Maiden Quartet! For Atlanta's sake he had finished up by playing a Swedish country waltz she was fond of. He had been rattling that dreadful stuff off when the two distinguished visitors entered the room.

And so here was this Østermann, this so-and-so. Never mind Count Oldendorp. But Østermann. This stuck-up theologian. This future bishop. This political and theological careerist. This quintessential mediocrity who had even had the audacity to write on Søren Kierkegaard. And incidentally just the trick you could expect from an old woman of a theologian: after all, you accept this priest-devouring philosopher because when all is said and done he is a theologian, and for all his sharp edges with a little skill he can be forced into the system! And because it makes an impression to be seen in the company of this unapproachable celebrity! Like a good housewife you mix a little sugar and sentimentality in his gall and place the main emphasis on his undoubted conservatism: he was after all a *believer*, the old stick-in-the-mud. So we can use him in our politics.

Kierkegaard!

Mortensen had of course read Østermann's fuddy-duddy little work and made some venomous notes in the margins of it. "Positive Aspects in Søren Kierkegaard's Concept of God!" Ugh! Mediocre from end to end. What is it Kierkegaard says somewhere: Mediocrity . . . mediocrity is the deepest perdition, oh all crimes are preferable to this self-satisfied, smiling, glad, happy demoralisation called mediocrity! Ha, ha!

Yes. But as this wretch Østermann really was mediocrity

incarnate, why should Mortensen be so fussy about his dress and so on. Inconsistent and middle class!

Mortensen had so far taken refuge behind a sad, fierce mask and only vaguely taken part in the vapid conversation that Østermann and the count had tried to get going. But he suddenly sat up as though awakening from some profound preoccupation and said in a tone that even he found a little false and somewhat jauntily polite: "I say, what may I offer you, gentlemen? Unfortunately I have no cigars here, but . . . what about a little glass of cognac?"

Østermann neither smoked nor drank. Of course. But Mortensen found a couple of glasses and poured drinks for the count and himself. They were two tumblers. But what the hell! The alcohol seemed to re-establish his normal composure. He breathed deeply, ready for battle.

"Here you are, you cheap little intellectual snob, to see for yourself how deep Kristen Mortensen has sunk in the mire," he thought. And in his mind's eye he saw how, on his return to Copenhagen, Østermann would get together with others from his student days, all of them now high-ranking and mightily prosperous . . . with just a little spiritual concern: "By the way, do you know who I met up there? Mortensen. The Kierkegaard man, you know." And so on.

"But just you wait, you mediocre creep," thought Mortensen ferociously.

In secret, he was just dying for the conversation to turn on to Kierkegaard. It was surely bound to sooner or later. Oh yes, and it even happened almost immediately, and it was Opperman himself who started it: "Your thought-provoking, percipient little book on Kierkegaard . . ."

"You flatter me," said Mortensen with a hard little smile, adding in a more excited tone than was really his intention, "But I would hardly say that that bit of scribbling was thought-provoking or percipient. It was written on the basis of a young man's academic grovelling to that man Kierkegaard. It really almost makes me sick to think of it."

Østermann cleared his throat and said with a concerned smile, "Oh, I don't know, I don't know."

"Ah, here we go," winked the count with a smile.

"Well, of course I mean Kierkegaard as a thinker and human being," continued Mortensen settling himself energetically in the dilapidated basket chair beneath the bookcase. "As an artist, a stylist, as a brilliant purveyor of aphorisms and a self-analyst, of course, he is fine. But otherwise. This everlasting, petty self-absorption he stumbles around in. This piteous, barren megalomania."

He had not originally intended expressing himself so intemperately, but the words flew out of his mouth. It was the sight of Østermann there on the chaise longue that did it. He went on: "For instance where he talks about his God-given qualifications . . . how does he put it . . ."

"Yes, but my dear Mortensen," Østermann interrupted him gently. "Irrespective of the way in which it is said – Kierkegaard is right: he was quite unique."

Mortensen stroked his thin face with a show of tranquillity: "Yes, he was in any case extremely keen indeed to demonstrate he was unique and to gather evidence for it . . . to throw it in people's teeth."

Østermann shook his head with a smile. Mortensen got up and flung out his arms excitedly. "Yes, but that is what Kierkegaard does all the time, without ever stopping. He's at loggerheads with a little group of theological numbskulls, all his activities are aimed at convincing these midgets that he's always right and is absolutely unique and number one and cock of the middin. And he's merciless because his innermost nature is one of hatred and evil!"

Mortensen leaned back and gave a brief, scornful laugh.

"But don't misunderstand me," he continued. "The sermon Kierkegaard preaches to the clergy and the masters of theology, it is so truly one they deserve."

He sat down in the basket chair again and said with a sigh, "And then that basilisk Kierkegaard finally comes to grief, of course, because it all ends with him being devoured after all . . . *devoured*, yes, for he ends in the stomach of his enemy the clergy . . . as a great, indigestible lump, but there he is in spite of everything, even if he does weigh rather a lot and hurt a little. There are certain boas that are able to swallow a whole lion lock stock and barrel. Mediocrity . . . mediocrity always has the final say, Sir. Kierkegaard was piteously drowned in his own gall, but the mediocrity that gall was intended to kill . . . mediocrity spreads far and wide and still dominates the highest seats of learning and sits in the most lucrative posts."

The count let out a great, uncertain guffaw. Mortensen refilled the glasses. He sent Østermann a look full of loathing. The minister smiled cordially. Of course. What else was to be expected? He shook his irremediably foolish and stuck-up noddle with an all-forgiving smile.

"Well," he said with a little sigh. "I understand that you have changed your opinion of Kierkegaard since writing your elegant little book."

"*Cheers*," said Mortensen. He felt just a little embarrassed at his excited behaviour.

During the rather embarrassed silence that now arose, the count made an attempt to conciliate, commenting: "Aye, you philosophers, you know about these things. As for me, I never got beyond Kant's Kritik der Urquellskraft . . . and that was quite a thing, ha, ha."

Østermann cleared his throat and asked in an amiable tone, "Is your new *book* about Kierkegaard as well, Mortensen?"

Mortensen caught his eye and said sternly: "No, Your Excellency, it's about *Satan!*"

"About Satan," echoed the count and again exploded in boisterous laughter.

"What the hell are you laughing at?" Mortensen burst out. "My work is about evil. About human evil and fault-finding and cruelty and pettiness and shrewishness and careerism. Which are inextricably linked to and form the basis of all theology, of all clericalism throughout the ages. And that scourge of humanity known as confessional religion."

Østermann flushed scarlet. Oh, at last.

The count took out his handkerchief and blew his nose loudly. "By the way, what was it I was going to say. . how's the star-gazing going, Mortensen?"

"Ah . . . I'm told you take an interest in astronomy as well," said Østermann with a smile. A little nervously.

"Yes, and in music," added the count. "Mortensen is very musical. He is quite a master on the viola. He plays in Boman's little band down in the cellar."

Østermann nodded and looked at his watch. His hand was trembling: "Oh, is it as late as that? I've no fewer than three cases to pack, so . . ."

He held out his hand to Mortensen: "Well, then I'll say goodbye and wish you well, Mortensen. It was fun to see you again."

"The *fun* was all mine," replied Mortensen scornfully. The minister jumped slightly, as though he was afraid of being struck or pushed. There was a stiff smile on his lips.

"Well, goodbye old chap, and thanks for the drink," said the count. "We'll get together some time and have a chat."

"Oh, shut your ridiculous trap, you stupid hippopotamus," snarled Mortensen.

The count gave him a hearty slap on the shoulder, "Oh, steady on, old man."

The minister quickly opened the door and slipped out, his eyes wandering about anxiously . . . this could lead to blows.

Mortensen went out on to the landing; he was deathly pale and in a harsh voice shouted after Østermann as he hastened down the stairs: "I don't give a *shit* about your religion! It lacks both seriousness and reality! An old pro helping some poor bugger up from the gutter is worth more than all you theological nitwits and cowards put together."

The minister was now out of sight. Mortensen shouted so that it resounded down the empty stair well, "*Goodness* is bloody well a reality! But canting careerists and castratos like you will never in all eternity learn anything about that."

"Well, what did you think of the – beast?" the prefect asked his brother-in-law. They were about to sit down at table.

The minister smiled concernedly.

"Poor Mortensen," he said absent-mindedly.

He added, nodding as he sought for the words, "He's

turned into a very bitter man, and there are probably obvious reasons for it. He talked a good deal about Søren Kierkegaard. But they were the strange, hateful words of a broken man. He's turned into a nasty piece of work, our good Kristen Mortensen; he doesn't hesitate to use the most vulgar expressions. No, unfortunately, that man has changed a great deal, a very great deal, since he wrote his elegant little book. But then that was probably only to be expected . . ."

Østermann unfolded his serviette and fixed the corner between his collar and his chin: "In truth, Mortensen is a profoundly unhappy man, a man to be pitied."

5

A great and happy event that nevertheless ends in a wake

Orfeus was making steady progress on the violin.

Old Boman didn't exactly spoil him; on the contrary, he was often quite unreasonably harsh, but when all was said and done, such was his method and it had borne fruit. Both Moritz and Kornelius were good at music. Of course, you could not call them real musicians, but at any rate they were excellent players. Indeed, they were even more than simply players, for they had both their ears and their hearts in the right places.

But Orfeus was even more than that; the boy was music through and through; he had a quite amazingly fine ear, and he was easy to teach. He was musical to his fingertips, and indeed he played Schubert's Serenade like a little angel. Boman was moved as he sat and plucked out an accompaniment on his cello. This was nothing less than unique.

"That was wonderful, my boy," said the old teacher, grasping Orfeus's hands. "You are undoubtedly the best pupil I've ever had, and now I'll tell you something: you've got a future in front of you. You mustn't stay in this hole; it's nice enough here, but . . . you've got to get *away*, Orfeus. You must have air beneath your wings. You must become something *great*, my boy; you must *experience* what the rest of us have simply gone and dreamt about and messed about with; you must become a real musician, a real champion."

Boman's wrinkled old cheeks had become quite flushed; there was an elated look in his eyes: "You must become the *meaning with it all*."

He shook his head with a smile and gave his godson a gentle thump on his backside. "Well, we'll see how far you can get if you really put all your strength into it and concentrate on your music, for it makes demands on you; it demands staying power and determination; you can't sleepwalk your way to great things, Orfeus. You first have to work like a slave; you have to be obsessed; you have to be as mad as a hatter and believe you're another Paganini, even when things look completely hopeless."

Boman had assumed his gruff look again; he caught the boy's eye and said in a stern voice: "Will you promise me that, you rascal? Do you realise that being called Orfeus gives you a responsibility? And then having had old Kaspar Boman as your teacher?"

Now, the old man's face was once more one large, melancholy smile.

"Oh, well, off you go."

As the summer progressed, Bomann became bedridden. The zealous old man had gone seriously downhill, and the painful heart attacks became increasingly frequent.

Every Sunday afternoon saw a large number of visitors at Boman's; no one could say his friends left him in the lurch. Occasionally, the string quartet gathered in his living room and played his favourite pieces.

But at the beginning of August there was a musical event of a quite unique kind, something that wrested Boman and his players out of their little world and exposed them to a breath of fresh musical air that left them almost speechless.

The great day started like a quite ordinary Saturday with overcast skies and a mist. At lunchtime, Moritz came home quite out of breath and demanded that his wife and children should dress in their Sunday best and get ready, for there was nothing less than a *symphony orchestra* on board the steamer heading for Iceland, and in all probability this orchestra would give a concert ashore while the ship was loaded. It was the Hamburg Philharmonic Orchestra, famous, first-class players.

Moritz hurried on to Boman's to give him the news and to do his best to get him to the concert. The old man's sunken cheeks flushed like those of a young girl, and in his enthusiasm he sat up in his bed.

"Well, I'll have to go to that, whatever happens to me, even if you have to carry me."

Moritz sat there as excited and happy as a sandboy. He pressed Boman's hand: "That's a promise. Then we'll come and fetch you."

At midday, Mortiz ferried the foreign musicians ashore with their instruments in boxes and cases. The men were dressed for travelling, sunburnt and weather-beaten after the long voyage. They looked like quite ordinary people and were dressed in the ordinary way. Many of them were elderly gentlemen, worn and bald, a few had great handlebar moustaches. They puffed away at pipes, some long, some short, and one of them cut himself a quid. You couldn't understand what they said, but they carried on a jovial conversation. They were fine chaps.

The concert had to be given in one of Consul Hansen's warehouses; it was the only room big enough to hold so many people. Moritz together with Kornelius, Sirius and Lindenskov the dancing master, had fetched Boman in good time and made sure of a good seat for him in the hall. Flanked by Moritz and Eliana, the old man huddled beneath his great overcoat, with all his features radiating happy expectation. Orfeus, together with his friend Gravedigger Peter had found a place to stand on top of a couple of coils of rope in a corner, and from there they could survey the entire tightly packed hall.

The sun had come out and sent batches of oblique rays in through the tiny, dusty windows. A hissing lux lamp was burning above the orchestra, bathing it in a whitish, restless sea of light. It was the count who had set this up; he himself was walking around red-faced and sweating, putting the finishing touches to his work.

It almost took Orfeus's breath away to see all the instruments. At the front sat a double row of violins, and behind them the cellists and viola players, then the flautists and horn players. At the very back sat the timpanist with his drums, a fat, little near-sighted man who in some funny way reminded him of a cook busy with his pots and pans.

Merely to hear all these men tuning their instruments was strangely deafening. The din coming from the orchestra was like that from an enormous poultry run where there were not hens but all kinds of strange, unknown birds. The clarinets made their contribution of clear, deep trills that sounded like the singing of supernatural snipes; the bassoons moved in a joyful profundity; issuing ecstatic gurgling sounds from their smiling throats; and the double basses were even further down, right down in tones redolent of the day of judgement. And yet it was the violins that were heard most: the familiar festive five tones that were so poignantly homely and familiar.

Now the conductor stepped up on to his flag-decorated packing case. He was a fairly young man, and he had a piece of sticking plaster on his neck. A profound silence reigned for a moment. Then the music burst forth! It was Gluck's Iphigenia Overture. It started high up in the violins, painful sounds, fateful sounds, but then the bass notes suddenly joined in like big, rough excrescences, angular and jagged, assertive, indignant, but yet curiously good-humoured, as though it was their joke after all. And now the music *glided*, like a huge, well-oiled machine . . . like a furious colossus yet moving on lightly tripping feet.

And again the dark double basses emerged, threatening and ominous in their masculine self-assuredness, angry, almost grim. And again they merged in supple harmony with the gentler voices and rose up in a noble and happy dance to the conductor's baton, which moved with infinite gentleness and sensitivity, like the antennae of a butterfly.

When the piece came to an end, the applause burst forth with a noise like collapsing piles of gravel. Then the good-humoured tuning and plucking returned, the hurried cackling of clarinets, flutes and oboes, the subdued blare of the horns and the rumble of the double basses as though they were emerging from some grim repose.

The count stepped forward and announced the next item: Schubert's eighth symphony.

Orfeus quite forgot to watch the instruments – the deep complaint of the double basses tightened his throat so he had to close his eyes. The sprightly, genial theme that arose now and again was mercilessly overcome by the dark powers and was not allowed to play to the end. It was like experiencing a little clump of resplendent, red flowers fighting against a tempestuous wind blowing over them, a wind that was perhaps not cold and biting, but nevertheless implacable in its dark hunger. Orfeus had to think of Boman's potted plants that were always in flower, even in the darkness of winter. These flowers, which always stood listening to music . . . aye, they almost sang! He was happy on Boman's behalf and looked for the old man's white bald pate in the crowd.

It felt almost like a relief when cheerful piles of gravel again collapsed in applause, and he hungrily absorbed the outlines of all the familiar, everyday figures in the audience: Effersøe the Prefect with his white ram's hair, young Consul Hansen with his great disapproving features, the Chief Administrator with his carefully tended grey vandyke, Fähse the apothecary and his enormous parrot-like wife, Judge Pommerencke and his daughter Leonora, Dr Manicus with the gentle countenance beneath a silk skullcap . . . Ankersen the Bank greedily bending forward with pulsating nostrils, Mac Bett the painter with the white sideboards and wearing an embroidered waistcoat . . . Janniksen the blacksmith, Berg the editor, Captain Østrøm, Mrs Nillegaard the midwife with her husband, Pontus the rose painter, Magister Mortensen and all the rest of them, whoever they were. And further back in the hall Lindenskov the dancing teacher with all his daughters, the Misses Schibbye, Sirius and Kornelius, Jakob Siff, mine host from The Dainty Duck. And right down in the semi-darkness at the back were Fribert the Coal, Ole Brandy and Olivarius the Sail, all in their Sunday best.

Now the count came forward again and announced the final number: Boccherini's minuet. A shudder of delight ran through Orfeus when he heard the familiar melody, borne by carefree violins, while all the other instruments simply sat and chuckled. No storm to make anyone tremble, nothing but homely good humour and the sound of gentle humming; the orchestra's many-headed monster surrendered to cheerful, good-humoured indulgence that both warmed and cooled. But when the minuet was past the heartbreak returned.

Gone, gone . . .

Gone, never to come again. Never more, never more.

The orchestra broke up. The instruments were returned to their cases and boxes. On behalf of the audience the count thanked the players for the unforgettable time and also spoke a few words in a foreign language. Alas, alas. Never again. . . .

Orfeus and Peter stood where they were while the hall emptied. One by one, the instruments made their way out of the wide warehouse door and disappeared in the void of the afternoon. There was at last nothing left but the gently murmuring gas lamp.

Gone, gone. But they could go down to the jetty and watch the music go aboard. The two boys hurried down there. Moritz was standing in the boat, carefully receiving the big double-bases in their man-like cases. A wind had got up. The water was full of bluish black banks of choppy sea. The steamer sounded its horn impatiently. The musicians stood chatting in small groups while they waited for their turn to go on board.

Evening was approaching. The lighthouse out on Seal Island was lit. There was a silent, slow movement of clouds across the heavens, lit from below by the light of the setting sun. It was like a final, visible echo of the symphony . . . as though it lived on in some ghostlike manner up in the pale and distant light of the evening, but immortal nevertheless, while the steamer sounded its horn for departure and became smaller and smaller out there in the boundless grey ocean.

Boman was happy that it had been granted to him to be present on this great event. He lay smiling with closed eyes, and it was clear that he was very tired.

"If only it's not been too much for him," commented Moritz.

Kornelius thought they might ask the doctor to come and take a look at the old man, just in case.

The count was at home in the basement of the Bastille. He was a little tipsy and had a couple of bottles on him. "Let's drink to music," he shouted enthusiastically to Moritz. "To music!"

He emptied his glass and filled another one, the veins were swelling in his temples. He drew Moritz aside and nudged him: "Can you get hold of Black Mira? Tell her to come out here. I bloody want something beautiful to look at this evening."

As time went on, more people gradually gathered in the big room. Lindenskov the dancing teacher and Magister Mortensen had been across to see to Boman. "I'm a bit afraid he's not long to go," whispered Lindenskov to Moritz, shrugging his shoulders. And then he added: "But I still don't think we should regret getting him out there with us . . ."

Later that evening, Moritz looked in on Boman again. His old housekeeper fiddled nervously with the buttons on his waistcoat; her eyes were red. "The doctor's been," she said, "and he looked very worried."

Moritz decided to keep watch by Boman's bed just in case. Kornelius, Sirius, Lindenskov and Mortensen had obviously had the same idea; they turned up one after the other and sat down in the little room, silent and sad. Among the many potted plants there was one that was just coming into flower; it was an amaryllis, standing showing off its red buds as though in silent contentment. The composers on the wall looked down with the faces of men listening intently. Boman's housekeeper was restlessly bustling about in the kitchen, occasionally lifting a corner of her apron up to her eyes. At about midnight, she disappeared for a moment, and when she came back, she had the Weeper with her. The two women embarked on a husky, gloomy conversation out in the kitchen. The visitors were offered coffee, but were not in the mood for anything. The Weeper wept silently and whispered reproachfully to Moritz: "What on earth were you thinking of, taking a dying man off to that nonsense?"

At dawn, the sick man woke up and looked around him, though it was clearly an effort. When he discovered Moritz, a surprised and almost appreciative smile spread across his pallid face, and in a thick voice he said, "Franz Schubert! Oh, how kind of you to come and visit me. It's really far too much. But at least you must have a cup of coffee if you will be content . . ."

He look enquiringly at Moritz, who nodded helplessly. Then the weary man lay back. Soon afterwards, he breathed no more. Old Boman had gone to his rest.

And with this, the first and oldest of our musicians slips out of the story. Old Boman was a good man; he was a source of strength; he lived on in what he had achieved, and he retained his place in the grateful hearts of his friends.

Moritz and Kornelius and Boman's other friends had decided to do everything within their power to ensure that the old teacher's funeral should be as dignified as possible. The male voice choir gathered to practise hymns and songs, and it was also the intention that a small brass ensemble should play Mendelssohn's funeral march. But nothing came of it all, for just as the preparations were well under way, they found an envelope among Boman's things. It was inscribed *Afterword and Will* and one of the things it said was: "As for my funeral, I want no speeches by the graveside and no singing. I just wish the enclosed serenade by Schubert, which I have loved since my early childhood, and which I have arranged for violin with a little base pizzicato, to be played at not too slow a tempo, least of all a mournful tempo, by my dear boy Orfeus and by some of you other old friends at my grave after it has been filled in, and not too late in the day, perhaps in the morning or during the forenoon if this can be done without too much fuss."

And so it was that Boman's funeral took a form that was quite different from any other. The old musician was laid to rest one sunny afternoon in late summer, and the comforting, almost merry tones of the serenade mingled with the fresh soughing of the wind in the shrubbery and grass of the churchyard.

Orfeus felt proud to have managed this, his first major

performance as a musician, without stumbling. He had played almost without thinking of the music; he thought only of Boman.

As he walked beside his mother out of the cemetery gate, someone grasped his head from behind and patted him on both cheeks. It was Magister Mortensen.

"It was lovely," he said. "Thank you, my boy."

After the funeral, Boman's friends held a little memorial celebration that lasted for most of the day. But it all took place in a most seemly manner; they refreshed memories of their late friend, and no one forgot for a moment that this was a wake.

6

How Kornelius, treasure seeker and musician, played and won a treasure and took it home one stormy winter's evening

Unlike his brothers, Moritz and Sirius, Little Kornelius the composer lived to quite a good age. It is only a few years since he died at about seventy. But those many years were not a blessing for him. A strange fate decreed that already as a young man poor Kornelius would bid farewell to the light of the world.

But we will return to his youth and to those good days when simply to be alive was the most natural thing in the world, and when the future tempted him with the most remarkable prospects.

In the case of Kornelius, one of these prospects was, as we already know, linked to a certain hidden treasure. The hope of finding this treasure enveloped a considerable part of his youth in an enviably magic and happy light. But after the visit to Ura the Brink another secret source of delight had also started to flow in Kornelius's breast.

It had begun in quite a small way, like a silent and tender trickle in his mind at the thought of the blind young girl whose name was almost the same as his own and who had stood listening to the music from the basement of the Bastille . . . stood out there in the dark so alone and deserted. And this trickle soon grew into a mighty stream which before long so occupied him that his search for the treasure was pushed quite into the background for a time.

Not long after the visit to Ura, he returned with an invitation to the old woman and Kornelia to come across to the Bastille and have a cup of coffee and listen to some music.

But no – Kornelia wouldn't. She sat twisting on her bench, quite overcome by the thought, and she refused to be persuaded. Kornelius had to leave without achieving his objective and with a pain in his heart. But he continued to see the girl in his mind's eye: her shy, chaste face, her huge eyes with their almost supernatural look, her slight figure with the mass of blonde hair. He longed eagerly to get to know this creature better and to be something for her, to take her under his protection and bring her close to his music, to fill her darkness with sounds and harmonies.

Then he had the idea of taking his cello and going over to play for her at Ura's home. Perhaps it was a foolish idea, but he knew of no other way.

"I was passing," he lied, stammering as he did so. "And then I thought that . . . since she's so fond of music . . . Kornelia?"

"Oh, you kind, kind soul," said Ura in a voice full of emotion. "Thank you so much, but this is too much." Kornelius took a seat and set about tuning his instrument. The young girl looked as though she was terrified; she simply shrank into herself, and when he started to play – it was "The Dance of the Blessed Spirits" – to Kornelius's horror, she burst into tears.

He stopped playing and said nervously, "Yes, but . . . yes, but . . . perhaps it was wrong of me to . . . to force myself on her . . .?"

Ura looked a little dubious, but she brushed it aside: "Nonsense, just you carry on, Kornelius."

Despondently, he started again. He was so strangely confused; the girl was sobbing; the black cat was walking about restlessly and rubbing against his legs, and in the midst of it all he came to think of the famous picture of Beethoven playing for the blind girl. He felt for a moment as though he had shown himself to be too presumptuous. More than anything else he wanted to leave, but he forced himself to play the rest of the minuet.

Kornelia had stopped weeping, but sat catching her breath in small sobs like a child that doesn't know what to do with itself. Deeply confused and ashamed, Kornelius put his cello back into its case and as it were tried to treat the whole thing as a joke: "Well, you know, I was just passing, and I looked in, and then I thought . . . just for fun . . ."

"Wasn't it just lovely?" Ura asked Kornelia plaintively.

The young girl made no reply, but heaved a long sigh.

"Well, then we'd like to say thank you again," said the old woman and shook his hand warmly. "Now give him your hand, Kornelia, and say thank you very much."

Kornelia gave him a warm and hesitant hand and with her eyes closed shook back her heavy head of hair. She was sniffing, and her eyes were red from weeping. Kornelius felt heartily sorry for her and pressed her hand between both of his.

Ura went out with him to the Brink.

"It was almost as though she didn't really . . . didn't really . . ." whispered Kornelius uneasily.

"She's a bit silly sometimes," the old woman wrinkled her nose. "But when all's said and done, she's really not much more than a child, and one thing with another . . ."

Ura gave a long and as it were hopeless sigh: "And she is a woman as well, and . . . you know, half in love, naturally, like all girls of her age."

"She's what . . .?" asked Kornelius eagerly.

Ura shook her head and answered evasively. "Well, you understand, she never sees anyone and never goes anywhere, and now *you've* come Kornelius and turned everything topsy turvey for her."

She smiled sadly and shrugged her shoulders. "No, you see, the poor thing's crying mainly because she feels that everything's pretty hopeless for her."

Kornelius was completely confused once more; the words stuck in his throat, and it was a while before he could make himself understood: "No, hopeless?" he burst out laughing and stuttering: "Oh, but dearest Ura, it's just so much . . . the opposite!"

He most of all wanted to go inside and put his arms round the girl and hold her fervently to him. But it was suddenly as though his feet had become frozen fast; he had as it were to pull them up by their roots to move off the spot.

"No, hopeless?" he repeated as he desperately pressed Ura's

bony hand. "No, surely not, no, she mustn't think that . . . do tell her . . . tell her I'll come again and play for her . . ."

Holding the cello tight, he staggered off, intoxicated with joy.

Kornelius was radiant with a sense of experience and enormous expectation and felt the urge to celebrate this event, and when he met the Crab King on his way home, he flung his arms round the little man with tears of joy and took him into The Dainty Duck and ordered a meal for them both. Later, Ole Brandy and Olivarius the Sail turned up, and the little company ended in The Dolphin, where they sang and made merry until the small hours.

During the following period, Kornelius was a frequent guest in the Brink House, and it was not long, either, before Kornelia thawed out.

Kornelius was now at the height of his happiness; his days passed as though in a state of intoxication, and he could often not fall asleep at night for sheer joy.

During this time, as though of its own accord, the string quartet had become reality in him; he had two movements almost finished in his head, and he was well on the way with the third, which he was going to call *allegro vivace*. It was to be a wedding march for him and Kornelia. And the entire work was to be dedicated to the memory of old Boman; indeed the quartet was simply to be called *The Boman Quartet*.

As the days gradually grew shorter and the autumn storms and gales set in, Ura's little house became ever more insecure and frightening to be in; all the joints creaked as in a sailing ship, and far below at the foot of the slope, the turbulent waters seethed and boiled.

"You know, there's no sense in staying here," said Kornelius. "Kornelia and I are going to get married now, and then we'll all three move out into the Bastille."

"Yes, just you get married, my dears,. That's how it should be," said Ura. "And you just move out into the Bastille and set up your own home. But you'll never ever get me out of this house until they carry me out feet first."

"And perhaps not even then," she added, and now she had another of those strange, unmotivated attacks of laughing that Kornelius didn't like.

"Yes, but why not?" he asked, pressing Kornelia's hand in confusion.

"Why not what?" laughed Ura loudly, and he didn't know what to answer to that either. Ura had the habit of speaking in riddles and vague hints at times, and there was nothing to be done about that.

The church was filled to overflowing on that dark and stormy December afternoon when Kornelius led his young bride to the altar. The whole town was eager to go and see the odd couple, and the general opinion was that Ura had bound them together, perhaps not without the help of supernatural forces. For who, in the prime of his life, will go and marry a blind girl who is as poor as a church mouse into the bargain and perhaps not even quite right in the head? The only person likely do to so at least is someone like Kornelius, a daft musician with a stammer.

Kornelius's wedding was long remembered, especially as it coincided with a night in which there was one of the worst gales in living memory.

This storm was already well on the way while the ceremony was taking place in the over-filled church, where the male voice choir sang in competition with the howling of the wind, while children and young people made joyful sounds and the Weeper wept. But as the evening advanced, the storm increased enormously, sweeping in from the south east, and surf and foam spread across Skindholm in wild fans of salt water. The newly-weds and the wedding guests were all in danger of not reaching the Bastille in one piece, and some of the guests turned back of their own accord when the rumour spread that the Adventist Samson family had fled for all they were worth before the raging storm, and that Ole Brandy had been found injured and with a broken arm out near the High Warehouse. He had intended visiting his friend Olivarius, but just outside the entrance door he had been knocked over by a barrel that had washed ashore and with which the gale was playing ball.

But even to the few brave souls who battled their way through the flooded alleyway and with more or less dry feet were pulled in through the door to the Bastille, this wedding celebration was a mixed pleasure. Fountains of salt water were seething in through the leaky windows, and there was no keeping the heating going in the draft-ridden rooms.

Things were especially bad down in the studio, where the celebrations were otherwise to have taken place. The floor down there was under water, and lamps and candles flickered and threatened to go out. It was like being aboard a ship in distress. The entire festive event that had been arranged by Eliana and Moritz together with Atlanta and Sarina came mercilessly to nothing, and the little party consisting almost exclusively of those who lived in the building, sat huddled together up in Kornelius's little sitting room.

Moritz, Kornelius, Mortensen and Josef the Lament did their best to keep their spirits up with the help of wine and song, but it was no easy matter, and for a time it looked quite hopeless. Josef's wife, Sarina, was especially close to despair, insisting that they should follow the Adventists' example and get out of the building, and the terrified woman was difficult to keep under control. Finally, they had to let her have her will. She was carried shoulder high through the pitch-dark, foaming night, across the seething alleyway to safety in The Dolphin.

When this was done, people quietened down a little. Moritz and Kornelius took out their instruments and entertained with duets, and Magister Mortensen, who by now was very tipsy indeed, sang an old love song from Southern Jutland, the text of which no one understood a word. But by virtue of its melody and Mortensen's emotional voice it went to the heart of everybody and produced tears in the eyes of both the bride and the bridegroom.

But . . . what the deuce is *that*? Suddenly from the stairs there is a clatter of hasty footsteps and weaponry. There is a knock on the door, and a bearded man in oilskins and sou'wester pokes his head in. It's Constable Debes. He stands there for a moment breathing heavily and beckoning Kornelius across.

Kornelius gets up with a start, with the result that he shoves the table so hard that glasses and bottles overturn and roll on the floor to the sound of breaking glass.

"What on earth's wrong, Debes?"

"Take it easy," says the constable, who has regained his breath by now. He pulls Kornelius out into the corridor and closes the door behind him, after which he undoes his overcoat, revealing his uniform and sabre. "There's been an accident," he says. "An accident that has perhaps cost a life . . . yes, Ura the Brink. Her house has blown off its foundations and fallen down the cliff."

Kornelius is speechless. The constable continues in a calm voice. "Ura's safe though, and they've taken her to hospital. But she's unconscious."

Kornelius is still incapable of saying anything. He stammers a few, incoherent sounds, but he can't help thinking to himself: "But it's jolly well her own fault, the stubborn creature; she could have moved over here with us . . . She could at least have been here this evening, but she couldn't even be persuaded to do that. She wanted to be at home, all on her own, impossible creature . . ."

"I . . . I'm coming," he finally manages to say. "I must just . . . a coat . . . my boots . . ."

"There's not really anything you can do," the constable says to calm him down. "As I say, the house *has* fallen into the sea, and Ura's in bed in hospital, and the weather's so awful, so you might as well stay where you are. It was just my duty to come and let you know what's happened."

But Kornelius already had his coat on. He opened the door in to the living room to give the bad news to Kornelia and the others, but his voice refused to obey him, and Debes had to come to his assistance: "Well, it's the Brink House that's blown into the sea," he says calmly. "But Ura's safe for the moment at least."

The gale lasts into the next day, and the surf fills the air with its dull coughing. Inquisitive folk make a pilgrimage out to the Brink to look at the site left by Ura's house and the pitiful pieces of wreckage that are being drawn out and in by the foaming waves down at the bottom of the cliff and bit by bit are being deposited like splinters and driftwood on the flatter cliffs further inland.

Concerning Ura, there are rumours that she is hovering somewhere between life and death.

As for the catastrophe itself, there are the most amazing rumours circulating from house to house. People shake their heads, huddle up together or brush it all aside with a smile, according to the mood they are in. There are those who doggedly maintain that Ura has been playing with magic. There was a lot of smoke coming from her chimney on the night of the accident, and you could see sparks, and a neighbour who went past the Brink House about midnight clearly heard Ura quarrelling with someone in there, and you can imagine who that was, it was hardly the cat, but rather a certain shady personage, the same one as gave her the power to find things that had been lost, to see into the future, to tie people together so as to bring about their misfortune and to give sickness and trouble to people she didn't like. So now those two had presumably got to quarrelling, perhaps about poor, foolish Kornelius's soul, who knows. And the Devil had naturally been the stronger and had given her something to remember him by.

Mrs Midiord, who was Ankersen the Bank's housekeeper and Ura's half-sister, entered Ankersen's office in despair and wept as she told him what people were busy saying.

Ankersen listened attentively. He nodded: "Aye. Yes, Mrs Midiord. But suppose there was something in all that?"

He looked at his watch. "Visiting hours start in the hospital at about three o'clock. Let us go out there together and see if we can talk to her. Let us at least *pray* for her.

114

Orfeus is introduced to the sad remains of his grandfather's Aeolian harps and is plunged into disturbing thoughts and evil visions, but finds some consolation in the phantom Tarira

The southeasterly gale that started on the evening of Kornelius's wedding appeared unwilling to stop again; it lasted for days and for weeks. The little town by the sea was enveloped in a frenzy of foam that dimmed all windows with a coating of sea salt, and the ceaseless seething of the surf made all ears deaf.

Christmas Eve started just as wet and windy as all other days, but by midday it suddenly cleared up, and the wind began to drop. Eliana had decorated a Christmas tree, and Orfeus had been given permission to bring his friend Gravedigger Peter and his sisters home with him for the Christmas Eve celebrations. Lukas the gravedigger's son was ill, and Lukas himself was drunk, so the children wouldn't find it much fun at home.

Orfeus met Peter up in the church tower. He was sitting up there with Poul the sexton, who was busy fitting some new hinges on a trapdoor. Orfeus and Peter were inside in the dark church loft. Lying there was a pile of curious things that seemed to be alive and to produce some strange sickly sighs in the wind as it blew through them. Orfeus drew back in fear, but Peter shouted, "It's only your grandfather's Aeolian harps. Isn't it, Poul."

"Aye, they're his grandfather's Aeolian harps," the sexton confirmed, mumbling something to the effect of "Kornelius the Kelp Trench, the daft thing."

"Aye, your grandfather was *mad*," Peter explained in a kindly voice, while the two boys went down the steps in the tower. "He made Aeolian harps, and you only do that when you're daft. And your father and his brothers are all a bit mad as well."

"But you don't have to worry about that, Orfeus," he added encouragingly.

Peter could not come to the Christmas Eve party in the Bastille, and in confidence he told Orfeus why: he had a Christmas tree of his own. He suggested he should go with him to see it.

Orfeus was cold. The strange sound of wind in the old Aeolian harps continued to haunt his ears. Full of excitement, he went with Peter. They went north, out of town; the fields were glistening with hoarfrost, and the stars were trembling in the cold air.

"Just look how they're moving up there," said Peter. "That's because the angels are playing with them and making them go off."

The Northern Lights came sweeping down over the hills to the north, spreading out rapidly and billowing across the heavens like a turbulent sail.

"Be careful not to look around you too much," warned Peter in a whisper. "The place is teeming with ghosts."

They passed a frozen stream with a rickety old wooden bridge across. Peter stopped and said in a hollow voice, "Look, Orfeus, it's specially haunted near this bridge; you often see the ghost of a dead man walking with a stick in his hand and driving a long line of geese in front of him. They're ghost geese. They shine in the darkness. Look, I think they're there now. Oh, no, it wasn't them. But you might see them afterwards. But just look over there."

Peter pointed to a ramshackle barn: "Have you ever noticed that before?"

Orfeus couldn't remember whether he had.

"No, I thought not," said Peter. " 'Cause it's only there on Christmas Eve. Otherwise it's disappeared. It belongs in heaven. For that's the stable Jesus was born in."

Orfeus became lost in thought and stopped to take a closer look at the barn. Of course, he didn't believe what Peter was telling him, for Peter was always full of big talk and tall stories.

And yet the derelict house looked so strange as it stood there: the gable end rose frozen and insubstantial in the clear air, glistening silver and grey as though paled by the Aurora and the starlight.

"Come on, you'll see," whispered Peter. " 'Cause this is where I've got my Christmas tree."

He went across and opened a creaking door. Orfeus went inside; he was numb with excitement; there was a pungent, mouldy smell, and there was a sound of giggling in the semi-darkness. It was Peter's sisters who were waiting for them. Peter struck a match, and they could all see the little Christmas tree standing in a barrel and sparkling with tinsel and streamers.

"Now you've seen it," said Peter when the match had burnt down. "We're not lighting it until later."

"Where did you get it?" asked Orfeus.

"It's always here," whispered Peter, " 'Cause it's a real Bethlehem Christmas tree."

"No, he's pinched it," came a giggly voice from the darkness.

"Now just *you* keep your mouth shut, Grethe," commanded Peter gloomily. "Otherwise I'll let the ghosts and the Devil in, and then it'll all be spoilt."

He struck another match and quickly showed Orfeus some coloured things in a cardboard box. They were Christmas candles and tinsel and some cookies and biscuits.

"You can stay if you want," said Peter amiably. But Orfeus had to go home to his own Christmas tree.

"All right, but be careful when you leave," warned Peter, and again assumed an ominous voice. "You know there are spirits lurking everywhere."

At home in the Bastille basement there was a wonderful smell of food and fir, and the candles on the big Christmas tree were lit. Sirius, Kornelius and his wife and old Fribert the Coal and his dog were sharing the Christmas dinner, and later Josef the Lament and his wife and daughter came along, as did Ole Brandy, Olivarius and the Crab King. There was beer and schnapps to accompany the food. Sirius read the Christmas story, and they sang and made music, but in the midst of it all, Ankersen the Bank turned up, dressed as Father Christmas and holding a thick stick in his hand.

"You're singing hymns", he said in an emotional voice, but at that moment he discovered the glasses and burst out in an ominous complaint: "Oh, even on this holy evening, Moritz. Even at this, the most sacred moment of the year."

Ankersen worked himself up into a kind of resentment, but it was quite obvious that this evening he was not out as some kind of castigator, but was filled with the peace of the Christmas message. He looked remarkable in his red bonnet. Little Amadea was frightened of him and started to cry.

"What's wrong with the little one?" asked Ankersen, taking off his spectacles to polish them. "Wait a bit, children. You at least can't help it if the grown-ups abuse the festival and besmirch sacred things."

Breathing heavily, he sat down and beckoned to Fat Alfred, who was out in the entrance holding a basket over his arm. Ankersen placed the basket on the floor between his feet, blew his nose and took out some small tracts from his pocket: "See here, you grown-ups should read these and do something about it. It can easily grow too late, for as the good book says, he comes like a thief in the night."

It developed into quite a little diatribe that was heard in silence. But Ankersen gradually thawed out, patting the children on the head and giving the little ones gifts and goodies from the basket, and when he discovered that Sirius had already read the Christmas story aloud, his eyes became quite mild, and he allowed himself a glass of beer. The little girls were not afraid of him any longer; he took them on his knee and tickled them under the chin.

"Well, we've a lot to do and we must get on," he nodded to Alfred and got up. "Let's finish by singing 'Silent Night'."

The hymn was sung. Moritz, Kornelius and Josef the Lament provided the harmony; it sounded beautiful, and Ankersen's spectacles clouded over. He shook hands with all those present. Even Fribert's old dog received a friendly pat from the fleshy hand of Father Christmas.

When Orfeus went to bed that evening, he lay there and could not get out of his mind the strange remains of the Aeolian harps in the church loft, and he was filled with fear and frightful thoughts.

The words, "Your grandfather was mad," resounded in his ears. "And so are your father and his brothers." He lay listening in a dull half stupor on the verge of tears to the din from the studio, where the grown-ups were still up. Fribert the Coal sang "Ole Morske lies dead in the loft", an indeterminate song of misery and distress, fights and doleful darkness. He wished it was morning already, and that it could always be light and like everyday so that the world could really be allowed to fall into place and become *ordinary*. He clung to this ordinariness: to the morning and the veiled winter sun, to people's talk and laughter, to meals, to school – no, he could never have enough of ordinariness, but all the time he dreaded what was *behind* it, the invisible abyss of horror and grimness, death and madness. When you fell asleep, the gate to this abyss was opened wide, and you had to wander alone in hidden, spreading lands, to tread a solitary path on twilit, windy roads and through boundless wastes, where departed souls lived their restless lives and all manner of madness had free rein.

And yet, in the midst of this confusion of horrors there was one friend who never failed him.

Orfeus turned over on his stomach and pressed his eyes against his arm, making it start to snow with a many-coloured fire; magnificent flowers unfurled, and then there was what he had secretly both expected and feared: Tarira's eyes, staring at him and capturing him in their smile of dreadful familiarity.

Tarira was no evil spirit and no ghost. What was she? One thing was certain: all melancholy thoughts and visions of horror had to give way before her power. But then you had to give in to her whims as well and follow her on the dizzying journey through her realm.

Whoo . . . now we are taking off, Tarira and I, like two birds swooping up into the vast moonlight high above the earth where it resonates with solitude and distance and immensity!

8

*In which fate prepares new surprises for Sirius, but
where he behaves in a manner that does credit to
his character*

Sirius Isaksen's star has been slowly but surely rising over the
past few decades. Lovers of literature have gradually awakened
to the profoundly original quality of this poet who has been so
long ignored, and according to The News there has recently
been a proposal in the city council that the now refurbished
Blacksmith Lane should be renamed as Sirius Isaksen Road.
The News supports this proposal and maintains that we should
be proud and grateful for having fostered this famous poet,
whose life was as short as it was unhappy.

But it is not quite right to say that Sirius's life was as luck-
less as it was short. On the contrary, at the bottom of his soul
he was in reality often boundlessly happy, indeed in a way,
despite his sensitive understanding, he was at heart strangely
invulnerable.

This was related to the fact that as a poet he lived in two
worlds, the world of reality and the world of poetry, and he
was familiar with the amazing art of moving at will from one
to the other. And while doing so he would sometimes take up
a position at one of the border crossings between the two
mighty and, each in its own way, cannibalistic, all-devouring
empires.

As Magnus Skælling perspicaciously observes in his mono-
graph, Sirius Isaksen was what is called an *escapist* in our
modern language. The same was naturally – mutatis mutandis
– the case with the other musicians in this book. They avoided
the pressures of reality by taking refuge in art and the imagination or, in the case of Magister Mortensen, in the philosophy
of religion.

The explanation of Sirius's being able for long periods at a time to go around in a state that the uninitiated could only denote as torpor was in fact that the poet was lingering on the borderline between spirit and matter and surrendering himself to that indescribable feeling of active equilibrium that can be associated with such lingering.

This naturally never occurred to Mac Bett the master painter, and so it goes without saying that a constantly tense relationship was inevitable between the young poet and the old master, who never had a thought for anything but his craft and his picture frame shop. It says a great deal for the old Scot that for about two years he allowed Sirius to carry on with his elementary school in the rear of the shop, although the business had long been in need of an extension, and that in addition he ensured board and lodging for the poet in his own home in return for an extremely modest payment.

But when Sirius started to become less attentive to his teaching while the number of pupils fell alarmingly at the same time, resulting in a similar decrease in their teacher's already incredibly meagre earnings, the master painter's patience was no longer sufficient for this harsh test. And so in an attack of fury one unusually irritatingly dark and foggy day in November, he asked his protégé to pack his bags and go his way.

Sirius for his part felt both relieved and liberated.

Both the school and his everyday dealings with the decorator, whom he regularly had to help mix paint or frame pictures in his leisure hours, had long been an intolerable straightjacket to him. So it was with unadulterated delight that he took leave of the children and told them not to come back, but to explain to their parents that the school no longer existed. And for some time he went around and totally surrendered to his complete independence.

At night, he went long walks, observed the starry sky and the sea and listened to the waves breaking against the shore, and during the day he slept on a sofa in the Bastille. He took his meals in a desultory fashion in a range of different places, at Eliana's, at Kornelius', at Ole Brandy's or at Lindenskov the dancing master's, or on board the fore-and-aft schooner, the "Lalla Rookh", the skipper of which was his school friend.

This free life continued throughout the winter.

It was an unusually mild oceanic winter. Even in February the grass was turning green, and the heavy spring snows that were expected to come in retribution completely failed to materialise: springtime had arrived by mid-April, and the big red currant bushes in the smith's garden were in full bloom.

Spring shook Sirius out of his nirvana. In his isolation throughout the winter he had devoted himself to his two women, Leonora and Julia, or rather to his unhappy love for these two beings. Scarcely a night had passed without his lingering for a time outside the railings around the blacksmith's garden and staring in the direction of the reddish light from Julia's bedroom window. Leonora had gone and was in Copenhagen.

But now, one mild, misty evening as he walked past the blacksmith's house, he chanced to hear Mrs Janniksen severely scolding her daughter and calling her a shameless slut. There was also the sound of something falling and breaking, and now Julia appeared in the doorway and disappeared into the garden. Sirius heard the blacksmith's wife mumbling vengefully and threatening the girl with Ankersen, and after a while he also thought he caught the sound of subdued sobbing in the garden. He clambered cautiously over the fence and whispered, "Julia. Don't be afraid . . . it's only me."

It was some time before he found the girl. She had hidden deep within one of the perfumed bushes; she was crying bitterly and was very unhappy. He stroked her hair and kissed her wet cheek.

It was a long time before Julia could say anything for weeping and distress, and when she finally regained her power of speech there was a sharp call from the smith's house: Julia! It sounded like an ominous stroke on a cracked bell.

Sirius remained beneath the bush for most of the night. He heard sounds of scolding and the slamming of doors from inside the blacksmith's house. But finally quietness reigned.

The flowers in the redcurrant bushes gave off a penetrating spicy scent in the misty air, and once more Sirius felt his heart swell in earthly and painful sympathy and a dull longing for tenderness. It was on this occasion that he conceived his poem "Darkness Speaks to the Blossoming Bush", which has been likened to the gentle quivering of tender leaves in a nocturnal breeze.

The following day it poured with rain, and towards evening the wind rose as well. Sirius sat for almost three hours in the blacksmith's garden before Julia finally appeared. He was wet through from the heavy, constant dripping from the branches of the bush. Julia took her raincoat off, and they both crept down under its shelter.

"You're cold, you poor thing," whispered Julia, clinging tenderly on to him. A refreshing warmth issued from the young girl's ample body, and the passionate kisses she pressed on his cheeks and lips felt like delicious flowers of fire. But when they had been sitting there for a while, Julia, too, became wet and started shivering.

"It's not really very nice here," she said and shuddered. And suddenly she started sobbing.

"What's wrong?" whispered Sirius in distress.

"Oh, it's all so dreadful," replied Julia with her mouth close to his ear.

It emerged bit by bit what a pitiful fate the poor girl had suffered. Her fiancé Jartvard had gone off, no one knew where. The unprincipled lad had jilted her and left her, but that didn't matter, for Jartvard was a nasty piece of work whom it would have been a misfortune to have as a husband.

"Aye, so it would," said Sirius.

He stroked her thick hair, which was damp from the rain. "You'll get over it easily enough, love, you're young and healthy. Things could have been much worse for you."

Julia swallowed her tears and answered in an impassioned voice, "Things *are* much worse, Sirius, they're as bad as they can be. 'Cause the idea was that we should get married this spring. And now I'm left behind with the shame. And what's going to become of the poor child?"

"Are you expecting?" asked Sirius timidly.

It had stopped raining by now. The wind was tearing at the bushes and trees in the garden. Julia was weeping silently and trembling. Suddenly she started. "Wasn't that them calling me?" she asked and held her breath to listen.

"No, it was nothing," said Sirius.

They both sat silent for a while. Julia stopped weeping, but a sob went through her breast now and then. Finally, in a voice full of warm, calm determination, Sirius said, "But you and I can get married, Julia."

"No, that'll never work," she replied and hugged him tight.

"Why not, love?"

"It's more than I can ask of you, Sirius. And besides . . . besides . . . what would we live on? Have you thought about *that*, my love?"

"There's always a way round that," said Sirius. "In any case, leave that to *me*. There! Cheer up, Julia, and trust me; I shan't let you down. Shall I go in and have a talk to your father straight away?"

"No, no," pleaded Julia, hugging him in terror.

"Then we'll wait till tomorrow," said Sirius cheerfully. "You'll see, it'll all be all right, Julia. Trust me."

"You want to marry Julia?"

Janniksen used both hands to ruffle up his vast ash-coloured mane and stared at Sirius with two bloodshot eyes that extended below into two or three red bags. When he seemed to have had his fill of staring, he turned away, took a piece of iron from the furnace and started beating it on the anvil. Now and again he glanced at Sirius through the smoke and sparks, and Sirius returned his glance openly and politely. The smith rammed the iron into the embers.

"Come here, come with me a moment," the blacksmith beckoned to him and went across and opened a stained door at the back of the smithy. Sirius went with him into the dim closet. There was a box in there with a round hole in the lid, and from the lid there rose a clear sound of rippling and babbling water from a brook running beneath the floor.

"What on earth is this?" asked Sirius. But the blacksmith tapped him gently on the back to soothe him and said affectionately, "Sirius, my poor boy. It's best that we two have a talk about this on our own. You do realise that the girl has *slipped up* and that the wretch's done a bunk?"

"Of course," Sirius confirmed.

The smith went on: "So it's to help the girl out of her difficulties that you . . .?"

"I feel sorry for her," replied Sirius "She's my old pupil, you know. But I'm very fond of Julia as well. I really am, and I think she's a good girl. And she's fond of me, too."

The blacksmith sighed and spat into the stream below.

Sirius went on: "The only trouble is that I haven't got a permanent job at the moment, but that . . ."

"Oh, never mind that," said the smith thoughtfully. "We can always get round that side of the problem."

Janniksen suddenly revealed his black stumps of teeth in a thoughtful smile. "But there's another confounded aspect, and do you know what that is? It's my wife."

He leaned his shoulder against the wall and raised his thumb in explanation: "You see, she has a habit of mucking everything up, for she's a real bungler. And now she's had the blooming stupid idea of taking the girl with her and confiding in Ankersen. And of course I won't hear of it . . . but what good's that when the *yangtsekiang* comes over her?"

The blacksmith spat passionately into the hole and went on, "You see, now she and Ankersen are putting their heads together and deciding that Julia's got to go through with it and turn up in the Christian association and confess her sins. In front of everybody, damn it. What good's that sort of *pisspressing*? Isn't it only something for people to gloat over?"

"It shan't happen," said Sirius emotionally.

"No, of course, but it's easy for us two to stand here and say that," said the blacksmith with a shrug of his shoulders. "But you don't know Rosa; you don't know what she's like when the confounded *klammerang* comes over her. If only we could get her to sing a different song! Yes, if only we could get her to sing a different song."

The blacksmith stared longingly down into the hole and continued in a low, confidential voice: "You understand, this isn't really so much about Julia herself. No, it's *me*, damn it, that's got to be hung out to dry. It's me that's got to be put through the *incimincing machine*, isn't it. The fact that I have a drink now and then and go a bit over the top has to be blown up, you see, as the real reason for these sordid events. 'The toper's daughter'. And so on. And you know what Ankersen's like; he's capable of anything when he comes over all holy."

The smith twisted his body vehemently and clenched both his big mercury-grey fists: "I'd crush every bone in his body, you understand, and I'm sure you don't doubt it, do you? But Rosa, now, I can't manage her, there's no limit to her mean tricks and her *squiddling*. . . . Aye, you lot don't know much about that, but as for me, Sirius, I'm having a dreadful time. I'm having a dreadful time."

The blacksmith groaned and ruffled his hair.

"I think we'll be able to manage things when I've had another talk to Julia," said Sirius in consolation.

"Sshh," whispered the blacksmith, opening the door slightly. His face assumed a listening and at the same time strangely impotent expression: "They're damned well here already! They're rummaging around in the flat and calling for Julia."

"Wait a minute," said Sirius and ran through the smithy and out into the garden, where Julia was waiting for him behind the big bush. She was trembling as she got up.

"I thought so," she said in a lifeless voice. "They've thrown you out. I knew they would."

"Not at all," whispered Sirius consolingly and put his arm around the girl's waist. He briefly explained the situation to her. "Well, that's how things are," he concluded. "And now there's only one thing for us to do, and that is to say that it's my child, and I'll say that that's how it is and everything's all right. We're engaged, Julia, and we'll get married as soon as we can. We've got your father on our side."

"Julia," came a resounding voice from the house.

"Just you go," whispered Sirius. "I'll come later."

Ankersen the Bank had seated himself in a rocking chair in the blacksmith's living room. He was sitting in a brooding position and breathing heavily through his hairy nostrils. His hands, which were folded across his stomach, moved slowly and forebodingly up and down with every breath. He did not alter his position when Julia entered.

"Aye, here's the poor child," sighed the blacksmith's wife. "Sit down, Julia."

Ankersen remained silent. Mrs Janniksen went on in a sombre voice: "Yes, Julia, Mr Ankersen knows everything, and he has promised to help you out of the mire. We have decided to take the only path still open to us. Haven't we, Ankersen . . . you're not saying anything."

Ankersen nodded. He cleared his throat with a hollow sound, and his voice came from deep down as though from the bottom of a well: "The wages of sin . . . the wages of sin is death, yes. But for those who repent of their sins and confess them, there is still a door ajar to the inconceivable gift of grace."

Julia sat with her head bowed, staring down at her feet. She heard Ankersen's ponderous words as though through a great feeling of languor. He spoke of the woman taken in adultery, of the curse of drunkenness that broke up homes and brought the children out into the impassable jungle of sin.

"What is it I've got to say?" thought Julia in confusion. No questions were asked of her, either. Ankersen's works were one long dull accusation: "You must start a new life, woman, you must take the path of the penitent. You must confess your sins to your Christian brothers and sisters so that they can first be a warning to them and then a spur to edification and liberation . . ."

Julia fought against her tears. Finally, she could no longer hold them back, but abandoned herself to a hoarse and perplexed sobbing. She heard Ankersen say, "All right. It is only good that repentance should come in all its strength and power. That is the first step."

But now there came a nervous knock on the door, and Sirius entered. She heard his voice explaining; it sounded so strangely frail and defenceless. He stammered and coughed: "As I say, Julia and I are engaged, and the child is mine . . . and so that's surely an end to the matter?"

He was overcome by violent coughing.

"What is it this young man says?" asked Andersen with a kind of ominous laugh in his voice. "The child is his? And the girl has been engaged to another? In other words, she . . .? No, no, this is just too inconceivable. So she has in truth lived the life of a *whore*, worse than any of us imagined. She has given herself to two men? No, this is indeed too indescribably dreadful."

He rose and fumbled to take hold of Julia's hand: "My child, my poor lost sheep. What on earth are we to do? So this is how far you have strayed from the fold."

"I'm going to marry her," said Sirius, who had now recovered from his coughing. "I have her father's permission. We shall be married as soon as possible."

"But why have you kept all this to yourself, Julia?" asked Mrs Janniksen. "Why haven't you confided at least in your own mother? So perhaps that's why Jartvard went off? But of course, that changes everything. If I'd had the slightest idea. . . ."

"No, it doesn't make things better at all," moaned Ankersen angrily, turning to the blacksmith's wife. "It makes it just twice as shameful. The girl's . . . the woman's actually been taken in adultery."

"Yes, so she has," confirmed her mother sombrely and took up a position beside Ankersen, facing her daughter.

Ankersen took Sirius by the arm and forced him across beside Julia.

"It is fundamentally a good thing that the truth has been revealed in all its atrocity," he said in a hollow voice. "And whether you marry or not, the path for you both is through repentance and penance and confession of your sins. You must accept responsibility for your dreadful actions, and I will do everything in human power, indeed more than that, to help to put you on your feet again. I will not refrain from any means, God help me. But then you must humble yourselves before your Christian brothers and sisters. Do you promise that? And let what must happen, happen soon. Let it happen this very evening. Let us together . . ."

Ankersen was suddenly interrupted by the door being flung open and the blacksmith entering the room. His face was purple, and his eyes were blazing furiously in their bags.

"Get out," his wife warned him in a hoarse voice.

The blacksmith stepped across to the table and thumped it with his fist so that it resounded throughout the tightly packed room.

"I am master in this house," he shouted threateningly. "I have given my agreement to Julia's marrying this man, and that must be the end of all this *idiotic nonsense*."

"Get out," screamed his wife breathlessly.

"Out with *him*, that nosy parker, that *twerpish twit*," thundered the blacksmith.

He took hold of Ankersen from behind and shook him so that the starched dickey was revealed beneath the neckline of his waistcoat.

"Oh, he's murdering him," wailed Mrs Janniksen, collapsing in a chair.

"Rubbish," said the smith, rather nervously letting go of the savings bank manager. "I only demand that he should leave this house of his own accord."

Ankersen collapsed first on to his knees and then remained on the floor with his short legs stretched out. He fumbled for his glasses and drew his breath heavily.

"Now," growled the blacksmith. "Get a move on."

"My glasses", said Ankersen severely.

His glasses were on the floor beside him. Sirius took them and handed them to him. Ankersen remained seated there with his glasses in his hand. He was breathing heavily, but otherwise seemed to be remarkably calm. He turned his huge face up towards the blacksmith and said in a low, tormented voice twirling his glasses in the air, "You needn't be so upset, Mr Janniksen. I have not forced my way into your house as a thief and robber, but because your wife asked me to come and because I felt it was my duty to come. A duty that is anything but pleasurable. I only want to help. To help. I will most certainly not try to prevent these two young people from becoming joined in holy matrimony. But let us also think of the *spiritual* side of the matter."

He rose with some difficulty and went on, still addressing the blacksmith: "Or is sin not sin? And does sin not always carry its punishment within it? Have repentance and grace no meaning then for us frail and helpless beings? Where will it all end, Janniksen? Well, perhaps *you* have something better to offer?"

Ankersen held out a hand to the smith as a kind of reconciliation. Janniksen hesitantly took it. "Yes, but go now," he said. "And we'll forget the whole thing. Let that be a promise."

"Do not believe I consider myself free from sin," continued Ankersen, looking the blacksmith in the eye. "No, on the contrary, I have been a captive of sin as dreadful as anyone, Janniksen. Perhaps . . . perhaps worse than . . ."

"Than *me*," said the blacksmith, laughing uproariously. "No, get away with you, Ankersen. But now buzz off while the going's good, like we agreed. Eh, Rosa? 'Cause now it's all been fixed, so to speak. Yes, by God it has. Hasn't it, Rosa? Come on, be reasonable. We two can have a bit of fun together as well now and then, can't we?"

He nudged his wife and winked.

"Yes, what . . . what do *you* think?" Ankersen now also turned to the blacksmith's wife.

Sirius stared anxiously at the hefty woman.

"It was mainly to be a support for *you* that I came," said Ankersen impatiently, looking at his watch.

"And it shall not have been in vain," said Mrs Janniksen warmly, turning her back on her husband. "No, indeed it shan't. For we won't yield an inch, Ankersen. Not an inch."

Ankersen put his glasses on his nose and held out his hand to her.

"God bless you," he said and sighed in relief.

He turned to the two young people. "Well, young lady and young gentleman. It's up to you now whether you do your simple Christian duty and open the door that stands ajar. It is still ajar. God is indescribably patient. But not . . . but not limitlessly so, no, for there *is* a limit, and woe to those who know not the hour of their visitation."

He shook hands with them both. The smith touched his shoulder to remind him. He accompanied the savings bank manager into the hall and handed him his hat and walking stick, and then went back to the smithy.

When Sirius went out to take leave of him shortly afterwards, the blacksmith was standing at the anvil. He winked merrily and prodded Sirius in the stomach: "Hmm, so it almost worked, eh? You managed your part well, I must admit. And provided we two stick together, we'll get their" – and he struck the anvil – "*fustypusties* put in place. And then we'll bloody well make their" – and he gave the anvil another enormous blow with his hammer – "fancy parrots jump up."

9

The return of the prodigal son

Johan Wenzeslaus Ankersen, this savings bank manager and lay preacher, in whose person pettiness and greatness for ever fought a bitter but hopeless duel, was naturally something of a mystery to those around him: a kind of dual creature or a centaur. On the surface he was an impeccable and quiet official who skilfully and punctiliously managed the financial institution whose welfare had been entrusted to him, but beneath the surface there was a turbulent, merciless being whose unpredictable moods were feared by all.

Ankersen also had the unusual and surprising quality that he grew worse as the years passed. People who knew him in his younger days describe him as having been reserved and polite, an almost shy young man who was reluctant to interfere in other people's affairs, and who everyone knew to be fighting a constant struggle against a weakness for alcohol that he had inherited from his father, Captain Napoleon Ankersen. It was only on very rare occasions, especially during the festive seasons, that Johan Wenzeslaus surrendered to this fateful tendency, and even when he let himself go in this way it was by no means in any violent or provocative manner, on the contrary. On an occasional evening he might be seen drifting around in the streets, lonely and hopelessly drunk, or hanging out in a dark corner of The Dolphin. Then, for the following days, he would completely withdraw from the world and in profound isolation behind rolled-down blinds he would abandon himself to contrition of a kind known by all to be unusually vehement.

It was in reality only when he was in his forties, that is to say at an age when others tend to quieten down and become more staid, that Ankersen suddenly began to show signs of the impetuous behaviour that was to characterise him for the rest of his life. As far as is known, this transformation in his behaviour was not due to external events of the dramatic kind that can otherwise so often bring about psychological eruptions in people: unhappy love and the like. But there it was – the savings bank manager turned up one day at the home of Mr Lindemann, an inoffensive, delightful clergyman of the old school, and tried to persuade him to take a different path in his religious teachings. When Lindemann turned out to be unwilling to do this, Ankersen took things into his own hands and from now on started appearing as a hell-fire preacher, sometimes speaking in the open street and sometimes – with various, often strangely contorted excuses – turning up at meetings or visiting families and individuals in their own homes.

People shook their heads at this new, self-appointed spiritual adviser to begin with. But it was not long before they were obliged to recognise him as a force it was difficult to ignore. He acquired adherents and formed his own congregation. At first he held open-air meetings, especially on Sunday afternoons on Shoemaker Ground. Later, they acquired a permanent meeting hall, and over the next few years Ankersen's ridiculous little congregation grew slowly but surely. But he only made his real breakthrough when he allied himself with the Ydun Christian Temperance Association and adopted the total prohibition of alcohol as part of his programme. From now on, his star rose steadily; his activities became more extensive, and indeed, as everyone knows, he became a man of considerable power and influence.

Ankersen achieved the greatest triumph of his life on the day on which, in the presence of a large group of witnesses, he was able to receive his son Matte-Gok on his return home.

It was generally known that Ankersen had been seeking this lost son for a long time and with untiring energy. Indeed, practically the entire town had followed these determined efforts of his with touching interest and curiosity, and on the day when it was rumoured that the savings bank manager

133

had at last made contact with his son through the Salvation Army, this even became the dominant theme of conversation everywhere.

Have you heard? He's had a letter from Matte-Gok! He's expected home from South America in April! Yes, that's certain, he announced it in Ydun himself, and Mrs Nillegaard has confirmed it. He'll be on the Mjølnir on the 11th of April.

Good Lord, good Lord, went up the sigh, and there were smiles and tears, and the number of Ankersen's followers rose. The Ydun meeting room was crowded. Everyone had to go and see Ankersen. After this, he was the man of the day as never before.

Even Ankersen's bitterest enemies had to fall silent, or at least keep out of the way for the time being. "Aye, let's see," said Jacobsen the editor. "Let's see how it all pans out. Let's have a closer look at this prodigal son. I can well remember that lad."

"Ahah," said Captain Østrøm, opening a bottle of port with an amused mien.

"Yes, I remember him damned well," the editor replied. "A weakling. A miserable lout. Always with a drip on the end of his nose."

Captain Østrøm looked slightly disappointed. He was ready for greater sensations. "Cheers," he said, rubbing his up-turned little moustache.

Jacobsen felt a terrible urge to say: "And he *stole*. That's why he went away." But it was best to keep quiet and see what happened. First of all because when all was said and done, he was the editor of The Messenger, which is a progressive radical newspaper that doesn't see it as its duty to stab the lower classes in the back. Secondly . . . hmmm. As a young man he had himself known the creature's mother, Ura the Brink. And suppose that it was neither Ankersen, as he himself maintained, nor old Consul Hansen, as the local gossips would have it, who was the father of this Matte-Gok.

Jacobsen emptied his glass and, so as not to disappoint Østrøm too much, started telling him about Ura. Østrøm had not been born and brought up in the little town here; he had come from abroad and was originally a Swede; he had not known Ura the Brink as a young woman.

"Ura comes from a very fine family," Jacobsen informed him.

"The devil she does!" Østrøm livened up.

"Ura is notoriously the daughter of the old trade commissioner Trampe, about whom it would be ridiculous to maintain that he doesn't belong to a highly regarded family," explained the editor in a low voice. "And *her* mother again was the daughter of none other than Commander Zenthner-Wättermann!"

"Well, I'll be damned," laughed Østrøm. His laughter continued for a long time and ended in an agonisingly amused fit of coughing.

"And you could damned well see that on the girl when she was young," continued Jacobsen. "She was *distinguished*, she was, slender and agile like a . . ."

"A jellied eel?" proposed Østrøm and followed this with another attack of his lecherous laughter.

"Precisely," said Jacobsen. "Damned seductive she was; you couldn't resist her, and she went for the upper echelons. Aye, she really did have a certain standard. The Ole Brandy type didn't have a look in. Even Pontus the rose painter, who's a son of old Trampe as well . . ."

"But then he's her half-brother," spluttered Captain Østrøm and raised his glass in the air, filled with amazement.

"Aye, but I'd say that there was nothing doing there either," said Jacobsen, turning slightly away to protect his face from the rain from the captain's coughing and laughing, which now seemed to be approaching the stage of serious spasms. The bulky man's eyes were staring stiffly ahead as though asking for help; he looked like a drowning man battling with a wave.

"Well, well, so this Matte-Gok is a man of the finest pedigree," he resumed, exhausted.

"Yes, he bloody well is," confirmed the editor as though thinking of something else.

"And then, the heartbreaking thing about it," said Fähse the apothecary, rising from the bridge table to offer a new round of cigars, "The heartbreaking thing about it is that this Matte-Gok isn't Ankersen's son at all. Most certainly not. And not old Consul Hansen's either, as some people believe."

He leant forward a little and lowered his voice: "No, the matter is far more seriously complicated than that, for his progenitor is none other than the old Royal Trade Commissioner Trampe!"

"But I say," said Berg the teacher excitedly. "In that way he's the son of his own grandfather. Or however else are you going to explain it?"

Kronfeldt, the Chief Administrator and Springer, the Deputy Prefect, both assumed a gawking, attentive expression. The apothecary sniffed deeply as he nodded in confirmation. Almost regretfully, he added, "The old libertine was over seventy at the time."

"Oh go home and change your nappy," Janniksen thumped Lindenskov in the stomach. "'Course he's neither Ankersen's son nor Old Bastian's nor Wenningstedt's, no one knows that better than me, 'cause I've got it from Ura herself. She didn't really want to admit it, but then I tickled her till she couldn't take it any more, and she had to give in. No, you chump: you see there were no less than seven of them after her, but it was Fähse who got the bull's eye."

Then the great day dawns.

It is a busy Saturday, but everyone seems to have taken the day off; there is a throng on the quayside, there are heads to be seen in all the nearest windows, indeed you can even see people on the roofs.

All the windows in Fähse the Apothecary's long, elegant façade facing the sea are wide open, and the faces of notables can be glimpsed inside: Count Oldendorp, young Consul Hansen, Berg the senior teacher, Kronfeldt the Chief Administrator, indeed even Doctor Manicus. There is also a crowd in the Bastille, and Janniksen and Mac Bett are fighting over

Magister Mortensen's astronomic telescope. According to Atlanta, Mortensen himself has gone out for a walk. The old stick-in-the-mud isn't even interested in being at home with his wonderful toy on this unique day.

Ole Brandy's boat is moored just off the landing stage, and here Jacobsen the editor and Captain Østrøm have reserved themselves the best seats in the entire show, front stalls par excellence. And the stern looks and irascible shouting of Ole Brandy and Olivarius the Sailmaker, who are sitting at the oars, keep the others at a distance. Those others include Olsen, the editor of The News, who has set himself up with his camera.

And now everything is ready. The curtain has been raised. The show can commence.

Ankersen is standing by himself. He polishes his spectacles and replaces them on his nose, straightens his tie, adjusts his cuffs, hangs his walking stick on one wrist, folds his hands, raises his head, sniffs solemnly, looks grave and unapproachable, fundamentally a handsome man, greying with dignity, not entirely unlike Gambetta, not without certain features reminiscent of Henrik Ibsen. A man of consequence. An idealist who goes through fire and water for what he believes in and is not afraid of making himself look ridiculous in people's eyes if it can further his cause.

Who else apart from him could take a situation like this so calmly? A mighty wave of silent sympathy sweeps over Ankersen as he stands there waiting for his lost son, whom he has brought home from those filthy hovels where hunger and misery are rife. The centaur is forgotten, as are the excesses and the bellowing madman. Something unusual is happening, an act of greatness, a cleansing of sin.

And then the moment arrives. The ferryboat berths, and the passengers get up and clamber ashore to a complete, breathless silence. There are no fewer than three young men here in addition to some ladies and an older man. Two of the younger men are well dressed, one small, the other large, they are in checked ulsters, the bigger one wearing a stiff bowler hat, with beard and pince-nez, and smaller one thin and blotchy. They are quickly identified as Egholm, the head clerk and Hjort, the post office clerk. Then there is the third man; he has also got up, but now he sits down again, or falls . . . yes, it looked as though he fell, yes, indeed he did fall, and he is lying in a strange bent posture across the thwart. The ferryman helps the ladies and the old gentleman ashore, and then he beckons to Ankersen and goes across and shakes the collapsed figure, shouts something to him and gets him to his feet.

And suddenly the stranger comes to life, flailing with his arms and crawling ashore. Yes, crawling. He crawls across to Ankersen and throws his arms round one of his legs.

It is *he*, Matte-Gok, the prodigal son. He is obviously blind drunk. A subdued, suppressed murmur of sympathy runs through the entire assembly. The tension becomes almost more than they can stand. Now the shameless wretch has knocked Ankersen down! No, that was not it. It was only Ankersen bending down, crouching down and taking his son's head in his hands.

And now Little Kornelius arrives and helps him to get the drunken man on his feet again. They take him each under one arm, Ankersen and Kornelius. An avenue opens up for them. Several male onlookers take off their hats as though at a funeral. The Weeper and other women weep. Matte-Gok is bare-headed and dressed in a very soiled blue suit. Good heavens, what a mess he looks: his jacket is creased and stained, his darned trousers are frayed at the ankles, the heel is loose on one shoe, yes, indeed, he really looks like what he is: a lost and exhausted sinner!

Ankersen has forgotten his walking stick down by the landing stage, but now Mrs Nillegaard the midwife comes and picks it up. She is weeping profusely and holds a handkerchief pressed to her mouth and nose. A couple of young people are grinning a little at her. But suddenly, she takes away her handkerchief, raises her tear-blotched face and with a piercing voice proclaims: "This is *great*! It couldn't be greater!"

"Great! Great!" she repeats in ecstasy, holding the walking

stick aloft, hurrying up the street and joining Ankersen. Her husband, Nillegaard the junior teacher, follows her hesitantly.

Up in Ankersen's small, spartan but well-kept house in the new district in town, everything had been prepared for the reception. Mrs Midiord the old housekeeper was standing in the doorway, wearing a black dress and a decorative white pinafore and bonnet. An appetising scent of caramelised potatoes emerged from the kitchen. Matte-Gok was placed on a velvet-upholstered rocking chair. He sank back with his eyes closed and wearing a little exhausted smile.

"Let him just sit like that for a while," said Ankersen gently. "Then he'll probably be all right. And as for the rest of you – do sit down, my dear friends, and you, too, Kornelius, if you wish. Then there'll be a bit of veal for all of you."

But Mr Nillegaard could unfortunately not stay; he had to attend a staff meeting in the school, and before long there was an urgent call for the midwife. Kornelius wondered whether he ought not also to leave, but he decided to stay. In a way, he felt it a duty, for he was a kind of brother-in-law to Matte-Gok, of course.

Ankersen went back and forth across the floor with his hands behind his back. He appeared to be elated and happy. Matte-Gok sat with his eyes closed. Kornelius looked at him. Matte-Gok was a tall, sinewy figure with a powerful nose and chin. He looked weatherbeaten and healthy, but he was much in need of a shave. His reddish hair was unkempt, but it was thick and healthy. There were blue and red tattoos on the hairy backs of his hands. Matte-Gok was a thin and well-built, good-looking man of about thirty. "He doesn't look a bit lost," thought Kornelius. "In fact, he actually looks almost sober as well . . ."

Finally, he opens his eyes and looks around as though in amazement. Ankersen takes up a position in front of him. He stands with his stomach protruding and his thumbs hooked into the armholes of his waistcoat, and in his beard there is a satisfied, benevolent, indeed actually enamoured smile. He looks like he does when acting Father Christmas.

"Well?" he says encouragingly. "All right now?"

Matte-Gok looks at him as though in horror and hangs on to the chair arm.

"Where . . . where am I?" he groans.

"In your father's house," nods Ankersen warmly.

And now Kornelius must turn away and hide his emotion. He simply cannot take this scene. He hears Matte-Gok plaintively begging forgiveness and Ankersen answering with prayer and biblical texts. It goes on for a long time. Kornelius feels himself strangely out of place and feels how he misses a father. He can dimly, dimly, remember his own father . . . a couple of sad eyes, a poor, stubbly chin.

Kornelius was again on the verge of abandoning himself to sentiment and tears; he sought to regain his composure by staring fixedly at the motionless, white kitchen door. It was not entirely closed, and inside the crack the observant eyes of the old housekeeper could just be discerned.

The experienced reader will probably already by now have a certain suspicion that Matte-Gok was not the prodigal son he pretended to be, but a swindler and cheat with considerable talents as an actor. It is by no means a pleasurable task to be compelled to give an account of the knavish tricks this terrible person was able to carry out over the coming period to the irretrievable ruin of others. All that can be said in defence of Matte-Gok is that he had poor forbears to take after on both his mother's and his father's side. There would have been nothing to choose between that shady and greedy man of enterprise, Consul Sebastian Hansen, the dishonest and narrow-minded Royal Trade Commissioner Trampe or indeed the farcically overblown and war-crazed Commander Zenthner-Wättermann, if they had been alive.

It is perhaps possible that if more favourable conditions had been granted him during his upbringing Mathias Georg Anthoniussen could have brought his undoubted abilities to fruition by applying them to a different and more generally recognised career. Who knows – an astute and daring businessman, an outstanding lawyer or diplomat had perhaps been lost in Ura the Brink's dissolute son, who left home at the age of seventeen and embarked on the chaotic existence of a vagabond.

However, Matte-Gok has now returned to the place where he was born and is behaving as an apparently artless young man, friendly, with polite eyes and a modest composure, pious and contrite, indeed there is really something touching about the whole of his outward appearance. Matte-Gok is really a handsome young man with well-formed features, a hooked nose and a cleft chin; he closely resembles his great-grandfather, the Commander. And he plays the part of the prodigal son with talent, naturally slipping into the Ydun association, suitably slowly and reluctantly, but one evening he has allowed himself to be moved to throw himself on his knees and, to the accompaniment of weeping and sobbing, to confess his sins and his lack of faith hitherto.

And – all in accordance with his knavish plan – he becomes a faithful support for the naïve folk in the Christian Temperance Association. He reveals a quiet, but obvious ability to touch hearts. Simply and unostentatiously, and without putting himself in the foreground, he talks of the wild life in the strange American jungles, where false gods are still worshipped by the ignorant population, and murder and robbery are part of everyday life. And he tells of missionaries' self-sacrificing, dangerous work to save souls among crocodiles and poisonous insects.

Matte-Gok's reputation quickly spread far and wide, and the evening meetings in Ydun were actually often overcrowded.

This was not only because of Matte-Gok, however. We are now in general approaching those remarkably fateful times when Ankersen the Bank and his fellow warriors could seriously feel they had the wind in their sails and glimpse the achievement of their great ambition: the complete prohibition of alcohol. It was a time full of pamphlets, popular meetings and newspaper polemics, and during this period Ankersen won a host of new supporters in virtually all levels of the population. He gradually emerged as a kind of standard bearer for all right-thinking persons, and people in general began to realise what dangers they could be exposed to if they tried to put a spoke in the wheels of his advancing triumphal chariot.

Thus Jacobsen, the editor of The Messenger, ran into serious trouble. He first had a law suit against him because in a leading article he took the liberty of doubting Ankersen's good intentions and calling the savings bank manager a vain, unprincipled tyrant who brushed aside all human dignity and at times applied methods that were nothing less than bullying in order to put a limit on personal freedom.

Despite these unjust words, Ankersen managed to have Jacobsen offered an out of court settlement. However, as the editor nevertheless refused to climb down from his high horse and withdraw the word *bullying*, while at the same time his newspaper published a new leader under the provocative title of *Holy Hooliganism*, his fate was sealed. He was given a fine, which he simply refused to pay and so had to face a spell in prison. And as a result of this The Messenger was also dealt a mortal blow: its subscribers cancelled their subscriptions, at first in small numbers, but then in droves, and one day the newspaper simply folded.

However, it was not long before The Messenger reappeared, with roughly the same appearance as before, but on the inside completely unrecognisable, and with *Ankersen* as its editor. The Ydun Association had simply bought the newspaper and turned it into its own mouthpiece.

Yes, Ankersen had certainly achieved a new victory that was noised far and wide, and it is easy to understand that Mr Jacobsen's fury was so boundless as to be almost majestic. The ageing man forced his entry into his former composing room and personally destroyed an entire edition of the new paper.

During the wild skirmish that arose in connection with this violent act, the remarkable thing was that *Kornelius* took Jacobsen's side, which resulted in the young compositor being sacked from the newspaper. When he was later compelled to provide an explanation of his strange behaviour in court, he merely said with a sigh, "Well, I don't know, but I really felt so sorry for Jacobsen".

This statement gave rise to uncontrollable laughter in the court and in time achieved almost proverbial status.

10

*Kornelius is mocked by Ole Brandy for his treasure
seeking but receives support from Matte-Gok*

However, it was without complaint that Kornelius once and
for all took leave of the dark, unhealthy little composing room
with its bleak atmosphere of black fingers and fiddling with
trivial bits and pieces. He had his garden to fall back on, and
then there was his music, which always provided a little extra
income. He had been teaching a couple of Boman's former
pupils for some time, and it might be possible to expand that
activity. And in addition, there were the dances.

And then, finally, there was the great project. His mind was
still secretly on it, and it provided him with sweet moments of
ecstasy which he shared with no one. It did not force itself on
him and make demands all the time. There were periods
when it was only like some vague longing. But it was always
there, and sometimes it flared up and made him hot and sleepless. It was good to have, and it might become more than
good; it could become great and ungovernable and change
everything. And now that the ridiculous drudgery on the
type cases was gone once and for all, he could really pull
himself together and devote himself to his speculations and
plans.

He had naturally never been able to afford diving equipment, so he had to dismiss that approach. But he could
presumably manage with less expensive methods if he was
inventive, determined and patient enough.

For instance, you could take a counterpoise weight or some
other heavy object. And then you would fasten it to a line.
With the help of a *sound weight* like that you could drag the
weight along the bottom and *listen*, provided you could hear
clearly enough. To carry out this experiment it was necessary

to have a boat and two men, one rowing while the other looked after the weight and listened. The Crab King could row, of course. The work would have to be done at night and in still, calm weather. An ordinary stone would make a certain sound to which one would gradually become accustomed. A copper chest, on the other hand, would make a sound of its own, a sound that was not to be mistaken.

Then, when the spot had been found, you would place a little buoy there. That was no problem. But the next part of the attempt would then have to be undertaken in daylight; you look to see whether you can see anything. Fine, you can; you can make out the outlines of a square object covered in verdigris. Then it's a case of fishing it up, and there is no denying that that will be the most difficult part of the operation. You need skilled help here, and the Crab King on his own isn't enough. But then there are men like Moritz and Ole Brandy. Of these, Kornelius would prefer to ask Ole Brandy, for he would like it all to come as a lovely surprise for Moritz; he and Sirius mustn't have the slightest idea before it's fixed.

If he could get Ole Brandy interested, it would be a great step forward.

No.

Ole Brandy isn't the least bit interested.

"No, you're not going to get me to swallow that idea, Kornelius," he says dismissively, adding apprehensively: "And incidentally, I didn't expect that of you. I thought you were my true friend."

"But so I am," says Kornelius in amazement.

Ole turns away from him and goes on chewing. "Well, perhaps so," he finally admits. "But in that case there's someone or other having you on and wanting to bring me in as well. But he can think again."

Kornelius says with a warm smile, "No, no, Ole, really. It's only me, I've thought it out all on my own."

Ole Brandy fills his pipe and grunts disapprovingly. Finally he turns broadside on to Kornelius, thumps his stomach and says, "All right, Kornelius, all right. I don't care in any case. But between you and me, what you're talking about is sheer nonsense. For even if that chest might once have existed, it's not there any more. It's long since been eaten by the fishes and vermin down there."

Kornelius now makes an attempt to voice his objections, but Ole breaks him off impatiently: "Fish can't eat their way through copper, you say? Well, that's simply because you're a landlubber and don't know anything about the sea and all the bloody things that live in it. Don't you think a catfish has good teeth? No, come off it, but tell me one thing: Doesn't a quite ordinary catfish have better teeth than you or me? Well, there you see. And I only talked about catfish, and they're among the gentler things down there. But what about rays? And what about sharks? Oh, get off with you. And have you never seen a shipworm?"

"Yes, but they only live on wooden posts," objects Kornelius in a timid but slightly hopeful voice.

Ole Brandy has to admit he is right. But then he takes another approach: "All right, there might be something in that, Kornelius. But, you don't know the *power of the ocean itself*! Don't you know the surf can throw an entire ship ashore and smash it to smithereens? Eh? No, my friend, the sea can grind even the biggest cliff to a stone smaller than one of your buttocks, and it'll put paid to a miserable undertaking like the one you seem to be planning."

"Aye, perhaps so," admits Kornelius. He takes of his pince-nez and surrenders himself to a cheerless contemplation of the situation. "I suppose so when you say so, Ole, 'cause you know the sea . . ."

But then he thinks of Ura. Ura doesn't make a mistake. She has said the treasure *is* there. That it is in some damp place. And she keeps on insisting on that. Well, this damp place doesn't strictly speaking need to be the Commandant Deep. There are other damp places. There certainly are.

He gets up; his face is flushed: "No, Ole, I suppose not. I'll think about what you say. Then we can talk about it again."

"Yes, just you think it over, Kornelius," says Ole in a

paternal voice. "And you'd do well to give those ideas up and not make a fool of yourself in your own eyes. I once knew a man who thought he could spin gold from the red in a common mussel! And believe me, that man ended his days dependent on his wife and spent his time messing about and achieving nothing. And he was a highly gifted man otherwise. But once you start on that path instead of using your brain and looking at God's nature as it's been revealed to any healthy, thinking person. . . .!"

"Yes, of course," nodded Kornelius penitently.

But he was by no means completely convinced. On the contrary. All that was clear to him was that Ole was the wrong man to turn to with that kind of idea.

But things can take a strange turn. This failed attempt of Kornelius's to get Ole Brandy interested was nevertheless to bear some fruit, though as the result of a strange series of coincidences.

One afternoon, Ole is standing chatting to Matte-Gok. Matte-Gok is always to be seen chatting to someone or other; he has so many old friendships he wants to renew and is generally very popular. And here is Ole Brandy who, as a boy, he used to spear mussels for and occasionally go out fishing with. And then, Kornelius chances to go past, and Ole shouts to him "See, there goes our treasure seeker!"

Kornelius blushes and rejects the accusation and is on the verge of tears, so disappointed is he at Ole for exposing him in this way.

Oh well, Ole's remark does not appear to have made any impression on Matte-Gok, thank heavens. He thinks it's some joke on the part of the old man, of course. He doesn't ask what all this about treasure seeking means. The conversation moves by chance on to gold-mining in general.

"Well, you ask how you go about it when you want to find out whether there is gold in the ground?" says Matte-Gok. "It's simply quite straightforward. You take a divining rod. All you need is a perfectly ordinary forked branch. But you see, Ole, it's not everyone who can use it. We were tested, several groups of us, hundreds of men. And then to my amazement it

147

turned out that *I* had the gift. And you can bet they found a use for me, Ole. I so to speak didn't need to lift a spade, but I still had a good percentage of the gold we found. Aye, it was a wonderful time."

"Well then, why didn't you stay where you were when you were doing so well?" asks Ole brusquely.

Matte-Gok does not reply immediately. He looks down penitently for a moment and looks quite sad and tired.

"I couldn't cope with my good fortune," he says finally. "I got into bad company, I turned to drinking and gambling and evil women; I sank deeper and deeper, and if I hadn't . . ."

Ole Brandy suddenly utters a vicious, scornful laugh and turns away to knock out his pipe. "That's a pack of lies, Matte-Gok," he says. "The whole lot of it from one end to the other, your divining rod and the lot. Don't start telling us that kind of rubbish."

Matte-Gok and Kornelius exchange glances suggesting something like: "Aye, we all know how Ole Brandy can talk."

Matte-Gok is not surprised, and certainly not hurt; he is simply kind and forbearing. Ole Brandy taps him on the stomach: "But for all that you might have been a gold-digger! And an undertaker's mute! And a shoe-black for the Queen of Brazil! But this story about the divining rod, no don't try to kid me with that one."

He lights his pipe and strolls of along the quayside, puffing vigorously. His earrings flash merrily in the afternoon sunshine.

Matte-Gok eyes Kornelius steadily but amiably and says, "But that story about the divining rod *is* true, even so. Ole doesn't want to believe it because he's such a one for telling yarns."

"Aye, so he is," Kornelius confirms with a smile.

"But what was it he was saying about you?" Matte-Gok went on with a yawn. "Are you looking for treasure of some kind, Kornelius?"

Kornelius blushes again and looks down. The question comes so unexpectedly. What is he to answer? Should he just brush it aside as a lot of nonsense? Or . . . perhaps he should rather confide in Matte-Gok and hear a bit more about his divining rod?

He takes Matte-Gok by the arm and says quietly, "Can you keep a secret, Matte-Gok?"

"Of course, Kornelius," replies Matte-Gok. "You know me."

And this is where the shameful drama is launched. Kornelius talks and Matte-Gok listens. He shows no particular interest, as though it were all about something extraordinary. On the contrary, he nods pensively; he has obviously heard the legend of the old treasure, but he is not so terribly interested in it. As is naturally to be expected of such a widely travelled and experienced man; Kornelius actually feels embarrassed at having shown himself to be so keen.

"Of course . . . well really," he stammers. "I realise that even if . . . that whoever found the treasure . . . couldn't really keep it all for himself, but would have . . . would have to hand it in and be satisfied with some kind of reward for finding it."

Matte-Gok shakes his head and says, "You're wrong there, Kornelius. The treasure belongs to the man who digs it up. No power can take it from him, neither by force nor by law."

Matte-Gok hides a slight yawn and looks at his watch. "Oh, I'm supposed to be up in Ydun at seven o'clock."

He gives Kornelius a little tap on the shoulder: "But it could be fun to try with the divining rod, you know. It's such a long time since I had one in my hands. I wonder whether I'm still any good at it. Suppose we meet again and talk about it tomorrow evening?"

They agree on this. Matte-Gok hurries away. Kornelius remains on the quayside. He feels strangely confused, but a sweet sense of excitement wells up inside him. "At last, at last. But, don't get excited too soon. It can still go wrong. But give up? Never."

The following evening.

At first, Matte-Gok stands fumbling with the divining rod, which he has taken from the blacksmith's garden. He stands and pretends he has forgotten the art or has lost his remarkable

149

skill. But then, yes, there is something left of it. . . . Yes, indeed. It trembles and moves just as it used to do when there was gold around.

"It's looking good, Kornelius."

The rod points towards the north east. And they go in that direction, excitedly observing the movements of the forked branch. It is a cloudy, windy evening with a greenish light over the northern horizon. Several times it looks as though the divining rod will make a definitive judgement, but nothing comes of it after all. Meanwhile, they are moving in a north-easterly direction out of town.

"There you are, Kornelius, we'll soon be at the place; there's no mistaking it. Here, out in the fields, this is where the old boy hid his treasure. Of course. Don't you think?"

"Yes, of course," says Kornelius.

"The old smithy's out here somewhere," says Matte-Gok.

"No, it's not there any more," Kornelius can tell him. "It blew down, and there are only the ruins left."

"Well, that doesn't make any difference. Let's go a bit further back again." Matte-Gok sighs. It sounds as though he is growing tired and is not far from giving up the search.

"It's a demanding job," he smiles. "It drains your brain power."

But then, suddenly, the divining rod starts dancing about as never before, and Matte-Gok is on the point of uttering an oath: "I've bl. . . .! No, just look here, Kornelius."

Kornelius's heart is beating wildly.

They are on a lonely, marshy moss-green place, not far from the ruined smithy.

It is right. This is the place. The divining rod is pointing vertically down and can't be moved.

"Oh, this is amazing," says Matte-Gok. "I really thought, between us two, that all this talk of the treasure . . . was perhaps just an old wives' tale. But . . . Oh, well, let's take it easy, whatever we do, Kornelius. Don't you think? And not a word of this to anyone else. Promise?"

"Of course," says Kornelius. He is trembling all over by now.

"Hey! What was that?"

"What?"

Matte-Gok stands listening for a moment. "No, perhaps there wasn't anything. But I thought it was as though something rattled up near the ruin. There can't be anyone watching us, can there?"

They go across to the ruin. But there is nothing unusual to be seen.

"Tell me, you're not frightened of ghosts and that sort of thing, are you?" asks Matte-Gok jovially.

"Not in the least," stammers Kornelius. "I never have been."

"You're fortunate there. I'm terribly afraid in the dark myself. It's a bit silly, isn't it?"

Matte-Gok gives Kornelius a friendly nudge: "But . . . well, I can't really get over my amazement that we should find your treasure after all. You're a fortunate chap, so you are. But as I say, we'll take it easy now. We'll sleep on it for a time. I'll have to have a good think. The first battle's been won, but there's a long way to go. We must just be careful not to spoil it all."

They start moving off towards home. Kornelius walks as in a dream. It is as though he has completely stopped being excited; indeed he actually feels strangely cold and relaxed, as though none of it concerns him any longer. He hears Matte-Gok going on talking about various treasures he has helped to track down and find. And so on and so forth. Kornelius is strangely sick of it all.

"You're very quiet, Kornelius."

"It's because I'm thinking about things. And do you know what I'm thinking about?"

"No."

Kornelius sighs. "Well, you see, I can't help thinking that that treasure . . . doesn't really belong to me."

"Oh, is that all?" smiles Matte-Gok.

Kornelius goes on, "No, for it's not my land it's buried in, but someone else's. That's one thing. But then there's another, and that is that it's you and not me who's found it. So in that way it belongs to you, not me."

"Rubbish," laughs Matte-Gok. "I'm not in need of money. And the treasure belongs to the man who digs it up. Every treasure-seeker knows that."

"Oh, does it?"

"Yes, of course. And no one ought to know that better than I. You dig it up, Kornelius. All on your own. I don't need to be there at all. So don't go and spoil it all for yourself with your silly worries. Think of all the things you can do with the money. Good heavens. Just think, Kornelius."

"Yes, of course," smiles Kornelius. "I've hardly thought of anything else for years. But . . . but at least I must say thank you very much indeed, Matte-Gok. For without your help . . ."

"Oh, nonsense, there's nothing to thank me for. It simply amused me to see that I've not forgotten my skill. But before you start digging, there are various little things to consider. For instance, you have to do it when there's a new moon. And the actual date is of importance. You mustn't do it tomorrow or the day after. Preferably not this week, Kornelius. Perhaps not even this month at all. It will be too light. On the other hand, though, it doesn't need to be pitch dark. Only a dark twilight. And then there's that question of the stars."

"The stars?"

"Yes, the planets. I must get hold of an almanac and work out how they're aligned. This is a very old treasure, you know."

Matte-Gok gives a good-humoured, friendly laugh. "It's jolly interesting is this. Fancy experiencing this. Here in this God-forsaken place."

And suddenly Kornelius also starts laughing. They both laugh and secretly enjoy the situation.

"Yes, it's fun," says Matte-Gok nudging Kornelius. "Some benevolent forces have helped us here. Do you know what I think? I think that God has appointed you to find this treasure. You and no one else. And do you know why? Well, because you have so much wanted it. What people go and want for a long time is granted to them. Have you prayed that you might succeed?"

"Yes," Kornelius had to admit.

"There you are. And then I was sent. Yes, I've had a feeling about it all the time. The whole project is blessed. Let's not neglect to thank Him for it. But we'd better both go home now. And it's most important we both keep mum about it. And that we don't talk to each other about it until the time arrives. In general, we have to purge ourselves and prepare ourselves."

"What do you mean, prepare ourselves?"

Matte-Gok shakes Kornelius warmly and firmly by the hand: "By looking forward and being humble. Oh, well, good night, my friend, and sleep well. Hey, Kornelius, are you crying?"

"It's all so strange," stammers Kornelius. "I hadn't expected it to be like this. It's like it's all too much."

"That's a good sign," says Matte-Gok emotionally. "I mean your crying. I had secretly been hoping that would happen. That's the best thing that could happen. Now I know for certain that you're the right one."

Kornelius walks slowly home. He is overcome and cannot really pull himself together again. After supper, he sits lost in thought. If they become rich, what then? It's almost too good to be true. A fine new cello is one of the things he'll buy. He suddenly catches himself thinking that it was really a lovely time when he was still working for The Messenger and came home tired and hungry each evening and washed and had his supper and played a little for Kornelia and went to bed and slept like a log. New times are on their way now, strange new times.

Kornelia comes and snuggles up to him, sits on his knee and takes his hand. He repays the pressure of her hand, but catches himself feeling irritated that this woman never says a word. . . . As though she were not only blind, but deaf and dumb as well. Only these soundless, child-like hands pressing his. And then this silly nervousness every time he wants to really hold her in to him . . . as though she were merely a girl of twelve and not one over twenty years of age. Perhaps she would never grow up, perhaps she would remain his *daughter* instead of his wife for the rest of her life. But then he immediately regrets his thoughts and presses a kiss on her cheek. "My Kornelia," he says contritely.

"Play a little," she whispers in his ear.

Kornelius takes out the cello. Kornelia seats herself on the stool over by the stove and with an open mouth surrenders herself to the trembling that always comes over her when he starts tuning his instrument, and which he has always found so sweet until now. But this evening he simply doesn't like to see her sitting and trembling and blushing and becoming beautiful. "Oh, it's a bit much," he thinks and is not far from weeping at the thought. "It's a bit much after all that it's the cello she loves, and not *me* . . .!"

11

Magister Mortensen receives an unexpected letter and at first goes completely haywire

Magister Mortensen's great philosophical work is naturally not only about Satan, but also about God: God as the principle of the good in the soul, in human life, in social life, in history. About how this principle of the good is ceaselessly taken over by pettiness, self-satisfaction and evil, which in the name of religion and charity feather their own filthy, blood-stained nests with vanity and lust for power. About how, over the years, the Church and its careerists and hangers-on have distorted and mutilated and still neglect and disregard the true core of Christianity . . . at the same time as simple goodness, honesty, self-sacrifice and love of one's neighbour are practised anonymously by people every single day – not with any thought of heavenly reward in the life to come, but as the most natural and innocent thing in the world. Every day you come across jewels about the existence of which you would perhaps have remained ignorant if a truly generous fate had not hauled you down from those oh so important pedestals of barren theological speculation . . .

Mortensen has been writing all morning and has felt in good form, but now, as he reads through what he has written . . . dear God, it is not what he had thought; it is just nothing at all. So, as usual, he has simply sat paddling in the ocean with a teaspoon.

He gets up, filled with despondency and self-contempt, and crosses over to the window with a sigh. Dust, dust and literature compared to life, life that is grey and yet secretly sparkling with diamonds, life with its *actions*. True Christianity is not literature, but action. Did Jesus Christ just sit and write? No, but that monster of an apostle Paul did immediately afterwards, St Paul, the first great swindler!

But what the hell . . . as soon as you settle down to act in a true Christian spirit, you bang your head against all those very things you are trying to avoid: pettiness, egoism, vengefulness, brutality . . . usually well hidden by Satan behind fair phrases . . .

Outside, the sun is shining, the cocks are crowing from the ragged turf roofs on Skindholm, and everywhere where there is a bare patch in the greenery the hens are lying digging their way down in the dry soil as though possessed of some sudden madness. Or perhaps rather like theologians rummaging around in the philosophy of religion in order to get rid of the fleas of their bad consciences.

And there, God help me, comes Wenningstedt the solicitor, the property owner, the landlord. And he's coming here. The old swine. "Well, let him come," thinks Mortensen savagely – "this money grubber, this man of many words, this erotic nosy parker!"

Mortensen was fuming inwardly, and it was some time before he was able to put on a comparatively accommodating face. But what the hell, you couldn't cut up too rough when you owed the man seventy-five thousand kroner and in fact hadn't a clue as to where you were going to get them from.

Mortensen grimly adopted an attitude of wait-and-see. Unfortunately he did not have the money and was forced to ask for a further respite.

"Of course," said Wenningstedt. "Provided we can agree on a date. Or . . . if it should turn out that you have something you might like to sell, then I'm always at your disposal."

Mr Wenningstedt had a gentle, watchful face and thin, projecting ears that moved attentively like those of a dog. He took his time, humming and drumming his fingers on the chair arm, talking about the bad times and of how impossible it was to collect his rent, especially here in the Bastille. For instance there was this ferryman in the big, really rather splendid basement flat. ". . . Can you imagine, he owes me over a hundred kroner, and he owes another hundred to Siff the grocer? He's one of that impossible category of tenants who always promise to improve and never keep their promise."

The solicitor exchanged a brief glance with Mortensen, looked down a little and went on with a stiff smile: "And then you can hardly take up a hard line with him after all, for he's so charming, of course, not to mention his wife. And then you always have to think of his beautiful music. I love music. And then there's that brother of his up in the attic, the one who married the blind girl. He's fundamentally a nice person, too, but hopeless when it comes to money. . . . since he lost his job at the printers. So you understand, Mr Mortensen, by comparison with these tenants, you are a pure angel in a way, ha, ha, and I don't doubt we'll sort things out between us."

The solicitor took a look out of the window. "This is actually a lovely place to *live*, Mr Mortensen. And what a view! You can really sit here and . . . stargaze, eh? For you have an astronomic telescope, I gather?"

"It's only an ordinary terrestrial telescope," came the informative reply.

"But you do look at the stars, don't you?"

"Yes, stars." Mortensen looked up at the ceiling and exhaled gently.

"If it's not inconvenient to you, Mr Mortensen . . . I would so much like to see a big beast like that," smiled the solicitor.

Of course. That could easily be arranged.

The telescope was up in the attic, in the "spire". They had to go through the kitchen to get up there, and here Wenningstedt took the opportunity to inspect Atlanta at close quarters. "Oh, she's quite young," he thought. "I wonder what a young thing like her sees in this good-for-nothing middle-aged failure."

They climbed a ladder, and Mortensen focused the telescope. A confusion of roofs, glimpses of water, blue and flashes of sunlight . . . oh, there was Seal Island, so clear and so close that you could see ducks and poultry in the alleys. If you turned the telescope a little, you had the sea and the sound. Fine. Wenningstedt turned a little further, and now the nearby houses in the town came into view, and suddenly he was looking into an attic where a young woman was standing in her negligee, indeed, as far as he could see, in her shift.

"Oh, but that is quite amazing," he said emotionally. "It's quite unbelievable how close the island is, and how beautiful it is out there."

"Yes, it's fun," confirmed Mortensen in a tired voice.

"Yes, by God it is, quite unique, quite unique. A sight for the gods. You are so close to . . . nature. To eternity. It is quite outstanding."

"Wouldn't it be fun for you to see the moon?" asked Mortensen, concealing a yawn.

"No, thank you very much," laughed the solicitor with a disparaging movement of his elbows. He laughed politely: "The moon, in broad daylight?"

But it was not meant as a joke; the moon was really high in the sky. Mortensen turned the telescope a little, and something indeterminate and misty appeared.

"Oh, there it is?" smiled Wenningstedt sourly, vainly trying to turn the telescope back to the attic window. "No, astronomy is something I don't understand and I'm not interested in it. On the other hand, I take a great interest in old houses . . . they are what I might call my hobbyhorse. Yes, for you know it's interesting to live in an old town, a town that's a thousand years old, and not in a . . . a mushroom . . ."

A sleepy, sad child's face suddenly showed itself in the stairs up to the loft. "That must be the idiot." The solicitor was all eyes.

"No, not up here, dear," said Mortensen. The face hesitantly disappeared. Oh, she didn't look as daft as all that, this daughter. Wenningstedt had imagined something more in the way of a grotesque cretin.

"Tell me, if it came to the point, how much would you have wanted for the telescope?" he asked.

A hunted, but composed expression came over Mortensen's lean face. The solicitor cleared his throat and said, "Listen, I have another suggestion. What would you say to hiring me the apparatus for a time, a short time or a long time? We could arrange it so you paid off part of your debt to me in that way."

"Yes," Mortensen also thought it might be an idea. They discussed the matter for a while and came to an agreement.

"Well, you see," said Wenningstedt in a sprightly tone, "I quite fell for it. I have to admit that I just love the sea; I never get tired of contemplating nature and all that life rustling out there. And I have quite a good view myself. You just see; it won't be long before I become quite lost in the firmament. I understand you, Mortensen. It is so inexpressibly good for mankind to dwell on lofty things, don't you think, and to turn its back on the drabness of everyday life."

There was a benevolent look in the lawyer's eyes as he stared into the distance.

Mortensen lit his pipe. "Oh, what the devil," he said as he flicked the burned matchstick into a corner. "It's as you take it, Wenningstedt. In reality, it's generally speaking the same up there as down here. It's just the distances that are greater. The everyday routine's just about the same."

The solicitor smiled in some confusion, and Mortensen went on, puffing eager little clouds of smoke up in the air, "Yes, all this about the 'eternal stars' is just a romantic cliché. The stars aren't eternal at all; they are born and live and die just like you and me, they drift around and cut up rough for a time and knife each other in the back and are guilty of all sorts of hanky panky . . . until they finally burn out, and then that's the end of that."

"Oh, is it?" said Wenningstedt with a little deprecating laugh.

They climbed down the ladder.

Magister Mortensen went back to his writing desk. But it was impossible for him to concentrate on anything sensible; he felt finished for today. Perhaps it would do him good to go for a walk. A short, stimulating walk in the good weather. He put on his old stained summer coat and filled his pipe again. But on the steps up to the apartments he met the postman, who came along waving a letter.

"A letter for me?" said Mortensen. "Good Lord, that's a rare event."

He quickly opened the yellow envelope. Lauridsen, High Court Solicitor, Ribe . . . who the devil's that? Oh, no, good heavens. God almighty!"

He suddenly felt dizzy. For a moment he really thought he was dreaming. He leapt up the steps. "Atlanta!" he called and was unable to recognise his own voice. Atlanta had not heard him. But heavens above, heavens above.

Mortensen was so dumbfounded and confused that he felt sick and had to go into the bedroom and drink a glass of water. It tasted lukewarm and stale. He poured a few drops of cognac into it, but it still almost made him sick. But this was no nausea resulting from illness and sorrow. It was the result of pure delight. As though it were meant symbolically. "It's . . . it's all your life so far that you want to spit out," he said half aloud to himself. He felt weak from overwhelming emotion.

"Vibeke," he called, and the girl came into the room and looked at him questioningly, with her head back and her mouth open.

"Vibeke," whispered her father. He lifted the girl up on to the chaise longue and whispered into her ear, "Oh, Vibeke . . . we're *rich* . . . we're *rich*, Vibeke! You've no idea what that is, you poor thing. But you see . . . you see . . .!"

She stared at him with her sad, misty eyes. He pressed the poor, melancholy head to him and kissed her forehead. Then he lay down on the chaise longue, weak and sleepy from giddy humility. Oh, but it was strange how sleepy he felt. He lay for a moment and actually fought to stay awake. But then he suddenly leapt up, rushed to the writing desk and grabbed the letter, ran through it breathlessly and broke into a sweat.

No, it was right enough. There is was in black and white, dry and sober, that he had inherited a hundred and forty-six thousand kroner. Uncle Andreas had finally died at the age of ninety-two, and he was the sole heir.

"So people can really live that long," he said aloud to himself and had to laugh at the ridiculous implication in the remark. "Of course they can live to be ninety-two and a hundred and eleven," he bumbled on. "I'd really given up his dying long ago," he laughed. "That's to say that I would live longer than him."

"I want to play with bicks," said Vibeke.

"Oh, so you want to play with bicks," said her father, rummaging around to find the tin box containing the child's empty matchboxes. You shall have some new bicks, daddy'll buy you some nice new bicks and a geegee and a rocking horse and . . . everything you want."

"And just imagine, 146,000 kroner," he went on, talking to himself. "I'd have imagined something in the region of, say four thousand. And I'd even have been very happy with that bit. But this, it's completely ridiculous. Completely ridiculous!"

"Where are nice new bicks?" asked the girl plaintively.

Chuckling to himself, Mortensen shook his head, and tears came to his eyes. "Oh, what the hell is there really to laugh about here?" he scolded himself. But he couldn't put a stop to the hysterical laughter. It came of its own accord, just like the nausea before. He glanced nervously at the kitchen door.

"Could it possibly be that I'm going daft?" he thought, and for a moment everything actually went black for him. Again, he had to throw himself on the chaise longue. No, nonsense, he wasn't daft. He'd like to see the man, the penniless wretch, the tormented creature who wouldn't go crazy in his situation.

But just fancy that old stick-in-the-mud Uncle Andreas had been so well off! In his young days, Andreas had been a farmer and later the owner of a plantation in America. At some time in the fifties he had sold his business and come home, broken by illness, bent quite double by rheumatism, like a wheel. But he had been able to hold on to life in spite of it all.

There had at one time been certain rumours about the incredible amount of money Andreas possessed. But rumours of that kind easily spring up out in the country where people have so little to talk about. But still . . . well, here was a proof of it all.

For a moment, Mortensen could see his uncle, alive, almost as in a vision: the old man, his grandfather's brother, bent double as though beneath some evil, unreasonable burden and with tired, bad-tempered and searching eyes in a whitish face. It was almost as though the old man had come to ensure he was remembered and acknowledged. Funny. Mortensen again felt unwell for a moment and sighed long and hard. He had never been able to stand the old boy and his hard, tormented smile.

Oh well. Enough of that.

Mortensen settled himself more comfortably on the chaise longue. He was not the least bit sleepy any longer. He was simply worn out. Worn out and calm. He lay there with his eyes closed and sought to gather his thoughts in some reasonable manner. But he could not really manage. He lay there and reviewed his life. It was all past now, something to be taken leave of. Good bye and thank you.

His childhood in Jutland. His taciturn father and his timid, strictly religious mother. His two brothers, both of whom had died young. Alas, alas . . . it was all so far away and unimportant, and yet it forced itself on him and wanted to be remembered one last time as it were. A time filled with a dull longing to get away and a hunger for something . . . for something *great*. The training college, where he attracted attention by virtue of the ease with which he learnt. His years as a student in Copenhagen, the time when he went hungry while living in Regensen. Religious crises. Kierkegaard. The theological studies that he gave up as gibberish. The first boozes and women. Music. Friends. Witty companions. Stupid girls, though he couldn't leave them alone even so.

Magdalena Herz . . . the enchanted sun of his youth.

Nonsense!

The examinations. The Master's degree. More drink, decline, dissoluteness . . . after Magdalena's scandalous betrayal. Night and misery and long hungry days full of the light of spring and a resounding void. And an echo, a merciless, crazy echo of Beethoven's sonata opus 31 number 2, the "Midnight Sonata" as he and Magdalena had christened it . . . the midnight sonata with its torrents of passion and tenderness and boundless pain.

Flight! The long journey to that far-off land where out of desperation he had applied for a vacant post as a middle school teacher . . . in a little town where he had thought it would be possible to abandon himself to solitude and philosophy and regain his strength and write the great philosophical work. Oh, no! A school that was hell and a small town that was hell. The malicious persecution to which he was constantly subjected as a "free thinker". His confrontations with Berg, the senior master, that opinionated jackass, that stupid over-blown nobody, which ended with that ridiculous fight in the playground that was the reason for his having to leave his post.

Kind little dishevelled Nikoline, the teacher who was his only consolation during this grotesque and ignominious time and became the woman he married. New poverty, degrad-ation, soul-destroying private tuition. The job as librarian that was given him as a kind of charitable act. The poor little pungent-smelling library with its eternal stench of paraffin stove. Nikoline's death in childbirth. The sentimental and overdone worship of his daughter, and the dreadful blow when it turned out that she was . . . that she was . . .!

Well, so now he was almost up to date.

Of course not, no!

Long years of suffering. Bold decisions once more to escape from it all. All coming to nothing on account of his total lack of money and of . . .

Well, of what?

On account of Vibeke? Rubbish. You could quite well have taken the poor, daft kid with you and had her placed in some suitable home. The great work? No, not that either. You could have blathered on with that anywhere in the world. No, my fine friend, the cause lay much, much deeper than that. In an accursed fatal inertia. A sickness of the soul. Something that had gone to bits. It was a case of pupating ever deeper in some metaphysical cocoon and then later trying to work your way out again without bursting the cocoon open. Until you finally pulled yourself together and blew it apart . . . after which you were then left cold and homeless to blunder about in the real world while secretly longing back to the pupal state.

Well. Go on.

Resignation. The telescope that he bought or was half given by Sundholm the photographer, that straight-dealing and noble human wreck. Telescope, philosophy and music. Serenity and unruffled peace.

Never mind . . . that serenity soon turned out to be a foolish illusion. Serenity is a wishful state that can never be established, least of all in a small town hell among insensitive folk with their gossip and chatter, their conceitedness and their disregard for the spirit, and their tireless attempts to corrupt one's meagre, dearly achieved peace.

Desperation. Hatred of the poverty that made one dependent on every Tom, Dick and Harry . . . and that banal counter-jumper and man-eater Consul Hansen or the obsequious creep Wenningstedt. Hatred of fate, of Vibeke, of everything. The decision to commit suicide. The lonely trip out to sea with the poor girl. God help me! The wretched capitulation and tear-dripping return to life. And Atlanta's dismay when in a fit of self-contempt he had confided in her and told her what he had been intending. Her despair, her surprising tenderness . . . something like the sparkle of rare, genuine diamonds in an otherwise banal bargain piece.

"Atlanta," he called.

Atlanta looked simply amazed: "Why are you lying down there? In your overcoat! You're not ill, are you?"

He felt a dull need to weep on her lap, to enclose her in an embrace so strong and ardent as though it were to be the last, to tell her what had happened, to make her wild with joy. But he simply lay there and said, "No, Atlanta, I don't feel too well at all. I don't want anything to eat, and would you tell the two pupils coming this morning that I'm ill."

Mortensen suddenly got up and made a deprecatory gesture with his hands: "No, better not, Atlanta. Just let the two drips come. I'm not really the least bit ill. It was only a bit of a headache, and I'm all right again now."

. . . Well! Now it was behind him, as it were. The comedy was ended. Peace and quiet established again. Now he would look forward. Just look forward. Look forward to telling Atlanta the great news. To make her wildly happy. To share her joy, rest in it, feel the pulse of life, live, *live*!

At long last it was as though he was on top of things. Hic Rhodos!

"This evening," he said to himself. "It shall be this evening. And we must be alone. Gloriously, gloriously alone."

The rest of the day passed in the usual way, as though nothing had happened. But in the twilight, when the last pupil had gone and quite contrary to his own wishes, Magister Mortensen slipped back into the strange feverish condition he had experienced during the morning. In his thoughts, as in a vision, he saw the dreadfully big, quite unmanageably big fortune that now, contrary to all reason, had fallen to him . . . bundles of banknotes, pile after pile, a snowstorm of ten kroner notes, of hundred kroner notes, of five hundred kroner notes . . . he felt dizzy and had to throw himself on to the chaise longue, where he fell into a restless, dream-filled sleep. He dreamt that he had bought himself a new telescope, a real telescope through which he could see the planet Saturn so near that it covered the entire sky.

When he woke up again, it was dark. Atlanta was not at home. He was suddenly taken by a fear that she might not return, but that she had left him for good and surrendered him to a void he could not bear. "Atlanta," he groaned to himself as he wandered restlessly around the empty flat.

He went into the bedroom, where Vibeke was asleep. The sleepy little bedside lamp was on the chest of drawers by her bed. The poor child almost looked like a human being when she was dozing. She ought really always to be dozing.

He kissed her forehead and suddenly burst into tears, and he laid himself on the bed, sniffing as he did so.

Before long, he bounced up, lit the table lamp and set about reading what he had written that morning before all this confusion had begun. Before the deluge. Before the Flood.

"As an intellectual type in the broadest sense, Kierkegaard thus belongs to the Mephistophelian category. Like the Devil's chargé d'affaires in Goethe, he is in possession of a superior intellect that he applies with the same deftness and tirelessness. Each in his own way, they are both at once witty, impudent and dazzling. Indeed, Kierkegaard is in fact more than a match for the Devil in that he is unsurpassed in the art of attacking reason with its own weapons. He is not only Mephistopheles, but he is at the same time Mephisto's victim, Man, Faust. He not only directs his weapons at others, but he finally turns them on himself, without mercy, standing there like a mortally wounded flagellant, whereas Mephistopheles dissolves himself in a miasma of brilliant conversation. And Kierkegaard suffers horribly under his own Satanism. He is what one might call the tragic Satan . . ."

There was someone coming upstairs now. Atlanta, presumably, coming home.

Mortensen pushed the manuscript aside. Yes, it was Atlanta. She was in her best clothes, but looked infinitely sad. She sat down hesitantly on the chaise longue. There were fresh raindrops forming pearls on her overcoat and in her heavy head of dark hair. She looked at him, pleading, as though she had something she had to say to him. What could it be that she had on her mind? She blinked her dark eyelashes in the light. And suddenly, her eyes were full of tears, and she turned away and looked down timidly.

"Hey, what's wrong?" he asked. "What, Atlanta? What's upsetting you?"

He went across and sat down by her side, took her hand and said tenderly: "You're naturally fed up with going here and messing around . . . in this miserable flat . . . together with a middle-aged man . . . yes, Atlanta, that's what's bothering you. Because it looks as though there's no future in it, doesn't it?"

Atlanta nodded and looked away.

Mortensen sighed deeply. Then, with a little smile, he said, "Yes, but that's all over now, Atlanta. It's in the past, and it will never come back."

She glanced at him, full of amazement.

He went on, caressing her hand the while, "Yes . . . I know it sounds like a bad joke . . . but even so, it's a fact that I've

166

been told today that I've inherited a huge fortune, no less than 146,000 kroner. You can see the letter for yourself."

He held out the letter to her. She stared at it without reading.

He got up and shook his head impatiently. "Well, as you know, I hate sentimental scenes. But, to put it briefly, the situation has improved beyond recognition. We are well off now. We can start afresh. We can travel. We can do just about anything we want to do."

He tenderly absorbed the picture of the young woman on the chaise longue. She looked like something on the lines of a neglected Spanish princess: slender and ardent and young and neglected. Ah, this soul with its hunger for life, in whose grey everyday life a *fairy tale* had suddenly appeared . . . like a sunbeam in a dark back room.

He went across and placed a hand on her shoulder, seeking to capture her eye, but she avoided him. She did not look happy at all. She was weeping.

"Oh, so we're going to have a scene after all," he thought. "But never mind. The situation isn't really entirely ordinary. And besides: haven't I myself gone and created various scenes all day?" But now he felt he was in equilibrium again. *This* was all that had been missing. Atlanta. The woman. The link between a man and reality.

"Atlanta," he said, doing his best to apply the least poignant tone he could manage. "We two have gone through a lot together for a long time, and we deserve to have a bit better life, don't we?"

She leaned towards him and surrendered to him, passionate and silent, without meeting his eye.

For a moment Mortensen felt a profound and fervent sense of peace in his soul, of good, healthy balance . . . It almost felt as though he had gone twenty years or so back in time and was in his youth again, in his twenties . . . this inexpressible feeling of primitive happiness between a man and a woman, of measureless reserves of future prospects.

And yet, deep down within him, a dull feeling of dawning middle-class idyll, of banal satiety, of mediocrity . . .

And – incredibly – a smouldering longing back for the old ways, an unhealthy longing for the mess he had been in, the worries, the hatred, the despair . . . the *work*! The book about Satan! What about that now? Must it be abandoned? No, it shall bloody well not be abandoned!

And yet – was he not now as it were disqualified from writing that book?

"Well, my girl," he said suddenly and gave Atlanta a friendly slap on the shoulder. "Shall we sleep on it for the time being? I'm tired out, and you look as though you are, too."

Yes, Mortensen was really tired, completely worn out and devoid of all thought. Sleep came upon him like a night of gusts and showers, and he blissfully surrendered to it.

12

*More about Magister Mortensen, who during these
days was indeed exposed to unusual events, and
about Josef the Lament, for whom an abyss also
opened one fine day*

Magister Mortensen awoke half dressed on the chaise longue
and noted that he had overslept by two hours. It was some
time before the events of the previous day again reappeared in
his memory, but oh! It was true, by Jove . . . Oh yes. That's
fine. Unless it was something he had been dreaming . . .?

He bounded up, shivering with cold and uneasiness, and
quickly opened the drawer in his writing desk where this
ominous letter would be hidden if it were all true. Yes, there it
was. Shivering, he laughed to himself . . .

Curiously enough, Atlanta was not up yet either. It was
cold and damp in the kitchen. He knocked on the door of her
room and went back into the living room The sun was already
high in the sky, and the bay and sea were one great shining
platinum mirror. Out in the sound there were two fishing
boats that almost completely disappeared in the enormous
shimmer, but then they appeared again, filigree small and
clear. And out on the horizon he could see the smoke from a
ship. Presumably the Mjølnir, the big steamer that was here
yesterday on its way to Copenhagen.

"You could have gone on that steamer, sir," laughed
Mortensen to himself. "You could easily have got a loan on the
strength of the *letter*. Aye, they'd even have bowed and scraped
to you and congratulated you and looked mightily up to you."

The sunshine poured into the room, warming it and dazzling his eyes. Mortensen yawned and stretched and uttered a
long, pensive sigh. But what was *that*? He suddenly discovered
that just under his nose on the table there was a sheet of paper,
written in a clumsy, childish hand.

It was a letter. He sat down and quickly ran through it. It was from Atlanta.

"Dear Mortensen, When you read this letter I shall no longer be here, but far away, I have left on the Mjølnir, I should have told you long ago, and then yesterday evening, but I couldn't get it said, but I decided a long time since that I can't be with you any more as I'm engaged, and now I must go with him, he's twenty-six, I shan't ever come back. Josef's wife Sarina is going as well, thank you for everything, now it's past, I am terribly fond of you and of Vibeke as well, I'll never forget you, my heart is filled with sorrow, but don't be angry, it must be as it is, and congratulations on your inheritance. Yours Atlanta."

Mortensen got up with a short, harsh laugh.

"Go to hell," he murmured. "And good luck."

"Never mind," he consoled himself. "She was a harpy after all. And besides, far too young for you. And one thing with another."

But what now? Light a paraffin stove and put some water on for some coffee.

He got hold of the stove, but he could not find any matches. The box in his pocket was empty, and there were no matches to be seen in the kitchen. Perhaps there was a box in Atlanta's room. He flung the door open. There stood her bed. Carefully made, with clean sheets.

"Oh, you . . . you perfidious bitch," he groaned menacingly. "But I don't care. It's a good job I got rid of you in a nice way."

There was a scent of cheap perfume in the air. A touching scent.

Umgiebt mich hier ein Zauberduft . . .

He sat down for a moment on the empty bed, shaking his head, and something moved in his neck or his chest . . . as though a string had broken in there. . . . One of these decadent romantic harp strings you hear about in really fine poetry.

170

"You little devil," he repeated and pressed his face down in the pillow. He saw before him in thought, her ardent young face, her full lips, her warm, desperate eyes, soulless of course . . . and yet they contained both goodness and tenderness, indeed a diamond-like glittering depth of womanhood! Her young, strong hair and small, well-formed ears, her neck and shoulders, her skin that was matt white and remarkably *intact*, yes, without a blemish . . . virginal skin, ha, ha! Her good, well-formed feminine hands, her living, electric breast . . .!

'My heart is filled with sorrow.' Yes, thank you very much. Enough of that nonsense now."

He got up, stood in the doorway for a moment and abandoned himself to dull self-contempt. "Ugh. You old layabout. What the hell had you really expected? She's twenty-four, and you're forty-seven. You weren't married or anything. She was sick and tired of you. And she didn't care a damn about your money. Which, incidentally, shows what an outstanding girl she was. 'My heart is filled with sorrow.' They were undoubtedly honest words. She had hesitated, but finally made up her mind like the healthy, upright person she was . . .

"While you . . . you drift aimlessly about, dull and cold, like a sick moth that regrets having got out of its cocoon and longs back to its metaphysical pupal state . . ."

He went out into the kitchen. But here again he fell into a reverie. An irritating voice inside him said, passionately and imploringly: "You *loved* her. You *still* love her. This is unhappy love. . . . Whatever you want to call it."

He sat down heavily on the kitchen bench and stared out in the air with raised brows. The sunshine was pouring into the sitting room and warming it. He got up, shaking his head, and went in. Well, this was the situation.

And what now? The first thing was to get hold of a box of matches. He got up and said in a hollow and plaintive voice, "Good God. There *must* be some matches somewhere in the place."

But no, there were not.

But he could go down to Jakob Siff's shop.

Vibeke had wakened up and lay waiting, good-natured and

hopeless, for someone to come and look after her. She never got up of her own accord.

Mortensen went across to the waste paper basket and took the crumpled letter from it, smoothed it out, but crumpled it up again without looking at it. "Matches, I need some bloody matches."

Down in Jakob Siff's little shop, the sun was shining on the worn counter. Mortensen bought his box of matches and hurried back. The paraffin stove was lit and the kettle put on the flames. Then, bloody hell . . . there wasn't any coffee anywhere either. Back to Jakob Siff.

"Aye, your housekeeper's gone, hasn't she?" said the grocer, and Mortensen nodded without replying.

"Josef the Lament's in a terrible way," said the grocer. "His wife's run off."

Mortensen started. He remembered that there had been something about this in Atlanta's letter as well.

"He's completely beside himself," said the grocer.

"Oh well, what the hell," said Mortensen and hurried back with his coffee. On the stairs he bumped into Josef the Lament, who was standing in the door to his flat. Mortensen glanced nervously at the little albino who looked completely done in and as though sleep-walking.

Up in the kitchen the paraffin stove was smoking. How the blazes do you make coffee? He thought a while, had an idea and went and knocked on Josef the Lament's door.

"I say, Josef, do you know how to make coffee?" he asked.

Josef the Lament stared at him. "Coffee? Yes, I suppose I do."

"Lovely," said Mortensen. "Just pop up into my place for a moment."

Josef shook his head dully. "Yes, I suppose so, but . . . Perhaps you've not heard what a dreadful thing's happened?"

"Yes, I have," said Mortensen,. "I know all about it. But that doesn't prevent you from making a cup of coffee."

"I suppose I could," said Josef and followed him hesitantly. The kettle was already singing,

"It took me completely unawares," said Josef starting to

172

weep. "Completely unawares. We've been married for twelve years."

"Yes," said Mortensen. "But we'll talk no more about that now. We'll put it completely aside, Josef. Here's the coffee. Now show me your skills."

"Yes, that's what Eliana says as well," sniffed Josef the Lament. "She also says I mustn't let it get me down. There's no one like Eliana. She's looking after Rita, my poor daughter. How could I manage, alone as I am."

Mortensen found a couple of cups, and the coffee was poured out. They both drank in silence. Mortensen took Vibeke a cup of warm coffee to her bed and lit his pipe.

"I simply don't know what I'm going to do," said Josef with a sad little smile. "I was just going to start on a stand . . ."

"Well, then, make that stand, Josef."

"Yes, but I can't for I've completely forgotten what it was going to look like and what it was to be used for, and neither can I remember who was going to have it."

"It'll come back to you," said Mortensen, giving him a little slap on the back. "It'll be all right, Josef. Just look at me, I've also been . . . what shall we say: made into a bachelor! Atlanta's bloody gone as well. But I don't care."

"But she wasn't your wife," objected Josef.

"I suppose not." Mortensen puffed heavily at his pipe. "But, what the devil . . . there's nothing as easy to forget as women, whether you're married to them or not. Wait a week or two. And then you'll see you were really fed up with her."

"I wasn't," protested Josef the Lament in a whisper and assumed a fanatical look in his pale eyes.

"Then you ought to have been," said Mortensen. "She was nothing for you. She was a harpy."

Josef suddenly got up and shrieked, "She was my wife! We were married! We were man and wife! She ran off! She's never going to come back any more!"

"There, there," comforted Mortensen.

Josef the Lament shrieked even louder, moaning and weeping: "She was my wife! She was my wife!"

"Ife! Ife!" came the echo from the bedroom. It was Vibeke lying and talking to herself: "Ife, ife, ife."

Josef the Lament listened, and there was fear in his eyes.

"Now, now, that's enough," said Mortensen and took him gently by the arm. "Sit down, Josef, and we two will have a little dram."

Josef the Lament sat down. Mortensen fetched glasses and a bottle.

"Cheers, Josef."

Josef the Lament raised his glass in a trembling hand. It rattled against his teeth. Mortensen sat staring at the wall with its great, diffuse, geographic ink stain. Curious about this stain, which in many respects looked like a well-drawn, carefully detailed map, the work of reasonable beings, and yet it had arisen as the result of pure stupidity.

"Typical," he thought bitterly. "Typical of all of this life that we fools find it so difficult to understand because we're sufficiently deluded to attribute its deepest origins to divine wisdom."

Ugh!

"What have the elemental forces in nature to do with wisdom? With meaning and coherence? The world came into being in the same way as this daft ink splash: as the result of a blind and foolish eruption."

Mortensen took a certain comfort in this thought. He dwelt on it pleasantly while lighting his dead pipe. Josef also started to thaw out a little. He gave Mortensen a trusting look and took a fresh drink from his glass.

"Sing something, Josef," suggested Mortensen. "You can sing."

"Sing?" Josef the Lament hesitated a little. "What on earth should I sing?"

"Something cheerful," Mortensen nudged him. "Something about joy and happiness and freedom and all that stuff and nonsense. A song from the choral society, a drinking song. 'Muses love joy and the grape'." He started humming and tapping his fingers on the table.

Josef the Lament shook his head and stared ahead as though

174

searching. But suddenly, he closed his eyes and sang in his high, penitent, lugubrious voice:

> Here in this world, midst all its tears
> You notice not the passing years
> Your days approach their bitter end . . .

Mortensen made a deprecatory gesture, but Josef the Lament continued undaunted and unctuously went on with the lugubrious hymn. Mortensen filled his glass and let him go on to the end. "My heart is filled with sorrow," he thought. He went across to the waste paper basket and once more took out the crumpled letter. He unfolded it, and his eyes passionately sought this sentence . . . yes, there it was, it was right enough: "My heart is filled with sorrow . . ."

At the last moment, Mortensen managed to prevent an attack of sobbing by taking a chair by the leg and lifting it up to the ceiling. He balanced it on the flat of his hand while dancing round the floor like an equilibrist.

"Nothing artificial," he thought. "No literary affectation, no pretence at education, but a poor young girl's ballad-like, simple and honest sigh. 'My heart is filled with sorrow'."

A true gem. It must be kept as a priceless jewel, something to be cherished.

Thank heaven, Josef the Lament was now finished with his cheerless funeral hymn. Mortensen nudged him: "Now, Josef, have a drink, and then we'll both sing this one: 'Like finest crystal'. Do you know it? You must know it from your choral society."

Yes, Josef knew it. The two men raised their heads and passionately started rendering the old love song.

> Like finest crystal blessed by the sun,
> Like the stars that shine in the sky.
> A maiden I know that lives close by
> A girl who dwells here in this town.
> Dear love of mine, my heart's tend'rest flower
> Ah, that we were but joined and never to part,

And I were your faithful friend
And you were my dearest love,
You noble rose and crown of gold.

"Yes, and then she buzzes off from us, this finest crystal,"
laughed Mortensen derisively and slapped Josef the Lament
on the shoulder. "And here we sit, two lonely, deserted
tomcats caterwauling at the top of our voices."

Josef the Lament burst into tears.

"For God's sake have a drink," Mortensen nudged him
furiously. "We've not come here to blubber, but to take it as
men. To force ourselves to face the truth. 'Das Weib, das ewig
weibliche . . . ein bloss imaginäres Bild, an den allein der
Mann denkt!' We idealise her to justify and enhance our
raw rut. We anoint the harlot with our confounded flawless
sentimentalising, and then we are quite happy to kill her off so
as to indulge in the perverse enjoyment of remorse and loss
and longing . . . like that man Kierkegaard. Being in love,
Josef, being in love is always masked self-pity. It's yourself
you're in love with. This finest crystal . . . it's yourself, Sir."

Josef the Lament sat in deep thought. He looked like an
ancient Chinese philosopher.

"I'm thinking about my frame," he said.

Mortensen nodded. "All this about that frame of yours
is fundamentally extremely interesting," he said. "There's
something symbolical in your not knowing what it's to look
like or what it's to be used for or who's to have it. But . . . well,
you're already feeling a lot better now, Josef, aren't you?"

"Yes, I'm feeling better," Josef the Lament confirmed, looking up at Mortensen with a grateful little smile. "But now I
think I'll go down and see to Rita, my daughter, for a while."

"Oh, are you off now? Aye, Josef, do as you want, for
heavens sake. 'My heart is filled with sorrow'," thought
Mortensen and stamped on the floor. " 'My heart is filled
with sorrow'."

He went into the bedroom. Vibeke had fallen asleep again.
How was he going to manage her now? How was he going to
manage everything?

"One hundred and forty-six thousand kroner. 'My heart is filled with sorrow'. Money, delirium and farmhand sentimentality. The man of reason . . . is he now dead and buried beneath all these eiderdowns of general confusion? Is there not as much as a drop of human decency left in you, Sir? Is it not you who wrote those bloody true and appropriate words: 'The heart is always a bitch. The hallmark of the honest man is this: that he feels with his reason'."

Mortensen went back into the living room. He started walking up and down the floor, the customary six or seven strides, the rapid turns at the door and the bookcase. The wild animal in its cage. Has the tiger not yet discovered that the bars have gone and the hour of freedom has struck? Then why doesn't it break out?

"Wait a bit, wait a bit, there's no great hurry now. And in any case, you're no tiger, no aimless wild animal, no old woman, but a grown man who takes himself seriously. And damn well knows how to behave. Even if a pauper suddenly becomes rich, he doesn't have to renounce all shame. He remains true to himself and his convictions.

Or is it a lie, this idea that you fundamentally believe in goodness as the only really relevant thing in life? The absolute supremacy of the good deed? Verily, verily: What is a man profited if he shall gain the whole world, and lose his own soul?"

Mortensen poured a glass, but left it untouched.

"Wait a bit," he said to himself. "Go to Rio de Janeiro or Hong Kong or Honolulu, buy your freedom and love and all sorts of enjoyment. Or – for you are also a man of the spirit and something of a connoisseur – go to Vienna or Milan and hear the world's most wonderful symphony orchestras; go to Rome and see the eternal paintings. But don't think that *that* is freedom and happiness. Freedom and happiness only come from within. Purge thy soul, humble thyself and be good. Go and sell that thou hast, and give to the poor, and thou shalt have treasure in heaven. Which bloody well doesn't mean that you can buy security in shares in Paradise, but that you should muck out your filthy soul and make it suited to the

177

only happiness that exists, the only freedom that exists: the peace of the good deed. For that's what your bloody book on Satan is about. That's the sum total of it."

Mortensen went across and opened a window, leaned out over the window ledge with wide open eyes, though without seeing anything. "Oh well, it's not as easy as that, either," he thought with a little smile. "But no one can expect that. It must take its time. But it will be interesting to see which power wins in you, God or Satan. Or neither of them."

He quickly steps back from the window, clenches both his fists, makes some furious gestures in the air and utters a long, savage hiss: "Neither of them? Mediocrity? No, in *that* case rather Satan . . .!"

Suddenly he notices that someone is standing over in the doorway . . . It is Eliana, the ferryman's wife.

"What the hell do you want here?" he blurts out. But he immediately regrets his outburst and becomes confused. "My dear Eliana, is it you? You must forgive me . . . I'm a little . . . a little . . ."

Eliana comes across and lays her hand on his to calm him down, smiling as though it were the most natural thing in the world that she should come and interfere in his affairs . . . like a midwife summoned by the cries of the woman giving birth . . . He hears her say something about Vibeke. She will take Vibeke with her. A bit of lunch. A bit of lunch and coffee for them both. Josef had told her . . .

Mortensen sits down on the chaise longue and buries his head in his hands. "Just a moment, Eliana," he says. "I seem to be a bit confused."

Eliana goes into the bedroom to Vibeke. He hears her kind voice. Her infinitely kind, naïve voice. And the little girl's happy chattering. He suddenly gets up and goes in and embraces Eliana; he takes her hand, kisses it emotionally and puts it to his cheek.

"It's all going to be all right, Mortensen," she says gently. "It's going to be all right. It's just a bit difficult at first. It'll all work out, you'll see. Just you both come along and have a bite to eat."

178

News travels fast in a little town. Already that afternoon, Magister Mortensen has a visit from Olsen the editor, who is all puffed up and so awe-struck as to be quite unrecognisable, and the following day The News gives a prominent place to the great sensation of Mortensen's inheritance. "A Happy Man!"

The nauseating, snobbish article fills Mortensen with disgust. And it is even worse when the *congratulations* start to pour in. People obviously go in for congratulations in this town. It is not only from Count Oldendorp or Captain Østrøm that the congratulations arrive, no, it is from the most unexpected quarters, Fähse the apothecary, the Reverend Fruelund, Dr Manicus, Nillegaard and his wife, the Misses Schibbye! A sheer epidemic of congratulations.

Here he had gone around in his innocence imagining he was something on the lines of friendless Job . . . no, no, in no way; he was in reality a popular figure, surrounded on all sides by gushing well-wishers. For once it's about something that people can *understand*: money. Money ensures prestige, friends, absolution for all past peccadilloes; indeed even Berg the senior teacher sends . . . oh, dear, this is about the end . . . sends a bunch of flowers, a bunch of white and red roses!

The only thing missing before long will be a greetings telegram from Østermann, the Minister of Culture! But there is bound to be one. Just be patient. It will all come.

In short, a profoundly ridiculous and shocking time arrives for Mr Mortensen. It's no use his wishing with all his heart that what had happened should not have happened. He has to put up with being the hero of the day. He has to put up with standing sniffing at a bunch of roses, indeed, even endure putting the bunch in a jug . . . for where the bloody hell was he to put them otherwise? It would be cruel to the innocent flowers to throw them out of the window or put them in the stove. He could, of course, have sent them back, accompanied by a note bearing the inscription "Delivery refused". But it wasn't worth making so much fuss about such a little matter.

And then came the worst of all: you peer deep into yourself

and, to your sorrow and anger, note that you are really feeling curiously *honoured*. You catch yourself thinking that you have basically deserved all this homage. In short, for a fleeting moment, moved and lost, you peep briefly into the holy of holies in the bourgeois world, to which you have suddenly been given access. First row in the stalls!

And then comes the reaction. Lurking there. A dull mental confusion, something that moves slowly, reluctantly developing into a painful chiaroscuro, just like the old pictures of the Day of Judgement. Or like the largo introduction to the Midnight Sonata, the one with the reverberating depths and the little, lonesome, hesitant recitative. . . this timid and hopeless little declaration of love in the midst of the darkness . . .

"My heart is filled with sorrow."

13

On spiritual torments caused by honourable people having offered a helping hand to an errant count

Kronfeldt, the Chief Administrator, stood wide-eyed and with an expression as though he were staring into a bottomless pit of stupidity. Indeed, he rose up on his toes and stretched his hands helplessly out as though he wanted to take off and like some doomed booby fly off into this void of idiocy.

But suddenly he clicked his heels together and uttered a brief, bitter laugh, "Nnoo! There are limits after all. That's enough. *That's enough.*"

He turned towards Constable Debes: "Yes, Debes, you can go to your office now. You have at least done your job well. Thank you."

"Not at all, sir." Debes bowed, well trained as he was, and withdrew to the guardroom with his hand on the hilt of his sabre.

Kronfeldt went to and fro excitedly, flung out his hands irascibly, rubbed his little vandyke: "Never heard anything like it. And what have we done for this monster – we've accepted him and looked after him and introduced him all over the place and got him engaged to an excellent lady of the best family."

He sank wearily back in the chair at his writing desk, but he got up again straight away and hurried out into the living room to his wife.

"Charlotte," he said gloomily. "Sit down, Charlotte, and be quite calm. I have an unpleasant piece of news for you. It's been ascertained now that Karl Erik, Count Oldendorp, is carrying on with that woman known as *Black Mira*! Yes, you might well open your eyes wide, and I understand that. But it has been ascertained. Debes, you understand. We've been keeping an eye on him."

The Chief Administrator laughed bitterly: "But this will be the straw that breaks the camel's back. We're finished with Oldendorp."

Mrs Kronfeldt got up with folded hands and sighed, "Oh, good heavens. Oh, good heavens."

"Yes. We'll have no more of this maddening comedy now. He must be punished. He must be exposed. Hung out to dry, the cad."

"But what are you going to do then?" asked his wife anxiously.

Again there came this hopeless expression over Kronfeldt, and he began to walk backwards and forwards: "Yes, that is just the question. What will I do? Now then, woman, stop blubbering. This is nothing to blubber about. It gets much worse! Much, much worse!"

"I am not blubbering," said Mrs Kronfeldt, assuming a brave look.

Kronfeldt continued: "Yes, what is to be done? It is not easy. It demands a great deal of thought. Oh well, don't go and get lost in your own thoughts. Rely on me. I have this miserable creature's fate in my hand at the moment."

He went back into his office.

"Now for it! Now for the case of Count Oldendorp! How can a scandal be avoided? *Can* one be avoided? And even if we do, who is going to guarantee that he will not be guilty of new and perhaps even worse scandals? Could he be quietly got rid of unnoticed, and if so, how?"

Kronfeldt stretched out slowly and pensively on the leather-upholstered sofa and surrendered himself to profound concentration.

Well. Yes – at one time they had been truly happy at the prospect of having this *count* in their home. There was something amusing and unusual about it. Something really grand. Effersøe, the Prefect, had his Minister of Culture to boast about, Judge Pommerencke his uncle, who was a professor of law. This had all to be taken into consideration when the Oldendorp account was to be drawn up fairly. A count is and always will be a count. Indeed, Kronfeldt admitted to himself without embarrassment that he had been deeply happy when he received that letter from the old Count Oldendorp of Krontoftegaard with the plea that . . . oh, *plea?* Yes, plea it really had to be called. The letter was easy to find, and the Chief Administrator bounced up and took it out of his well-organised filing cabinet:

"My dear Emanuel,

I hope I may still be allowed to call you by your Christian name! I was recently informed that you have become nothing less than *Chief Administrator* in charge of a distant country.

Congratulations, Emanuel; it pleases me to the bottom of my heart that you have achieved so much. To be truthful, I do not know what a Chief Administrator is, but it sounds almost like a governor, but I always had a feeling that you would go far in this vale of tears. How terribly sad that your father, our delightful old gardener, who was a true friend to us children (and the same applies to your mother, of course, that delectable Mette the gardener's wife!), that these two old people of whom I was so genuinely fond, should not have lived to see this good fortune! Yes, now I am sitting here writing to you and thinking of the old days when we played cops and robbers and all those things, and I was always the robber and you the cop, or the *policeman*, as we called it.

But now, Emanuel, a few serious words while we are talking of robbers! My son Karl Erik is my life's greatest misfortune. He cannot fit in anywhere – not because he was not originally a thoroughly kind nature, but because he has turned to gaming and drinking and in general is leading a life that will put me in my grave.

Now, it was my idea that if you, now you are a governor at the other end of the world and presumably still the 'policeman', I assume that if Karl Erik came up to stay with you and, as it were, were left alone for a time and collected his thoughts in a place where there can presumably be no question of major temptations: that it would probably have a beneficial influence on him. He will probably go along with this, for as I say, he is fundamentally a good lad and always full of those

183

good intentions with which the road to Hell is said to be paved, God forgive me.

But write to me and tell me what you think. I shall be waiting eagerly. God will reward you, and so will I, you must not doubt that. He comes home from an extremely dubious visit to the forbidding city of Copenhagen tomorrow, the poor boy. I dread seeing him again, he is probably an awful sight. But now I will look forward to hearing from you very soon.

Yours sincerely, C.F.W. Oldendorp."

A touching letter indeed. The Chief Administrator carefully folded it up and put it back in the drawer.

Well. Then you agreed, and along comes this Karl Erik, this *lout*.

And to begin with it all went extremely well. He was amenability personified, and he was pleasant and charming to his "Uncle Kronfeldt" and "Aunt Charlotte". It was a pleasure to introduce him as "the young Count Oldendorp, the son of my old friend the titular Master of the Royal Hunt".

Yes, it actually also looked as though this dissipated son would reform and become a new and better person. He quickly recovered and soon looked the picture of health. This was thanks to Charlotte, that kind soul who so took everything to heart; she coddled him with egg and milk and all kinds of good things and in general was so touching in the way she looked after him. And when he even became engaged to the Reverend Schmerling's daughter, a big, quiet and capable girl, they were really so naïve as to believe . . .!

Well, the first couple of times he let himself go and ended in up bad company . . . they thought these were just minor relapses that would not be repeated. Until the beast began to show his true face! Stumbling around blind drunk among the worst drunkards from Skindholm. Showing himself in public in the lowest company. And then finally, his most recent escapade: visiting this Mira after dark, a simple harpy, the daughter of the woman known as the Weeper, illegitimate, of course. A count! Heaven help us! A man he had introduced into the best company the place could boast of and of whom he had been genuinely proud. A man who had solemnly entered into an engagement!

And this was by no means all. Once the less respectable side had seriously been revealed. Oh, scandal after scandal!

Kronfeldt lay writhing. He rubbed his eyes with clenched fists and for a moment put on a childish, sulky expression. Had he not already begun to feel a certain coolness on the part of the Prefect's wife? And did he not sense a certain biting irony in Doctor Manicus's reference to: "Your protégé, the *ethnographer*"?

Of course, it had been a dubious idea when he talked of Karl Erik's pretended interest in ethnography. It was intended as a way out. It was no good introducing this count as a poor, deported good-for-nothing. It was purely for humanitarian reasons he had thought of this idea of ethnography, a plan of which Karl Erik had been only too heartily pleased to approve!

The Chief Administrator abandoned himself to melancholy thoughts. He ought to have dissuaded the Master of the Royal Hunt from sending him up here. But he had acted with the best of intentions.

But what now? Get him out of the country as quickly as possible? He could put all the cards on the table to Miss Schmerling and get that situation behind him. In general, he should reveal the beast and simply get rid of him. It would still be a scandal, but one of limited proportions . . .

And yet a scandal on the grand scale!

Mr Kronfeldt's protégé, the count, the ethnographer, found in Black Mira's bed and sent away like a whipped cur.

Oh, he had deserved it, the wretch. But what about one's own reputation? The whole matter would be turned over from top to bottom, and the entire comedy would be seen through, and he would be made a figure of ridicule. "Uncle Kronfeldt", the friend of the Master of the Royal Hunt, would be reduced to "the Krontoftegaard gardener's son". And so on . . .! Effersøe, the Prefect, who was the son of a doctor; Judge Pommerencke, whose father had been the owner of the well-known Pommerencke Works ... they would have a quiet, sympathetic laugh. And the postmaster as well. And the apothecary and his wife. And Doctor Manicus.

No, then there was presumably nothing to be done except to patch up the misfortune as far as possible and to make the best of a bad job. It was bitter. *Bitter.*

Yes – or, good heavens: can't a born count properly speaking not be allowed the liberty of having extravagant habits? You could take a broader view and shrug your shoulders ... something of a Don Juan, of course. And between ourselves, Black Mira isn't bad looking, let's be fair, and after all she is the illegitimate daughter of a naval officer. And her mother, the woman known as the Weeper, is no less than old Consul Sebastian Hansen's daughter, by Jove! You can understand the lad in a way. And – as an aside – the Master of the Royal Hunt was like that in his youth – oh, get off with you, of course. All these counts and barons are like that, gentlemen. Oh, I know. And what haven't we seen even with members of the royal family? Oh, I'm sorry. But let's rather keep our mouths shut about young Oldendorp's goings-on ... for the sake of his fiancée, for she deserves that. And the Reverend Schmerling, too, that brilliant man.

The Reverend Schmerling was the son of an admiral.

Kronfeldt got up and rubbed his shiny beard. Yes, of course. And he was the man to manoeuvre his boat away from the rocks instead of navigating so clumsily that it went bottom up!

Kronfeldt chuckled and went across and opened the window. The matter had been thought through. Fixed. Simply nothing is going to happen. Karl Erik will be given a sharp reprimand in private, and if all this about Black Mira comes out, well one is a diplomat. One is a man of the world.

Kronfeldt rubbed his hands and sighed, humming the while. Then he went to join his wife in the living room.

"Hey, Charlotte, what are all these tears about? We really can't have this."

"Oh, Emanuel, I am so upset for your sake."

"Rubbish." Kronfeldt tapped her arm and with the kindest

of smiles said, "Well, Charlotte. Don't you think I'm the man to solve this problem? I think you do."

He added seriously, "No, you see – we'd better continue to be patient with . . . with this barren fig tree. It's our duty. It's about a human being, after all. We can't simply abandon him just like that. I can't break my word to the Master of the Royal Hunt. Now, we must be patient with him, Charlotte. For his own sake and for his father's. And for that of his future wife."

A ring of emotion had crept into Kronfeldt's voice.

"No, Charlotte, we must . . . we must bear our cross. And then we must hope for the best outcome nevertheless. He is after all a count and the son of a count."

THIRD MOVEMENT

In which there are scenes of a great and eventful if rather confused wedding celebration, during which the monster Matte-Gok starts feathering his nest in earnest

1

Preparations and dress rehearsal

It is a rare occurrence in our days that a wedding is really *celebrated*. It is usually no more than the bridal couple spending the evening in the bosom of their closest relatives. At the most, they will drink a glass of mulled red wine and make a watered down speech that is listened to without pleasure. The age of the grand weddings, the vigorous age of the real *welcoming weddings*, is past.

These old wedding festivities never followed a previously determined pattern but developed freely in the manner of wild flowers, without any great attention to spiritual or civil ceremonies, indeed often even so to speak without any particular regard to the bride and bridegroom. For during the real, old, enormous welcoming weddings, the bride and bridegroom really played a subordinate role. Rifles were fired in their honour, and their health was drunk, and songs were sung for them when they returned from the wedding ceremony, but once the *bridal dance* was out of the way they quickly ceased to be the centre of the festivities and for that matter could quite well retire to the peace and quiet of private life without causing any surprise.

This circumstance was not due to a lack of tact or gratitude on the part of the guests. People showed their gratitude in other ways than by hanging over the newly married couple and tiring them out. People gave solid presents, really generous pledges of friendship. The better off gave money, and those who could afford less gave useful, practical items, anything from furniture and kitchen utensils to sheepskins or thick woollen overstockings. Other gifts again consisted of personal services: a cobbler could thus offer to shoe seven pairs of shoes free of charge as the need arose; a glazier or carpenter undertook without payment to replace broken windows after the festivities came to an end, and so on. Naturally, among the many guests there would be a few who surreptitiously took part in the pleasures of the feast without contributing anything in return, but parasites were regarded with contempt by everyone – if they were even noticed at all in the confusion.

In general, a welcoming wedding always led to a sizeable profit for the hosts, and so it was a feast in which everyone had every right to participate. And it was in this that the loyal sense of brotherhood existing among the participants had its origins.

The wedding between Sirius Isaksen and Julia Janniksen was just such a welcoming wedding in the good old style.

It took place in an array of different places and in many very disparate sections. Thus, part of the wedding was celebrated in the Christian Temperance Association, Ydun, a second part in Janniksen's home, smithy and garden, a third out in The Dolphin, a fourth in The Dainty Duck, a fifth in the sail loft in the High Warehouse, and so on.

In the course of the night, these various sections spilled over into each other with the exception of the first of them, which kept itself resolutely to itself all the time. And yet . . . as time went on, that, too, slipped.

This first section had originally attempted to claim a kind of sole prerogative of being the real one, the official one, thanks to determined collaboration between Ankersen the Bank and the bride's mother. Their battle plan was simply that immediately after the wedding ceremony they would appropriate the bride and groom, take them across to the Ydun assembly hall and keep them there throughout the night, ensuring that the association's building was closed to undesirable elements. This was taking a huge risk; they would be attracting Janniksen's anger and risking his vengeance, but they would have to put up with that, for, as Ankersen put it, "It is after all our duty to oppose the powers of darkness, and God helps those who help themselves."

The blacksmith, who naturally assumed that his daughter's wedding would have its true centre in her own home, had for several days been busy with preparations, which resulted in a great deal of fuss and ordering about. He had a lot of men working for him; they fetched flags and pennants and coloured lanterns, ribbon and knickknacks. Count Oldendorp had undertaken to organise an orchestra, and excited men went in and out of the smithy carrying drums and horns and remarkable apparatuses. Staid neighbours, who were sitting watching in the twilight from behind potted plants in their windows, saw eight men come dragging something that looked like a canon.

Finally, when the finishing touches had been put to the job – it was the evening before the solemn day – the blacksmith and his friends and helpers congregated in the smithy, which had been fitted out like a kind of bar. Janniksen opened eight bottles and issued his final commands:

"Friends and kinsmen! We have done a good job, as is fitting for men and comrades, and now this evening we are going to let ourselves go and have a proper *stag party* as a kind of dress rehearsal! It will take place out in The Dolphin. But before we completely lose sight of each other this evening, I want to impress on you what is to be done tomorrow, and woe betide the wretch who doesn't remain at his post! So: As soon as the church bell starts ringing, we will all be ready, the count's band and the male voice chorus at the entrance to the garden, the marksmen on the other side of the smithy so as not to frighten the bridal procession out of their wits. And for heaven's sake make sure the canon doesn't misfire – that would be a disgrace to us all from which we would never recover. Agreed? Good."

"Cheers".

At the same time as the smith and his loyal companions form a merry cohort and wander off to The Dolphin, a disgraceful scene is being enacted down on the shore, in the profound darkness between two old boathouses, where Matte-Gok and Kornelius have agreed to meet.

"Yes, tomorrow evening between eleven and twelve," says Matte-Gok. "Of course, it's a bit unfortunate that it should coincide just with your brother's wedding, but there's nothing to be done about that, Kornelius. I've sized up the situation, and it's now or never."

"As far as I'm concerned it can just as well be tomorrow evening," says Kornelius.

"Yes, I'm sure you'll agree. After all, it's something you have to get over and done with. You've fiddled around with that treasure for so many years now, Kornelius, and it would be a shame if you missed your chance now it's finally there. You can easily see an opportunity to go for a walk during the course of the evening; you're not responsible to anyone."

"No, of course not," says Kornelius. "But how are we going to get the treasure home?"

"You won't have to do that at all, Kornelius," says Matte-Gok, placing a firm hand on his shoulder. "When it's to be brought home, I'll come myself and help you. No, you don't even need to dig it up tomorrow evening. You only have to dig down to it until you feel the copper. Then you must draw three crosses on the lid. Three crosses like those on a poison bottle. Understand? Drawing these three crosses is very important; it's what's known as the signification. I could have told you this before, but it wasn't possible; it has to be said at the very last moment. Once the treasure has been signed, it will stay where it is, and then, as I say, the two of us together can get it up and move it."

"Well, that really changes everything," says Kornelius in relief. "I'd been worrying so much about how I would manage that heavy chest alone."

"See here," says Matte-Gok and presses a hard little thing firmly into his hand. "Take this, it's an iron ring, a finger ring, but you don't need to have it on your finger. Just keep it with you, in your pocket for instance. It's my ring of fortune. When you've got it with you, you can't go wrong. And every time you feel any doubt, Kornelius, just take the ring, close your hand firmly round it and squeeze it, and then everything will be all right. But I must go now, I've got to go out with Ankersen on missionary work."

"Wait a moment," says Kornelius eagerly. "It would all be easier for me if you at least agreed to share the proceeds."

"I don't need it," smiles Matte-Gok. "But if it will help you, then let's say that I get a fifth for helping you. But then I'll be on hand to help you organise it all, I promise.

And otherwise: good luck, Kornelius, and may it bring you blessings."

That evening, the stag night, was one of the great, memorable evenings in The Dolphin. It gave a festive glimpse of the world that the colourless generation from after the introduction of total prohibition has never known, a world that turned its back on all the barren and snobbish petty jealousy and spite that is otherwise a characteristic of life in a small town.

Alas, you young people, you who grew up in the anaemic part of town with its chapels, temperance hotels, nice little shops, notices and police regulations: never have you experienced the thunder of the mighty wave of singing and banging on the table, the chink of glasses and the disorganised praises sung by blissful spirits, the declarations of friendship and love, the scuffles and meritorious forgiving tears and the loyalty that emerged from Captain Østrøm's hostelry when it was having one of its so-called *crown evenings*.

You haven't known Ole Brandy when he was at the height of his powers; you haven't seen his earrings glisten golden through haze and tobacco juice in the men's great basement, the one known as The Kitchen. You haven't seen the drunken glow of delight in his eye and heard him sing the sorrowful ballad of Olysses. Nor have you heard the wild and wondering howls that swept through the general tumult when Janniksen the blacksmith danced his colossal solo dance. It is impossible to conceive of the superhuman power and passion with which this happy man, filled to the innermost realm of his soul with sensuous recklessness, twisted his giant body in the turbid air while unrestrained scraps of verse and songs and blasphemous challenges poured out of his breast in inexhaustible waves.

A secret ring of resolute mariners surrounded the mammoth as he culminated and ensured that he did not lift the building from its foundations, and once the performance was over, the blacksmith was carried out into a side room so that he could gather his strength in peace and quiet for a new, demanding day's work. Ole Brandy placed a brimming glass beside his couch.

When Ole arrived at The Kitchen, something completely unforeseen and not forming part of the programme was taking place: the silhouettes of Ankersen the Bank and his son Matte-Gok could be glimpsed through the smoke and stir of this dim spot.

"I'd better take care of this," thought Ole Brandy. He forced the two uninvited guests to take a seat at a table and poured a glass of beer for each of them.

"I suppose it's non-alcoholic?" said Ankersen. However, he emptied the glass without waiting for an answer, for he was very thirsty. Matte-Gok left his glass untouched. In a low, compelling voice, Ankersen started on Ole while polishing his spectacles: . . . "And how is this going to end, Ole? Tell me."

"With the *milk remedy*," replied Ole.

Ankersen placed his spectacles on his nose. He had an uncomprehending rattle in his throat, but Ole went on good-humouredly: "The milk remedy? Well, you see, it's when you've drunk yourself as flat as a pancake and as it were can't *manage* any more, but you can't stop either, so you so to speak stand throbbing deep in the mire. That's when you get hold of a quart of milk and drink it down."

"Milk?" asked Ankersen suspiciously.

"Well, you know, not pure, unblended milk, of course," explained Ole. "Is that what you thought? Oh, get off home to your pot of tea piss! No, there has to be some extra good stuff in it to brighten it up, first class stuff like really strong white rum. And then you'll be completely clean inside for a time, as clean as a newly born baa-lamb. You won't have an evil thought left; you won't talk nonsense. You'll be like an honest man. You won't roar and lament any more; you won't get your poisonous fang into decent people, you won't frighten the life out of young girls any more, you mad monkey! And you, Matte-Gok, whoever you're the son of, you're at least not his, this fine specimen here, and then to finish with I'll tell you a thing that's as good as ten . . ."

Ankersen interrupted Ole Brandy's speech by noisily clearing his throat and scraping his chair. He made a fierce sign to Matte-Gok; they both got up and burst into song at the top of their voices. A silence suddenly fell on The Kitchen; everyone listened open-mouthed to the hymn. Matte-Gok had a good, healthy voice; Ankersen virtually only shouted:

> The blind can see and the deaf can hear
> The timid believe and no longer feel fear
> The mute now sing in joyful key
> And the lame spring merrily on the lea

Ole Brandy adopted a comfortable position as though listening. But when the long revivalist hymn was finally over and, at a sign from Ankersen, Matte-Gok moved forward to deliver a penitential sermon, it was too much for Ole in his present state; he got up and delivered a well aimed blow on the young shit's jaw. It came as a complete surprise to Matte-Gok; he fell back and lay outstretched on the ground.

"And will you now get out!" roared Ole Brandy, approaching Ankersen with bloodshot eyes.

Ankersen whimpered as he bent over his son. "Have you hurt yourself, Mathias-Georg? Now, now, no, you can support yourself, you're a strong lad, aren't you? Now, just get up again and we'll be off, my boy. Lift high your head, my lively lad, as the song says. No, no, just take it quietly; we'll acknowledge defeat in this first round. This was only a little foretaste of what's to come. Come on. We'll go home and gather our strength."

"Well, get on with it," roared Ole Brandy. "Eh? And see about locking that door, Jeremias, and let's have a double to clean the deck!"

2

Other signs of approaching trouble

The wedding day dawns with the most beautiful late summer weather, sunshine and a blue sky with patches of lovely fleecy clouds, pure and delicious like the wrinkled film of cream on top of a bowl of junket.

Mrs Midiord, Ankersen's old housekeeper, is standing on the savings bank manager's stone steps, tying the ribbons of her black bonnet under her chin while dwelling on the sight of all this heavenly purity. Alas, her eyes are not so good any more; she notices this on a day like today; the air immediately starts shimmering and is filled with rising and falling little figures, filigree clear and moving, and with the most curious shapes: hairpins, musical notes, hooks and eyes . . . perhaps it all means something? Mrs Midiord is nervous and has had bad dreams in the night. And now this morning she has had a message from the hospital asking her to go out and visit her half-sister, Ura. What can it be that Ura wants to talk to her about? She is not usually keen on having visitors otherwise.

But now, since falling down and losing the use of her legs, Ura has in every way become more peculiar and unbalanced than ever before. Indeed, she is simply terrible, so unreasonable and stubborn she has become. Just fancy she has simply refused to see her own son, Matte-Gok. He has visited her several times, both alone and with Ankersen, but each time she has lain and turned her back to them, made herself deaf and blind and hidden under the blankets. Indeed, she won't even as much as take her son's name on her tongue. He simply doesn't exist for her. And no one knows better than Mrs Midiord how this upsets the boy.

Mrs Midiord has comforted him the best she can: "Dearest

boy, you know your mother isn't quite right in the head, and as you know, she hasn't been for a long time. And I also know when it began. It goes back to the first time she was in hospital to be operated on for a boil in her abdomen. For, you see, she couldn't take it, the stubborn woman, but there was no alternative, and since then she's had the idea that Dr Manicus took her spleen. A lot of nonsense, I'm sure. But now it's far worse, she's completely mad now, but don't take it too much to heart, you're a fine, strong young man, and you've got a clear conscience . . ."

Ura smiles grimly. Her eyes are quite small, her cheeks flushed; she is scarcely recognisable.

"Are you running a temperature?" asks her sister anxiously. Ura shakes her head. She looks with distaste round the fully occupied ward that is milling with visitors. "Sylvia," she whispers eagerly, taking her sister's hand. "Sylvia. What on earth's brewing?"

"Nothing," says Mrs Midiord soothingly. "Nothing, Ura. Just you relax."

"Rubbish," says Ura. She shakes at her sister's hand and pushes it away. "Then tell me what's going on today. Why are you hiding it from me?"

"You mean Sirius Isaksen's wedding? There's no secret about that."

"No, it's not *that*," snaps Ura. "That's not *all*, Sylvia."

She takes her sister's hand and whispers. "What's he up to, that beast, that swine? Watch out for him, Sylvia. He's up to something. It's something to do with Ankersen. They're up to something, I know. Tell everyone they must watch out. In particular, tell Kornelius as well; tell him not to get mixed up in anything. Ask him to come to see me here tomorrow. It's true what I'm saying, Sylvia, as true as I'm lying here. If only I was in top form. Oh, if only I was at least able to walk . . ."

There is a look of desperation in Ura's face, and suddenly she bursts into tears, and her sister has to kneel by her bed and do her best to comfort her.

Mrs Midiord has a feeling of what it is Ura is getting at. She dreads it herself. For the situation is that a war is brewing between the Ydun association and Janniksen the blacksmith. Oh dear, it can turn into terrible things, and it seems to be a terribly daring idea on the part of Ankersen to kidnap the bridal couple. He is completely out of hand, and perhaps the main sufferer will be Matte-Gok. He was not far from having the living daylight knocked out of him by that old thug Ole Brandy . . .

Mrs Midiord herself is on the verge of tears, but she pulls herself together and says, "I think you're a bit feverish, my dear. They'll give you something to bring your temperature down, and then you'll feel better."

Memories of a certain piece of music keep ringing in Magister Mortensen's ears. A strange, furious piece of music, swirling, tempestuous, energetic, devil-may-care . . . what on earth is it? It is the remarkable, ferocious figurations that introduce the march from Tchaikovsky's Symphonie Pathétique!

Mortensen is carrying a file under his arm. And in this apparently completely everyday file there are two large envelopes, each of which contains fifty thousand kroner in notes. He is on his way up to Wenningstedt's office, where he will deposit one of the envelopes, which is intended for Atlanta. He has tried in vain to discover the girl's address. But sooner or later she must surely turn up, and she shall have this gift, even if she did once spurn his money. Or perhaps for that very reason. And Eliana is to have the other envelope.

The lawyer is not in. Oh, never mind, then it must wait. He's plenty of time now. So he can take his time going back and see if Eliana has come home. She has gone a walk with her four daughters, the two real ones and the two new ones, that is to say Josef the Lament's daughter Rita and then Vibeke. Eliana is without equal. Women like her stand as it were at the centre of the world. Their warmth radiates out in all directions and reaches right up to the arctic regions. In a way, they represent the meaning and objective of life. They are more true than all theology and all philosophy. They are simply *action* . . .

And now she shall have her reward. She and Moritz shall not only be able to afford to find a new and better apartment, but there will be plenty left, some of which can be used for their son's musical training. For the boy is a little wonder, and he must be turned into a great musician. And poor Vibeke; she is better off now than ever before, for she is in the best possible hands.

The rest of the money is going to Sirius and Kornelius, the two co-musicians, with ten thousand for each of them; they are meant as thanks for the music. And then Josef the Lament must have a little, and Lindenskov, and then Boman must have a splendid gravestone.

And so this is the final, unshakeable decision, after a fortnight's consideration, after a fortnight's lonely inner struggle . . . after a fortnight's self-examination and putting on a confounded act and a wearying struggle with the trolls in what Ibsen calls the vault of his heart and his mind. Some of these tireless little devils have still have not even been silenced; they scuttle around and get at him with their poisonous sharp little nails: "Ha, ha, Kristen Mortensen, I must say you're a man who knows how secretly to address his 'good deeds' to his own benefit. Both in the case of Atlanta and Eliana. The first of them is a sentimental final declaration of love, a heavily underlined *declaration of how fond you are of her!* Pinning a splendidly gilded forget-me-not on the breast of the loved one. And the other means simply: *And do please look after Vibeke.*

And with this, you hope now that your spirit has found peace. Peace to return to yourself, to your work, to your isolation, to the *work*!

Rubbish, you're simply deceiving yourself."

Mortensen stops briefly and grinds his teeth. At this moment he could kill someone. At least kill himself. "The only result," he admits icily, "the only result of your agonising considerations is that you recognise your own helplessness and misery. But that's a result as well, of course. You are incapable of helping yourself out of your dilemma. And you've always been like that. A peasant's primitive hunger for life does battle in your sadly messed-up soul with a brooding intellectual's sombre inclination to sacrifice and asceticism. It's impossible for you to achieve any sort of liberation. You were born unfree . . . a pitiful offspring of generations of glutinous Christianity . . . never, never will you succeed in liberating yourself from the musty old moral obsessions . . . you reek of them; they're like sweat in clothes that are never changed, filthy, old hand-me-down underclothes . . .!"

"Yes, but what the bloody hell do you want me to do?" he mumbles to himself in a low voice, confronting the grinning assembly of devils. "The money's in my way, it's ruining my peace of mind, and so it has to be turned – turned into action, good actions; *that* at least is certain. And can it be wrong of me to give it to the people who need it and have deserved it? Ought I perhaps to have given it to the Reverend Fruelund or to Ankersen?

Oh, enough of that. You've puzzled your head long enough to discover how to practise simple goodness. You've played cops and robbers with yourself long enough. Now you had better go out and have a bit of fresh air, whatever else happens . . ."

"And that decision stands," he says in a peremptory tone, and the little devils are swept aside and lie down pretending to be dead, as spiders do when you blow tobacco smoke on them.

"Oh well, then that must wait as well. But never mind, I've got plenty of time. I can go and have a lie down on my chaise longue for a time while I'm waiting."

Mortensen calls to Vibeke, who is running around playing with the ferryman's daughters. She doesn't hear him. Yes, she probably hears him all right, but she can't be bothered coming.

"Come to Daddy, Vibeke," he shouts sadly.

The little girl shakes her head energetically: "Not to Daddy, no. Not to Daddy!"

"Hello, Mortensen," comes the sound of a happy, elated voice behind him. It is Ole Brandy, and he is accompanied by

Moritz, Josef the Lament and Jakob Siff, all of them on their way to the High Warehouse to see Olivarius. Come with us, Mortensen, and have a dram . . . unless you've become too self-important with all your money! Eh, old boy? Do the same as the rich man who said 'Eat, drink and be merry' "

Mortensen gives a friendly nod.

But what about the file? It will have to be locked in his writing desk drawer meanwhile.

He does that. And the flat is securely locked up. So it's all right. Mortensen has been up in Olivarius's sail loft a couple of times before; it's really cosy up there with those old blokes. The weather is delightful. The devilish figurations from the Russian march are reverberating in the emptiness of the air. God in His heaven knows that you need to forget yourself. Not in a theoretical sense, which demands a constant Herculean effort, but in a practical way, the absolution provided by Bacchus, aye, the conversation of doughty men and soothing stuff and nonsense.

"Just a minute, Mortensen," comes the sound of a commanding voice up through the stairway. "Wait a moment, I simply must talk to you on your own."

It's Oldendorp. What does he want now?

The count takes Mortensen by the lapel of his coat and says in a low voice, "Mortensen. Could you lend me five hundred kroner?"

"Course I bloody can, provided we can get a move on, for there are some fine chaps waiting for me down in the street."

He opens the door again and then the drawer in the writing desk.

"Only five hundred kroner?" he says, waving a note.

"Yes, thanks." The count presses his hand. "You might never get them back, Mortensen. Can you forgive me for *that*? If not, you shall have them again, for I'm an honourable soul. By the way, can you keep a secret, old man? Yes, of course you can."

The count puts his mouth close to his ear and whispers, "'Cause then I'll say goodbye to you now, Mortensen. For I'm off tomorrow morning on the Mjølnir. Simply buzzing off.

203

Together with Mira! In deepest secrecy. Because I simply can't *stand* them any longer. There'll be a fuss, but I can't help that. So goodbye, old boy, and look after yourself, wherever in the world you go, because I suppose you'll be off soon as well? And make sure you finish your book so they can have something really shattering to read, the nincompoops. Well, let's go down again now and say nothing about it. And then, to be on the safe side, I'll shout 'see you again soon' to mislead any spies. Constable Debes has eyes everywhere!"

"Goodbye, Mortensen, see you before long," the count waves, turning the corner with a happy face. Mortensen absent-mindedly joins Moritz and the others.

"Ha, there's Matte-Gok," comments Ole Brandy, nudging Mortensen. "I socked him a beauty yesterday evening."

Ole Brandy jeers at him and shouts, "You can have some more if you like, my boy; just come over here to dad!"

Matte-Gok actually stops and goes over towards them, the fool. Ole Brandy's expression becomes embarrassed by his innocent look and says in a gentle voice, "Coming up for a drink, Matte-Gok?" But Matte-Gok merely smiles and shakes his head. "Don't drink. Thanks otherwise."

"Hm, can you stand to attention when you're talking to a superior officer, you scumbag," Ole snarls and turns his back on him contemptuously.

Matte-Gok exchanges friendly looks with the others and strolls on without hurrying. As he passes the Bastille he finds it difficult to prevent himself from popping up into Mortensen's flat and seeing what it looks like when its owner is not at home. But damn it, it's too risky in broad daylight, it must wait. But he won't miss it. He has a sneaking feeling – no, he is certain – what it looks like. A miserable writing desk of the kind that can be forced opened with a finger, and then the entire fortune is in his hands, ready for the taking. Unthinking and confused people like Mortensen look after their money themselves.

He greets Mrs Nillegaard the midwife with a winning smile as she hurries past carrying her bag.

3

On the course of the battle. The flight of the bride and bridegroom. Speeches and processions. The bridegroom's strange dream. The bride's loneliness and consolation

Ankersen the Bank had expected that his battle plan would encounter resistance, even considerable resistance, for Janniksen the blacksmith was a tough nut. But the fact that it went wrong from the start certainly came as a surprise to him.

Just at first, things went beautifully according to the programme: the carriole, which he had borrowed from Fähse the apothecary after some hard bargaining, was waiting very conveniently outside the door of the church. The bride and bridegroom stepped happily into the carriage, and the coalblack horse set of at an elegant pace. But when the bride saw which way it was going she got up and ordered the coachman to stop, an order that he obeyed with some surprise. Then she got out and made clear to the bridegroom that he should go with her. Sirius hesitantly followed his wife, who had already hidden in the alleyways behind the nearest houses. He found her in Sexton Lane, where she had concealed herself behind an open cellar door to wait for him.

"What's all this about?" asked Sirius uneasily.

She took his arm and forced him to go on: "This way! We're not going to have any standing and confessing our sins in front of Ankersen's association. Mother's up to her tricks. Well, let's leave them to it."

Ankersen, who together with the bride's mother, the Nillegaards and other friends had followed the two-seater carriole on foot, was beside himself when he was told what had happened. He waved his stick about with such fury that the horse took fright and bolted with the empty carriage.

"Aye, go to He . . . – blazes," shouted Ankersen and flung

his stick after the departing carriage like a spear. Then he raised his empty hands and turned imploringly to his followers: "After them. Catch them. Yes, that's right, Mathias–Georg, my boy: after them! We mustn't loose this. It's a good cause! We must sacrifice ourselves in this cause, each one of us."

"Yes, I quite agree," Mrs Janniksen chimed in.

"No, no," Nillegaard the junior teacher cleared his throat and shook his head. "No, no. It's no use, Ankersen. We'll come off worst, Ankersen. We'll make fools of ourselves."

Ankersen approached this rebellious follower, gesturing threateningly at him. Nillegaard looked down, but stubbornly continued: "We mustn't act too hastily, Ankersen. We must gather our forces. They are expecting us over in Ydun."

Ankersen was too angry to reply. A gentle wail emerged from his dilated nostrils.

Suddenly there was the roar of a cannon being fired. Followed by several rifle shots.

Nillegaard was trembling all over. In his confusion, he grasped Ankersen's arm.

The cannon was fired again. Nillegaard screwed up his face and held on to Ankersen's arm. Then another shot, and one more . . . nine altogether! A murderous stench of gunpowder filled the air. The sounds of horns and an infernal din of weaponry. Nillegaard groaned and kept his eyes closed.

"Right," said Ankersen.

The sound of a male voice chorus could be heard in the distance. Nillegaard opened his eyes and saw he was alone with Ankersen.

"It's terrible," he said.

Ankersen grasped his hand and said warmly, "Yes, but we two remained at our post, Nillegaard. All the others fled. But let us quite calmly proceed to Ydun and together devise a plan of action. We'll stick together, Nillegaard; we won't let each other down in the hour of our need. Is that a promise?"

The two men moved off, hand in hand.

Matte-Gok had returned. He could tell them that the bride and bridegroom had ended up in the smithy, where they were singing songs and giving speeches.

"Wait a bit," said Ankersen. He took Matte-Gok by the lapel of his coat: "It's best that you keep an eye on their movements. It can be of the greatest importance to us. You don't mind, do you? Off you go again, my boy, and then keep us fully informed."

"We *must* win this battle," shouted Ankersen, raising both his arms in the air. "We *must* gain victory, whatever the cost."

There was already quite an atmosphere in Janniksen's smithy. The male voice chorus had sung "In the wondrous hour of the dawn", and now Oldendorp's fantastic tinny band was playing a march that was so never-ending that the count had to stop the playing with a heavy hand, for now was the time for speeches. He himself wanted to make the first.

The count spoke of the sense of fraternity represented by the celebration, also calling it a fraternity of humanity. He also quoted some of Schiller's ode to joy, famous from Beethoven's immortal symphony. He raised his glass: "And this evening, we will especially raise our glasses to Janniksen the blacksmith, the father of the bride, this Hercules, this Vulcan, in whose smithy we are gathered together. And so we will raise our glasses and . . ."

It was at this moment the count interrupted himself and, holding out his filled glass threateningly at the entrance, shouted, "Yes, I can see you all right, Constable Debes. Spying for the teetotallers! But I would advise you to withdraw as soon as you can if you don't want us to start setting about you. Cheers!"

All faces were turned in astonishment towards the door, but Constable Debes had sensed the situation and had already made himself scarce.

"Never mind him," said the blacksmith with a little smile. He got up. Now it was his turn to give a speech.

This was a very rare occurrence, indeed one that perhaps was taking place here for the first and last time in history. The blacksmith looked splendid, dressed as he was in a tight-fitting frock coat that emphasised his muscular body, and with a fresh poppy in his buttonhole.

"We have here among us a *count*," he said. "A count of blue blood, a man whose fathers rode on gold-bronzed horses and buried the tips of their spears in their enemies' bellies, who were also counts and barons and fine knights, as we can all read in our good old books, and as is also heard far and wide in the wonderful ballads with which we are all familiar."

The smith worked himself up as he spoke, waving his great, scarred fists and staring mightily up in the air. He spoke in grandiloquent turns of phrase and used words that no one would have attributed to this simple man.

"Then they rode out against each other, dressed in armour and cuirasses and beating their immaculate shields. And whoosh! There went their lances through the ribs in their armour, and their opponents toppled off their horses and writhed in the mire, while their horses returned from the battle bloody but triumphant. Those were the days! You didn't accept a mean insult, as is done now. No, it was the power of the fist that determined things, and the victor returned in pomp and circumstance to his beloved, who was watching from the balcony. And now, as said, we have a descendent of those times among us, and what is more: he comes here with his own band, the biggest, the only one, the best he can produce, and with that he does us all an honour for which he deserves our fulsome thanks. And now we'll let the corks pop and drink his health and intone a nine-fold hurrah for the count!"

They drank, and the power of the hurrahs made the iron and tin in the smithy vibrate and rumble and reverberate. Then the smith took the count by the arm, and headed by the band and the male voice chorus, they went in procession through the illuminated garden.

Sirius had stayed behind in the smithy. He sat on the settle over by the cold anvil and looked pale and out of sorts.

"It's as though it's more than I can manage," he said with an attempt at a smile.

"You always have to ruin everything," snorted Julia. "What's wrong with you now?"

"Oh, I don't know; I'm just so out of sorts and tired, Julia."

Sirius looked genuinely penitent. "Perhaps it'll pass. Let's catch our breath for a moment."

"Catch our breath!" snarled Julia. "Catch our breath. *Now*, before we've really got going."

Julia had a vexed expression in her eyes; she resembled her sourpuss of a mother in a way that hurt Sirius. He sighed, "Yes, but dearest Julia, just *you* go out to The Dolphin, and I'll come later."

"Oh, wouldn't that look fine," laughed Julia derisively, with a catch in her throat, but she suddenly changed and in doing so assumed an attractive similarity to her father. "Come to think of it, you do look really miserable, Sirius. Have you drunk too much? Are you feeling sick?"

"No, no, it's not that. But just you go, Julia, as I say. No one'll notice that I'm not there for a short while. And then I'll go up and have a lie down on the bed."

"Well in that case I'll come with you," said Julia, looking at him tenderly and irresolutely. This was Julia through and through. "That's what she's like," he thought.

They went up into their little garret. Sirius threw himself on to the bed, worn out, and Julia sat down by him. "You'll see, it'll be all right," she comforted him and stroked his pale, freshly-shaven cheeks.

It was not long before Sirius fell asleep. Julia shrugged her shoulders and went and arranged her hair in front of the mirror. Before long, she was on her way out to The Dolphin.

Sirius dozed for half an hour. He lay dreaming and imagining, but suddenly he was wide awake, remembering with dreadful clarity a dream he had had.

. . . He was walking along the banks of a lake on whose dark surface floated some strange, bluish white birds, and all around, as far as the eye could see, there was a throng of exotic birds. There were pink flamingos strutting delicately around each other and issuing deep, harmonious sounds, birds of paradise sparkling in diamantine clear colours, slowly floating birds of pure, radiant mists. He turned towards Julia and said triumphantly, "What do you think!" But it was not Julia standing with him now. It was – Leonora!

"Leonora," he said. "Are *you* here?"

She smiled. "Of course I'm here." And in a divinely warm and clear voice she started to sing . . . a song of many beautiful verses, all of which ended with the words: Your wedding night.

Sirius knew the verses; they were his own; he listened captivated and was completely lost in the melodiousness of it all, a polyphonic, blissful melodiousness to which the strange birds also contributed like the swelling sounds of an orchestra.

. . . Your wedding night.

Leonora. Good God!

Sirius got up. Everything went black, and he had a prolonged attack of coughing; but then it passed, and he felt better. He went across and opened the window. Trees and shrubs in the blacksmith's garden were soughing gently in the mild evening breeze, and the coloured lanterns were flickering, ghostly and unreal.

. . . Your wedding night.

Sirius abandoned himself to profound wonderment and felt inexpressible gratitude to Leonora, who in this way had come to him in his dreams and sung for him. The firm and familiar melody of her voice, "Yes, of course I am here" still sounded in his ears.

Now came the sound of singing and excited voices from the smithy, tedious and foolish drunken exchanges that as it were grated and lacerated the divine, resplendent, memory-filled solitude. He shut the window.

What now?

He felt no desire to be together with others, not even with Julia. He just wanted to be alone for as long as possible.

He lay back on the bed and through his weariness felt the boundless comfort of being alone . . . alone with his dream, with the song, and with Leonora.

Julia wandered around aimlessly. First out to the visitors' tent, where people were sitting eating and drinking in a weltering stench of cooking and drink that was distasteful to her and filled her with a sense of loathing for food. Then she came to the dance floor, where the dancing had already started. She stood there for a moment and wished that she could throw herself into the dance like any other girl.

Then back home. But here, Sirius still lay asleep.

Off again.

There is nothing on earth so lonely as a bride who has been abandoned by the groom. Everyone she meets assumes that for some reason or other she is waiting for her groom and that her loneliness will only be short-lived. Those who are sufficiently sober give her a friendly nod and congratulate her, but most scarcely notice her, all the more so as it is a fairly dark evening. She wanders off at random.

She is alone, alone.

The coloured lanterns in the garden go out one by one. The odd one catches fire. She stands watching it devour itself, leaving it to burn until there is nothing left but a few whitish strips of ash drifting off in the darkness.

Then, that, too, is past.

She goes back to Sirius, who lies there with his eyes closed and is very pale. She is suddenly afraid: is he still breathing, or . . .? Yes, he is breathing; he opens his eyes and gives her a gentle look and strokes her hand, and she settles down beside him on the edge of the bed for a moment. But then he dozes off again, and she is drawn out again, out into the night with its milling crowds and the festive din, a night that nevertheless can only offer solitude to a wandering bride.

In time, she is overcome by the sense of loneliness; she sits down morose and cold on an old decayed bench in a hidden corner of the garden and surrenders herself to strange, hopeless thoughts.

But it is at this moment that Matte-Gok appears in the half-light.

"You're sitting here all on your own?" he says.

Julia doesn't know what to reply. She says nothing.

"Where's your husband, Julia?" he asks gently.

She remains silent.

"You needn't be frightened of me," says Matte-Gok, without more ado settling down beside her on the bench. He grasps her cold hand and in a low, intimate voice says, "Julia. You oughtn't to have gone off. Do you understand? Be a good lass and let's see about getting hold of Sirius, and then come with me up to Ydun, where it's both cosy and warm, and we would all so much like to have you with us."

He holds her hand tight and moves closer. She feels the warmth of his body.

"You're cold, you poor thing," he says, and hugs her protectively. She smells his breath; she tears herself away and flees, but in the altogether wrong direction, in behind the bench into the dense bushes. He follows. It leads to a confrontation, a silent and tender battle which ends with her surrendering . . . but not until she has forced him to promise that for God's sake this must remain a secret . . .

So it happened that on this night Matte-Gok succeeded in adding a new and rare item to his long and terrible list of sins. Seducing a bride! That was something he had never tried before. Fancy, that this should be granted to him . . . in this ridiculous, miserable dump!

4

More on the course of the battle. Sectarian deliberations

The meeting in the Ydun association, which of course was originally intended to be a wedding celebration, had gradually developed into a kind of war council.

Everyone was agreed that some move should be made against the dissolute revellers. But there was a division of opinions as to how this was to be done. As usual, Ankersen represented the most extreme view and insisted that after finishing their coffee the entire company should break up and go out together to find the bridal couple and bring them back. "We know we shall encounter opposition and perhaps be exposed to terrible things," he said, "But that is something we must suffer."

"Yes, I quite agree," urged Mrs Janniksen.

Mr Nillegaard, however, was strongly opposed to this plan.

"The idea is attractive enough in itself," he said. "But the time to embark on such a crusade has not yet come. I will very happily indeed go along with a demonstration of our good cause, but let us wait. Let us simply wait until this wedding feast has worked itself out in a couple of days, let us wait until reaction, weariness and repentance have announced their presence. Then and only then will it be the fullness of time."

The murmuring in the assembly suggested that Nillegaard's standpoint met with general approval. But Ankersen held his ground.

"There might be something in what Nillegaard says," he acknowledged. "But in a case like this, I do not believe that cold calculation is appropriate and it should not be tolerated. On the contrary. Nothing ventured, nothing gained,

Nillegaard! I for my part have learned that it is the *sacred fire* and nothing else that leads to great results. When you meet a mad bull, you can do one of two things: you can run away and let the bull rage on and do immeasurable damage to your fellow creatures while you yourself shut yourself up in your closet. Or with your head held high you can turn on the ungovernable beast and meet its eye and do what is in your power to overcome it."

"That's right, every word you say is right," confirmed Mrs Janniksen,

Nillegaard shook his head and replied earnestly and most emphatically: "In no way do I underrate your genuine willingness to take up the fight, Ankersen. I only believe that we will serve a good cause best if we put our common sense at its service. A bull – yes, the image is excellent. A bull is a bull, and in the face of the blind fury of natural forces no persuasion, no argument, no proclamation of the truth avails."

Ankersen rose and swept out his arms. "Natural forces," he shouted contemptuously. "To *the Devil* with natural forces."

"Oh well, no offence meant," remarked Nillegaard with a wan smile.

Ankersen laughed exultantly: "It's easy to see you are a teacher of *mathematics*, Nillegaard. But believe me these sums you have to work out are of no avail when confronted with the blind fury of sin! Sums are sums, but the sacred fire is infallible. It is miraculous. Or is it perhaps not true that faith can move mountains?"

"Yes," shouted Mrs Janniksen triumphantly.

Nillegaard gave a weary nod. "Yes, Ankersen, you're right in a way – in a way and at the right time. And in a figurative sense. And I also well understand your . . . your remarkable way of thinking. But I do not believe that every ineffectual gesture serves God's purpose. We must not, for the sake of desperate valour and a reckless willingness to sacrifice, get ourselves into a fatal mess. The day when, through our well organised and untiring work we have established *complete prohibition*, Ankersen, that day will be the true day of our victory.

214

And we are not so far from our goal after all. Indeed, the sands of the dissolute have almost run out. What is taking place during this dark night is the beginning of their last convulsions. So be a wise commander, Ankersen, do not fight blindly, do not carry out your attacks in the wrong places. You know we have confidence in you; you know we will follow you when . . ."

"When there is no longer any risk entailed," Ankersen bit him off. "When there is no longer a skin to be risked! Thank you, Nillegaard. Let me tell you, and let me tell this assembly, that I profoundly disagree with you. For, Nillegaard, the fact is that you are *afraid*! You are not only a cautious and calculating man, you are a timorous person, a man of little faith! No, in truth, it must not be said of us that we lost a battle and turned our backs, that we looked after ourselves and went home hoping for better luck next time! We won't have that stain on our reputation."

"No, we won't have that stain on our reputation," echoed Mrs Janniksen ecstatically.

Ankersen held out his arms in a gesture of embrace: "Therefore I implore you for the last time, all of you: *Follow me!* Follow me now at this hour. And if you hold back . . . well, then I will go out and do battle *alone*!"

"No, you shall not go alone," shouted Mrs Janniksen, giving the savings bank manager an intense look.

Nillegaard blew his nose and then said in a dry and accusing tone: "Well, what is it really you want us to do, Ankersen? You really do owe us a more detailed explanation."

"No," shouted Ankersen. His voice was trembling: "We need no more detailed explanation, Sir. What must happen shall happen!"

Nillegaard had turned pale. In a low, but unusually clear voice he said, "The only thing you will achieve, Ankersen, thanks to your *insane* behaviour, is to sow dissent among us, us who could otherwise have stood as a united block, a dangerous block that no one could dodge around."

"Dodge around," roared Ankersen, raising his clenched fists. "Dodge around! Aye, there we have it. What else are you doing, Nillegaard, except dodging around? For you are so terribly afraid, Sir, afraid for your fair looks and what bit of a position and respect you enjoy. That's what it is."

Nillegaard gave a restrained smile, but he was totally incensed. With a grating voice he replied, "You think you are a kind of prophet, Ankersen. But let me tell you that you are just about the only one to believe that, Sir. But do as you like. The most you can achieve is that people tomorrow will shrug their shoulders and say, 'Oh, that man Ankersen, *that madman* went over the top yesterday evening.' And the only thing you will achieve is precisely to damage your own cause. Just so that you can be allowed to capitulate to your unfortunate urge to *make a show*."

Ankersen burst out in a great laugh that was something between a roar and a moan. "Thank you, Nillegaard. Thank you. I think by now we all know you to the bottom of your jelly-livered heart. You coward. You wimp. Oh . . . I despise you. Just think how you shook and trembled just now when the cannon was fired."

He turned to the assembled company and said in a plaintive, hollow and ominous tone: "Choose then, brothers and sisters. Then choose between *this man and me*! If you choose him, then I shall understand the message. Then I will leave and go my own way."

"No, Ankersen, you mustn't go," came a voice suddenly.

It was not Mrs Janniksen's. No, it was Mrs Nillegaard who spoke. She had got up and stood wringing her handkerchief between her hands. "Ankersen must stay. Ankersen mustn't go."

Mrs Nillegaard's appeal had a powerful and immediate effect. There was a palpable movement among those gathered; many got up, and one woman wept loudly and provocatively. Nillegaard had acquired a strangely foolish expression; his lower lip hung down limply.

"Yes," continued Mrs Nillegaard in a fanatical and high-pitched singing tone that could melt the heart even of a roof tile: "I disagree with my husband. I believe in Ankersen. He is right. *For the letter killeth, but the spirit giveth life.*"

She almost howled these last words, shaking her head violently at the same time.

Ankersen, too, stood speechless for a moment. But then he suddenly began to speak in a deep and gentle voice, like someone who is moved and profoundly satisfied. "Thank you Mrs Nillegaard, thank you, my friend and sister. Thank you for those words. But hear another word now, my dear friends and fellow-believers . . . a word that applies to our brother Nillegaard. I want to make an apology to Nillegaard for my harsh words. Of course, I know Nillegaard from a long and loyal period during which we have worked together. I know his good disposition, his clear understanding, his tireless industry. We cannot afford to do without him."

Ankersen now turned directly to Nillegaard: "I will use this opportunity to express my most heartfelt gratitude also to you. Let us hold out our hands to each other, Nillegaard, in the sight of this gathering. Let all bitterness be forgotten. I believe we do best in giving way to each other in the name of Our Lord. *You* are right in that we ought not to lose sight of our ultimate objective. *I* am right in that we should not give way in this single instance."

Ankersen again turned and addressed the congregation. "So, dear friends, I propose that this evening we go together through this town. . . without drawing attention to ourselves, without accosting anyone, merely singing quietly. We will make a round and then go to our homes. I think it will be best so."

The assembly rose quietly. All faces were marked by profound relief, by gentle and confident resolution.

5

Of the further progress of the battle. Nillegaard's bitter thoughts and misgivings during the procession. Ole Brandy's seductive singing. The great confrontation. Sectarian victory

Quietly singing, the procession from Ydun moves out along the shore towards the old part of town. Ankersen leads, glancing watchfully to one side or the other or turning round to look back, inspiring and singing.

"What a ridiculous undertaking this is," thinks Nillegaard to himself. "How crazy. For heaven's sake, what good is it going to do? It's the result of an idiotic compromise. All right, Nillegaard, you could have refused to take part. But the fact is that once more, for the umpteenth time, you are a victim of Ankersen's *coup*."

Nillegaard becomes more and more upset at the thought that he is now dancing to Ankersen's tune and submitting to his deranged will. For the sake of the *cause*? "Never mind, the cause would only have gained by Ankersen's being put in his place once and for all in the presence of the entire association. And this was just about to happen and would have happened if Ida hadn't had that attack of hysteria! Crazy people and hysterical women – preserve us from them! If you did what was right, you'd buzz off from it all. And yet here you are traipsing along with them. Contrary to your better understanding. You old fool."

And if only it had all ended without complications. But it is useless to believe you can play with fire without burning yourself, especially when a firecracker like Ankersen is leading things.

Nillegaard clenches his fists in his pocket and mumbles to himself, filled with dark forebodings, "Just you wait. Just you wait."

Up in the sail loft in the High Warehouse, the bottle has passed regularly from hand to hand. They have talked and sung; Ole Brandy and Olivarius have tried to overdo each other with old ghost stories and hair-raising memories from the storm-tossed life of a seaman, and by request Moritz has several times recited the wonderful old wedding hymn "In the wondrous hour of the dawn". In the course of all this, they have several times agreed to break up. But they have got up and stamped the stiffness out of their legs, moved around a bit, moved coils of rope and other rubbish standing and getting in the way, and drunk the irrevocable last dram. Indeed at one time they went so far as to start looking for the trapdoor to the steps down.

But then these heavily burdened men have gradually lost contact with each other, becoming withdrawn and morose, victims of that strange remoteness that always lurks after extreme joy, and as time has passed they have found their way to that vast loneliness that is the final experience of all living organisms.

However, this did not apply to Ole Brandy.

He fought his way through this portentously threatening solitude, sitting astride a cogwheel. Then he determinedly made his way through sleep and mist and all manner of confused concepts, and managed to push one of the hatches open. The fresh air transported him to a kind of ponderous balance; he took a dram from his hip flask, again felt the dawn of life in his soul and felt an irresistible desire to burst out in a hopelessly pessimistic song:

> Sounds of mourning, notes of black
> Evermore my harp must play
> Babylon's river's watery track
> Hears my sad playing every day.

The Christian temperance procession, which was at this moment turning the corner by the High Warehouse, stopped and listened to this melancholy song echoing in the night. Ankersen stood in wonderment with his head raised, seeking the hidden source of the song.

"Upon my soul, it's a hymn" he said in an enraptured voice. "I wonder who it can be up there singing hymns?"

"It's a drunken man," Nillegaard informed him with a certain malicious glee in his voice. "And it's not a hymn, Ankersen, it's *Olysses*!"

Ankersen nudged him with his elbow. "Sshh! A drunken man certainly doesn't sing like that. So movingly! Only a soul in torment sings like that."

Nillegaard laughed to himself, sarcastically and bitterly. Ole Brandy went on singing, his deep bass voice resounded emotionally as he sang his anguished song.

> Then fare thee well, my angel sweet,
> In bliss and joy you now can rest
> In mournful garb 'tis only meet
> I dress my sorrow to attest.

> Let but the fish thy flesh devour
> Thy soul rests with the Lord,
> My dearest love, my precious flower,
> Still hear my mournful chord.

"What did I say?" Ankersen turned round triumphantly. "Was it not a hymn, Mr Nillegaard?"

"No," said Nillegaard wearily. A sense of powerlessness and despair welled up in him, and he was not far from weeping. It *was* only *Olysses*, a dreadful sentimental old sea shanty. But he couldn't be bothered arguing with Ankersen any longer.

The savings bank manager cupped his hands and called out in an unctuous voice: "Who is it singing up aloft there?"

No reply. The voice fell silent. The procession moved slowly on.

Of course Nillegaard was right. His presentiments turned out to be forerunners of appalling and inevitable events.

There is an infernal din outside Janniksen's smithy, the sound of singing and shouting and tramping like wild animals, the clinking of iron, the chinking of bottles, blasts on trumpets, howls of laughter.

Perhaps the worst can yet be avoided. Nillegaard shakes Ankersen violently by the arm and says excitedly, "Listen, there is no reason whatever deliberately to go right past the smithy, is there? The agreement was that we . . . that we . . ."

"Of course," nods Ankersen. He turns round, surveys the procession and proclaims in a threatening voice, "But here, then, you can hear. Truly, Sodom and Gomorrah cannot have sounded worse. Let us stop here for a moment, let us collect ourselves."

Nillegaard is trembling with excitement. He glances at Mrs Janniksen. The expression on her face is indescribable. She is staring towards the entrance to the smithy like a wounded animal.

Ridiculous and dreadful. And all Ankersen's fault. Nillegaard stares in horror, as though he were a man with the gift of second sight sensing that a dreadful vision is about to reveal itself.

And then it happens.

An assembly of reeling torchbearers, convulsed with dark, throaty bursts of laughter, appears at the door to the smithy. Then comes a man in shirtsleeves. He is carrying a flag on a pole. It is Count Oldendorp. It is not a real flag fluttering at the top of the pole. It is a signal flag, yellow with a black ring. A strange fateful symbol of destruction.

Then more torchbearers appear. Followed by a horn blower, blowing as loud as he can. Then a man rattling two bottles against each other, and another one devoting himself to the same skill. Then a man with an iron bar, from which he creates some long, debilitated sounds with the help of a hammer. Then yet another man with an iron bar that seems not to produce any sound at all. Then a new crowd of torchbearers.

Then a man with a pair of hand bellows, which also makes no sound. But then a man with a deafening horsy laugh, followed by a young lout producing piercing whistling sounds from a bottle. And finally three or four men drumming on tin pails and saucepans.

Then more torchbearers and some men heartily laughing and pulling on ropes. What is that they are dragging along? The cannon! The *cannon*, of course. And now comes Janniksen the blacksmith himself, illuminated on all sides by spluttering torches and *wearing a woman's red dress*! Good God! No, less than this would never suffice, of course. He issues spluttering commands; his coarse voice is out of control with amusement beyond belief; he is howling like a girl being tickled.

"Keep quiet, for God's sake, and stay where you are, all of you," shrieks Nillegaard.

But it is too late. Mrs Janniksen is already on her way. She approaches her husband. Collision! Indescribable confusion, in which Ankersen is involved of course. Mrs Janniksen tears and scratches at the smith's dress. Ankersen is wailing. No, he is *singing*.

Nillegaard turns away, stooping, flailing like a drunken man.

"Ida," he calls. "Ida. We must get away. We must all get away. Quick."

And he starts to run. He hears footsteps around him without knowing whether they are pursuers or companions, at any moment expecting to hear the roar of the cannon . . .

Not until he is over on the other side of Skindholm, at the foot of the hill leading up to the High Warehouse, does he stop and look back and discover that he is alone.

From over in the region of the smithy there are shouts and bangs, songs, oafish roars of laughter, howls and an infernal din. The battle is raging. Mrs Janniksen has succeeded in tearing the dress off her husband. Mrs Nillegaard, too, has thrown herself into the battle and in a grating voice is demanding that the bridal couple should be handed over.

"Julia! Julia!," her voice cuts through all the racket. And Mrs Janniksen joins in: "Julia! Julia!" So does Ankersen, and soon the entire Ydun community join in a rhythmic chorus: "Julia! Sirius! Julia! Sirius!"

Sirius is awakened by the loud shouts; he goes over to the window just in time to see Ankersen raised aloft by powerful hands and borne shoulder high. An incredible sight, like a vision in a dream. Ankersen offers not the slightest resistance; rather, he helps them with it, his face expresses a certain grim, expectant delight. And when the bearers start off with him, jeering and screeching, he turns his head back and shouts with all the strength in his lungs: "Be of good cheer! Hold out! Victory is assured for us!"

"Sirius, Julia" is still the repeated cry. And now Julia comes in through the door. She is out of breath and dissolved in tears. "Come on," she says. "Come on, Sirius. Mother's here."

Indeed ... now Mrs Janniksen appears in the bedroom door, with Mrs Nillegaard behind her. They are both weeping. Mrs Janniksen is holding a short iron bar in her hand and has a crumpled bunch of red clothing under her arm. She flings the bundle of clothes at Julia and raises the spear at her threateningly at the same time as revealing a madly distorted face and screaming, "Come on, Julia. You're both coming with us, this minute."

Mrs Nillegaard places a comforting hand on her arm and says imploringly, "Oh no, Mrs Janniksen. There's no reason to threaten the young people; they're not objecting to coming with us ... are you?"

Sirius sighs and meekly says, "No, there's no objection on my part. What do you think, Julia?"

Julia steps across and takes his arm, weeping profusely.

Sirius puts on his jacket and shoes, trembling the while. Mrs Nillegaard goes across to the window and proclaims in a loud voice: "Quiet! Everything's all right now. We'll be coming in a moment."

"Everything's all right?" groans Mrs Janniksen. She has sat down on the bed and is close to a breakdown. "Everything's all right, you say? Then what about Ankersen?"

"*He*'ll manage all right," replies Mrs Nillegaard with

223

conviction. "He's not alone either, Mrs Janniksen. His son's with him. I saw him. He was fighting like a tiger."

She bends down over Mrs Janniksen, shakes her and shouts ecstatically, "This is *great*, this is, Mrs Janniksen. It's *great*. It's *victory*!"

Before long, the abstinence procession was on its way home with the bride and bridegroom at its head, flanked by Mrs Nillegaard and Mrs Janniksen and singing loudly and cheerfully.

Nillegaard stood hidden in an alleyway and watched the procession go past. Alas . . . so it had still ended in victory for Ankersen.

Nillegaard ground his teeth. Unjust! Crazy!

But then, where was Ankersen? Nillegaard felt driven by a curiosity he could not resist. When the procession was out of sight he crept out from his hiding place and cautiously approached the smithy. It was empty. There was not a soul to be seen. Yes, there was the Crab King. The little chap was standing in the semi-darkness of the smithy, staring at him in the light from the pitch-spitting forge.

Nillegaard went up to him and said politely, "You haven't seen anything of Ankersen by any chance?"

The dwarf made no reply.

But there came Constable Debes and two assistant constables hurrying and rattling their sabres.

"Do you by any chance know where Ankersen is?" asked Nillegaard.

"No," came the surly reply.

Nillegaard joined the policemen. He was thinking to himself: "Perhaps they've killed Ankersen." This idea gave him a curious, spicy taste on his tongue.

"Oh . . . ooh," there came a hollow sound in the darkness. They stopped and listened.

"Uhm," it came again, dull and half-stifled. And then, subdued but clear: "Here. Help! I can't . . . I can't . . ."

The police moved in the direction of the sound, Nillegaard following, hesitant, trembling with excitement. He thought it sounded like Ankersen's voice and imagined the savings bank manager lying in a ditch, drenched in blood. But no, it was not

Ankersen. It was Matte-Gok. He was lying on the ground, alone in the darkness, curled up.

"Have you hurt yourself?" asked Debes.

Matte-Gok had difficulty in speaking but otherwise seemed to be calm and composed. He mumbled something about his back, about an iron bar on his back. Lost his breath. "But it feels a bit better already now, I think. No not the doctor. It'll be all right."

The policemen helped him up. He found it difficult to support himself. "Thank you, thank you very much," he said. "If you would be so kind as to help me home. No, it feels a bit better, it'll be all right when I get to bed. I'm simply so dreadfully confused and bruised. I fainted."

"Oh," said Debes. "Carry him home and put him to bed. Hmm!"

The two men disappeared with Matte-Gok. The constable and Nillegaard hurried on to The Dolphin. "Ankersen," thought Nillegaard. "Ankersen, what's become of him?" And suddenly he had no doubt that Ankersen had been killed. Dead. Fallen. He wouldn't listen to the voice of reason. Stubborn and desperate, he had gone to his destruction in this dreadful night of murder.

But no, Ankersen was by no means dead. On the contrary, he was in the best of health. He was standing on a table in the full and stuffy hall and speaking to his people.

It was not the hellfire sermon that might have been expected. No, there was reconciliation and tenderness in his voice: ". . . It is never too late, dear friends, *never*. The door is ajar even at the twelfth hour, indeed even when the twelfth stroke has rung out."

"Aye, Ankersen's all right," came a loud voice. It was that of Count Oldendorp.

"Aye, long may he live," roared Janniksen the blacksmith, and the entire company shouted hip, hip hurrah.

Without realising it, Nillegaard was stooping as he tiptoed away. He felt the urge to weep in a place where he was on his own.

6

How things finally went for Magister Mortensen

Alas, once more now, one of our dear musicians is going to make his exit from of the story. Not just an ordinary exit, for he leaps! He leaps up the steps to eternity, for although he is both wounded and tired, he is no clammy, miserable soul, but to the end a man with a passionate hunger for life.

Worlds come to an end and re-emerge and again come to an end; values are revalued and skewed; all things are subject to the inscrutable laws of decay and rejuvenation, but at all times tar and pitch retain their penetrating, harsh smell of harbour and ships, heroic maintenance and undeniable everyday life.

Mortensen lies inhaling this aroma; for a moment it completely dominates his consciousness: this safe and thoroughly reliable smell is all there is; there is nothing else. Yes there is, there is a dryness in his mouth and throat and the resultant thirst. And then the extraordinary figurations from this march, whatever it's called . . . the death march.

But then, slowly and as if in a dream, he is confronted with a hanging sail, whose vigorously emphasised, twilight-filled folds lead his thoughts to a bird's-eye view of a spreading mountain landscape at dawn. The next of the things of this world to appear to his dawning consciousness is the rusty horn of an abandoned ship's siren. He automatically expects it to produce a sound, but it emits only silence and darkness.

Then the stillness is broken by a couple of sharp, close screeches from gulls, and his ear, suddenly brought into intense activity by this, now registers other sounds: a deep, polyphonic snoring dully and sultrily combined with the refreshing sounds of waves breaking against a shore.

He raises his head and looks around. Olivarius's sail loft, of course. He gets up, shivering with cold and thirst. Over by the foot of a pile of discarded pieces of canvas lies Josef the Lament asleep. The expression on his face is reminiscent of that of the man who has frozen to death in the well-known painting "All Quiet at the Shipka Pass". A little further away lies the inoffensive little grocer Jacob Siff with a sweetly devoted smile beneath his grubby moustache. And yet further away lies Moritz the ferryman, he, too, asleep, but sitting up and leaning against a coil of rope; and even in sleep his gaunt face retains its cheerful and incorruptible expression. And over by an open hatch, Ole Brandy! He is reminiscent of something like a Stone Age man who has risen from the grave; he does not look as though he is really asleep, but on the other hand he is not in a state one would dare to call awake. He is staring ahead, paralysed but immortal. Now he raises an arm and bends his fingers to beckon, and Mortensen goes across to him.

Ole nods profoundly satisfied and speaks in an adenoidal voice: "There's a vottle, a pottle in ma back pocket."

A bottle in his back pocket? Mortensen grabs the bottle and takes a gulp. The lukewarm drink makes him shudder all over, as though he had swallowed a live fish.

"Me one . . . me one . . ." mutters Ole Brandy indistinctly, but immediately falls back asleep hugging the hip flask against a waistcoat covered with fluff from the ropes. Mortensen drags him across to the pile of canvas and covers him with the soft old foresail under which he himself has slept.

Over among the coils of rope stand the empty bottles, glowing green in the semi-darkness. There is still a good dram left in one of them. Mortensen takes another gulp and draws his breath, deep and liberated. All nausea is dissipated – it feels as though a clear and pleasing light has been lit within him.

He allows his thoughts to float freely around the huge loft.

"You're free! You're free, free from Satan himself. *Flieh! Aus! Hinaus ins weite Land!* No more of this confounded private tuition or grubbing around in libraries. No one to explain to or to try to keep out of the way of. And no more women's nonsense and sentimentality. No financial delirium.

227

It's all so far away and irrelevant now. Done with. At last you managed to slough your old skin. The cocoon's burst! You no longer go around festering with some small-town infection. You don't hate anyone, not even Berg the head-master. Nor Østermann. You are totally independent! You are totally independent until further notice. Enjoy your freedom, man."

Mortensen gets up. He sashays across to the open hatch. The gulls out there are floating on rose-pink wings in the sunrise. Magnificent. Homeric. Incredible how long a gull can float without moving its wings. Paradoxical. It is the symbol of unfettered, complete freedom. Of the art of an independent life.

"You're free, man. You can afford to buy yourself the fastest motorboat in the world."

It must be called *Hell Hound*!

The two fastest motorboats in the world, *Hell Hound* and *Satan Himself*.

The three fastest and most ruthless racing boats: Hell Hound, Satan Himself and *A Match for the Devil*!

Gaping faces on the shore. Puff! In a jiffy you've disappeared into infinity . . . sea on all sides and drifting clouds. And puff! Back to the gaping crowd. And puff. Out of sight again.

"Mr Berg, Headmaster, you with your small-checked suit and your shiny trouser seat and your sweet-and-sour tea cosy of a wife and your middle-aged daughter, you can stuff the lot!! Much good may it do you all! And you, Østermann, expert in authorised mediocrity. I wish you all the best, and may you stagnate in vapid and conceited idyll. Yours sincerely, Hell Hound. P.S. Satan Himself also sends his greetings. P.P.S. The Devil's boss sends his most cordial greetings on the occasion of your silver wedding."

The sun is shining on the western side of the cove. A wonderful morning. The small dusty, mildewed windows in the warehouse are fighting a hopeless battle to keep the sunshine out. But it is too powerful for them. It has the vic-torious power of goodness in it; it thaws them out along with

228

all their green mildew and theological cobwebbery, just as the good act destroys the intrigues and knavish tricks of mankind.

The free, untrammelled light forces its way into the spreading loft in long, sovereign wedges, endowing the confusion with new and hope-filled life. It plays on the nap of the strong golden manila; it clothes the mountains of canvas in light and shade and conjures up formations that remind one of those distant and inaccessible mountain reserves, the Rocky Mountains, the Himalayas . . . or of the still more distant and lofty virgin ridges and pinnacles on the moon. Or of that geographical insanity called Saturn. Morning on Saturn four hundred years ago! Or in three hundred and thirty one million years!

It is indeed good to live and die here. Here is joy, joy!

> Sing of joy and exultation!
> Sing of joy in all creation!

hums Mortensen. The old hymn has always reminded him of mighty journeys through the world, of Sindbad the Sailor's preposterous travels in sunshine and surf.

"Yes, it's good here. Here, you are finally completely yourself, full of life, freed from your shackles.

The only pity is that the bottles are empty. And it's a shame for those fine men sleeping there that they'll have to wake up to empty cups."

But something can be done about that. He has a couple of bottles at home. And now they are needed.

Mortensen opens the trapdoor and climbs down the many steep steps. It is only just turned four o'clock. But the town is not dead by any means. The air is full of singing and of indomitable whirlwinds of multitudinous sounds. He can hear they are dancing out in the Dolphin. Two hopelessly inebriated men come staggering along, arm in arm, weak-kneed with affability and happiness.

"The key!" Good heavens, has he lost it? No, it's in the door. So he must have forgotten it there yesterday . . .?

And suppose someone . . .

Yes. Of course. Mortensen sees the drawer in his desk has been forced open. And the folder and the envelopes have gone. And the thirty or forty thousand that were on their own at the back of the drawer. Of course. Of course.

And that is the end of that.

"There's nothing you can do about it," he says persuasively to himself. At least the bottles are untouched. He opens one of them and fills a dusty glass. "Let's drink to that. It was probably a good solution. Now there's no need for any more of this intimate hocus-pocus . . ."

He notes an undignified attack of fury working its way up in his breast. *My money!*

"Shush," he says to calm himself down. "What do you want with all that money? You were destroying yourself over it when you had it. You were not suited to it. Do you have to *weep over it* now on top of everything else?"

But the demon in his breast begins to complain and show its dissatisfaction. "My money," it rasps, stamping on the floor. "My gifts." And then suddenly he goes all sentimental and starts snivelling: "My heart is filled with sorrow".

He gets up and rummages feverishly in his inner pocket and takes out Atlanta's letter, unfolds it on the table and traces the naïve girlish writing with his finger until he finds the ominous phrase: "My heart is filled with sorrow". Yes, here it is, here it is: "My heart is filled with sorrow".

He smoothes the letter out, folds it gently together and raises it to his face several times before putting it back in his inside pocket.

And now it feels as though the most important thing has been saved after all.

He cautiously places the two bottles in his coat pockets. And then back to that blessed, cosmic place where freedom dwells, where all need and sorrow is silent and forgotten,

> . . . to the land where never again with sadness
> souls take leave of souls.

Out in the sail loft, Josef the Lament had woken up and sat staring ahead like a dog on the point of death.

"Cheer up," said Mortensen, taking out the bottles. "This is an extra fine three star cognac. Just brought down from Orion's Belt."

"It's all so strange," said Josef down-heartedly.

"Cheers," said Mortensen in a commanding tone.

It was not long before Josef recovered his good humour. Mortensen took his arm, and they made a quiet perambulation through the morning-lit room.

It was in the course of this walk that Mortensen discovered the stairs to eternity. This flight of steps was no different in appearance from the quite ordinary, roughly constructed flights of steps seen in all warehouses. It stretched from floor to ceiling in the south-western corner of the room. But as there was nothing above it except what is known as space, this flight of steps served no purpose whatever, but only stood there as a kind of enigmatic new creation of nature or as some work of art of remarkable and profound symbolism.

Mortensen tried to convey to Josef an impression of the indescribable magic implicit in the fact that the steps led nowhere. And he succeeded . . . just as, against all expectation and reason, there came a glimpse of delight in Josef's pale eyes; they flashed with red sparks, and the whole of the spectrally transparent face became radiant: "Yes. Exactly!"

"Yes, isn't it?" said Mortensen and almost had tears in his eyes at meeting such understanding so quickly.

"Yes, 'cause it's like my *frame*," said Josef and rubbed his hands together in child-like glee. "My frame . . . that isn't going to be use for anything; it's just going to be there, just like a . . . well . . . an eternity frame!"

He laughed shyly and a tender expression appeared at the corners of his mouth.

"It'll be a good frame," he went on. "I can already see it before me in my mind's eye. It'll be the best frame in the world, Mortensen."

He had a serious, determined, almost fanatical expression in his eyes and, nodding furiously, he added, "And no living soul shall ever come and say: yes, but that's a perfectly ordinary frame, Joseph, that can be used for this and that. Not on your life."

Josef held out his frail hand to Mortensen. The two men exchanged handshakes. Glancing at the steps, Josef said: "And of course, it will be a lot better than steps like those."

He kicked the steps, not without a certain contempt.

"Aye, but why just that?" asked Mortensen.

Josef wrinkled his nose: "Well, because those steps can be used for something."

"Yes, but how?" asked Mortensen nervously.

"Well, to get up on the roof." Josef was now regarding the steps with unconcealed contempt.

A shadow of disappointment crossed Mortensen's face. He doggedly objected: "Yes, but what would anyone want to do up there?"

"Yes, what would anyone do?" Josef had no answer on the spur of the moment.

"There you are," nodded Mortensen.

The two men quickly mounted the steps as though filled with the same idea. It led up to a kind of deckhouse in which there was a hatch. Mortensen opened the hatch, and they looked out on the great sun-glittering tiled roof that sloped down at a dizzy angle and suddenly ended in a blue nothing, like the road to the end of the world.

"Aye, what the devil does one do on a roof like this?" asked Mortensen.

"Aye, what does one do?" admitted Josef.

"It's not bad up here, though," said Mortensen. "Just look how the sun is shining. And if you slide down, you'll land in the blue water and go to the bottom like a stone. It must almost feel like being shot out of a cannon, eh? Ugh, let's go down and drink to that."

They went slowly down the stairs. The hatch was left open. Mortensen quickly emptied his cup and poured another and yet another.

But then something dreadful happens. Mortensen goes up the stairs again, quickly, almost at a run and disappears through the hatch! Josef hears how he slips down the smooth tiles. And then the sound ceases.

Josef the Lament opens his mouth to cry out, but he is unable to make a sound. He staggers across the floor, stumbles and remains stretched out there with his face buried in a pile of spare bits of canvas.

7

General confusion interspersed with new harrowing events. Kronfeldt, the Chief Administrator, is on the point of a nervous breakdown, and for the first and last time in his life the Crab King bursts into human speech

You can become so incensed that it is so to speak impossible to react. You shut yourself off. You laugh just a little. You pick your teeth. You hum a little. You grab a newspaper, yawn and read an advertisement. A light, well-paid job available for a willing and reliable young lady.

There, there. Now, now.

That is how things went with Kronfeldt the Chief Administrator on the morning when he received the triple news of misfortune telling him of the count's flight together with Black Mira, the break-in in the savings bank and Mortensen's suicide.

The first two of these might conceivably be connected. Karl Erik simply had no money to pay for a ticket. It's so obvious. In that case, you break in and steal forty-nine thousand kroner.

"And then there's us two, Charlotte," says Kronfeldt quite calmly in an everyday voice. "Then there's us two. We'll pack our things. We are finished. I am finished as a civil servant. But we'll manage even so, my dear. You are good at *knitting*. You can knit for people. I can get a job in an office. That little change might even be a good thing for both of us. We have been too foolish. We must take the consequences. It is nothing to weep about. Things could in fact have been much worse for us. He could have murdered us both, for instance."

Constable Debes comes back from the savings bank with important news. The thief has left his jacket and cap behind together with a crowbar and a pair of tongs. In one of the jacket pockets there was a perpetual calendar belonging to the savings bank.

"Cap?" asks the Chief Administrator with a poisonous little smile. "You mean *hat*? He wore a hat, not a cap."

"No, a cap," says the constable in surprise. "A quite ordinary cap with a shiny peak."

The Chief Administrator sits down at his writing desk. He chuckles to himself. "No, of course," he says, suddenly blushing all over his face and down his neck. "Naturally. It's a cap man who's been at work. Not a hat man. Not a hat man."

He gets up. "Well, then we must see about finding the owner of the jacket and cap. Do you suspect anyone in particular, Debes?"

The constable shakes his head despondently.

Kronfeldt looks at his watch. Things are whirling round for him. For a moment he feels very happy.

"We'll manage this like we've managed everything else," he says in a most kindly voice to the constable. "Just do your best, Debes."

"Yes, sir." The constable withdraws with a slight bow.

Kronfeldt goes into the flat. "Charlotte," he says warmly. "Charlotte. I think we made a mistake. It was not *he*. It was a cap man."

"Yes, but hasn't *he* left?" whispers Mrs Kronfeldt.

"Oh, yes. Oh, yes. Thank God. That's something we have both been looking forward to for a long time, isn't it? Ever since Miss Schmerling broke with him. We have every reason to be pleased, Charlotte. Our most ardent wish has so to speak been fulfilled."

"I can't forget how calmly you took it . . ." says Mrs Kronfeldt. She sits down, dries her eyes and sighs deeply.

"Yes, but of course," smiles the Chief Administrator. He suddenly feels weak at the knees. The reaction! He feels dizzy. He straightens himself up and goes back to his office. There, he lies down exhausted on the sofa. There are fireflies dancing before his eyes.

The police embark on a search for the owner of the jacket and cap. But this owner makes himself known of his own accord during the early part of the morning.

It is Kornelius.

"Yes, it's my jacket and cap," he says. "But I don't know anything about the crowbar or the tongs, or about the perpetual calendar either."

Constable Debes cannot hide his amazement: "Yes, but . . . then it was *you*, Kornelius."

"No, it wasn't me who broke in, if that's what you mean," replies Kornelius, looking him in the eye. "I don't know who it was. I've had nothing to do with it."

"Wasn't it terrible about Magister Mortensen," he adds and sighs, shaking his head.

"But then you were up in the savings bank last night and . . . and . . .?" asks Debes.

"No."

Kornelius makes no attempt to hide anything, but relates everything just as it happened.

"Yes, but wait a bit," says Debes. "The Chief Administrator is coming himself."

Kronfeldt is very agitated now. His calm has vanished completely; his hands are shaking terribly, and he has hectic red blotches in his face. He gives Kornelius a glance that is full of disgust and entirely without mercy.

"Get a move on, man," he says in a flat voice.

Kornelius makes his statement and hides nothing. He is calm, indeed he speaks almost without stammering. The Chief Administrator shuffles impatiently in his chair: "A divining rod? A buried treasure? . . . You've got another thing coming if you believe you can put that one over on me. And then you were *attacked*? By whom, sir?"

"By some . . . person, or whatever I'm to call it, well, because I really don't know how to explain it. It was so dark, and I thought his face was all black. And when he took hold

236

of me and seemed as if he was going to choke me, I was very frightened. Not that I believe in ghosts. But it seemed to me that he reminded me of the Devil himself, or I don't know what. And then I got away and ran home. And my jacket and cap . . . I left them behind. It wasn't until later I discovered I'd lost them."

The Chief Administrator snorts and says harshly, "Oh, I see. That's what you did. Yes, that's probably enough. But where's the money?"

"Well, I don't know anything about that," replies Kornelius, trying to catch Kronfeldt's eye. "There *was* no money! There *was* no treasure."

"You'll do best to produce the money straight away and without beating about the bush," says the Chief Administrator, bouncing impatiently in his chair.

"Yes, but how can I when it *wasn't* me . . .?" objects Kornelius dispiritedly.

Kronfeldt gets up, but sits down again, spreads both his hands and becomes quite distorted in his face: "Good heavens, man. Who do you think you are dealing with? Do you think you'll get anywhere here with your idiotic tales?"

Kronfeldt is now so furious he is on the point of tears, and he speaks in a voice choking with sobs. Kornelius meets his hateful look with equanimity. "But I *am* innocent," he repeats.

But this is too much for the Chief Administrator; he collapses into a kind of convulsive laughter, gets up and dances around the floor with his hands raised.

"Listen, little man, will you do as you're told?" he snarls. "Will you? Will you tell me where you've hidden the money? Won't you? All right, then you must take the consequences. Debes! Debes! Heavens above! *Debes*. Oh, you *are* still here. That's good. I thought you'd perhaps gone home to play patience. Now we'll put this thick-skinned little chap under lock and key. And then you carry out a *search of his home*. Understand?"

"Yes, straight away . . ." says Debes, looking extremely unhappy and dubious.

"Yes, Chief Administrator!" snarls Kronfeldt.

Debes takes Kornelius by the arm.

"What do you say, Debes?" repeats Kronfeldt with a cry.

"Yes, Chief Administrator!"

"Thank you for remembering."

Breathing heavily, Kronfeldt puts his hand up to his collar. He is sweating profusely. His heart is throbbing and hurting. He goes across and flings open a window: "God preserve us. God preserve us!"

"But thank God, now. Thank God. Oldendorp at least wasn't guilty of the break-in. And his flight together with this woman Mira . . . . Yes, that must be ascribed to the incredible extravagances that counts and barons could allow themselves. It's not easy, but it will be all right, provided I can manage to take it in my stride and not lose face. 'Aye, it was dreadful, good Lord. And yet basically splendid, incredibly daring. Almost like in an opera, ha, ha! Il Seraglio! The young man's incorrigible. But we did our best. We didn't fail the confidence placed in us by the Master of the Royal Hunt. My poor old friend. But the fellow was too much for us.' And so on and so forth. We know how to manage things. We take it calmly. One is a diplomat . . ."

The Chief Administrator sits down calmly at his desk and to his inexpressible satisfaction notes how the whole affair is gradually falling into place, coming together in a pattern that can only be to his advantage. The storm is subsiding. The sea is calming down.

Until new waves arise, a new breaker, if possible worse than the first . . .

For it turns out that Magister Mortensen's money has disappeared without trace. Where is that money? And who says that this was really an accident or a suicide? Why not a murder? A carefully planned murder in furtherance of robbery?

Interrogations and witnesses' evidence suggest the worst. It really looks as though there has been a careful plan here. Mortensen has been tempted up to the warehouse, been plied with drink until thoroughly intoxicated, robbed of his money and then quite neatly edged down from the roof and out of play.

The great question now is: Was the *count* part of that plot?

"No, there can obviously be no doubt about it, Charlotte," says Kronfeldt in a voice as matter-of-fact and dry as a pencil sharpener. "He consorted with that very crowd of course. He identified himself with those dregs of society. He was into the bargain seen that same afternoon together with Mortensen."

Kronfeldt has again grown quite calm and collected, just like this morning. He has postponed his reaction. He whistles a little, sits down, grasps the newspaper and reads an advertisement for coal and coke. He yawns and puts his hand gently up to his mouth.

"It's no use crying, my dear," he says casually. "We must accustom ourselves to the thought that he has not merely behaved towards *us* as an ass, but that he is a first-rate scoundrel into the bargain. A thief and a murderer. Ha, ha, ha! You've been spoiling a degenerate animal, a murderer, my dear Charlotte. You have been fostering a *serpent* at your breast!"

"A serpent?" he repeats. "No, a Midgard serpent! A sweet little Midgard serpent . . ."

Matte-Gok has played his cards with impressive dexterity. His alibi is firmly established. He is still in bed after the simulated attack, indeed he has even had the effrontery to send for Dr Manicus and has had his chest listened to and been given a bottle of medicine to calm him down. And now both Ankersen and Mrs Midiord are spoiling him with good food and words of encouragement.

"One must suffer for one's faith; one must have the courage of one's convictions," says Ankersen. "One must risk one's skin. Then one receives the reward that is worth more than gold, that is to say the wondrous bliss of eternal life. Yes, even if you had had your back broken, Mathias-Georg, that would have been preferable to your holding back with your tail between your legs like poor Nillegaard. You've shown now that you will risk your skin, and if you go on in this way, I prophesy a splendid future for you, my son. Alas, alas . . . if I were young like you, I know what *I* would do! I wouldn't remain in this small place; I would go out to heathen lands and become a mighty proclaimer of the Word."

Matte-Gok lapses into his own thoughts. A glow gradually emerges in his eyes. He knows the trick from countless films he has seen. Until finally both he and Ankersen are overcome by ecstasy. It is so simple and straightforward; indeed it proceeds so smoothly that Matte-Gok has to hold back a little, to have attacks of doubt and fear and pretend he lies awake all night in prayer and doubt.

But finally, the decision is made. The decision to go to darkest Africa as a missionary to the heathen.

And now the decision has finally been taken, his impatience grows. The *call* forces itself on him and leaves him no peace. Let that which must come to pass, come to pass soon.

As will have been realised, Matte-Gok is a very considerable confidence trickster, a hypocrite and unscrupulous rogue, and anyone is entitled to wish him all the misfortunes in the world on account of his evil deeds. But then it must be said in his defence that he is after all only of modest dimensions. He will easily be outdone among the strugglers of this world: so to speak every third lawyer can beat him when it comes to smartness, even without going beyond the bounds of the law. And in comparison with the armaments manufacturers, diplomats, generals and clergymen who during these very years were preparing for the world-wide slaughter of 1914–18, Matte-Gok's person fades completely . . . a tiny, pale centipede among the tigers, lions and poisonous snakes of the jungle . . .

The search carried out in the Bastille has produced an important new element in the case: the papered-over door linking Mortensen's sitting room and Kornelius Isaksen's kitchen turns out to have been broken open, and, judging by the fresh tears in the wallpaper, this must have been done quite recently. The thief has obviously entered by this route, and so

Kornelius can in fact have been responsible for it all. And this is supported by the fact that his wife remains stubbornly silent. She has obviously been well trained.

On the other hand, it is so striking that Mortensen was kept away from his flat that very night that there is no reason to abandon the hypothesis of a plot and to cancel the arrest warrant for the men who spent the night and morning up in the sailmaker's loft together with the late Magister Mortensen. They all protest their innocence, but there are signs of an incipient breakdown in both the carpenter Josef Simonsen and the grocer Jakob Siff.

As for Count Oldendorp, there has still been no mention of his name in this connection. But Kronfeldt, the Chief Administrator, becomes more and more convinced that the count is the leader and that this will be revealed before long. Seized with dread and secret tears, he looks forward to the moment when the first of the conspirators breaks down and points to the count.

The dreadful day finally comes to an end and an even more terrible night arrives.

The Chief Administrator takes a powerful sleeping mixture and lies there in a nightmarish stupor, in the course of which he utters terrifying dying howls. Mrs Kronfeldt gets not a wink of sleep. She tries to wake her husband by means of strong coffee, but it is in vain. Then she puts cold compresses on his forehead, but that, too, fails to help. And the dreadfulness of it all is simply compounded when Kronfeldt suddenly sits up, climbs out of bed and with closed eyes and open mouth begins to dance around the room in his long, spooky nightshirt. Constable Debes has to be called to help Mrs Kronfeldt get the sleepwalker back to bed.

Then, finally, he falls into a deep slumber.

His wife looks at him in his torment. Even in sleep, his face betrays suffering, and his open mouth wears an unspeakably piteous expression.

It is in every way a night of distress and fear. The town lies veiled in an impenetrable mist, both in a figurative and

241

tangible sense, a treacherous and oppressive mist in which the apprehensive light of lamps from sleepless windows appears like luminous rays at the bottom of the sea.

If the wedding festivities had not come to a complete stand-still, they had at least been toned down until they could hardly be recognised. Out in The Dolphin there sits a small group of meditative men with their tankards of beer, talking in subdued voices, as though it were a wake. They never drink to each other, for there is nothing to drink to; they do not call for the waiter, but absent-mindedly and with a suffering mien raise their glasses in the air if they want more.

Even Janniksen the blacksmith is speaking in subdued tones. His eyes are stiff; his rubicund face is gathered in infini-tely sad folds; again and again he shrugs his shoulders, for the whole thing is so completely inconceivable.

"I can't think it's the count," he says. "And as for Kornelius and Moritz, we *know* they're innocent. Aye, I'd put my head on the block here straight away to their being as innocent as sucking pigs. Then there's Ole Brandy and Olivarius . . . my dear friends, my dear friends: it can't possibly be them, can it? As for Ole, we know he goes around grumbling and he can dot people one if the mood comes over him, but *dishonest*? No, there's more chance of the moon falling out of the sky. And then Josef the Lament and that little twit Jakob Siff . . . no way. No, it's none of them, that's as certain as the Devil's under the church floor. But then, it *must* be the count after all."

The blacksmith curls his finger at Jeremias the waiter and makes a silent movement of his shoulders, meaning a round of schnapps. "For it's so hellishly upsetting," he murmurs. They drink in silence, and the blacksmith continues whispering: "If that confounded slimy toad Matte-Gok hadn't been beaten up, as he truly deserves, I wouldn't hesitate to say it's him."

The blacksmith draws a heavy breath and glances sideways reflectively. "But can't it have been him even so? Can't he have managed it with the help of some minion?"

"I've been thinking just the same thing," says Mac Bett the decorator.

"But who could that minion be?" says the blacksmith with a wan smile.

"No, that's just it."

"There's this matter of the divining rod," says Mac Bett. "It's a curious story. Matte-Gok says it's all a lot of nonsense on the part of Kornelius, all this about a divining rod and the treasure. And perhaps he's right. 'Cause Kornelius *has* got a screw loose. I think we can easily agree on that. We know that."

"What do we know? What do we know?" says Jacobsen, the editor, who has just come in through the door. He sits down at the table in high spirits, and the blacksmith makes a sign with his elbow to the effect that he must have a dram as well.

"One thing we do know," continues Jacobsen elatedly. "One thing we do know is that it's Matte-Gok or Ankersen behind it all."

They all stare tensely and hopefully at the editor.

"Do you know anything definite, or is that only some ordinary inane newspaper gossip?" asks Mac Bett sternly.

"It's Ankersen and his bloody henchmen," replies Jacobsen fanatically. "Prove it? No, I bloody can't. But . . ."

"Then you'd better shut up," Mac Bett breaks in. "You're not sitting with a crowd of gossiping women, Jacobsen, remember that. We're serious men sitting here. We think serious thoughts."

Jacobsen scratches behind his ear and falls silent.

The blacksmith's words are bitter and vicious: "That we all *want* to see Matte-Gok and Ankersen ride off to Hell on stinking black horses, that's another matter, Jacobsen."

"There's a prayer meeting up at Ydun this evening," Jacobsen informs them. "You know, they're going to celebrate the defeat of their bitterest enemy now. The monstrous fiend of old, they were singing when I went past just now. That monstrous old enemy of theirs is now seriously angry."

But what suddenly comes over Janniksen? He gets up and his face is all contorted; he pushes his chair so it overturns on the floor, throws off his jacket and rolls up his shirt sleeves, and quite beyond himself, he snarls, "Just let me get at them, the dogs. I'll . . . I'll . . .!"

"Janniksen! Keep a grip on yourself," says Mac Bett in a commanding voice.

The blacksmith looks at him as though in amazement. He slowly sits down at the table again. But there is still something distorted about his face, and his eyes are full of tears.

From his position on the couch against the wall in the now dark studio, Orfeus can see into the lighted kitchen. There sits his mother. She is simply sitting and staring ahead. Behind her sits her shadow, huge and gentle like a good spirit.

The boy feels a great urge to get up and hurry across to his mother, to comfort her, to take her hand and comfort her with a thousand kisses. But he stays there and makes himself resolute. When he screws up his eyes a little, his mother's face is changed; it becomes stiff and marble-like, like the face of the figurehead Tarira. Weeping, he turns to the wall; he weeps until his pillow is quite wet, but finally he falls asleep, and now he dreams a strange dream that at once is full of suffering and inexpressible happiness.

He dreams that both he and his mother are dead, but live on like two shadows, two drifting and gently whispering shadows holding each other by the hand and moving about unseen wherever they wish. In the manner of ghosts, they go in the silence of the night to familiar places, out to Stake Point, where foam from the sea is gently blowing in, further out across the cove, where there is a rush of water and unfurled sails, and further on across the roofs of Skindholm, which is bathed in a pale, empty light.

But then, suddenly it is no longer his mother with whom he is fleeing; it is Tarira. She stares at him with her pale eyes; thrilled, he follows her up in the church tower and further on out into the vast chasm of clouds, where the spirits of the dead wander. He keeps close to Tarira; he longs for her to show him some kindness, but she merely stares at him.

And suddenly she is gone, and now he floats down among

the graves in the churchyard. Graves and graves and more graves ... some green, others framed with black wood or bluish white zinc. Or recently filled graves topped with withered leaves that whisper dryly in the wind as though in silent dismay. White figures rise from the graves and wave to him in long garments. Other spectres appear in the form of bare skeletons dancing among the graves and beckoning him to join the dance. They look wild and fierce; they launch themselves into long, lingering leaps over graves and paths; they pull tufts of dried grass out of the ground and launch it to drift in the wind. Some of them play violins, white and yellowing bone violins that produce plaintive notes in a minor key, descending harmonious minor scales.

There are entire orchestras of spectral players. They sit nodding their bald craniums as they play. They wave to him: "Where are you going, boy? Come and join us; you're musical like your father."

"No, for I'm not dead," shouts Orfeus in fear and hurries on.

But now, at last, he is standing by the familiar double grave, where his mother waits for him, silent and pale, but secretly happy to see him and have him with her. "*Here lie*", it says on the tombstone: "*Here lie the mortal remains of Eliana and Orfeus Isaksen, mother and son*".

But up on a tall gravestone, indeed a whole rocky pinnacle, sits Tarira, waiting for him. She just sits and waits with her mighty wings at the ready, and he feels with sadness that she is stronger than his mother and that he must now follow her and leave his mother alone and sorrowing behind in the grave.

He wakes up and feels a hand stroking his hair. It is his mother.

"Why are you crying like that, my dear?" she asks gently. "It'll all be all right, you'll see. There is justice after all."

He takes her hand and presses it to his cheek. Before long he slips back into sleep.

Eliana goes back into the kitchen. She is sleepy and weary, but she refuses to go to bed. She sits nodding and dozing.

Suddenly she gives a start on hearing someone slowly clearing his throat with a hollow sound. Before her, in the middle of the kitchen floor, stands a small, black figure. It is the Crab King.

"Good heavens," she exclaims. "You gave me such a fright, Poul Peter. You came in so quietly. But do sit down, Poul Peter. I'll make a cup of tea."

The Crab King does not sit down, he remains standing, shuffling his small bent legs a little. He is silent, as usual. His face is indescribably mournful; his eyes are burning like coals, like black, shining fragments of coal. Suddenly, he opens his mouth, as though to speak, but nothing comes of it. And yet . . . something does come of it nevertheless . . . he utters a couple of deep, hoarse sounds as though from the throat of some strange sea-bird. And then a remarkable thing happens: the Crab King starts to speak, almost like a normal person.

It sounds so incredible. Eliana starts at the sound; her heart races, and she goes all hot and cold, for it seems so strange that the Crab King can speak. He is a human being.

"It's not good, all this about Kornelius."

"No, Poul Peter," she replies. "It's not good."

"But it was Matte-Gok that was in the bank."

Eliana looked at him. She was speechless.

"It was Matte-Gok," repeats the Crab King. "I saw it myself. I saw it myself."

"Good heavens," exclaims Eliana. "If what you say is true, Poul Peter, then you can save Kornelius if you go and tell the Chief Administrator what you saw. You can, Poul Peter. I'll go with you if you will. You will, won't you, Poul Peter?"

The Crab King stares at her for a moment, but then suddenly turns away and waddles out of the door.

"No, you mustn't go now, Poul Peter," says Eliana imploringly. "Do you hear? You must help us. You will, won't you? You will help Kornelius?"

But the Crab King is already through the door though he has not quite gone away, for he is now standing outside, peering in through the window. He looks as though he is considering things. He supports his heavy forehead against the crossbar and stands there staring. Eliana is feverishly tense; she dare not go out and try to tempt him in again; she is afraid of spoiling it all. She fetches two cups and puts them on the table in front of the window. And then she hurriedly butters some slices of bread and puts them alongside the cups. She puts jam on the bread. Really tempting. The Crab King loves jam. And then she fetches the steaming teapot. Her hands are trembling, and she is close to tears. The Crab King is standing in the same position. She daren't beckon him, but just ignores him.

After a short while he comes back. He sets about the meal, silent as is his wont. But he nods to himself several times, and in time he again starts to speak. He slowly tells Eliana what happened when he saw Matte-Gok. Slowly, slowly so that she almost comes to a standstill over it. He listens as though nervously to his own words. But what he says is coherent enough.

He was standing outside Ankersen's house, and here he first saw a window being opened and a man creeping out of it and staying hidden for a long time. The Crab King himself was standing so that no one could see him. It was dark, but it was just light enough for him to see that the figure coming out of the window was not Ankersen but none other than Matte-Gok. But when Matte-Gok came into sight again he had blackened his face and was walking like an old man. But it was him all the same.

The Crab King makes a long, long pause. She pours another cup of tea for him. She dare not ask questions, but in her great excitement hopes that he will continue his account.

And so he does. But he doesn't say whether he followed Matte-Gok or how . . . and now we are suddenly at the savings bank, where Matte-Gok lets himself in with a key. Then a long time passes, during which Poul Peter stands outside, waiting. But then Matte-Gok comes back through the door and hides in the garden. And before he disappeared, he went and smashed a window.

"And then I went," concluded the Crab King. "Because it had nothing to do with me. But then they came and took Kornelius and said it was him. But it wasn't. It was Matte-Gok."

Eliana wept with delight, quite literally. She could not remember ever having felt so happy and relieved, and in overwhelming gratitude she took Poul Peter's hand. That was a thoughtless act; she had forgotten what the Crab King was like, and that no one was allowed to touch him except Kornelius at a pinch. He blew out his cheeks, blew her angrily in the face and trudged quickly away. In despair, she called to him, imploring and tempting, but he did not relent and did not return.

And yet: in a way the Crab King did relent. Towards morning he did return and was given a fresh cup of tea, though he would only stand in the door to drink it. But he had completely stopped saying anything. Not a sound came over his lips. And in no way would he consider going up to the Administrative Officer, not even when Eliana said that Kornelius's life might depend on it. Persuasion was useless. Only Kornelius could have persuaded the Crab King. It was hopeless.

So Eliana went up to the Chief Administrator's office alone. She wanted to inform Constable Debes of the situation.

"What, did he really *speak*?" Debes has to sit down and pause for a moment, so amazed is he, too, that the Crab King has spoken.

"But unfortunately, unfortunately," he says finally. "The Crab King isn't exactly a man to be relied on. He's mad, you know."

"No, he's certainly not mad," maintained Eliana, though she could already sense how hopeless the situation was.

"But heaven prevent me from putting obstacles in the way of Kornelius being found not guilty," added Debes. "*I* don't think he's the criminal. And for that matter, I'm very willing indeed to inform the Chief Administrator of what you've told me and hear his opinion. But there's not much hope, Eliana, I can tell you that beforehand. There's not much hope if the Crab King is the only witness you can produce."

"It's no use wanting to produce him as a witness," said Eliana in a broken voice.

"No, but surely he'll confirm what he's told you?"

Eliana shook her head and hid her face in her apron.

"Well, then it *is* hopeless," said the constable in a voice that betrayed some relief. "Then there's nothing to be done, Eliana. But let's just see how things go. Justice must nevertheless prevail."

During the afternoon, however, Eliana returned, and this time she had the Crab King with her. Constable Debes was not there, but Hansen, the bespectacled young head clerk who was new in the job stared numbly at the fantastic creature and could not refrain from a frightened little laugh, and Eliana knew already at this point that it would be of no avail. Poul Peter stood and blew out his cheeks as he looked around and trembled.

"We've got to save Kornelius," whispered Eliana encouragingly to him. He gave her a look full of fear.

Immediately after this, the inevitable happened. What Eliana herself could have said would happen.

Kronfeldt himself put in a noisy appearance.

"What sort of a pantomime is this?" he says with an unsmiling laugh. "Are you trying to make a complete fool of me?"

He flings out his hands, adopts a loose, gawping expression and turns his eyes up to the heavens. But then he suddenly pulls himself together, points at the door and shouts, "Get out. That dwarf's an idiot."

"No, he is not," Eliana dares to counter. She gets up and stamps on the floor. In impotent fury she stares at the irate, pink-skinned man with the little pointed beard and the false teeth. She hates him. But it is no use even so, for now the Crab King starts howling. He howls and twitches violently just like an infant, but in a coarse and rough voice . . . it sounds dreadful; never in his born days has Kronfeldt heard the likes. And suddenly the Crab King sets off and waddles out of the door like a clockwork toy.

"There, you can see for yourself," says Kronfeldt in a gentler voice. For a moment he almost looks human. "There, there, don't cry, my dear. You doubtless did it with the best of intentions, but . . . to come running here with sheer idiots

. . . no, it's bad enough as it is. Dreadfully bad. Dreadfully bad."

He withdraws, breathing heavily, to the interior of the house.

And the Crab King had now once more grown implacably silent. He had withdrawn into himself like a hermit crab into its shell. No one ever heard him speak again.

But perhaps this doesn't mean the battle is lost after all?

Meanwhile, several days now passed without anything new occurring.

8

Matters take an unexpected turn

Yes, time passes. Count Oldendorp and Black Mira have long been far away, and poor Magister Mortensen was laid to rest one foggy day in the churchyard to the words of the hymn, "A pilgrim I am and know my journey's end".

But Matte-Gok had received great visions and inspiration. Ankersen has made an enormous thing out of the once pro-digal son's decision to become a missionary to the heathen, and all right-minded people give their support to these two, the father and the son. Even those who have been lukewarm, even they have started to be inspired, for the violent events of recent weeks have shown that Ankersen was right, indeed that the place had, if possible, been even more dissolute than he had painted it.

The great criminal case is taking its course. Slowly, slowly. Far too slowly. The tension is intolerable. It is now up to Pommerencke, the *judge*. All eyes are on this one man. It is not without a dutiful shudder that people pass the big grey house in which they know that the tall grey man with the kindly and ever-attentive eyes sits considering the case.

But has this Pommerencke come to a complete standstill?

No, not at all. But the judge is a thoughtful man, and the case is an extremely complicated and unusual one.

In Pommerencke's view, the accused, the former typo-grapher Kornelius Isaksen, was not the crafty malingerer that Kronfeldt wanted to make of him. There was a great deal to suggest that he was a naïve daydreamer. It was most unlikely that he would have taken part in a *plot* of his own free will. He was no brigand. On the other hand, he could have acted as the tool for others in the plot.

If there were indeed a plot. There was a great deal to suggest that the other accused were also innocent. They were not brigands either, even if there were some dubious creatures among them like the drunken hothead Ole Olsen.

The judge did not believe there was any connection between Mortensen's presence in the sailmaker's workshop in the High Warehouse and the disappearance of his money. He did not believe this was a murder to carry out a robbery. It was either an accident or a suicide. Nor could there be any reason to believe that Count Oldendorp was implicated. A man like Oldendorp, despite his less fortunate aspects, was no brigand either.

Was there a brigand implicated at all? If there were, it must be this Matte-Gok who, according to Mr Isaksen's statement had helped him to seek the so-called *treasure*. But the man had been able to produce an alibi. He had the police themselves as witnesses. The "attack" on Kornelius had happened *after* this Matte-Gok had been taken home after being beaten up. But the judge was very much aware of this mysterious man – the so-called son of Ankersen, the savings bank manager, a man with an unknown and allegedly shady past.

If it *was* he, who during the excitement surrounding the wedding of the blacksmith's daughter, was guilty of the two break-ins and had manipulated the evidence to implicate Kornelius, then here was indeed a very dangerous man, an almost incredibly cunning man, a master thief. Fantastic hypotheses should never be brushed aside. But this hypothesis was nevertheless almost too fantastic. And yet, and yet.

But Judge Pommerencke was also working with another fantastic hypothesis. This was that Isaksen the typographer and "treasure seeker" was the victim of some kind of self-suggestion and could have worked in some state of somnambulism.

When a man has gone around for years talking of a treasure that at a stroke can make a poor wretch as rich as Croesus! When day after day he exposes himself to this intellectual *pressure*, must it not actually automatically lead him into criminality?

The judge discussed this possibility with Dr Manicus, who had considerable experience of pathological phenomena, and the doctor on the whole agreed with his theory.

The judge also touched on the other hypothesis, the one about Matte-Gok's dual role.

"Can you confirm, doctor, that the man really had his back injured during that wedding night, and that he could not have been simulating?"

"Oh yes," replied the doctor with a little smile. "His back is black and blue like the sky during a thunderstorm. And there are also contusions in the upper part of one arm."

"But would he nevertheless not have been capable of walking unassisted that night?"

The doctor reflected. "Possibly," he said. "Yes, yes, he probably would. But a man who is out of breath after being thumped in the back is naturally somewhat confused at first and is inclined to believe he has just about been killed."

"Can he not have inflicted such blows on himself, Manicus?"

"Yes, if he's something by way of a pure fakir?" smiled the doctor.

"If this hypothesis is correct, then he *is* something of a fakir. He is quite outside the normal run of things."

The doctor quietly shook his head, and there was a fine play of light in the velvet wrinkles around his eyes.

"My personal impression," he said slowly. "My personal impression of the man does not point in that direction. He does *not* give the impression of being particularly bright. He is unreasonable, pampered, somewhat childish, quick-tempered, limited, like Ankersen. He resembles Ankersen all right."

"If it's not all play-acting," said the judge.

A new element in the case. Up among the ruins of the old smithy that was blown down by the wind are discovered the remains of two charred hundred kroner notes. A closer examination shows that a good deal of paper has been burnt here. The ashes, which also contain the corner of a banknote, have been thoroughly stamped down into the ground and further hidden beneath a couple of rotting sacks.

New mystification. New speculations.

This was just about the state of affairs on the day when Kornelius *confessed*.

Yes, for it ended with Kornelius confessing his guilt in both crimes. It sounds amazing. And yet, when all is said and done, it is not difficult to understand that the story of a treasure seeker of Kornelius's kind had to end this way.

You go around for years tending a fixed idea, which you carefully keep secret and which so to speak in time becomes part of your innermost being. It forces you into a strangely skewed relationship to reality. But you grow accustomed to this skewed relationship; you adapt to this curious dual existence that you have slipped into; indeed, you find pleasure in it, find yourself at ease in its dim element of fluorescent hopes, in which you can abandon yourself to a free and lonely process of imagining and making music, at which you become a true master in time. Just as your father in his day became a master of his Aeolian harps in the lonely church tower.

During this process, you develop within yourself a remarkable elasticity not unlike that which makes a deep-sea fish suited to living its life under the immense pressure of the ocean's watery masses. This elasticity means an enormous amount to you; indeed, who knows, without it you might have become a wretch who was unsuited to life, a kind of Crab King, and not a man who is known and appreciated for his easy-going, good-humoured and helpful personality.

And it all goes fine as long as it is only a case of imaginings and captivating future prospects. Indeed, you love these very possibilities. Fundamentally, you don't want them to turn into reality any more than an artist wants to see himself confronted with the products of his imagination as tangible reality. On the contrary, he wants and tries to turn reality into art so as in this way to keep it at a clear distance, sensitive, even hypersensitive as he is.

Then, one fine day, the potentials show signs of becoming reality. The effect is enervating and anything but pleasant. You are beside yourself. You lack the ability to redirect yourself in these new circumstances. Like a deep-sea fish forced by some natural turbulence up into an element to which it is not accustomed. It longs to go back into the depths.

And then you suddenly find yourself thrown into a third world, the existence of which you have not considered at all. You find yourself accused of misdeeds of a dimension with which you cannot cope, misdeeds of which you are innocent, but in which you nevertheless cannot deny having been implicated. It is about money, vast sums. And you have at that same time been out in the dead of night with your spade to seek a huge treasure that it was your intention to obtain, although deep down within yourself you felt you were embarking on a rather dubious undertaking.

Oh well, you are naturally at first convinced that you have at least not committed these unspeakable deeds. You think it is obvious and cannot understand that others might see things differently. Nor are you naturally blind to the possibility that the person who attacked you and stole your jacket and cap might have been Matte-Gok, who was the only person who was aware of what you proposed to undertake that night. But even if you are convinced that justice exists and that the truth will emerge sooner or later, you cannot entirely liberate yourself from the bad conscience that lurks inside you, for with all your peculiar qualities you are still a profoundly honourable man.

Your dream of the treasure gradually undergoes a strange transformation; it fluoresces fatefully and terribly in its depths; it is fertilised under the influence of unpredictable forces that have pushed their way into it along with harsh reality. It engenders a formless, dull self-accusation.

That is just about what happened to our poor Kornelius.

It did not make his crisis easier that during the interrogations he was asked the most fantastic questions, questions that were calculated to throw new, dark, ambiguous shadows into the world of his imagination, which was already under strain.

Are you accustomed to sleepwalking? Are you used to having very lifelike dreams? Have you ever suffered from delirium? Do you think a great deal about digging for treasure when you are under the influence of stimulants? Do you have visions? In the case of no treasure existing, could you imagine having taken the money from another source?

And Dr Manicus comes. As though it was assumed that you were suffering from some illness. He speaks to you as though to a child; he looks at you with a maternal eye that gives you goose flesh all over.

Then you are again left to yourself and your scruples. You ponder. You long to get out of all this. You feel terribly sorry for your wife, and it pains you beyond description that they have arrested your brother Moritz, your good friend Ole Brandy and poor one-legged Olivarius. And the fates of Josef the Lament and Jacob Siff worry you, too. In your mind's eye you can see the little grocer's shop standing empty, indeed, the sound of its emptiness rings in your ears. And emptiness resounds in the big room in the basement of the Bastille, which used to be filled with all that beautiful music and where you have had the happiest times of your life. And emptiness lurks in Ole Brandy's little hovel. And emptiness resounds dreadfully in Magister Mortensen's deserted flat. The desperate violins of loneliness play, moving and heart-rending, and the void's dull cello pizzicato thumps as in a fever. You are tormented by nightmares and fearful dreams. At times, you are overcome by icy terror. And during all this, your feeling of guilt puts out new shoots, new strange and aberrant suckers.

And Ankersen comes.

Yes, they are innocent or unthinking or unfeeling enough to let him come. He sits with Kornelius like a father, sings consoling hymns to him, reads from the book of books, impresses on him that everything that is happening now is happening for his own good.

"You have led a life of failure," he says. "You have drunk and fooled around with your so-called friends, who in reality have been your enemies; you have played music for dancing in that terrible place The Dolphin; you have been in the grip of evil powers."

"But that is all past now, Kornelius. The time for renewal has come; you are now approaching a purging and rejuvenation. You must soon confess your guilt. You know what is at play. If you are solely responsible for your evil deeds, Kornelius, as a Christian man you will not leave your innocent brethren and your other friends in the lurch. And if they have been part of the plot, then you can also save them by confessing. You can give them a chance, Kornelius, a chance through confession, penance and repentance of arising again with purified souls in the life beyond and of joining in the hymn of the saved:

> The blind can see and the deaf can hear
> The timid believe and no longer feel fear
> The mute now sing in joyful key
> And the lame spring merrily on the lea.

The disgusting hymn has a cooling effect on Kornelius, who after all is a musical person. But the thought of being able to save Moritz and the others . . . that lights a spark and grows inside him, for the only bulwark in his mind that does not give way in this night of trial and destruction is his kind heart. Kornelius is no great man, and he is only a poor amateur, in life and in music, but his heart shelters the simple grandeur of an honest man.

As the days pass, Kornelius gradually reaches the culmination of his scruples and establishes a certain balance. His speculations reach their limit and run in rings like fish in an aquarium. Finally be becomes dizzy and sickened by thinking a thought. He simply thinks: "Moritz will go back to Eliana as an innocent man, and they will look after Kornelia. Moritz will play for her. And he can play the cello as well. And when she hears the cello, she will be happy. For it's the cello she loves. And Ole Brandy will go back to his hut, and Olivarius to that lovely big loft of his, and Jakob Siff to his little shop, and Josef the Lament to his carpenter's workshop. And then all will be well again.

And the *treasure* – how totally irrelevant it is for you. If all those things about Matte-Gok and the divining rod were lies then it doesn't matter. If the money's been burnt, then it doesn't matter. If it never returns it doesn't matter. Finished with it. Now a new time is starting. Now you can rest."

So it goes with Kornelius. He sleeps abnormally long and often; he eats his food, lies listening to music deep within himself, in short, he starts to take comfort in the new life and to gather his strength to resists its pressures. He slowly falls back into place.

On Kronfeldt, the Chief Adminstrator, Kornelius's confession had the effect of a cooling shower of rain on a intolerably close and thundery summer's day. Kronfeldt had in truth recently begun to fear that one of Pommerencke's clever hypotheses might, contrary to all reason, be right and put his own simple and natural view to shame. But, thank God, it had once more been confirmed that the shortest way between two points is a straight line. The little wretch had made a clean confession of everything. Of course. It had all been totally plain sailing for him. The late Magister Mortensen's irresponsible carelessness with his money cried out to high heaven and so to speak issued an invitation to any convenient thief; indeed, not only was it tempting for his nearest neighbour to appropriate this homeless money, it was almost inevitable, so to speak, ha, ha. And the sloppiness in the savings bank had almost been on a level with Mortensen's. Now that madman Ankersen would get it in the neck, perhaps even lose his job, and that was something he richly deserved. He could look after the bank's money instead of going around and making an exhibition of himself. This was not the legendary age of knights.

Kronfeldt rubbed his hands and clicked his tongue.

"It's all right, Charlotte. *It's all right*."

The judge, on the other hand had certain hesitations about the little typographer's unreserved confession. Admittedly, it had generally speaking confirmed the pathological hypothesis devised by Dr Manicus and himself. And yet. Deep down inside him, he had no confidence in the confession and dared not take it at face value. But the strange case had to take its course. He gathered the documents together and gave a careful account of every detail. He enclosed a statement from Manicus to the effect that it was desirable that Kornelius Isaksen should be subjected to a thorough mental examination.

And so, one fine day Kornelius was sent out of the country, leaving his native town in a state of general confusion.

Those who saw him go on board were amazed that he was so calm and so unchanged. The kindly, slightly absent-minded smile, the underhung jaw, the pince-nez, everything was as before. Kornelius was just as he had always been. He was the old Kornelius.

A few days later, Ura the Brink was discharged from hospital. She was able to walk only with the aid of two crutches. For the time being, she moved into Kornelius's flat in the Bastille. The first thing she did on her return was to send for Moritz and Ole Brandy.

"Now, Kornelius has been sent off like a confounded robber," she said. "But who is the robber?"

"Matte-Gok," said Ole Brandy. "But can *you* prove that?"

Ura could not. She sat writhing.

"I think justice will be done at last," said Moritz.

"No," said Ura. "Not unless someone helps it on its way."

Ura raised a finger in the air, shook her head and said with closed eyes: "I have asked and implored my sister to go through Matte-Gok's belongings, to open his drawers, to search his bed, behind the wallpaper, everywhere. I *know* the money's there! I've had a vision of it and dreamt it time after time. But she *will not*. She is completely taken in by him, the foolish old bird. She thinks I'm the one who's mad. She talks to me like a child."

Ura pointed to Moritz: "But now, Moritz, you must get to the bottom of the matter. Understand? In one way or another you must get into his room."

"Has he got to break in?" asked Ole Brandy sarcastically. "You'll never ever get Moritz to do that. But, I've got a bloody good idea . . .!"

Ole slapped his thigh: "I know how, Ura. I know how."

Ura suddenly burst into laughter. She had one of her old attacks of laughing; she clapped her hands and suddenly acquired a quite young, bashful look in her face. "Ole's got an idea," she said. "Of course he knows how."

Ole Brandy had straight away thought of the gravedigger's son Peter. If anyone was good at breaking in, it was he. The boy simply never did anything else. And if he was always breaking in and doing damage to others and bringing disgrace to himself, why not for once commit a useful break-in in a good cause?

"I'll stand by you," he said to the boy. "If anyone ends in the clink, it'll be me. And I'll tell them why, as well. And even if you don't find a bean, my boy, you shall have five kroner as a reward."

The break-in took place that very evening. It was easy to do. The house was empty. Ankersen, Matte-Gok and Mrs Midiord were all three at a meeting in Ydun. The main door was locked, but you could get in through the cellar. But Matte-Gok's door was also locked, so it was necessary to start over again. His window was ajar. Peter clambered up the rowan trellis. Ole Brandy kept watch and kept the boy informed by means of various ways of clearing his throat and coughing.

Peter spent such a long time in Matte-Gok's room that Ole had to go right up to the window and cough and splutter to get him out again, for it was getting on for the time the sectarians would be coming back from Ydun.

Finally, the boy showed in the window. Ole ducked down and disappeared.

They met again a little later down in Ole's boathouse. Peter brought with him a small brown leather attaché case. "I looked everywhere," he said. "There was only one drawer, the drawer in the washstand, but it wasn't there. Then I looked under the bed and in the bed and in his clothes hanging in the wardrobe, and on top of and underneath the wardrobe and behind it and behind the washstand and under the carpet and in the seat of the chair and in the curtains, and I felt to see whether there were any lumps behind the wallpaper and the millboard lining the walls. There was nothing there, but I couldn't open this, and so . . ."

Ole Brandy could not get the attaché case open either. He took his knife and made a cut in the leather. Papers. By God!

But no money. Only religious pieces, tracts, issues of The Messenger.

Ole Brandy flung down the case, kicked it, stamped on it. Poured petrol on it and set fire to it. His eyes and earrings glinted in the light from the flames, and his broken nose was all shiny. At that moment he could have incinerated Matte-Gok and Ankersen in their home. He wished with all his strength that something appalling might befall them.

When the fire had been put out, he turned towards the boy, who was standing shrinking back in the darkness, tired and patiently waiting, and his thoughts were suddenly filled with regret and tenderness. He took the boy by the shoulder and asked him to go back to the hut with him. Here, he opened a drawer in the old chest of drawers and took out a shaggy, grey purse.

"See here," he said in a kindly voice and gave the boy two gold coins. "They're worth twenty kroner together," he said. "You shall have them. And then promise me to be a good lad in future. Come to me if you need money or if there's anything you're in doubt about. And then I honestly think you ought to go to sea and start a real man's life like I did at your age. And if you go along with that, then I promise I'll find you a job under a really fine, honest skipper so you won't come to regret anything."

And with a little sigh, he pressed Peter's hand.

Human charity and sacrifice are often to be seen at their best when there is a matter that enjoys popular support. There was hardly any end to the interest that was shown to Kornelia and her old mother now they had lost their breadwinner in such dramatic circumstances. Scarcely a day passed without their having visits, not only from friends and acquaintances, but also from people they had never before even exchanged a word with, and folk sent them eggs and milk, cakes, bread and coffee. Consul Hansen sent them eight sacks of coal. The Reverend Fruelund came and said a few consolatory words.

And the welfare committee from the Ydun Christian Temperance Committee with Ankersen at its head came and offered to find accommodation for them. The condition: they should become members of the Association, make public confession of their sins, promise penance and repentance, take part in public prayers and so on. And the town council also turned up with similar offers, though on different conditions. Ura thanked them emotionally, but was able to tell them that Ole Brandy had already long ago been kind enough to place his home at their disposal, just as he – together with Olivarius, Janniksen, Mac Bett and other friends – had undertaken to see to their everyday needs.

So much charity at one time can easily become a burden on the person who is its object. Ura was hard of hearing, old and handicapped and secretly wished that she could soon put the entire fuss behind her. She felt almost refreshed one day when a man came along with nothing apart from an old-fashioned bill. This man was Wenningstedt, the solicitor. He looked carefully around the little sitting room and sat down on the sofa with a nod.

"Well, it's about a quarter's rent," he said in a kindly voice. "What are we going to do about it? And then there's another thing: I've had several offers for this flat, and I heard this very day that the town council . . .? Oh, you're moving down to Ole Olsen? Well then, that's splendid. The day after tomorrow? Then perhaps Olsen will attend to this little bill? Yes, I'll have a word with him about that."

Wenningstedt again gave a kindly nod and waggled his ears while secretly looking at the blind Kornelia who, despite repeated attempts previously, he had never been fortunate enough to see at close quarters. Oh, so that's what she looked like. Not bad at all. Not at all. And rumours that she was expecting were simply nonsense. Not the least sign of it. As thin as a rake.

The solicitor shook hands on leaving. He went on thinking

as he went down the stairs: "Generous of Ole Brandy. Very generous indeed. Hm. Ulterior motives, I wonder? The girl doesn't look at all repulsive. And the old woman's deaf and slow. But . . . a blind person! It would be a disgrace. Fundamentally a disgrace. But perhaps it has a special charm for that very reason, who knows?"

A couple of days later, the two women moved down into Ole Brandy's shack. He had made sure he had mucked out and cleaned the sitting room and kitchen, and he had moved his own bed up into the loft. The sitting room was unrecognisable when he came home that evening. Curtains had appeared at the windows, and all Boman's composers had been fixed up on the walls. However, the old pictures of Vesuvius by Night and Vesuvius by Day, which had hitherto been the only decorations in the house, still hung in their places above the chest of drawers. As was only to be expected.

Ole Brandy was no angel, of course, and that evening when he had gone to bed up in the narrow loft where it had just been possible to find room for a bed and he lay listening to the womenfolk bustling about in the sitting room downstairs, he felt like a man who has to admit that his golden freedom is, if not gone, then at least greatly circumscribed. But that was how it must be. There was no room here for regret. He had felt it as his duty to look after those Kornelius had left behind so as to avoid their falling a burden on the parish. He had a perfectly good conscience.

And aboard his boat he was at least, thank God, still himself.

What thoughts moved in Kornelia's head will ever remain a secret. Outwardly she gave no indication. It might look as though she was entirely unaffected by the entire fuss. Even in the courtroom she was amazingly composed and showed no sign of emotion. This surprised a lot of people; indeed there was a small number who felt incensed by it and believed that the young woman was in reality a hard person without any deeper emotions. Others maintained that she hid her reactions behind a mask of studied calm. Others again believed that the poor girl, like Kornelius himself, had been subjected to Ura's magic powers in every respect. Doctor Manicus was inclined to the view that Kornelius Isaksen's wife was infantile both in body and mind, and that her understanding was that of a five-year-old child. But that, too, was only a guess.

Certain it is, however, that Kornelia bore her fate with a patience that is beyond the understanding of ordinary mortals.

FOURTH MOVEMENT

Relating the sad ending, but at the same time giving hope of something new and better

1

*New remarkable excesses in the Ydun Association,
speaking in tongues and ritual dance and finally what
we have all long hoped for: the downfall of the monster
Matte-Gok*

One has to associate something unreal with Matte-Gok; in a
way he has no face, no human soul. He is merely present as
a cold and incontestable force. With his hawk-like profile
he resembles the god *Ra* with the inhuman bird's head. He is a
monster, a lone bird of misfortune, a low-flying lurking bird of
prey.

Never mind that in comparison with other birds of prey
and vultures he is only a poor sparrow hawk. In his way,
he nevertheless represents a great evil in his day, the cynical,
brutal rapacity of mankind, the dark and demonic exploitative
forces that embrace our human world with their vast octopus
tendrils and feed on our foolishness and sentimental patience.

But in the case of Matte-Gok our patience is at an end. His
days are counted.

A noticeable change has recently come over Moritz. He has
become pale and forbidding, indeed he is greying at the
temples and has acquired sharp lines around his mouth. And
he has become restless and preoccupied, too; he never touches
the violin, and his good-humoured singing is heard no more.

He is no longer good company either at home or outside.
He is turning into an irritable sourpuss and pessimist; indeed
at times he can be so quick-tempered that his wife and children
can hardly believe their own eyes and ears.

And he has turned teetotal. That was not a bad thing in

itself, of course, if only he had not at the same time become such a crosspatch.

"He'll get over it," Ole Brandy says in an attempt to comfort Eliana. "You'll see, he'll get over it. It's this affair with Kornelius that's done this to him. It's Matte-Gok he's mad with. It's Matte-Gok and Ankersen we're all bloody furious with. But just you wait, just you wait."

Ole Brandy, Olivarius, Lindenskov, Mac Bett and Janniksen put their heads together out in The Dolphin. They agree that something ought to be done to cheer Moritz up. But how? They are all pretty miserable as well. In truth, it's a hell of a mess.

"Yes, a hell of a mess," confirms Jacobsen the editor. He, too, is experiencing a humiliating time; his face has become old and worn, and he has grown a straggly beard. "Injustice is having a heyday," he says. "That sectarian folly is spreading like an epidemic. Before long they'll even manage to introduce a total ban on alcohol. Then you won't be able to buy yourself as much as a perfectly ordinary beer."

"As long as they can't forbid ships to sail the seas," says Ole Brandy darkly, "every honest sailor will always be able to get the drink he wants if he can be bothered."

Ole Brandy empties his glass. He empties large numbers of glasses, and so do the others. But there is no joy in it any more, no singing and music, no brightness, only sweat and burdensome thoughts. Ole Brandy staggers home, blind drunk and angry, clouded by sorrow and inchoate thoughts of revenge. He drinks heavily for a week.

Then he suddenly completely vanishes from the scene. He is in gaol again. He has attacked Matte-Gok. He has been guilty of a brutal, foolish attack one dark evening in Sexton Lane, where he stood watching Matte-Gok and Ankersen on their way home from a prayer meeting. Matte-Gok made no resistance. He was struck straight in the face and bled like fury. He might even have been killed if Ankersen hadn't made an enormous fuss and kerfuffle and called for help while doing his best to harpoon the treacherous assailant with the ferrule from his umbrella.

Matte-Gok wanted the matter dealt with amicably. "The man's mad, of course," he said. Indeed he even went to the length of defending him: "Ole and I are good friends of long standing," he said. "There's nothing evil about Ole, he can just not take all this terrible drink. But the days of drink will soon be passed, thank God."

However, the authorities saw things differently. It was necessary to make an example in this instance as a warning to others. Ole Brandy was gaoled for fourteen days on bread and water.

Meanwhile, the time for Matte-Gok's departure is approaching. The mood among the sectarians varies between melancholy and elation at the prospect of victory.

The last evening in Ydun took the form of a sectarian orgy in a grand apocalyptic manner.

Ankersen had had the idea that Matte-Gok should be *anointed*. Nillegaard was very much opposed to this, which he maintained was a reversion to heathen barbarity, but Ankersen could triumphantly counter this by referring to an array of biblical quotations. It is a good old Christian custom, he maintained, excellent practice that has been neglected for far too long.

Attendance in the meeting house that evening beat all earlier records. Every inch of floor space inside was occupied, both in the hall and in the entrance, and outside there was a Babylonian confusion of inquisitive figures desperately seeking to ensure a place for themselves in the open doorway or in front of one of the windows. It was a raw, cold evening, and those who were standing outside in the dark shivered with cold, excitement and fearful misgivings. From inside came the sound of ecstatic singing, which gradually dissolved into shouts of joy. Strange things happened in Ydun that evening, things unheard of, indeed sheer miracles according to what some people said. Mrs Midiord, Ankersen's housekeeper, who until now had always kept modestly in the background, stood forth and spoke in tongues. She had brought with her a palm branch from Ankersen's sitting room, and she waved it about as she spoke. Mrs Ida Nillegaard, the midwife, answered her in the same language. It was so upsetting to see that several people fainted, and the Weeper burst out laughing.

While all this was going on there came the penetrating sound of a horn from a steamer. It was the Mjølnir, the ship Matte-Gok was to leave on. It had arrived earlier than expected, and a messenger had been sent ashore to announce that it was to continue its voyage south straight away; there was only an hour to play with. Moritz quickly made his boat ready. There were only four passengers to be taken out, and he quickly had three of them informed and ferried on board, but then there was the fourth, Matte-Gok. How was he to get in touch with him? It would be almost impossible to force his way through the crowd at the entrance to the meeting house. But it simply had to be done. Moritz elbowed his way forward; he was almost desperate. Hey, hey, said some and elbowed him in return; others thought there was a fire, and here and there there were signs of panic.

When Moritz had finally fought his way into the hall and made himself heard with his message about the ship leaving, Ankersen shouted back with the full force of his lungs: "*There is no ship!*"

Ankersen was flushed and puffed up as never before; his eyes were virtually boiling in his head. He repeated: "There can be no question of a ship here! All there is room for here is the living word!"

But Matte-Gok saw things differently. He was suddenly in a hurry. He managed to make himself heard and with a calm, bold voice shouted: "Friends! The time for parting has arrived. But be not upset that I am leaving. It is only my earthly flesh that is going, only my frame. I remain in your hearts as a spirit."

There were several who were unwilling to accept this, but Matte-Gok was adamant: he had to leave. "My heart bleeds," he said. "But you cannot drag me back from my calling. The call is stronger. The call is the strongest thing in a human life."

"Right," howled Ankersen. "The call is the strongest. The call is the strongest."

"Yes, the call is the strongest," screamed Mrs Janniksen.

"*Medefigis epa abetesda*," shouted a joyous Mrs Midiord, and Mrs Nillegaard replied with her eyes closed and almost without moving her lips: "*Esse eh! Esse eh!*."

Nothing like it had ever been seen before; it was all so strange, so terrible, so completely outside of ordinary experience. But the most remarkable thing of all, the most dreadful thing, came only after Matte-Gok had uttered a last brief prayer and started moving.

Alas, it ought never to have happened; it brought confusion and destruction in its wake, indeed it had the effect of an ugly black jet from a fire extinguisher in the midst of a living bonfire of wild rejoicing and unquestioning faith.

At first it was thought it entailed an unfortunate accident of the sort that might happen to anyone. It was thought that Mrs Midiord had got her blouse badly torn in the general mêlée. But when she also started ripping her skirt to pieces, people understood that something was seriously wrong. Those closest to her tried to interfere, but the old lady was completely beside herself; she tore herself away and started to perform a dance, dressed only in her black, half-length cotton knickers! Now, this was not in itself an inelegant dance; no, it was performed not without a certain dignity, and older observers also remembered that in her youth Mrs Midiord had had a slender figure and had been much in demand at balls at that time. She was a remarkable sight, but not really immodest, and it would not have been so bad if only Mrs Nillegaard had restrained herself. But she also suddenly throws herself into the dance, and she is virtually stark naked. In the confusion, people never really decided how naked she was, for it only lasted for a couple of seconds before her husband threw himself at her and covered her with his jacket. Others took care of Mrs Midiord. The old lady smiled, tired and compliant. But she was still talking in tongues. And so she did for the rest of her life.

When Matte-Gok had finally torn himself away from Anker-sen's embrace and got on board the ferryboat with his two suitcases, the steamer sounded its horn for departure.

"Quick," he nudged Moritz fiercely. He was sweating. His hair fell untidily down over his forehead. He looked fierce and forgot his part. "Get a bloody move on!"

"We've plenty of time," said Moritz to calm him down. "They've got to raise the anchor first. That takes at least a quarter of an hour. People often go out as late as this."

The boat slid out into the darkness. It was a cold but calm evening with clouds and stars. Matte-Gok was dressed in a new grey ulster and looked like a perfectly ordinary commercial traveller.

"You're going to have good weather," said Moritz. Matte-Gok nodded.

They were approaching the illuminated steamship. Matte-Gok was already rummaging in his pocket to find money to pay the ferryman, but Moritz now suddenly changed course . . . Matte-Gok immediately suspected trouble, and he got up. "What the bloody hell . . .?" he said, grinding his teeth.

Moritz took no notice. The boat sailed on.

"Oh, that's what you're up to," said Matte-Gok between gritted teeth. "But you've got another think coming, you lout."

With hands outstretched, he staggered towards Moritz, but at that moment the boat made a sharp turn so he lost his balance and had to sit down and lean back.

"You bastard," he hissed.

Moritz waited until Matte-Gok had got to his feet again, and then he again gave the boat a sharp turn and at the same time made it rock back and forth. Matte-Gok had to lean forwards and hold fast on the thwart. But at that moment Moritz got up, grabbed the handle of the club-shaped ladle and gave him a powerful blow on the head. Then another blow, and then another.

Matte-Gok collapsed without a sound. The boat continued at full speed out into the darkness. The sound of the steamer's windlass made itself heard. Silence descended. Moritz sat down. His heart was beating in competition with the engine. He was unable to collect his thoughts. For a moment he wished that Matte-Gok would get up again or even just move a little.

But Matte-Gok remained there. Moritz saw with horror how blood was trickling from his head and running in two dark lines down his coat. So it had happened after all.

Moritz got up blindly. He loosened the lamp from the prow of the boat, put it down on the floorboards and spread his jacket over it. Then he had to go back to the rudder, and there he sat, while the boat forged on in the darkness.

It had happened.

A bright star was shining ahead. The dog star. It twinkled and changed colour. The steamer issued three short blasts and started off. Before long, it had glided past. The lights slowly disappeared in the distance. Moritz was sweating all over, despite sitting in his shirt sleeves. He passed the northernmost point of Seal Island, moving out to sea. There was no way back.

A weak, bubbling sound came from the slumped figure on the thwart, a slight sign of life. Moritz started shivering; he curled up in disgust and horror; he had difficulty in suppressing a moan. Suddenly he got up, filled with agony; he lifted the limp body and with some difficulty managed to push it overboard. There was a little splash. Then it was done. So that, too, was done.

Now all that was left were the two suitcases. He took out his knife and cut one open, rummaging through it in feverish haste. A bottle. A pair of new shoes. Sobbing, he ripped a hole in the other. *The money* – it must surely be in that suitcase. Or was it all simply a lie?

Yes. There it was. It lay bundled together in a leather bag at the bottom of the suitcase. He uncovered the lamp for a moment and saw the golden brown and greyish green notes. He put out the light. The boat was moving rapidly further out to sea in this cloudy night. The great star could be seen again for a moment. It twinkled and changed colour, one moment ruby, the next bluish white, then the next again an icy green like death itself.

Moritz remained at his oars all night, completely stiff and drained of all thought.

When dawn came he got up with difficulty and took hold of the can containing the reserve petrol. There must be an end to this. Now this, too, must happen.

The thought enlivened him and almost did him good, crushing as it was.

He remembered the time he saved the seven men from the Karelia. He remembered the dark night when he had been thrown ashore at Stake Point and had felt death's teeth in his throat, and the wonderful afternoon of the church concert when he had drifted out to sea together with the count's red currant wine. And the rescue and the festive return. Oh well. All that was finished now.

It was not easy to utter those words: now it is finished. They stuck in his throat like fragments of glass; they couldn't be swallowed, they hurt and tore at him, they drove him to unworthy acts, he wept and howled madly out in the dark morning to give vent to his feelings, he turned the boat and steered back towards land, but it was in vain, he couldn't do that . . . He was himself again; he pulled himself together once more in his decision to put an end to it all. But first he would send Eliana a greeting. There was a bottle here, and he had a stump of pencil in his pocket; and there was paper, too; there were the banknotes for instance. He opened the bottle; it was a black bottle with no label; he smelt the contents; it was old rum, but that didn't matter, he had no desire to taste it. He emptied the bottle over the side of the boat. And then there was the question of what he should write.

Hours passed before Moritz came to a decision as to what should be written on the note. The sky was ready to burst forth in light grey, and the sun appeared in this showery grey like a veiled moon. Finally, he wrote the difficult words: "To Eliana. Love from your Moritz. We shall meet again."

He put the stopper in the bottle, threw it overboard and watched it with empty eyes until it had bobbed away and disappeared among the waves.

Then he took the can of reserve petrol again. With

trembling hands he poured the clear fluid all over the boat and put a match to it. He waited until the fire had spread so much that the heat was more than he could stand, and his clothes had started smoking. Then, with a wild cry, he leapt overboard.

2

The mangle house

So Moritz, in a musical sense the finest of our poor doomed musicians, has also left the story. The exact details of his disappearance were never known. The ferryboat was sought intensively and for a long time, but without result.

There would not really have been anything surprising about this if the evening in question had been stormy. It had happened before that the motor had broken down and the boat had drifted away. But in calm weather? The boat must have sunk in some way. But how? An explosion in the engine, fire on board? But that kind of thing would inevitably have been observed from the shore.

There was something fundamentally mysterious about it all. And still more mysterious did it become when, some time later, it became known that Matte-Gok had not been a passenger on the Mjølnir at all.

So the boat carrying the two men had for some reason never reached the ship.

And now the guessing game really gets under way. The entire town is seething and resounding with rumours. Again, something dreadful and mysterious has happened. But what?

"It's quite simple," says Ole Brandy to Constable Debes. "Moritz has killed Matte-Gok. It's as simple and straightforward as that. And then he's gone off to sea. It's like him. And then he's been fished up by some foreign ship. And of course he wouldn't admit who he was, 'cause he's not going to risk having his head chopped off just because he's done his duty. And you'll see, he'll come back one day when it's all forgotten. I know him."

"Yes, but what about the boat? It had both a name and a registration number," countered Debes.

"Aye, but he's taken those number plates off in good time, of course," says Ole. It's as easy as falling off a log. It might be that in his place you'd have forgotten to think about it, Ludvig, but Moritz wasn't such a fool. He was a stout fellow, and so he had to kill Matte-Gok, and God bless him for *that*."

"You'd better be quiet," warned the constable. "You'd better watch your tongue."

But Ole Brandy did not watch his tongue regarding what he considered to be justice and truth. As soon as he had been released from prison, he went straight to the Bastille to comfort Eliana and her children.

"He's not dead. He'll come back. As sure as my name's Ole Olsen, known as Ole Brandy, and my father's name was also Ole Olsen, known as Ole the Jib, and my grandfather's name was also Ole Olsen, known as Strong Ole."

Eliana opened her red-ringed eyes and surrendered herself to staring out in the air. He could see that his words were doing her good. He thought to himself: "Eliana is one of those hope people. People who hope. Always hope. People who hope never become completely unhappy, for they have the hope that they hope for. You've got to strengthen people of that kind by pouring more oil on their hope."

"I daren't believe that," said Eliana.

"Then what do you believe?" asked Ole sarcastically. "Do you think they've gone off together and shared the spoils? No, there you see."

"They might have killed each other," sighed Eliana with a shudder. She dried her eyes with a corner of her apron.

"And then drilled a hole in the boat afterwards?" laughed Ole scornfully. "Or what's become of it? Can you think of a better explanation? No, of course not – there you see again."

"The sea is so vast," sighed Eliana.

"You'll get a letter from him one day," said Ole, untouched by the size of the ocean. "Shall we bet? A letter without the sender's address, of course, 'cause he knows what he's doing. He'll write that he's well and living off Matte-Gok's money.

277

Because he has genuinely and honestly deserved that for his trouble. And then it might even be that he can buy Kornelius's freedom. We've heard things as mad as that before. You know the old songs, Eliana."

Eliana took Ole's hand and patted it gratefully. "I know you mean well by me, Ole."

"She has hope," thought Ole. "She's a hope person." He turned his face away. He was moved. He drew is hand back on the pretence of wanting to cut himself a plug.

That same afternoon, Eliana received a visit from Wenningstedt the solicitor. He came, he said, to talk about the future.

Wenningstedt had not been tactless; he had waited with this visit until it could be thought that the first shock had worn off and the mourning had glided over into the more contemplative stage of melancholy. Not only had he a certain liking for Eliana, he had in reality the deepest sympathy for her, indeed he was really fond of her. This woman was a tower of strength. The only positive one in the whole crowd. And at the same time, she was still not lacking in charm. What a pity, he had often thought, what a pity that this girl, who in reality was so splendid, should have sunk down in the mire, this girl who could easily have had nothing to worry about if she had behaved reasonably and followed well-intentioned people's advice at the right time.

Girls with her looks always had plenty of good chances, indeed wonderful chances. But the female mind is injudicious. Injudicious to a shocking, stupid extent.

And yet, when foolish girls have been married for a number of years or have been widowed, their reason sometimes seems to awaken. Especially when they have been slightly worn out. Which Eliana, however, had not really become although thirteen years had passed since this . . . oh, let us not say anything disadvantageous about him: this *ferryman*. There were really many good things to be said about him. Rash, somewhat stupid, but a fine man. A good-looking man. But . . . thirteen years, good heavens, is it really so long ago? Aye, time passes, and we grow old before we realise it.

The solicitor had taken a seat and sat staring before him in benevolent recollection. He had a good, positive proposal to make to the young widow. But that was not something you blurted out straight away. First a few words of sympathy, as an introduction, and a little silence and sadness.

On the occasion when this ferryman had disappeared at sea together with Count Oldendorf ... for a moment it had seemed to Wenningstedt almost to go without saying: she'll come to you. It's obvious. It's your fate that she'll come. It can't be otherwise. It was as it were in the air. And the same was true now. It was as it were a matter of course that it must happen.

To the accompaniment of suitable tact and caution, Wenningstedt gradually revealed his plan. It was that Eliana and her children should leave the Bastille and move into the house that had belonged to the late Marie the Mangle down by the stream. It was still for sale and was going cheap. He had himself been there and inspected the house. It was not bad at all, this place known as the Mangle House. And here, there would not only be a question of a roof over her head, but also of an assured livelihood for whoever was prepared to take on the mangling and perhaps also do a bit of washing and ironing for people.

Eliana was grateful for the idea and immediately agreed to it.

"Good, for you can hardly live in this place during the winter," she said. "The Mangle House is far nicer and warmer even if it is on the small side."

"But it's for sale, not for rent," said the solicitor, making a pause. "It costs just under 700 kroner," he added. "Which must be said to be a bit much for that house. But so much has been spent on it that it won't go for less."

Again a pause.

"Yes, it's a lot of money," said Eliana hesitantly.

"But I'll buy it," continued the solicitor, shuffling excitedly in his chair. "Shall we say that, Eliana? I'll buy it."

An emotional tone had crept into his voice. He was going to add: "And then I've thought that you shall live there rent free until we see whether the business succeeds. And if not, then we'll take things as they are."

But Eliana got in first: "And then you'll rent it to me, Wenningstedt! Oh, how kind of you. For we'll make a go of the laundry; there are five women here, and both Franziska and Amadea and Rita are ever so good with their hands and they'll soon be grown girls. And then we've something honest to live on while we . . . while we wait."

Eliana blushed, which made her look particularly attractive; indeed, at this moment she resembled herself as a young girl, when she was a waitress in The Dolphin and he used to frequent that grubby pub for *her* sake and only for that.

She added with a smile, giving the solicitor a sideways glance from her inclined head: "Well, perhaps you'll think I'm a bit . . . a bit too hopeful, Wenningstedt. But I have decided to wait."

"Oh, wait?" said Wenningstedt with a look of incomprehension. "How? Oh."

"Yes, wait for Moritz to come back," explained Eliana with a determined toss of her head.

"Oh, I see," said the solicitor, coughing several times as though he had a frog in his throat. "Yes, of course. Naturally."

"*Or*," added Eliana in a determined voice, "Or until we know for certain that he's not alive."

"Yes, but . . . no, of course," coughed the solicitor.

Eliana took his hand and, filled with gratitude, said, "I'll never forget your kindness to us, Wenningstedt. Many, many thanks indeed."

As he slowly strolled home through the cobbled alleyway again, Wenningstedt thought, "What optimism! Good heavens! Aye, it's all crazy. Completely crazy. Completely crazy."

A couple of weeks later, Eliana and her children and foster children moved over into the Mangle House. It coincided with a period of dark, oppressive rain; the river outside thundered on its stony watercourse outside the small rain-blinded windows, and the mangle rumbled inside the little room with the bare wooden walls. It was a big professional mangle, so heavy to handle that it only really got going when all the children helped out, but it was nevertheless a success – Orfeus, who by now was a big boy, made a useful contribution, and Ole Brandy, the Weeper and other friends and acquaintances often came and lent a hand.

One day, the Crab King turned up. He stood for several hours staring at the big boulders from the river, now shiny from wear, that lay in the upper part of the mangle and radiated a strange subterranean warmth. But he didn't think of helping Eliana and the children who were toiling away pushing the heavy trolley backwards and forwards over the rollers.

"Try to see how strong you are, just once for fun, Poul Peter," suggested Eliana merrily.

The Crab King immediately disappeared through the door. But shortly afterwards and looking rather tense, he came back and took hold of the mangle and showed what strength was hidden in his heavy torso.

The Crab King came back the following day, and it ended with his actually being permanently employed in Eliana's mangle business. When he came one day to see how the business was going, Wenningstedt started at the remarkable sight encountering him. Eliana was not at home, but the mangle was working all out. At one end stood the Crab King on a foundation consisting of biscuit boxes; at the other end was Ole Brandy, and up on the trolley sat Mortensen's daft daughter and two other girls, mangling with every sign of enjoyment. And over by the window stood the boy Orfeus scraping away at his violin for all he was worth.

Ole Brandy stopped the mangle for a moment, puffed some acrid, inhospitable clouds of tobacco into the solicitor's face and said, "Did you want something?"

Wenningsted withdrew, shaking his head, and the mangling started again.

"That's what you get for your kindness," he thought.

Well – kindness and kindness. Wenningstedt was no hypocrite, whatever else could be said to his detriment. He had lived too much in isolation and useful contemplation for that. He was a practical man, a rationalist who had spent most of his almost sixty years delicately pulling other people's chestnuts out of the fire in return for a suitable fee. And as he was by nature frugal, he had in time become a wealthy and relatively happy man. But occasionally, and in recent times more frequently, he was pestered by a painful feeling of having been cheated out of one of the most essential things. He would not sentimentalise and call it *love* – that sounded a bit too much like Ankersen. But then: *woman*.

He was fond of women in the way typical of men – that is to say in the same way as a lepidopterist is fond of butterflies: they are worthy of admiration and they must be caught. To do this demands both caution and resolute action. Wenningstedt had never been short on cautious consideration, but on the few occasions on which he had shown resolution he had not been favoured by fortune, and now he must really hurry if he was ever to have any hope of seeing a butterfly in his net.

It is not surprising that he had chosen Eliana, for she was one of those women whom it is no disgrace to have on the brain.

Wenningstedt willingly admitted to himself that he had got Eliana on the brain. The young widow had an electrifying effect on him in his solitude. Even though she was not particularly young any longer, but thirty-three or thirty-four, she was in fact still the lovely girl from The Dolphin, the girl he could never forget. And that this woman should now as it were come his way was not unreasonable; it was as it should be. It was his turn. It was quite natural. And he had made a good start. He had looked after her, shown her attention and given her positive and tangible support, and she had shown herself to be gracious and grateful.

Perhaps she might even quite simply have said yes if it were not that she had these foolish and ridiculous hopes that her husband would return. Was it possible in some cautious manner to convince her that this was in vain? But take it easy. The future would take care of itself.

But Wenningstedt was terribly wrong in this, for now fate again played a trick on him. It turned out to be none other than Wenningstedt who found Moritz's bottle message.

It happened on one of the solicitor's frequent lonely meditative walks along the shore, one bitterly cold and windy day in February. A shiny black bottle is bobbing about pointlessly among the stones in a little inlet, and he suddenly has a boyish urge to demolish this lonely bottle. He raises the handle of his walking stick to smash it, but realises at that moment that there is a cork in the bottle and that it might possibly contain a message.

And right enough, there is a piece of paper in the bottle. A five hundred kroner note! Heavens above! And across the note, in clumsy blue writing: "To Eliana. Love from your Moritz. We shall meet again."

Deep in thought, Wenningstedt folded the green note together and put it in his wallet.

"We shall meet again," he thought. "Oh. We'll meet again. But in what circumstances, my dear sir? Perhaps it'll be best to keep quiet about this."

He kept quiet. However, it must be said in his favour that he suffered to some extent as a result of this silence and had some difficulty convincing himself that he was maintaining it for humane reasons.

Wenningstedt remained silent for all of three months. Then the kindness within him finally got the better of him; he decided to sacrifice his own possible happiness and give Eliana the note. But before this was done, he suddenly died one day of a heart attack.

Wenningstedt left a considerable fortune of over a hundred thousand kroner. It went to his sole heir, his sister Alvilda, who was married to the young Consul Hansen. But – to be on the safe side – he had left the house with the mangle and the wash boiler to Eliana.

The two women showed their gratitude in the most pleasing way, the sister by erecting a tall, polished basalt stone in memory of her brother, bearing the inscription "Blessed are the pure in heart", Eliana by planting a wild rose at the foot of this stone. As the years went by, the wild rose bush grew up around the stone and completely covered the inscription with its exuberant profusion of greenery.

And days and nights pass, the mangle turns, the mill of time grinds on. It grinds new events, or perhaps merely the familiar grey dust of which everyday life is composed. Today is mercilessly ground into yesterday, yesterday to the day before and the day before yesterday into the grey mass of the past, which then can condense and assume a historical perspective that just as often merges into darkness and legend, hints and suspicions and secrets that are never cleared up.

3

The poet and the moon

Sirius lies contemplating the full moon.

He has again moved over into the house belonging to Mac Bett the decorator and is now living in the little garret above what was once the classroom.

Yes, Sirius had been coughing and going downhill for a long time, and at last he had gone to the doctor, who had examined his chest and discovered it was rather seriously affected. This led to his having to stay in bed, which in itself really raised a lot of doubts. But on the other hand, Sirius was genuinely happy to be alone again. His brief life together with Julia had been agony to him, partly because it had become increasingly clear how unsuited the two were to each other, and partly on account of the contempt and coldness constantly emanating from the blacksmith's wife.

As for Janniksen himself, he had throughout behaved as Sirius's friend and paternal protector, and the same could be said without hesitation of Mac Bett. After Julia had given birth to a healthy daughter in November and the doctor had pointed out to the family that Sirius's presence was undesirable as he must be considered infectious, the two men had conferred briefly and reached the decision leading to the present arrangement.

So now Sirius is lying in his old room and can generally speaking have things as he wishes. The blacksmith ensures that he gets what he needs apart from paper to write on. But here, Mac Bett has stepped in to help and given the poet a lot of old wallpaper off-cuts that he has cut and stapled together to make books.

These books are now to be filled with poems. There they

lie, hungering to be taken into use. It doesn't matter that it isn't shiny white paper. On the contrary, there is a certain charm to these flowers and flourishes on every page. It is almost like writing your way through an enchanted forest. And the moon is shining so brightly this evening that it on its own provides enough light to write in.

Aye, the moon! It rose a short time ago above the blacksmith's garden, heavy and red, as though it had run out of breath as it rose. Or as though it were not the dead moon at all, but a newly-born, live earth on the first day of creation. But little by little, the heat has drained from it, and now it has become itself, the lonely but happy and untroubled moon, the eternal nocturnal yachtsman.

Aye, what cannot be said about the moon, that magnificent, immortal old showpiece that every child on earth has dreamt of catching and having as a toy at one time? And yet no distance on earth is as vast as that to the moon.

Sirius lies staring up into the moon's blurred and inscrutable old face. This face is calm and curiously blank this evening, like a tempting sheet of paper. But otherwise it changes expression all the time. No face is so prone to change and so full of surprises. At one moment it is attentive and cunningly observant, the next sleepy and indifferent. At times a warm smile glides across it, but it can also be bad-tempered; indeed the moon can be irate and abandon itself to a certain silent and rather foolish anger, especially in a gale when the clouds unceasingly tickle its nose.

But it can also be solemn, not least when surrounded by a large, rainbow-like halo. Then it has an expression of distance and majestic gravity. And at other times the same moon can sink into the most basic indifference and turn into a sleepy old lazybones and sourpuss that wants nothing more than to be left lying in peace under its eiderdowns.

He thinks back on the time when it dawned on him that the moon was no anthropomorphic being, but a planet like the earth. It was said in those days that it was a marshy world of evil-smelling gasses, full of endless and impassable marshes, here and there cut through by slow-flowing rivers that lost

286

themselves in motionless lakes and oceans. During his youth, Sirius had absorbed this picture of a dripping and bubbling lunar world and in his thoughts sailed its hidden waters: The Sea of Clouds, the Sea of Fecundity, the Sea of Moisture, the Lake of Dreams and whatever else they were called.

Later, to his sorrow, he was told that the moon was an arid, ice-cold desert, nothing but a barren ruin in the incomprehensible wilderness of space.

And yet, the moon is naturally something more than a lifeless thing, and even though its light contains no heat, it nevertheless has its own living, magic soul. It weaves its eternal magic spell in earth's nocturnal waters, plays in the shiny tops of the seaweed forest, conjures up life in grass and gravel, gleams magically in windows, fills children's eyes with eager wonderment, lights mighty sparks of longing and dreaming in the minds of youthful lovers.

Yes, the moon, that mischievous old trickster – it knows everything, it sees the reverse side of things, nothing fools it. It knows all the past history of the world by heart; though silent, it is privy to the future and its infinite potential.

Indeed, what cannot be said of the moon? Sirius takes out his pencil and grasps one of Mac Bett's wallpaper booklets.

For the moon is a mirror reflecting the depths of space and the infinity of the universe, but at times it is dimmed by the profound sighs of the human heart. Alas, all transient creation breathes its silent woes to you, the moon, ancient yet everlastingly young. You watch over cradle and deathbed, you hum your eternal lullabies for the weary. You are loyal to the dead and know even the most neglected graves.

You are the friend of the ailing poet, you cool his damp forehead and generously fill his lonely mind with the great secret of the world.

4

Tarira the phantom takes on a kind of tangible form but is the cause of great confusion and a sanguinary struggle

We are now rapidly approaching the end of this story of the lost musicians. It might be said generally speaking to have been a melancholy account, and yet, like everything in the world, it has its brighter aspects, for even though our musicians finally came to an unhappy end, there was both happiness and a faith in life, music and youthful love in their early years, comradeship and solidarity, all those things that made life wondrous to live. This was no mere story of broken illusions or of the triumph of injustice. And something really great also finally emerged from it all, something that later, in the fullness of time, was to be met with appreciation by the wise and the bright, and by embarrassment if no more on the part of fault-finders and the apathetic: Sirius's poems and Orfeus's playing of the violin.

As is well known, Sirius never experienced the joy of being recognised. But then he encompassed a different mental joy, the immense joy bestowed on those who devote themselves to it by the power of poetry.

Sirius was not particularly bright, not calculating and ingenious, no, he behaved foolishly for the most part, and so it is not surprising that he became the object of prosaic midgets' impatience and contempt. But on the other hand, it fell to him to help to imbue things with a soul, to awaken insensate nature from aeons of torpor and to give it the power of speech that all unfulfilled creatures so crave and yearn for: the human voice of art.

It is this strange process that is taking place in the little garret where Sirius lies writing among the flowers in Mac Bett's wallpaper booklets. And a similar miracle is unfolding at the same time in Mr Lindenskov the dancing teacher's lumber-room, where Orfeus is practising on his father's violin.

A euphoric love of the violin came upon this boy like a furious winter shower, at the same time as he was acquiring a dark voice, big despairing features and painful religious scruples. It goes without saying that these latter were, if not awakened, at least nourished to an iniquitous extent by Ankersen, who after the disappearance of Moritz attended the little family in the Mangle House like a visitation of the plague. Nor is it easy to say how things would have developed if it had not been for Ole Brandy whose scornful words constantly played a helpful role as an indomitably curative and cleansing antidote.

In this connection it is also only fair that the name of Lindenskov, the dancing-master, should be crowned with honour. He placed his excellent large lumber-room at the disposal of the young musician and in general poured all the oil he could produce on the musical flames in the boy's mind.

Nor, in this connection must we forget Orfeus's friend Peter and his gramophone. The origins of this gramophone are lost in a somewhat dubious darkness . . . one fine day it was suddenly *there*, and another fine day a furious bookseller came and fetched it back along with some records that were worn beyond recognition. But for the three or four months the gramophone was in Peter's possession, it was of invaluable benefit. The deserted old mill where Peter hid his music machine was a true temple of art for that time thanks to the first movement of the Kreutzer Sonata, the Romance from Schumann's Fourth Symphony and the immensely amusing song with flute accompaniment entitled "When I awaken at ten in the morning". These three records constituted the entire repertoire; they were played through ruthlessly several times each evening, and without a change of needle. Yes, they were quickly ploughed to bits, but by then Orfeus had learned part of the violin sonata by heart, not to speak of Schumann's beautiful romance, while Peter had an almost magical ability to copy the flautist's playing and cheerful singing.

Ever since their school days under Sirius, Orfeus and Peter had been friends. There could be times when they had drifted apart, but something always brought them together again, and more often than not it was because Peter had some unusual and exciting idea. But one day something happened that at a blow turned the two boys into bitter enemies.

It started in a strange and oppressive way, as was so often the case when Peter was up to something. It started one greenish, twilit spring evening with Peter coming and telling Orfeus in confidence that he had seen *Tarira*.

Orfeus naturally did not exactly believe that; you never did when Peter told you something, but there was nevertheless usually something in it, and so there was now as well: "Up there! Can you see her?" asked Peter. "Aren't I right? It's *almost* Tarira."

They were down in Sexton Lane staring up at a gable window illuminated by the evening light, and here, immersed in thought by the open window . . . yes, there stood Tarira, the figurehead and the vision from the dream, a young girl, fair-haired and pale and with staring eyes. There stood Tarira staring out in the pale evening.

Now Orfeus knew of course that it was *not* Tarira, but he nevertheless ran cold with excitement. His throat tightened. His heart started to race.

"Ha," laughed Peter triumphantly. "It's only Olsen the watchmaker's daughter Titty. Did you really think . . ."

"No, of course not." Orfeus smiled wanly and was still far away. He went on staring until the girl finally closed the window.

In the following time, Orfeus would secretly cross over to Sexton Lane and stand watching from a hidden corner whence he had a view of the watchmaker's gable window. He would go in the twilight and often stand there for a long time. Only rarely was there anything to see in Tarira's window, and then it was not Tarira herself, but her red-haired sister, who was in the habit of whistling foolishly and who could boast of little by way of attractiveness. Tarira herself did not appear again. But when the lamps were lit inside, Tarira's shadow could sometimes be seen against the blind. At all events, he imagined it was Tarira, and at the same time he associated this idea with Schumann's romance. When in the evening he had gone to bed in his little triangular garret in the Mangle House, he lay listening to the heartfelt sighing of this romance, which is as though replete with twilight in which a warm and secret lamp is lit – the most wondrous sigh of longing in all music, the tale of incipient love.

One evening, he quite unexpectedly met the watchmaker's daughter Titty in Sexton Lane. She passed so close to him that he could feel her breath, and they chanced to touch each other's arms.

"Look where you're going, clumsy," said Titty.

Orfeus felt unspeakably embarrassed, and for several evenings he kept away from Sexton Lane. He surreptitiously took the mirror from the kitchen up into the little room where he slept and sorrowfully looked at his face, which he thought ugly enough to make him sick – big and grey and full of red spots and marks and pale down. Look where you're going, clumsy! Yes, that was the only way people could address that face; so much was obvious.

But *Tarira* herself – she is not like that. She doesn't speak. She remains silent. She comes to him in his dreams and takes him out into dawning space. She regards him with a distant smile in her eye and passes close to him so he can feel her breath.

Then there are many nights without a dream, and he longs so intensely for Tarira. Indeed, he lies whispering her name, the soft tones of her quietly drifting name.

New nights and days elapse over the sea and the winter-ravaged land. And in time, the distant northern chasms of cloud give birth to the first anaemic light of spring. With every morning that dawns, the roseate spring light gains in strength.

"Titty's taken a fancy to you," says Peter one evening. "Shall I give her your love?"

It emerges that Peter knows Titty well.

"She'd like to get to know you," he goes on to say. "She's been standing outside Lindenskov's garden listening while you've been playing. She says you'll certainly become a *Pakkenini!*"

Orfeus only half listens to Peter's promising words. But one day he meets Titty in Sexton Lane again, and this time she smiles to him as though wanting to say: "What Peter's said is right enough."

And from that moment a fire is lit in Orfeus's heart. It spreads and takes complete hold of him and for a long time he has no thought for anything but Titty. He avoids meeting her; and Peter as well for the same reason; he dare not see either of them; he blushes and turns pale and breaks into a sweat and blissful torment at the thought of Titty. He is almost on the point of shelving his violin playing. He is simply lost; he gives confused replies when people speak to him; he becomes increasingly pale and thin and he goes around with a sickly smile and lost eyes.

His mother forces him to see the doctor. But there is nothing particular wrong with him. "Puberty," says the doctor. "He'll soon be all right again."

It was up in the old mill on a bright evening redolent of fresh grass towards the end of April, that Peter told Orfeus that he was now engaged to Titty. "It's me she fancies, not you," he said brutally. "She says you look like a plate of burnt porridge."

"She and I meet up here in the mill almost every evening," he added. "We sit here and play the gramophone. I kiss her and all that. Oh, just you get mad, you squirt. You're no good; that's what she says as well. Your grandfather was mad, and your father was a murderer."

With a loud scornful laugh Peter ran out of the door. Orfeus followed him, blinded by tears and fury. Peter suddenly stopped up on the hill and confronted him. "Yes, come on then, you wimp, if you dare," he shouted and pulled the sleeves of his jersey up. "I'll show you . . .!"

Orfeus threw himself at him; they tumbled about in the fresh grass, rolled further down the hill, holding tight on to each other, and continued the fight further down. Orfeus was smaller and more slightly built than Peter, but he had the furious, primitive strength of jealousy on his side, and he won easily; he pressed Peter's neck down in the mud and planted his knee on his chest. Peter cried and spat in fury, but he was beaten. They were both bleeding from their noses and gums and glaring emptily and foolishly into each other's eyes.

"That was good," came the sound of a sharp, jovial voice behind Orfeus's back. It came from Mac Bett. The old decorator was out for his evening stroll; he was dressed up for the evening in an embroidered waistcoat and a blue, stiff bonnet that sat like a crown on his well-tended head. He was standing there swinging his white bone walking stick.

"Let him be now, and go and wash yourselves in the river before you go home. You look awful."

Orfeus released Peter, who immediately ran off down the hill.

"I was standing watching you," said Mac Bett with a hard little smile. "I saw that it was you all right, Orfeus, and I thought to myself: Let's see now how well he manages. Aye, for your father would have managed it all right, let me tell you, although he wasn't one for fighting. But your uncles, Orfeus. No! A poor reed like Sirius would simply have let himself be flayed to death, no doubt about it. And the other, Kornelius, well he *was* flayed, more or less. Nor did he put up any resistance. He'd no backbone either."

Mac Bett laughed sadly to himself. "It's no good at all with that sort of people. They just can't fight back."

"And so, my boy," Mac Bett turned his head and stared fiercely into Orfeus's eyes. "And so, my boy, it delighted my old heart to see Moritz's son knock that other rascal down. To see that you're made of stronger stuff than your uncles. That you can stand up for yourself. Yes, stand up for yourself, my boy, stand up for yourself when others are insolent to you or want to cheat you or knock you down. Don't forget that, my lad, don't forget what old Mac Bett said to you: stand up for yourself! Keep your back straight and let no injustice have any effect on you."

The decorator waved his walking stick elegantly in the air, gave a short laugh and strolled on with a smile.

This was about what Mac Bett said. It was a speech filled with praise, although it was stern, and it was intended as consolation and encouragement, but Orfeus felt anything but strengthened. On the contrary, he staggered back to the mill, and there he threw himself on the dirty floor, beside himself with pain and shame.

5

*Days that have vanished, broken dreams of happiness
and grief-laden longing along with mysterious music
in a lumber-room and great bliss*

A large proportion of the many more or less neglected little
gardens scattered around the old part of the town can boast of
quite considerable age. In his poem "Green Oblivion", Sirius
has expressed the peculiar atmosphere of age and dim memories characteristic of these old gardens, where past generations
have gone about and had their joys and sorrows, of which the
perfume of flowers or the soughing of the wind or the dripping of the rain can sometimes revive memories and give a
certain ghost-like half-life.

The house belonging to Lindenskov the dancing teacher
was surrounded on all sides by one of these overgrown old
gardens. At one time it had belonged to the well-known trade
commissioner Trampe, who had been passionately fond of
flowers, and here and there among the grass and the weeds it
was still possible to come across indomitable little patches of
fine decorative flowers from Trampe's day. Just as the impenetrable barrier of wild raspberry and rose bushes surrounding
the garden and the luxuriant rowan espalier with which the
house was hung were also Trampe's work.

The constant greenish twilight that dominated both Trampe's garden and Lindenskov's dilapidated big house had an
oppressive but at the same time calming and healing effect on
Orfeus's agitated mind. It was a strange, closed world, a hidden
and profoundly stifling world constantly *swarming* with a
growth of one thing or another. In the living rooms there was
an array of cloth, remnants and rags, pin cushions, rolls of
thread and thimbles. And then there were knickknacks of all

kinds, vases with everlasting flowers, small terracotta figures and statuettes, porcelain dogs, centrepieces and clammy old family albums in velvet bindings. In the dancing teacher's little study there was a host of pipes of every calibre from short, encrusted shag pipes down to enormous churchwarden pipes with flower-decorated porcelain bowls. In the daughters' rooms in the loft there was an array of coloured congratulatory cards which together with faded old cotillion bouquets were fixed in fans around the sloping walls, and the cellar was filled with a host of spiders, woodlice, centipedes and earwigs.

But nowhere was there such an array as in the lumber-room, where Orfeus spent most of his time at present. It was quite incomprehensible how much lumber of every conceivable kind had been packed in.

This lumber-room was moreover the lightest and best room in the house. There was a special reason why it was not used for living in: It was in this room that, as an old man, Trampe had put an end to his life by hanging himself.

Orfeus had at first felt anything but comfortable when he was alone in Trampe's room. But now, in his agony, he no longer felt any fear of ghosts; on the contrary, there was something almost consolatory about this lonely and light lumber-room with its countless odd bits and pieces.

And as the days pass Orfeus slips into a fertile state of dull, melancholy longing. He pretends that Tarira has also let him down. She flies alone now. He simply sits, longing, infinitely ugly and poor, despised and deserted. So it goes with all good people, he thinks. That was how it went with Sirius – he, too, was let down and deserted. But there is a certain charm in being one of the deserted ones who live in their own world of sorrow and disappointment and longing.

With tears in his eyes, Orfeus plays Schumann's romance. There is consolation in it. Green twilight sky and lighted candles in black gables. And behind closed doors and windows glows the world of love and delight that will never be yours.

Sewing machines hum in Lindenskov's tightly packed rooms; the seven middle-aged daughters, the "aunts" are all keen seamstresses. Occasionally, the aunts will sing, and Orfeus listens to the melancholy words of their songs about times that have vanished, flowers that have withered, and birds that flew past and were lost to sight.

> There flew a bird o'er the pine-covered heath
> Singing songs now long forgotten.

Old Lindenskov likes to join in these forgotten songs, and while doing so he takes on the same longing and lost expression as his daughters.

So much has disappeared and will never come back, however much you may long for it. The aunts long for times past, often falling into a trance with tears in their eyes. And the trees in the garden long, too, and the wind longs as well, on its eternal path.

And the jumble in the lumber-room longs. Indeed, nothing is so full of hopeless longing as Trampe's sitting room. The big damp stains on the faded carpet are pure longing that shows itself in the form of pale, swollen patches.

And the river that hurries past the Mangle House and fills the nights with its dark rushing sound, that too is full of voracious and storming longing. And the stones in the mangle lie waiting in hopeless, absurd longing for someone to come and drop them in the water again.

One night, Orfeus dreams that he is out in the basement of the Bastille listening to music like in the old days. But it is not the warm, roseate music from before, for it is strangely sweeping, lawless music, filled with sorrow and longing. And there is only one person present in the big, half-lit room. It is his mother. She sits there staring in front of her in longing, so alone and deserted . . . but suddenly it is not she at all, but Tarira!

And now Tarira gets up and comes over towards him, silently, gliding, and he has to follow her, follow her in boundless, sorrowful, almost desperate happiness.

They float out into the night and hover for a moment up in the church tower where the old, dried remains of the Aeolian harps in the pitch-dark loft give forth deserted tremulous sounds. And he follows her on her eternal journey through the realms of dream, where the resonances are lonely and vast. They both listen, and their eyes meet in silent dismay.

This Tarira, this vision – why is she so untiring in her pursuit? Is she one of those demons that do not relent before they have led their victim into damnation? Is she a good spirit – if not a kind angel at least an attendant spirit, unswerving and strong?

Later in life, he often had to ask himself these questions, but the answer was never a clear yes or no: Tarira was a gift you received, in which something of the deepest quality in yourself found expression.

She was a personification of sorrow, longing and love, the product of the restless longing of an artist's mind.

The days pass, and one beautiful evening Orfeus and Peter meet again, and everything is much as before. "All that about Titty and me was a lie," says Peter. "It was just something I said because I was so mad that Titty was going around with Kaj, Fähse's errand boy. She was not in the least bit interested in me either. So that's why I wanted to take my revenge by telling you that tale about me and her. And that's why I lost when we had a fight because when something's a lie you can't stand your ground. But you thought it was true, and so you were strong."

Orfeus absent-mindedly sets the gramophone going. He is not angry with Peter. Or with Titty. He rather feels a little disappointed at having been told this truth. It disturbs his longing.

"She *isn't* a Tarira," says Peter contemptuously.

"No," agrees Orfeus, and their eyes meet in common contempt and loyalty.

"A bitch, that's what she is," says Peter.

The summer passes and it is autumn again, sleepy, damp and dark days, days full of longing. Sometimes one of the aunts has a birthday, and then the sitting rooms are tidied up and the

Misses Schibbye and other elderly ladies come and have chocolate in little gilded cups and they prattle away . . . a noise and chatter as though of a flock of busy birds.

One afternoon, one windy afternoon with a pale sun, Orfeus had an unforgettable experience in the lumber-room. He had just put the violin down and gone over to the window when behind him there was the sound of some delicious music, a dying chord of inexpressible depth and gentle harmony. He turned round and sat for a long time absorbed in wonder. Where could these tones be coming from, this strange spirit music?

Ghosts? He felt slightly nervous, but wished more would come.

But none came. However, shortly afterwards a cat's head appeared in the midst of a pile of junk. It stared at him with its bottomless eyes, long and intently. Then it disappeared as silently as it had come.

Orfeus had a really unpleasant sensation. The silence began to resound around him, and across the faded walls of the room ghost-like shadows moved like long, groping hands. He felt himself caught in some strange sorcery and thought for a moment that he was dreaming.

But then there was suddenly a rattling noise and one, two, three, a large cat appears and leaps up on to the window ledge.

Oh, so it *was* a real cat. Orfeus let it out. He felt calmer and started thinking. Perhaps the music also had a natural source. Perhaps, for instance there was some stringed instrument somewhere in the lumber that the cat had happened to play. He became more and more fixated with the thought of this instrument and started rummaging in the pile where the head of the cat had appeared. But the fear of ghosts was still with him, and suddenly it rose to panic . . . running cold, he drew back and opened the door with a little cry.

On the steps outside he bumped into Aunt Lucie, the oldest of Lindenskov's daughters, and almost knocked her over.

"Was there something in there?" asked Aunt Lucie quickly.

Orfeus had to tell her about the music he had heard and about the cat that jumped out of the window.

"Oh, was that all?" laughed Aunt Lucie in relief. "I really thought that it was Trampe . . .! But it was only my zither you heard. It's in there somewhere. Come on, I'll show it to you."

After searching for some time, Aunt Lucie found the zither. "Ah," she sighed and struck a tone. "It still sounds quite good, but it's so rusty and covered in dust."

She sat down on a backless chair, took the zither on her lap and went on, staring out into the afternoon light: "Yes, it's been left alone in there for . . . well, how long? Twenty-three years. Yes, time flies."

She plucked gently at the strings and sighed again: "Do you know, my boy, I was once given this zither by my *fiancé*. Yes, for I was once engaged. But then he let me down, for he was a rotter. All men are. But that's all such a long time ago, and as for him, he's dead and gone. It was all very sad, but thank God it's all in the past now."

Aunt Lucie suddenly raised her voice and began to sing with a cracked voice while fumbling across the zither's rusty strings with her thin, veined hand.

> I am a stranger,
> A pilgrim I,
> Only one evening
> A single evening am I here.

But suddenly she got up with a little start and started to peck Orfeus on the cheek so that his ears tickled: "Trallallala. The world is faithless, but don't bother about *that* because it's something you get over. There. But now you can have the zither to amuse yourself with if you like. Then it will have been of some use after all."

"Thank you so much," said Orfeus, flushing with delight.

As soon as Aunt Lucie had gone, he turned eagerly to the instrument. All afternoon, into the gathering twilight, he lay on the floor plucking away at it. The long, singing sounds transported him to a state of almost tearful joy. You could make harmonies and make it sound like a whole orchestra.

That night, he had a wonderful dream.

300

He dreamt he was in a huge, empty room, the bare walls of which were bathed in brilliant afternoon light. But at the end of this room there was a stepped platform, and on these steps there was a mass of musical instruments: big, reddish brown and black brown violoncellos, glistening violins, glinting horns and flutes, and at the top of the steps a row of gleaming copper-coloured drums. And all at once, this mighty orchestra began to play of its own accord, without anyone touching the instruments ... a swirling torrent of sounds that almost bowled him over.

He awoke and lay a long while writhing in silent ecstasy.

6

Ankersen marks a new phase in his development by quite unexpectedly turning his back on the jubilant Ydun Association

On the day on which, after a great deal of struggle and trouble, the total prohibition of alcohol finally became law, the Ydun Assoction held a great festival of thanksgiving. As a kind of rounding off of the portrait of Ankersen the Bank, there follows in conclusion a brief account of the harrowing events that took place during this remarkable celebration.

"Well, all of you gathered here know the reason why this hall is decorated with flags and streamers this evening, and why we are all dressed in our Sunday best."

It is Mrs Nillegaard, the energetic vice-chairman of the association, who is speaking. Mrs Nillegaard is emotional and at the same time both hungry and suffering from a very bad cold. She blows her nose energetically, during the process dropping her pince-nez, which falls to the floor and breaks. But this is not the time to bother about trifles, so she frowns and continues in a loud voice: "Yes. The total prohibition of alcohol is now a happy fact. It has, as we all know, been first approved by a referendum and then established by law. So there are now no two ways about it."

Mrs Nillegaard's expression suggests that she is suddenly about to burst into laughter, but the reason is that she is about to sneeze. An attack of sneezing follows, and her handkerchief again appears. She continues, "As I say, there no two ways about it. No."

Mrs Nillegaard's expression now suggests she is being tickled, and a new attack of sneezing follows.

302

She continues: "It is under the leadership of Mr Ankersen, the savings bank manager, that we have achieved the objective we have so long desired. His fervour has infected us all. Like no one else, he has risked his skin and has gone through fire and water. His example has steeled our wills, and under his leadership even the weakest of us have been able to straighten our backs.

But now it has finally fallen to our enviable lot to place the crown of victory upon our head. Yes, dear friends! The race is ended. We are have reached our objective. We can now exclaim with King Solomon . . ."

Mrs Nillegaard is battling with a fresh attack of sneezing.

"Exclaim . . ."

Violent sneezing.

"Well, with King Solomon exclaim. . . ."

Yet another attack. Mrs Nillegaard pauses. Her nostrils are pulsating. There are signs of laugher from the most distant tables in the hall. Then comes yet another attack of sneezing, and she resignedly accepts it. But then the way is clear again, and she continues: "So with King Solomon we can exclaim: 'And I saw that there is nothing better than a man who is happy in his deeds, for that is his lot'."

There are already signs of a fresh attack of sneezes, and in order to get in first, Mrs Nillegaard delivers the last bit of her speech at breakneck speed: "And now, dear friends, we will rejoice with each other, and I ask you not to scorn the excellent roast beef that has been put on our table this evening. Enjoy your meal."

She descends from the podium with a sneeze of relief and sits down at the table between her husband and the savings bank manager.

During his wife's speech, Mr Nillegaard has been on tenterhooks. Since the great event, Ida has been in a worrying state of elation, and in addition she has been overworked during the preparations for this event, which she has been left to arrange. But, thank God, the speech went without a hitch, and now it is finished. Without any glossalalia. Without obscene scenes. So the worst is now happily over. There is a lovely smell of roast; knives and forks are taken into happy activity, and from the large, horseshoe-shaped dinner table a happy and carefree murmur can be heard.

Only Ankersen's plate is empty.

What is wrong?

"Aren't you going to have anything to eat, Ankersen?" asks Nillegaard nervously.

Ankersen makes no reply. He sits completely motionless.

Mr and Mrs Nillegaard exchange glances. Mrs Nillegaard frowns and demonstratively starts on her roast. But Nillegaard is suddenly not hungry. A remarkable frigidity is being exuded by Ankersen as he sits there brooding over an empty plate.

Mrs Nillegaard nudges her husband eagerly. "Well, don't you like the food, Jens Enok?" she asks, chewing away energetically. Nillegaard jumps inadvertently: "Yes, yes, it's an excellent roast."

"Then I think you should eat it."

Mrs Nillegaard pushes the dish closer to Ankersen's place, as a result of which a gravy boat tips over and surrenders a little of its abundance to the tablecloth: "Here, Ankersen, don't let it go cold."

But Ankersen takes no notice of her. And now he gets up, noisily moving his chair and walking with slow, ponderous steps up towards the rostrum.

"Ankersen is going to speak. Hush." The hall falls silent.

Ankersen surveys the gathering. He is breathing heavily and distractedly and gives himself plenty of time. At last his voice is heard. It sounds strangely lonely and plaintive.

"I had thought," he said. "I had thought that this gathering would be marked by solemnity. I had imagined it to be a quiet and reverent festival of thanksgiving coming from the heart. And not an . . . *orgy of eating*!"

"No, I say, that's *too* . . .!" Mrs Nillegaard puts down her knife and fork.

"Shush," warns her husband. "Let Ankersen say what he has to say."

Ankersen raises his voice: "Yes. I will be honest and say that when I entered this hall this evening and noticed the smell of vast amounts of food, I was deeply surprised in my heart."

"I don't understand that at all, Ankersen," interrupts Mrs Nillegaard, shouting from her seat. "We had agreed there should be a dinner."

Ankersen nods dejectedly: "Perhaps that there should be a dinner, Mrs Nillegaard, but not that the dinner, if I may put it this way, should take precedence over everything else."

Mrs Nillegaard blows her nose with renewed violence. Her blotchy face has now turned scarlet, and her eyes are wandering in confusion due to the loss of her pince-nez. Ankersen gives her a searching look that is earnest without actually being reproachful: "I had really imagined, Mrs Nillegaard, that the dinner would come *in second place*. But . . . well, it could not wait." "No, of course it couldn't wait," replies Mrs Nillegaard in a voice that sounded as though she is on the point of laughing, but which was the result of her sneezing and indignation. "Of course, Ankersen! The food was surely not to be left to go cold, was it? Just have a little thought, man."

There are signs of merriment here and there in the hall.

"Good," says Ankersen. "Good. Then I think I understand."

The merriment increases.

"I'm glad of that," replies Mrs Nillegaard, pursuing her triumph.

Ankersen's face adopts a weary and deeply pained expression. He nods and speaks to himself: "I see, I see. I will be brief."

Suddenly he looks up and raises his voice: "Yes, for I have long been aware of it. I have understood the direction it was taking. The sad truth is that the Ydun Association has increasingly become a secular institution devoid of serious thought. An association with no spiritual substance. And now that our *secular* objective has been attained, what is left of the spirit in which we started our labours? It was surely not the intention that we should stop here. But all right. Perhaps the mission of this association is complete. Perhaps we shall make no further progress this time round."

Ankersen sighs deeply. The association watches him with palpable tension.

"But, as I say, this is not what *I* had imagined. And so now, my friends, now I will resign from the association. I will therefore now have nothing more to do with this association. I will go my own way. My place is not at a table of diners. My place is not in the circle of the replete. My place is on the battlefield. I will be where there is struggle and blood. And so . . ."

Ankersen is moved. His voice sounds broken: "Therefore, dear friends, therefore I will now take my leave of you. Do not let me disturb you. Eat your dinner with a good appetite. You must simply realise that I feel myself to be superfluous here."

"Oh, no, Ankersen!" protests Nillegaard.

Mrs Nillegaard nudges her husband violently, shakes her head and starts speaking in her turn: "Listen. May I be allowed to make a comment? To begin with, I must repeat that Ankersen himself was among those suggesting that the menu should contain roast beef. Yes! I don't care what you say, Ankersen. You yourself said roast beef. And when you now come and ruin it all for us, let me tell you that that was a mean trick. It was *mean*. Yes, that's what I said. And your need to assert yourself is unbounded."

Nillegaard: "Now, now, Ida."

Mrs Nillegaard raises a crumpled, soaking handkerchief threateningly towards the podium: "Yes. This evening I *will* be allowed to speak my mind. It was a mean trick of Ankersen to come here and interrupt the meal merely to make sure of really drawing attention to himself. He can simply not countenance our eating and being merry here. Let me tell you, we have seen through you, Ankersen. You could have resigned quietly if you disapproved of the occasion. But it's too late now. You have spoiled it all now. There is no question of continuing."

Mrs Nillegaard has worked herself up into a powerful state of nervous excitement. She turns to the assembly: "God knows that no one has admired Ankersen more than I. I have been fond of him, indeed I have loved him. Yes, I have *loved* you, Ankersen. But now I *hate* you. For you are not a human being. You are a heartless, loathsome tyrant! And I suggest now that we all simply leave the table and go to our own homes and leave Ankersen to this frosty isolation. So . . ."

Confusion. Some of the participants get up; others remain seated; a few indignantly begin to eat again.

"Scandal. Scandal," groans Nillegaard. He puts his hands up to his head. But deep down in his soul a tiny, long suppressed fire starts seething and spluttering.

"Ankersen," he shouts triumphantly. "You should be ashamed. Ashamed. Do you hear?"

But Ankersen is happily already out in the entrance. He is putting on his galoshes.

"Listen," says Nillegaard. "Do you realise you have been acting in a *curmudgeonly* fashion, Ankersen? Your are a curmudgeon, so you are. Do you hear?"

No, Ankersen neither hears nor sees. He has an expression on his face as though he were far away in another world. He is not angry, he is merely far away.

The fire spreads deep down in Nillegaard, sooty and spewing smoke. He hisses scornfully: "Yes, but you're finished here now, Ankersen. You have disqualified yourself in every way. An obnoxious curmudgeon, that's what you are, a real heartless blackguard, between ourselves a demagogic thug, a poor, dense creature, a malicious old he-bitch . . .!"

Ankersen stares at him. He says nothing. He does not look angry. He is just far away. As though distractedly he takes Nillegaard's hand and says, "Goodbye, Nillegaard. I must go. Don't hold me back."

Nillegaard turns away in despair and makes his way to the outdoor clothes in the deserted cloakroom. He stands groaning for a moment.

Then a solitary sound reaches him from the otherwise totally silent hall . . . a dreadful sound . . . like the plaintive crowing of a cock that has been the victim of a failed attempt to chop off its head . . . a high-pitched, idiotic weeping.

He rushes feverishly back to the hall and sees the very sight he had expected, the sight of Ida leaning back in her chair and vainly trying to combat her hysterical convulsive laughter with the help of her handkerchief.

In the moonlit evening, shamefaced members of the Ydun Association on their way home through Shoemaker Lane after the interrupted thanksgiving dinner glimpse the outline of a little group of people gathered around a singing figure.

It is Ankersen starting all over again.

7

The poet and death

The sky this evening is a yellow, sickly colour that we know means a gale, as the level of the barometer also confirms.

Yes, for some reason or other there is to be a gale.

In the face of the weather, human beings are like children watching the lives and activities of grown-ups without really understanding what is happening. The weather this evening intends to be bad. It is preparing a gale, for some reason unknown. So there is nothing to be done but to resign to it. Resign to it as to fate.

Sirius lies reflecting on his lonely couch. He is in high spirits and cannot entirely deny looking forward a little to the gale that is to come. He has just had a visit from Ole Brandy and Olivarius. It is they who have told him about the unusually low state of the barometer.

Where was it we broke off? Resigning to fate. They also talk of fighting against fate. That was what Beethoven did, they say. But is that not a lot of nonsense, properly speaking? If you conquer your fate, as they put it, it is your fate to conquer it. Fate is what happens. What else?

Sirius is at once tired and uneasy. He stares into the dazzling square formed by the window, into the yellow chasm of light that has now acquired a touch of red, a touch as of distant trumpet blasts. Mountainous formations of clouds glide forward, silvery grey and grey as ash. For a moment the entire sky is of a colour like that of dirty bedclothes. But it would be fun to lie up there on one of the folds in the vast heavenly eiderdown and from that dizzying height look down into the abyss and see the gale's greedy broom sweeping the darkening sea.

Ha! The gale has probably already started; there are long, nervous whistling sounds around Mac Bett's gable, and the naked trees in the blacksmith's garden are rattling gently like skeletons rising from the dead. And suddenly a darkness falls like a shadow across the hastening train of clouds . . . it is like the shadow of a vast, restless, beleaguered mountain. Sirius thinks of the story of the mountain about to give birth. The showery darkness fills him with a feeling of wellbeing, and he makes himself comfortable in his bed.

Meanwhile, the great gale is increasing in strength. Whirlwinds dance in lonely, desperate intensity out on the ocean floor. Meaningless and enormous. Waves move in vast droves towards the north west as though to reach a goal, but, as everyone knows, no gale has ever had any objective apart from that of blowing a gale.

With his inner eye he sees how the gale progresses and whips up the sea to churn around lonely precipitous coasts. Columns of foam rise slowly and gently in the pallid twilight, unfold, hesitate for a moment and tremble, then calmly fall back into the depths, where the darkness breaks out in flowers and greenish foam. Some of these roses of foam are of huge dimensions and passionately extend their sparkling tentacles in the half-darkness. The entire coast becomes a miraculous living ocean of luxuriantly growing, fervid and merciless foam efflorescence.

Yes, it is seething and growing everywhere out there in the unreal doomsday light; thundering giant forests of dark blossoms emerge from the depths; heaven and earth grow together. Finally, all is darkness. A mighty, foaming gale-replete darkness.

Then come furious showers that reverberate with a myriad of tempestuous sounds against windows and fill the rills in the corrugated roofs with a flow of cold fresh water. Sirius thirsts to feel the cooling flow against his heated forehead; he longs for it and surrenders comfortably to the dense, wet, storming darkness . . .

When Janniksen the blacksmith came the following morning to see his son-in-law, he found him dead.

The blacksmith scratched his neck in bewilderment and his eyes became round and staring.

"Good lord. Poor thing," he murmured to himself.

8

*How it in time fell to that determined man
Ole Brandy to be the one who saved Orfeus from
the underworld*

Orfeus had become apprenticed to the decorator Mac Bett.
He was almost fifteen years old now; his school days were past,
and he had to start doing something sensible.

The old master's quick Scottish temper had in no way
become less with the years; he sensed a new Sirius in the
withdrawn, lanky boy. One day when Orfeus had happened
to overturn a tin of newly mixed paint, Mac Bett's fiery temper got the better of him, and he flung a role of gilt-leather
tapestry at the boy. It hit him in the face, resulting in a long
gash down his forehead and a mightily blackened eye.

"Oh, heaven help me," moaned the decorator. "You look
wonderful now. Oh dear, oh dear. And you're not even crying;
I must admit you're a tough lad even if you are a clown and a
clumsy fool."

Breathing heavily, he sat down on the bottom rung of a
ladder, drew the boy over to him and stroked his hair. "What's
going to become of us?" he groaned darkly. "What's going to
become of us two, boy? Perhaps one day I'll end up knocking
the daylight out of you and ending my days as a common
criminal and a ruined man."

"And you don't say anything; you just put up with it all,"
continued Mac Bett. "And when you get home, you'll perhaps tell your mother that you've fallen and knocked yourself.
Because that's what you're like; you're a kind, gentle boy. But
even so, I'll not give you any reason to *lie*. Come on, you little
devil, and we'll both go down to your mother straight away.
For even if I am a stupid old brute, Orfeus, I've all my life tried

312

to be an honest man. And then I've been fond of the lot of you, of Sirius and your mother and father and poor Kornelius. And that's why I wanted you as my apprentice. I wanted to teach you something useful, to turn you into a lad with a bit of method so you could start on something sensible and useful in your life."

Mac Bett closed his eyes and bent his head back. And in doing so, he looked really old and worn out.

"And then – I'd better tell you this now while I'm in the mood – for otherwise I might regret it later after all . . ."

Mac Bett took out a big red handkerchief, wet it with spit and set about carefully wiping away some spots of dried blood from the boy's forehead. "Aye, I'd really thought you should go on here and take over the shop later when I'm dead. I've no children or heirs, you know. I had the same idea with Sirius at one time, but then it all fell through because he was impossible. No, perhaps it doesn't sound nice to say that now he's dead, but he was impossible, through and through. He just lay there and wrote on the wallpaper, so he did, and I've kept everything he wrote in case it's worth anything. I thought at first of burning all that nonsense, but then a voice said to me: 'Suppose there is something in it after all? Suppose some learned man should come along one day and say: *Just look at this, Mac Bett, you can sell it for a good sum of money.*' One's heard of that kind of thing before. But what's that really got to do with all this? As I say, let's go down to your mother now. Are you feeling a bit better? Your eye's closing, but that's as it should be. It'll be all right, you'll see."

Ole Brandy and the Crab King were alone in the Mangle House. They were finishing their lunch. Ole Brandy lit his pipe. His eyes flashed through the sharp clouds of smoke.

"No, you don't need to say anything, Mac Bett," he snarled contemptuously. "It's not the first time you've given way to that *murderous* hand of yours."

"That's enough," said the decorator threateningly. "It's not you I've come to talk to. I don't owe you any apologies."

The two men glared at each other. Orfeus glanced nervously from one to the other with his good eye. They were

313

angry and each in his own way looked terrible and alarming, Ole with his broken nose and the contemptuous twist of his mouth, Mac Bett with his staring, stern eyes and white whiskers. On the verge of tears, he had to admit to himself that he was really very fond of them both, like a couple of grandfathers. He had to think of Abraham and Isaac and the other strange old men from the Bible; they, too, could be quick-tempered and unreasonable, but fundamentally they were good, kind men. It hurt him terribly to hear how Ole Brandy was now starting to let fly at Mac Bett.

But it did not turn into an ordinary, rough and shabby quarrel, even if Ole did use some harsh words.

"There you are," he said. "For fifty years you've painted and papered, Mac Bett; you've glued and stained and pasted and patched and scrimped and saved, stale and withered as you are, with poison in your eyes, and all so you could sit alone in the evenings and feel up to your eyes in money. And if a poor apprentice just happens to put a bit of snot on one of your pieces of wallpaper, you go out to kill him; you put your fangs into him and then you weep your crocodile tears afterwards, 'cause then your conscience starts stirring things up in you, and there is plenty to stir up – ugh, there's probably a whole muck heap to clear out."

"Watch it," warned Mac Bett.

Trembling with fury, he looked around for something to sit on. The Crab King suddenly got up and waddled out of the door. Mac Bett took his seat and grimly sat himself down on it.

"Aye, and now I'm going, too," said Ole Brandy. "For I won't stay under the same roof as you. But as a final word I'll say this: You let go of that boy! Understand? He deserves a better fate than getting your ruler in his eye. And that he shall have. I'll see to that."

Ole Brandy blew an angry cloud of smoke in Mac Bett's direction and disappeared through the door with a scornful grunt.

Ole Brandy knew that he had pledged rather too much by

314

promising to ensure a better fate for Eliana's son than that of being apprenticed to Mac Bett. That evening, he discussed things with Olivarius and Lindenskov. Olivarius was of the opinion that the boy was in good hands with Mac Bett after all. Lindenskov had originally been opposed to the idea that the boy should be apprenticed in the decorating trade, for it was after all music that was his forte. But there was no way they could afford to give him any other start in life. Though perhaps things might turn out better one sunny day . . .

"Perhaps he'll inherit Mac Bett," he said dreamily. "And for that inheritance he can go off and learn the violin and become a real musician. But on the other hand, it might be a long way off, for Mac Bett has still plenty of go left in him. He could live to be ninety, and by that time the boy will be almost forty – and by *then* it'll be too late, damn it!"

Ole Brandy lay thinking for most of the night. He was gradually starting to feel tired of thinking about this boy Orfeus. He had other problems. In general, things were going strangely wrong all around. Kornelius had been locked up in a hospital for lunatics. And Josef the Lament had gone completely barmy and built a daft little tower on the roof of his workshop. It was a ridiculous tower, a humiliating piece of work. It was just big enough for Josef to stick his head up in it, but it was furnished with pipes and valves and gear wheels and chains in a sort of corkscrew spire. And the black hole that Janniksen had so long had on his forehead had started swelling now, so he was in hospital with the whole of his head wrapped up in a steaming tea towel.

And there was no word from Moritz, so perhaps he was dead after all. But Ole still tried to maintain hope in Eliana, for she was a hope person, and you must never kill the hope in such people, for then they simply wither. Strange thing about hope, thought Ole, shaking his head in his nocturnal solitude.

And now, after the introduction of total prohibition, you could not even get as much as an ordinary beer out in The Dolphin. Østrøm talked about closing and selling the business and going off to Sweden.

And he had started to grow old; he was far from being the

man he had once been, and a flat non-alcoholic beer didn't improve things.

But there were still the ships; their world did not change. It never changed. Mariners are not to be fooled. They remain the same, generation after generation. Mariners are like the firm floor beneath your feet, like the deck planks that never fail. That is the essence.

And the following day the sea sends a gift to Ole Brandy and makes him happy and courageous and really puts him on his feet again. For what is this proud ship sailing into the roads other than that magnificent old bark the Albatross. The Albatross, on which he sailed for nine years of his life. The Albatross, the good, happy ship of his youth. The Albatross with the white and gold figurehead beneath the bowsprit. But the yards are gone and an engine has been installed, and there are other things as well. But never mind that.

The Albatross has been away for a long time, six or seven years at least. But now it is back.

However, the best and most remarkable thing is that *Uncle* still sails on the Albatross. It sounds incredible, but Uncle, 74 years of age, still sails on the same ship and is even almost unchanged, as thin and dry as a Red Indian and with his cap at an angle. Nothing in the world has been able to put *him* down!

Uncle is still an ordinary sailor, but he enjoys great respect and is free to do as he likes. When he offers rum, there is rum all round, and the mate and the skipper come and raise their glasses to the happy reunion with old friends.

It is a lovely ship in every way; kindness and warmth are there like flickering sunshine over the entire ship. "It's not used for anything any longer," explains Uncle. "It just sails. It's an ocean survey ship, but there'll soon be an end to that, too, now, and I'm afraid it will probably just be broken up."

Ole Brandy has a sense of nostalgic happiness such as he has rarely known before in his life. One of Uncle's ears still shows white marks after the time when the half-caste girl Ubokosiara bit it to bits almost half a century ago. "Aye," he shakes his head merrily and reveals a lonely tooth, the last on the quarterdeck.

There are so many strange people on board the Albatross; one of them wears glasses and sits writing a book. "All he ever does is write," says Uncle. Another is stretched out snoring on a chair on the deck; he is wearing a jersey and waterproof boots and has a Newgate frill on his horny face. "Aye, look at him," says Uncle. "That's the concertmaster."

"Do you have concerts on board?" asks Ole, once more having to chuckle at it all.

"All the time," says Uncle enthusiastically. "When he's not drinking or sleeping, he plays his violin, even during a storm. Otherwise he doesn't do anything useful. He doesn't even study the sea. But he's still signed on as an AB like me. Though he doesn't get any pay. But he doesn't care a damn about that, 'cause he's got a good job ashore."

Ole Brandy spends a lovely evening on board the Albatross, one of the best he can remember.

If remember is the right word. The only thing he really remembers is that he sang Olysses several times by request, and that someone played the violin a lot.

Violin!

It suddenly strikes Ole Brandy: *Violin!*

He nods to himself as he sits bent over shaving in front of the broken mirror in the low loft. Strange great and reckless thoughts flash through his mind. And as though in a distant, beneficent vision he sees old Boman and Moritz and Kornelius and Mortensen and the other doughty musicians from the good days with their bows and their violins. Now they are all dead and gone or have rudely been removed from the story. But you are left, Ole Olsen known as Ole Brandy, you son of Ole the Jib and Strong Ole, you efficient deckhand, you, who never in your long life have let an insult go unanswered. You didn't achieve riches and honour, so much is certain, not even in your playing of the Jew's harp, but wait, just wait. If you can get Eliana's and Moritz's son torn out of Mac Bett's clutches and fix him up learning music among good people – if you can get him made into an Ole Bull, sir, you will certainly not make a packet out of it, no, but noble hearts will joyfully surround your name for ever, amen.

"Now you're sitting here talking nonsense, Ole, almost as though you were an Ankersen. Besides, you've still got a hangover. But that's only a good thing. Now get to work. Bloody nuisance that you can't even stand upright in this rotten loft."

Ole shook his fist challengingly at his freshly shaven face in the mirror.

Among the many strange stories Andersen, the concertmaster, used to tell about his holiday trip in the North Atlantic on the Albatross in the summer of 1914 there was one about the old seadog Ole Brandy with the earrings and his protégé, the violin virtuoso Orfeus.

It was no ordinary anecdote; it was far too moving for that, as Andersen used to say.

"First of all, the old man came on board alone and sang some dreadfully mournful and tear-dripping songs for us about Olysses and Pimpleja; but how wonderful he looked, he resembled something between a Chinese pirate and the conductor Johan Svendsen!

And then, the following day, he came on board again and with a look as though he was about to admit to a terrible crime, he told us that there was a great violin genius living ashore there, held prisoner by a dangerous and evil-intentioned man called Mac Bett, and that we ought to devote all our energies to liberating him.

'Well, of course,' I said. 'If what you tell us is true, there is no time to be lost.' And so we went ashore in that remarkable little town where Ole Brandy lived, and we did our best to make our way up the narrow rocky alleyways without treading on all the eider ducks and other ducks. It was a lovely Sunday morning; there was poultry and sheep and goats grazing on all the roofs. And Ole Brandy – he stops at the absolutely smallest house in the world and asks for Orfeus. No, Orfeus isn't at home, he's in the lumber-room, came the answer.

So on again, up hills and through tiny gardens filled with flowers, until we reach a house that can't be seen at all for leaves and grass and pendant shoots, and then on again up to the lumber-room, and here, quite alone, we find a weepy boy with purple and green rings around his eyes and a black mark on his forehead that looked as though it had been made by a blow from a whip. He is lying there on his stomach playing a zither.

'Now you'd better play your violin the best you know how for this gentleman,' commands Ole Brandy. And the boy gets up obediently, not the least bit surprised or frightened, just so endlessly tired. He tunes his violin and plays the romance from Schumann's Fourth Symphony.

That wasn't exactly what I had expected to hear, and it gave me a kind of musical shock, for the boy played with great, naïve sensitivity. . . . Yes, it was child-like, and the romance can simply not be played on a solo violin, but I have seldom been moved by music as I was that day in that lumber-room. I went almost crazy and had tears in my eyes, and Ole Brandy and I agreed straight away that this boy should not pine and be lost here in Mac Bett's hexed shack.

'No, the best thing would be if he could get off straight away,' Ole Brandy said. 'Mac Bett's in church at the moment.'

Well, we talked it over with the boy's mother and the skipper of the Albatross, and then later with Mac Bett himself, who turned out to be an honest old man with an embroidered waistcoat and white whiskers à la Gladstone, and so we took the boy with us, and as we all know there has never been any reason to regret that."

So one afternoon of watery sunshine, Orfeus went off, with a fading black eye and large tears running down his cheek, and with his father's violin case under his arm.

A great number of people had congregated on the quay-side, and they all wanted to shake the boy's hand and wish him luck and give him their blessings on his way and further on through life. So he was completely confused, having to look into so many faces at once, even though most of them were those of old friends – Ole Brandy, Olivarius, Mac Bett, Lindenskov and his daughters, Peter the gravedigger and his mother, Josef the Lament and Pontus the rose-painter.

Many tears were shed, not only by those closest to him and by the Weeper, but by others such as Boman's old house-keeper and the youngest of the three Misses Schibbye. And Aunt Lucie was quite inconsolable, though she assured people that it was out of sheer delight on Orfeus's behalf. In general, there was incredible participation; some of the good wishes were underlined with generous gifts, for instance a hundred kroner from Mac Bett, twenty-five from Olivarius and from Lindenskov the dancing-master an old, worn but good pocket watch in a horn case attached to a chain.

Orfeus felt quite overwhelmed and could not utter as much as a thank you on account of the emotion stirring within his breast. But he remained brave until the very last moment, when he was to say goodbye to his mother, and then he broke down and had gently, but firmly, to be forced down into the boat by Ole Brandy, who accompanied him on board.

As the boat glided in under the bowsprit of the Albatross, Orfeus saw the face of Tarira through the rainbow-radiant lattice of tears. He had never before seen it at such close quarters. It was a lifeless face of painted wood, slightly cracked and battered, but for a tiny moment a reflection from the waves had played across its features and brought it to life, as though it was smiling to him in recognition.

Illustration by Zacharias Heinesen